We're a BAD IDEA, Right?

ALSO BY K. L. WALTHER

The Summer of Broken Rules
What Happens After Midnight
Maybe Meant to Be
While We're Young
A First Time for Everything

We're a BAD IDEA, Right?

K. L. WALTHER

First published in Great Britain in 2025
by Electric Monkey, part of Farshore

An imprint of HarperCollins*Publishers*
1 London Bridge Street, London SE1 9GF

farshore.co.uk

HarperCollins*Publishers*
Macken House, 39/40 Mayor Street Upper,
Dublin 1, D01 C9W8

Text copyright © 2026 K.L. Walther
Cover art copyright © 2026 Monique Aimee

The moral rights of the author have been asserted

ISBN 978 0 00 868848 6

Printed and bound in the UK using 100% renewable electricity at
CPI Group (UK) Ltd
1

A CIP catalogue record of this title is available from the British Library

All rights reserved. No part of this publication may be reproduced, stored in
a retrieval system, or transmitted, in any form or by any means, electronic,
mechanical, photocopying, recording or otherwise, without the prior
permission of the publisher and copyright owner.

Without limiting the exclusive rights of any author, contributor or the
publisher of this publication, any unauthorised use of this publication to train
generative artificial intelligence (AI) technologies is expressly prohibited.
HarperCollins also exercise their rights under Article 4(3) of the
Digital Single Market Directive 2019/790 and expressly reserve this
publication from the text and data mining exception.

Stay safe online. Any website addresses listed in this book
are correct at the time of going to print. However, Farshore is
not responsible for content hosted by third parties. Please be aware that
online content can be subject to change and websites can contain content
that is unsuitable for children. We advise that all children
are supervised when using the internet.

Sarah:
Thank you for pouring us glasses of Hogwash
and settling in for a few of the eighties' finest.
They're almost as iconic as you.

CHAPTER 1

THE HOT SHOP WAS *NOT* THE PLACE TO ZONE out, but I couldn't stop myself from doing it anyway. "Holly?" I heard Henry's voice, as if from a distance, while I stared into the furnace at the mesmerizing melting pot of sand, soda, and lime—or, in one word: glass. *Molten* glass, which had taken hours to heat to a balmy two thousand degrees. Sweat was beading on my forehead even though I hadn't technically started working.

Henry, again: "Holly? Are you okay?"

Don't you have something else *to ask me?* I thought, but instead I blinked, as if I'd looked at the sun too long. "That's not my name," I said, for only the millionth time.

"Oh, right," Henry said from behind me. His voice suggested a smirk. "Sorry, *Sabrina*."

"Try again, *Hank*," I replied, sliding the furnace's hatch shut before turning to look at Henry perched on the nearby workbench's stool. His thick black hair was tousled, ready for his *GQ* photo shoot, but his mouth had thinned into a straight line.

Because if there was one thing my dear friend Henry Chen hated in this world, it was being called Hank. We'd only known each other a year and change, but from the way we teased each other, it felt like much longer.

"What's up?" he asked after I drained my dented water bottle in three glugs. "You seem pretty out of it."

"I had a nightmare last night." I rolled my tense shoulders back. "And I can't seem to shake it."

"Really? I always kick mine the second I wake up."

I gave him a look. Henry had once told me that as soon as his head hit the pillow at night, his eyelids didn't flutter until his alarm went off in the morning. If only I were that lucky.

"Okay, okay." Henry shifted on the stool, offering me his full and undivided attention. "What was your nightmare about, Princess Anne?"

That one took me a second. I wasn't well versed in Audrey Hepburn's filmography, the source of Henry's ridiculous nicknames. It turned out sharing a name with the Old Hollywood star made for endless quips from my best friend.

Roman Holiday? I guessed silently, then said, "It's not just the plot; it's that this is now the *third* time I've had this nightmare."

Henry lifted an eyebrow. "Down to the last detail?"

"Down to the last detail," I confirmed, crouching on the hot shop's concrete floor. I traced the chalk drawing of a strawberry-shaped paperweight—what I'd fired up the furnace to blow—then spoke. "It always starts with Griff calling—"

Henry raised his hand.

"What?"

"You're categorizing this as a nightmare," he said. "But it's already sounding more like a *dream*."

I rolled my eyes but felt a thrill at the thought of Griffin Keeler's name popping up on my phone, the same thrill I always felt when we texted. Not only was he our school's star quarterback, he was also our coworker at the local catering company... and blissfully unaware of my crush on him.

The whole scenario fell just short of cliché, but I couldn't help it.

Hey, Audrey! I could almost hear Griff's upbeat voice in my ear, a flirtatious lilt to it. *I have the house to myself...*

Losing a battle with a blush, I said, "He asks if I want to come over and try the sugar cookies he's baking."

"Ah, so it *is* a nightmare." Henry nodded. "Griff's sugar cookies taste like sand, remember?"

How could I *forget*? Back in the fall, Griff had made a batch of atrocious cookies for the football team's bake sale. "They were blander than bland," I agreed. "So then I drive over to his house—"

"In Brigitta? Or the Spider?"

I groaned. "Will you shut up and listen?"

Henry held up his hands, as if to say, *Well, excuse me.*

"The Spider," I answered, another sign that this was a dream gone wrong. Unlike Brigitta, my beloved VW station wagon (named after one of the *Sound of Music* children), my parents' Fiat Spider was a manual. And driving stick was *not* my forte.

Finally satisfied with the visual, Henry dropped his hands and settled in for story time.

~

THE NIGHTMARE GOES LIKE THIS: I DRIVE Brigitta over to Griff's house. On the phone, he said he was home alone, but my stomach sinks when I pull up and see two cars in the driveway. *Maybe his family just got back...?* I hesitate before unbuckling my seat belt. It isn't that I don't like the Keelers; I'm just not used to all the parental attention. My mom isn't the type to "check in" every half hour under the guise of delivering snacks.

My eyebrows knit together as I make my way up the front walk and notice the wide-open yellow front door. I kick off my Nikes in the foyer. "Hello?" I call into the kitchen.

No reply, but then: "Audrey!"

It's Griff, thankfully, and it sounds like he's upstairs.

"Did you finish the cookies?" I joke, because there's a distinct lack of fresh-baked-cookies scent.

"Nah," comes Griff's voice. "I spaced and forgot to preheat the oven."

I can't remember climbing the stairs, but a wave of heat hits me on the second-floor landing. Goose bumps burst on my skin, and dramatic clouds of steam billow out of the bathroom.

"Be out in a minute!" Griff shouts over the running water. "I'm jumping in for a quick rinse."

Griffin Keeler in the shower, I think as the air grows thicker—heady, even. My mind makes a sharp, off-limits turn. *Is he a shampoo-then-body-wash guy? Or body-wash-then-shampoo?*

A blink later, the steam shifts into flashy yellow-orange flames that lick the hallway walls. "Griff!" I screech. "Griff, get out! The house is on fire!"

And since this is a warped dream and not real life, I sprint into the bathroom sans fire extinguisher . . .

The Keelers' hallway carpet suddenly turns into cold concrete under my socked feet, and the flames flicker and then burn out as I barrel into my hot shop. My heart rate slows, and I try to reorient myself amid the swift scene change. The space isn't very big; when we moved to Essex Harbor last year, my parents let me convert the guesthouse garage into a hot shop. "You've been such a trooper about the move, kiddo . . ." my dad said, even though I didn't feel like the permission was his to bestow. This house feels like my mom's.

Everything looks normal in my dream: the circular furnace in the far corner wrapped in sheet metal with a silver hood and cylindrical venting duct disappearing up through the ceiling. Its sliding hatch door is closed, no lava currently swirling inside. I glance over at the hot shop's equipment stall, where I store my long blowpipes.

Like a fishhook in my heart, I feel the longing tug I always feel in my workshop . . .

Only to be interrupted by a loud crash from my left. I spin to see my mother standing in front of the shelf of finished glasswork, near the candlesticks. There's shattered blue glass on the floor. "Mom!" I blurt.

"Oh, Audrey, relax." She waves her hand. "It wasn't your best one."

The back of my neck prickles. She isn't wrong; my candlesticks aren't good enough for Etsy yet, but they're getting better.

"What are you doing here?" I ask, because while the guesthouse is directly overhead, my mom isn't a regular hot shop visitor.

She takes a step toward my vases. "Your father and I need a wedding present for the Keelers," she answers. "Their registry wasn't very inspiring."

A hard lump forms in my throat when she taps a pink ombré vase only for it to effortlessly tip over and smash. "I posted that this morning," I whisper. "It's my most expensive piece."

"Oh, honey, I'm sorry . . ." My mom now assesses my drinkware. Rocks glasses are really popular come Father's Day, so I'm stockpiling them. "I'll take four of these," she says. "Griffin and his fiancée apparently like bourbon."

My heart twinges. Wait, what? Griff is getting married?

"I also saw you got a C on your statistics exam," my mom continues, but now it's my father's voice coming out of her mouth. "That won't cut it, Audrey. Wharton won't like that."

Again, what? I suddenly feel like smashing glass myself.

"I got an A!" I object, as if it even matters—I only have a month left of high school. "And Wharton can't wait for me to set foot on campus..." I drop my voice to a mutter. "Unfortunately."

"Pardon?" A third voice says, and Henry, of all people, walks into the hot shop. He's wearing a version of his typical ensemble: a black T-shirt with a pair of perfectly tailored stone-colored trousers (with Henry, it's never *pants*). There isn't a single scuff mark on his leather loafers. They must be new.

"Henry, hello." My mom is still speaking with my dad's voice. "Please tell Audrey she can't skip college to make glass."

"It's *blow* glass," I correct her. "I *blow* glass, not *make* glass." Sigh. "And it's not like I don't appreciate college; I just want to take a different path—"

"Okay, no." Henry shakes his head. "You're *going* to college. You *need* to go to college."

"Or what?" I challenge him.

"Or all this"—he gestures around the hot shop—"disappears."

I've never heard Henry sound so dead serious, and he's never told me what to do. "You're threatening to shut this down?"

He snaps his fingers. "Like that."

I glance toward my mother, but she has inexplicably vanished.

"Henry, you love Golightly Glass," I say. The name for my Etsy shop was his idea, after all. An ode to Audrey Hepburn's iconic *Breakfast at Tiffany's* character, Holly Golightly.

"I do. Of course I do." Henry nods, his face paling so quickly that it becomes translucent in the blink of an eye. "But . . ."

But . . .

But . . . ?

Nothing.

But nothing.

Because, for the third time in a row, the lights go off before Henry can finish his sentence.

⁓

"WELL, WHAT DO YOU THINK?" I ASKED, EAGER for Henry's opinion. Although I held up a hand before he could speak. "Do *not* ask about your outfit. I don't know where you got loafers."

"I suspect they were the bespoke pair from Portugal," he mused. "I showed them to you last month, remember?"

I glared at him.

Henry snorted. "I think it's relatively straightforward," he said. "You've got a massive crush on Griff . . ." He paused to see if I'd take the bait. I didn't. "But if you had to make a choice, you'd pick glass over him—"

"Untrue," I disputed. "Griff would never give me an ultimatum."

"Okay, then explain why you abandon him when his house goes up in flames, only to run into the hot shop."

"Because my brain is twisted" was my reply.

Henry kept going. "Your mom is there breaking your inventory because she *and* your dad—that's why she speaks in his voice, obviously—are against the Master Plan."

I grimaced. *The Master Plan* had been a point of contention in the Barbour family for the past nine months. I'd applied to college and gotten into not only the University of Pennsylvania—my dad's alma mater—but also its prestigious Wharton School, their business school. It had been a huge deal, and I'd worked my ass off and was really proud of myself . . .

But I didn't want to go there. Even though I could see myself strolling along Locust Walk to class, I didn't think college was my next chapter. Or even *a* chapter.

What I wanted was to blow glass—*seriously* blow glass. Golightly Glass was gaining traction, and after months of taking the train from my home in coastal Connecticut to Brooklyn for a Saturday class, I wanted to devote time to really learning and improving my glassblowing with the best instructors in the country. I'd always dreamed of honing my craft at the renowned Blue Ridge Glass School in the mountains of North Carolina or upstate New York's Corning Museum of Glass. Not to mention Pilchuck Glass School in Seattle. There were even residencies in Monterey, California!

My parents, unfortunately, weren't on the same page as me. "We're happy you've found a hobby you're so passionate about," my mom had said over Christmas break, when I first broached the subject, "but your focus needs to be first and foremost on earning your degree."

They didn't understand that, in a way, I *did* want to pursue business—I wanted to turn Golightly Glass into a real shop someday. But I couldn't do that if I wasn't a good glassblower, so my parents' reservations didn't stop me from researching Blue Ridge and Pilchuck and Corning, or having my Brooklyn instructor write a letter of recommendation. The next time I pitched my Master Plan of pursuing glass over college, I had a full PowerPoint featuring potential courses across the country.

No dice.

As far as my mom and dad knew, I'd accepted my fate—that I'd be moving into a dorm at Penn in two months and studying for an Introduction to Economics midterm come October.

What they *didn't* know was I'd been accepted to Blue Ridge's prestigious yearlong fellowship, and that I'd already paid my deposit, just to hold my spot. I hadn't given up hope yet.

"That's accurate," I told Henry. "I know the MP is a pipe dream in their minds." I paused. "But what I don't get is why *you* were in the dream."

Henry spun around on his stool. "Well, I'm your business partner," he said. "Maybe that's it."

I guess that made sense. Henry and I curated Golightly Glass's Instagram together, and we called the workbench his "base of operations." His mom's old iMac sat on it, along with an HP printer and an extremely organized filing cabinet containing who knew what. I blew the glass, Henry handled all the administrative work.

"I admit it *is* a little funny that you claimed you could shut everything down," I said, laughing and gesturing at the furnace. "I mean, you don't pay the gas bill."

"I shudder to even estimate the gas bill." Henry's lips curved into a sly smile. "Though I *could* end this party if I wanted."

"How, pray tell?"

He winked.

"Fine." I sighed. "Be that way."

"I most definitely will," he chirped, then checked his watch. "We should probably head out soon."

I consulted my phone; sure enough, it was nearing four. Dream dumping and analysis had taken longer than I'd thought. Henry had arrived in uniform, but I was still wearing my favorite Wildfang maroon jumpsuit. "We have leftover scones from breakfast," I said. "Wait for me in the kitchen while I change?"

GRIFF WAS LEANING AGAINST THE REAR bumper of his new but old (and hideously orange) Chevy Camaro when Henry and I turned in to Wicklow Mansion's staff parking lot. He somehow looked both silly and suave in his deep-green pants, standard white button-down, and not-yet-knotted gold tie. His black apron was casually tossed over one shoulder, but I knew that small embroidered stars outlined Orion across the chest.

(Despite my complete lack of musical talent, my apron featured Lyra.)

The three of us had seasonal jobs as cater-waiters at our town's event-planning firm, Constellation Catering. Even though it wasn't quite summer, our boss had texted us last week. Are you available Friday night, 5/10? the message read. All hands on deck for a wedding welcome party!

"Ready?" Henry asked after putting his car in Park.

He wasn't talking about the party.

Through the window, I watched as Griff locked his phone, slipped it in his pocket, and ran a hand through his chestnut hair before noticing us. His eyes brightened.

Who was he texting? I wondered. *Libby?*

Libby was Griff's on-again, off-again girlfriend. They'd broken up when she moved to Arizona last year but kept getting back together. Right now, they were supposedly off, but Griff had gone to Scottsdale for spring break. His tan suited him.

"Get hyped, guys," Griff said once Henry and I met him at his bumper. "Ellie said it's a barbecue vibe tonight, so the corn bread's on the menu!"

As if on cue, Henry and I groaned with intense longing. Constellation's corn bread was mouthwatering, always sliced into perfect wedges and served warm with our special honey butter. Whenever I circulated parties with a full tray, I had to silently scold my stomach for its incessant rumbling.

You couldn't work a Constellation party without a fortifying snack first.

"Fingers crossed there are leftovers," Henry said as Griff offered him a fist bump. He left Griff hanging for a beat, an inside joke, then knocked his knuckles against Griff's. They didn't have much in common, but they had known each other since kindergarten.

"Audrey." Griff turned to me, and my stomach flipped the second he smiled. One of his bottom teeth was chipped from a football game. I thought it gave him character.

"Hey." I smiled back, hoping he couldn't feel the elevated *onetwothree* beat of my heart when he wrapped me in a hug. He smelled like eucalyptus and mint. Our eyes locked after I stepped back, and instead of awkwardly looking away, I made myself hold his hazel gaze. "You need to pull yourself together, Keeler," I teased as I touched his limp tie, trying to flirt even though he never seemed to notice. Griff flirted with everyone. "It's almost showtime."

Griff tilted his head, bemused. "Help me, won't you?"

I sighed a dramatic sigh, but silently thanked my lucky stars that my father had taught me this particular skill when I was little. My mom had thought it was adorable—me tying my dad's tie before they went to a wedding or holiday party or out to dinner with friends.

Now that he lived across the Atlantic Ocean, I hadn't done it in a while.

"How do I look?" Griff asked once I'd finished tightening

the tie and dared to subtly smooth the front of his shirt for the finishing touch.

"First class," I answered as Henry deadpanned, "Like a grunt."

Griff chuckled, then raised his arm to wave at someone behind me. I glanced over my shoulder to see a familiar white Prius slide into a nearby parking spot.

Ellie.

Henry unsteadily shifted from one foot to the other, standing close enough that his hip bone sharply bumped mine—*ouch*. Griff might've been a strapping six foot three, but Henry and I were the exact same height at five eight. "Smooth," I mumbled.

"Is it just me"—Griff said when the Prius *beep-beeped* goodbye to its owner—"or does it seem like cameras flash every time she gets out of that car?"

"It's a Prius," Henry stated as I fought the urge to roll my eyes. Whenever Ellie locked her car, the headlights lit up like paparazzi cameras. "Not an Escalade."

Griff looked at Henry blankly.

"It's like driving a tin can," I rephrased. "Not rolling up to the red carpet."

"Mmm." Griff nodded, not totally getting it. The three of us watched Ellie Hopper sling her canvas tote bag over her shoulder before heading toward us. I absentmindedly plucked a piece of fluff off Henry's shoulder, and one side of his mouth tipped up amusedly.

"What was that?" he murmured.

I didn't answer, a little weirded out by myself. Because *that* was something Ellie used to do all the time.

Like Henry and me, she and I'd met last year, when my family moved to Essex Harbor, Connecticut, halfway through the school year. There'd been an empty desk next to hers in English, and on a superficial level, I took it because I thought her hair—wavy and blond with light pink streaks—was cool. It was my conversation starter. "I'll pass the compliment along to my stylist," she told me. "Also known as my sister." She introduced herself. "I'm Ellie. Ellie Hopper."

"Audrey Barbour," I replied, and over the next couple of weeks, we became casual friends. We didn't text much or spend a ton of time together outside of school, but Ellie and I sat together at lunch when there was drama between her theater friends, periodically studied at our favorite coffee shop, and exchanged the occasional meme on Instagram. She'd also introduced me to her boyfriend, Henry. He and I connected so quickly that I wondered if the three of us would become a true trio.

But it was not meant to be.

After Ellie broke up with Henry last month, she and I weren't as close (if we were even close in the first place). Our conversations sounded forced, and I couldn't stop picturing Henry in tears when he'd come over after their breakup.

"Hey, guys," she said now, pulling her long hair up into a high ponytail. "Did you read Jake and Cassie's story?"

"Who're Jake and Cassie?" Griff deadpanned. "Isn't it Jack and Casey?"

Ellie rolled her eyes. Whenever we worked a wedding, she was the first to find the couple's website and memorize all the details. Her mom was Constellation's cofounder, so Ellie was always invested.

I felt a small twinge when Griff winked at Ellie, but reminded myself there wasn't anything to be jealous of. Partly because he was still hung up on Libby, and definitely because Ellie wasn't interested. "He asked me out once," she'd told me, "but we have nothing in common. Sports put me to sleep, and he doesn't know what *thespian* means."

"By the way, congratulations, Henry," Ellie added after Griff grilled her about the rest of "Jack and Casey's" menu. "No one deserves that award more than you."

This past week, our school had announced Henry as this year's recipient of the Hearne Prize, which everyone summed up as the award for "best human." Perfect GPA aside, Henry played tennis, peer tutored, and was president of the improv club. He also did the morning announcements (Principal Ruiz thought he had a nice radio voice).

Henry slid his hands into his pockets, his too-cool-for-school move. "Thanks, Ellie," he said, and I watched her self-consciously shift her THEATRE IS MY SPORT tote to her other shoulder. When they were dating, Henry had always called Ellie "Pinks" for the same streaks that had caught my eye. Hearing him say "Ellie" had been an adjustment.

"Are your parents proud?" she tried.

A tight nod. "Over the moon."

Griff and I made eye contact. He looked amused. *On a scale of one to ten,* his face read, *how awkward is this?*

I checked my phone; we still had some time, but nevertheless I said: "We should probably head in for briefing."

"Good call." Griff followed my lead. "Who's our shift manager tonight, Ellie?"

Hearing her name made Ellie blink. "Oh, um, Mel."

"Ah, mighty Mel . . ." Henry mused.

". . . how we've missed her so!" I finished, making us both laugh.

Griff chuckled too, but Ellie stood there silently, expression annoyingly unreadable.

Was she thinking about Henry?

It was your choice, I wanted to remind her. *He never wanted it to end.*

And if Henry and I had anything to do with it, maybe it didn't have to . . .

CHAPTER 2

HENRY CHEN AND ELLIE HOPPER HAD ALWAYS seemed like a match made in high school heaven. Not prom king and queen level—that title belonged to Griff and Libby—but still, they were a really cute couple. Ellie played the lead in all the school musicals and Henry was her handsome, well-dressed film-buff boyfriend. They were the only people I knew who had AMC Stubs memberships.

Henry mostly sat with his improv friends at lunch, but he chivalrously walked Ellie to her cafeteria table of choice and came back to walk her to class afterward. She watched all of his tennis matches; he went to every musical and play. They did clever couples costumes on Halloween. Friday was date night, and they had dinner at her house on Sundays. "If you and Henry were a Taylor Swift song, which one would you be?" I'd asked Ellie back in March. We'd been working on a statistics presentation at Rise & Grind Coffee, and it seemed like Taylor was the only artist on their spring playlist—and fine, I was curious. How did Ellie see their romance-novel relationship?

She'd looked up from her laptop and given me a funny look. "Seriously?"

I shrugged, and figured she wasn't going to answer when she went back to her computer.

But after a moment, she mumbled the title of a song from *Fearless*.

"Oh, nice." I quickly tweaked something in our Google Doc to mask my surprise. Because unless its lyrics had changed since my last listen, the song was about *two* guys, not one. Sensible and so incredible, and then screaming and fighting and kissing in the rain.

Is Henry somehow both? I wondered. As far as I knew, they *never* argued.

That afternoon should've been the tip-off. I shouldn't have been shocked to get a text from Ellie in April, one that said: Henry and I broke up. It was mutual, so definitely not a big deal. Just wanted to let you know.

Pulse pitching, I immediately locked my phone and blinked before reopening it. Ellie and Henry breaking up? I'd misread the message, right?

Spoiler alert: I hadn't.

I'm so sorry, **I began to type.** Let me know if you need—

The sudden groan of the garage door rising paused my thumbs. Myself excluded, only three people knew the keypad code. But my father was in Vienna and my mom had braved the rain for book club.

Which left . . .

Henry walked into the hot shop, drenched from the downpour. His dark hair was plastered to his forehead, and water had somehow seeped through his impenetrable waxed raincoat. His boots left a footprint with every step. "Lose your umbrella?" I quipped.

Henry's voice was controlled but furious. "Did Pinks ever mention a 'someone else' to you?" he asked. "Because tonight it was brought to my attention that there is a *someone else*."

I opened my mouth, but couldn't even squeak out a syllable.

"Oh, right." Henry nodded. "My opening statement should've been something along the lines of 'Adelaide Hopper dumped my ass out of fucking nowhere.'"

Who? I almost asked before remembering that Adelaide was Ellie's real name. Adelaide Eleanor, after both her grandmothers. A little too old-fashioned for the twenty-first century.

"Yes, I gathered that . . ." I said slowly, grimacing. "I also had a heads-up."

He snorted. "Did she say it was *amicable*?"

I read him Ellie's text.

My heart twinged when Henry reached up and wiped lingering raindrops (or were they fresh tears?) from his eyes. "I have zero idea why she'd tell you that, Eliza—"

"*My Fair Lady*?" I guessed, another Audrey classic.

"Nicely done, Doolittle," Henry said, then sighed heavily. "*Why* would she say that when it's so far—like, *light-years away*—from the truth? Obviously she knows I'm going to tell you."

"Obviously." I slipped my hands into my jumpsuit pockets. If you wanted to pinpoint our origin story, Henry and I had become friends through Ellie during junior spring. When I'd finally been confident enough in my glasswork to open an Etsy shop, I asked Ellie to ask Henry to have lunch with us. He was a member of our school's Future Enterprisers club, so I thought he could give me some advice.

Three cafeteria table consultations and a negotiated twenty percent commission later, he quit Future Enterprisers to run Golightly Glass's affairs.

I sighed. "I think it's her way of saying she doesn't want to talk about it."

"Well, I do." Henry unzipped his raincoat, then shucked it off and hung it on a hook near the side door. It promptly drip-dropped. "May I?" He gestured to my supply of blowpipes.

"By all means," I said. Henry didn't blow glass often, but the hollow metal pipe was one of his favorite fidget toys. He held it like a scepter or spun it like a fire dancer sans dance routine.

I grabbed a pipe in solidarity, though not to work; after blowing glass for two hours tonight, I'd just put my last piece in the annealer—the kiln—when Ellie texted me the news.

"His name is Chase," Henry said.

I snorted. "Really?"

"I know." He rolled his eyes. "Makes it even better, right?"

"I mean, *a little*," I said. "'Chase' seems like the quintessential douche . . ." I trailed off when Henry stopped spinning the blowpipe and looked at me expectantly.

May I please tell the tale? his expression said.

I nodded.

"Chase Reynolds," he told me, "is *not* a new face. He's Pinks's ex-boyfriend."

Wait, what? I thought with a slight jolt. *Ellie dated someone before Henry?*

Henry and Ellie had always seemed so together, it was difficult to imagine either of them being with anyone else.

"It was before you moved here," Henry answered my unasked question. "She was a freshman; he was a junior. They broke up when he left for college."

"But kept in touch?" I surmised.

Henry shook his head. "She told me he'd drunk-texted her a couple of times his first semester, but other than that, no contact."

I waited for him to say more.

"Remember when she and her parents went to Davidson's revisit day?"

I bit the inside of my cheek. Davidson was in North Carolina, and Ellie had applied on a whim; she'd never set foot on campus. "Let me guess," I whispered. "Chase goes there?"

"Bingo!" Henry chirped. "Chase not only transferred there last year, but he also was her tour guide or orientation leader or *whatever* that whole day . . . and lo and behold, they've been texting ever since." He sighed. "She told me she's really sorry, but she's been *emotionally cheating* on me for the past few weeks, and they've talked about seeing each other this summer..."

A lump rose in my throat. "Oh, Henry."

His face twisted. No one put their girlfriend on a higher pedestal than Henry Chen.

I swallowed, and after confiscating his blowpipe, pulled him into a hug. He was trembling. "But it's definitely not a big deal," he said, quoting his ex's text. "It was amicable."

"Mutual," I corrected him.

His laugh sounded more like a cough.

"Are you hungry?" I asked after a beat. Henry and I didn't usually hug, so it was a little awkward. He was so angular, all edges and points. "Do you want to order pizza?"

Thankfully, the rain had let up and our food was delivered within the hour. Ottimo's brick oven pizza was the best in town. Henry and I had ordered our favorite white pie with grape tomatoes, mozzarella, arugula, and topped with shaved Parmesan, prosciutto, and basil. My mouth watered as I carried the pizza box to the back of the garage, which my cousins had dubbed the "groupie area" when I first set up shop. Grace and James had helped me arrange a mid-century leather couch and round aluminum coffee table—two of my mom's castoffs—on a fraying Persian rug to make the corner cozy. I flipped open the box as Henry inspected the contents of the tall minifridge, digging through some water bottles, seltzers, and a lone iced tea until he found what he was looking for: Stiegl Goldbräu.

Otherwise known as Austria's most popular beer. Since our expatriate experience in Vienna, my parents stocked a steady supply and turned a blind eye so long as I didn't touch their meticulously curated wine collection. "We trust you, Audrey" was my mom's recurring line. She knew I liked hosting friends but would never throw a party.

I wasn't extroverted enough for that.

The beers paired well with the pizza, and we each cracked open another bottle after the last crust had been eaten. Besides being heartbroken, Henry was a lightweight, so he now bounced from topic to topic: Golightly Glass's new stickers, his grandfather's dog chewing his sneakers, how Matt Rife was an overrated comedian, the LSATs (depending on the day, Henry either wanted to be an entertainment agent or lawyer). I confiscated the beer and switched us to water when he somehow brought everything back around to Ellie and Chase.

"It's stupid!" he sputtered. "She's going to *Barnard* next year, not Davidson. We were together almost two years, and she's throwing it away for what? A summer with him?"

Feeling all warm and fuzzy from the beer, I battled the urge to break into an off-key rendition of *Grease*'s "Summer Nights." Ellie had starred as Sandy last semester.

"It'll be a *long-distance* summer too," Henry added. "He has some internship in Boston."

"Wow," I said, straight-faced. "Tell me how you *really* feel about long-distance relationships."

"They're doomed," he replied. "Even with the best intentions and purest hearts."

What movie did he steal that from? I wondered. *Or is it a Henry Chen original?*

"Okay, so get her back in the fall," I told him after a long sip of water. "Let Ellie and Chase crash and burn, then make your move. NYU is only a subway ride from Barnard—"

"No way!" he said. "I want her back *now*."

I gave him a look. "You sound like an overtired four-year-old."

Henry groaned. "But, Audrey, I love her."

"I know," I said, then went all rom-com wedding on him. "But take comfort from the Corinthians! *Love is patient,* right?"

"Mmm," Henry mused. "Yes, unless . . ."

"Unless what?" I asked, something flipping in me when Henry's brown eyes brightened. What he was about to suggest would either be brilliant or brilliantly stupid—

"Will you go out with me?"

Okay, or just plain *absurd.*

My water went down the wrong pipe. "Oh my god," I said after I'd coughed my way to recovery. "Did you seriously just ask me to *go out* with you?"

Color creeped up Henry's neck. "Yes, Sabrina, but I don't mean it like that . . ."

"How do you mean it, *Hank*?" I asked, confused. He'd been wallowing over Ellie five seconds ago.

Henry shot me a stone-faced look. "You know I hate 'Hank.'"

"That's a shame," I said dryly. "Because I think it has a certain je ne sais quoi—especially if we're going to start dating. Nicknames would really sell it."

"Exactly." Henry snapped his fingers. "We wouldn't actually be in a relationship; we'd be *selling* one."

Oh, I thought. Henry didn't want to mix business with pleasure—he wanted to start another business.

"You want to pretend," I deduced. "You want to make Ellie jealous."

"*Jealous* sounds half-baked," Henry said. "I thought we'd spin it as us helping her realize who she truly loves."

"And you think us *dating* will accomplish that?"

Henry nodded.

I took a beat to think, blinking hard as I imagined Henry's fingers lacing through mine and tugging me toward him for a—

"Okay, *no*," I blurted, fueled by a sudden hot pulse. "No way, no thank you, absolutely not."

"Really?" Henry slowly raised an eyebrow. *"Absolutely not?"* He held my gaze until I started squirming—something in my gut requesting I reconsider.

Or at least help him realize how flimsy this scheme was.

"What would be in it for me?" I asked, folding my arms across my chest as if to hide my hammering heart. "Beyond potentially watching you reunite with the love of your life."

For all of three seconds, I thought I'd stumped him.

But then a stupid smirk spread across his face.

"Two words," Henry said. "Griff Keeler."

I felt my face warm but rolled my eyes.

Henry didn't buy it. "You have a crush on him," he continued. "I know you do, Holly."

"At least half of Essex Harbor has a crush on him," I countered. Not only was Griffin Keeler incredibly handsome, but he was also friendly, funny, and a glass-half-full guy—so damn delightful that girls were powerless against his grin.

And girlfriend or no girlfriend, he was a huge flirt.

"He thinks you're cool," Henry said. "Cute, too."

"He does?" I semi-squeaked. Griff and I weren't really friends at school, but we were pretty close from cater-waitering. He hung out with Henry and me after work and sometimes visited the hot shop. "When did he say that?"

"It was a tangent during a tutoring session." Henry gave me a look. "Honestly, being with someone—well, in this case, being with *me*—might put you on his radar."

"He's still more or less with Libby," I pointed out. "Spring break in Scottsdale, remember?"

"Yeah, and he came back lovesick because he got a *maybe* for prom," Henry reminded me. "Griff Keeler wants what he can't have."

Hmm . . .

I closed my eyes and leaned back against the couch cushions, thinking about Griff. I wouldn't say I had an all-consuming, overwhelming, can't-eat-or-sleep crush on him, but I was far from immune to his charm—and I liked the layer *beneath* said charm. I would never forget a couple of months ago, he'd stopped me in the hallway and asked for a favor. "Next week is the anniversary of my grandpa's death," he confided. "And Gram is in rough shape right now. I want to surprise her with flowers, but none of the florist's vases are special enough." He glanced away for half a second, as if nervous. "Would you be able to blow something one of a kind for her?"

The project had taken a full weekend, and it was the first time Griff and I hung out alone together. He'd been there every step of the process—from the initial sketch to blowing the vase to setting it in the annealer—and, later, his grandmother had commissioned three identical vases for her children. *Who needs Simon Pearce?* she'd written in an unexpected thank-you note. *You are going places, Audrey!*

"Come on," Henry tried, his voice a little hoarse. "What do you say?"

I snuck a peek at him from beneath my lowered lids. He looked hopeful, yet also full of despair.

Eh, what's the worst-case scenario? I wondered. *You and Henry discover you're the worst couple ever and stage a dramatic breakup?*

That didn't sound *not* fun . . .

Although I wasn't sure it was worth the risk. Henry and I were strictly friends, but what Ellie saw in him wasn't a secret. I got it, and even I'd felt the pull into Henry Chen's orbit. Not six hours after agreeing to partner on Golightly Glass, I'd run into him at the bookstore; he was buying a guide to glass-blowing. "You should watch *Blown Away* instead," I advised after he explained he wanted to immerse himself in the glass world. "It's a glassblowing competition on Netflix." I couldn't stop grinning. "It's a great introduction to glassblowing and also *extremely* entertaining."

In typical Henry fashion, he still bought the book, and late that night, he called me. "May I come over tomorrow?" he asked. "I finished season one and really think I can blow something..."

So much glass ended up on the floor that day, but I hadn't laughed so hard in—well, *ever*. To quote many a Minted Christmas card, Henry made everything feel merry and bright. I suddenly couldn't imagine the hot shop without him in it.

Luckily, I'd set myself straight before hearts filled my eyes—*He's with Ellie! They're perfect together!*—but now he wasn't with Ellie and nothing meant more to me than our friendship and business partnership. If we pretended to date, what would happen when all was said and done? Would we go back to being best friends? Or would this make things... different?

Maybe even *weird*?

I didn't know, and I didn't like that.

So I sucked in a deep breath, then said: "One month."

"One month?" he asked. "One month what?"

"You can ask me again in a month," I told him, then shrugged. "You can't get over Ellie *too* quickly."

Henry's lips slowly twitched up in a smile. "Good point," he said, and if he suspected I was stalling, he didn't let on.

TONIGHT MARKED FOUR WEEKS SINCE HENRY had suggested our fauxmance, and I was embarrassed I remembered without any reminders from him or my calendar. *What does that say about me?* I wondered as I folded napkins and arranged silverware. *That I think Henry's idea is such lunacy it's unforgettable? Or that it actually does have some merit?*

Hmm.

Thankfully, the welcome party distracted me. After service, per usual, all the high school workers left Wicklow and drove over to Hamburger Hill. On a side street off Essex's main drag and open till midnight, the diner was decorated with Beatles memorabilia. Paul, John, George, and Ringo bobbleheads greeted us at the hostess podium, Technicolor-pop art portraits decorated the walls, and every time I ordered coffee, it came in a different themed mug. My favorite was the yellow submarine. Thankfully, the old-fashioned jukebox played more than just Beatles songs.

"Hey, gang!" Heather, the owner, called from behind the counter. "Good night?"

"The bride and groom are made for each other!" Ellie called back, as I said, "The bride is going to eat the groom alive!"

"But the truffle mac and cheese was *electric*," Griff added.

Heather shook her head and smiled. "Sit anywhere you like."

Henry chose a big booth with a Union Jack painted on

the tabletop. While I wanted to sit next to Griff, to feel his arm or leg accidentally brush against mine, I ended up sandwiched between Henry and Jared. Jared, Mia, and Kenzie—all finishing up their junior year—were the Constellation rookies. Mia needed to work on her eye contact (or lack thereof), Jared had to control his Super Bowl–level enthusiasm, and, per Commander Mel, Kenzie needed to stop inserting herself into guests' conversations.

Across the table, Mia and Kenzie were all too happy to flank Griff, and Ellie took the outermost spot. She was feverishly texting someone—Chase, I guessed—but looked up from her phone once Henry flagged down a server. "Please tell us you haven't run out of salmon burgers!" Griff said by way of greeting.

"Salmon burgers?" I asked, caught off guard. Griff never wavered from Hamburger Hill's bacon cheeseburger.

"Yeah." Griff nodded. "Mia told me she doesn't do red meat."

Next to him, Mia beamed.

She was in luck, and our milkshakes and burgers arrived about twenty minutes later. "Can I have one of your fries?" Kenzie asked Griff, whose chili cheese fries took up half his plate. She blushed when he gave her permission to have *more* than one.

"Not to bring the mood down," he added, dramatically clearing his throat, "but I have a little announcement."

"You're getting the Camaro repainted?" Henry guessed.

"You've realized the orange is heinous?"

The table laughed. "Chen, I don't have that kind of money," Griff said, then shook his head. "No, I wanted to let you all know that Libby isn't going to make prom."

"Oh, Griff..." Ellie, Kenzie, and Mia chorused as everything around me turned to white noise.

Libby isn't going to make prom.

"Which means I'm in desperate need of a date," Griff continued before my heart could burst out in song. His eyes twinkled. "Let me know if you have any suggestions, okay?"

Under the table, I felt Henry's knee nudge mine. He didn't say anything, but I could hear his voice in my head: *If you don't do something soon, you might miss your chance...*

Unfortunately, Griff searching for a date suddenly made Henry's and my potential fake dating seem less moronic than when originally proposed.

Our burgers were so delicious that we ate them in near silence. "How kind," I told Henry when he offered me his black-and-white milkshake, and in return, I gave him my salted caramel. Our new thing was drinking half our shakes before trading.

"So, Audrey," Griff said as I dipped a couple of French fries into the creamy shake, "I heard your mom's headed out of town soon."

"Where's she going?" Mia asked before I could chew and swallow.

"She and my dad are going to France," I said. My father

had flown in for an extended visit two weeks ago. "They're celebrating their twenty-fifth wedding anniversary in the Loire Valley. If there's a wine trail, they'll follow it."

"C'est incroyable!" Ellie exclaimed as Mia, Kenzie, and Jared laughed.

"How long are they going to be gone?" Jared asked.

"Three weeks. Back just in time for graduation."

"Interesting . . ." Griff's eyes shined, so mesmerizing that I barely felt Henry's knee knock mine under the table again. "You have any special plans while they're gone?"

"Not really." I took a sip from my water glass. My throat had gone dry. "I'll probably blow a lot of glass, to be honest. And my cousin—"

"Audrey." Griff cut me off. "You have the house to yourself for almost a month and all you're focused on is *glass*?"

Well, I'll eat more pad thai than usual, I thought, since my mom hated the lingering smell. *But yes . . .*

Henry coughed, then leaned forward with a comically furrowed brow. "Griff, have you *met* Audrey?"

To hide my snort, I turned and accidentally nuzzled Henry's neck as he settled back into the booth. His warm skin singed the tip of my nose and he smelled of spicy-sweet cologne mixed with Constellation's corn bread and *why* were we sitting so close to each other?

Blood rushed to my cheeks when I noticed Ellie watching us, and as soon as our eyes locked, she shifted in her seat and spoke.

"Nice try, Griff," she said, almost coolly. "Just because Audrey's house is the size of an amusement park doesn't mean she should open its gates."

"Why not?" he asked. "It doesn't need to be huge..."

Ah, I realized. *He wants me to throw a party.*

That was so not my idea of a good time.

But Kenzie was already excited. "You live on the beach, right?"

"Kind of," I said. My house overlooked the Long Island Sound, and we did have a stretch of beach, but it was more pebbles than sand. My mom liked to read there, and in the summer, I loved taking a quiet dip after a long day.

"Audrey, Audrey." Griff grabbed my attention again. His energy was contagious, making my stomach spin. "Can I offer you some advice?"

"I don't know," Henry said, munching on a sweet potato fry. "*Can* you?"

Griff good-naturedly flipped Henry the bird. "*May* I offer you some advice?" he corrected himself.

I couldn't help but smile. "All ears, Keeler."

"Have some fun!" He grinned. "Like, I know you have your glassblowing stuff, and that's cool—*really* cool—but embrace your freedom, too. I mean, you have *three weeks*. Do something you've never done before. Say what the hell and shoot for the moon!"

"And don't worry if you miss," Henry stage-whispered, "because you'll land among the stars..."

Ellie stopped texting to grimace. "I'm pretty sure you're quoting a cheesy elementary school aspirational poster."

"Yes," Henry confirmed. "Mrs. Lipton. Fourth grade."

The table laughed again.

"Your wise words are much appreciated." I started giggling when Griff looked at me expectantly. "I'll definitely consider digging my astronaut gear out of the attic."

It took him a second to get it, but then he perked up. "Seriously?"

I nodded. "Seriously."

He raised his hand for a high five, and I stretched to meet him for a satisfying *slap*. The skin-to-skin contact sent a zing through my veins.

And when he smiled at me, with that adorable chipped tooth, I did think, *What the hell?*

HENRY WAS SURPRISINGLY SILENT ON THE

drive home from Hamburger Hill, and I kept my mouth shut, too. Half of me surmised he was tired from several hours of service with a smile, but without any exaggerated yawns to prove it, the other half of me suspected the wheels were turning in his head. He was quiet because he was *thinking*.

"Thanks for the ride," I said once he'd passed through the gate and slowed to a stop in my driveway. The house was dark; my parents had gone into Manhattan for dinner and a show.

"Brigitta should be ready next week."

My car was currently in the shop, thanks to its never-ending list of maladies. This time, all the electrical in the driver's side door had gone out. I wondered how hard that bill was going to hit my bank account. Every inch of my lifestyle screamed *privileged white girl* and my dad did make an incredible living. But I was far from spoiled and covered most of my own expenses. All the money in my bank account was thanks to my catering job and Golightly Glass. And admittedly, birthday checks from my grandparents helped. My American Express card was only for emergencies.

The Blue Ridge deposit hadn't *entirely* wiped out my savings, but I wouldn't be able to pay for the tuition by myself.

"Do you want to come to the city tomorrow?" I asked while unbuckling my seat belt. "We can go to a museum after my glassblowing class. You still need to find your mom a birthday gift, right?"

Henry nodded. "That sounds great," he agreed, then waited a beat before saying, "It's been a month."

A month? I thought about joking and playing dumb, but I knew I wasn't going to escape this conversation. As ridiculous as it was, it was too important.

"Yes," I said instead, stoic. "It's been a month."

"I *would* get down on one knee . . ." Henry said as my stomach started to swirl. "But being buckled in makes that a little difficult." He casually popped open the center console and pulled out a box of Good & Plenty, my favorite candy. I couldn't help but fight a smile: Good & Plenty had become hard to find. "Holly, there's no one like you." Henry's brown eyes caught mine as he shook the licorice candy. "Your love for this vileness is a testament of that." He grinned. "Please go out with me?"

No, I thought, my stomach tying itself into knots at the same time warmth flooded my chest. It was a bad idea.

We were a bad idea . . . right?

Red flags waved in my head, but over the last month, I'd really grown sick of Henry being sick over Ellie. I mean, he still had a photo of them as his phone wallpaper! If this charade helped him win her back, wonderful. If not, maybe he would finally get over her.

And, I thought, *if Griff suddenly feels inclined to flirt with me . . .*

Well, I wouldn't stop the backs of my knees from going weak.

"You don't think it'd be kind of weird?" I asked. "Us pretending to be together?"

Henry didn't flinch, let alone blink. "Why would it be weird?"

His five words said about a thousand. Weirdness between us would never cross Henry's mind because we were *just friends*. Had I imagined something sparking between us? Yes, but only for a moment, and that moment had been ages ago. Our friendship could withstand anything. Even stupidity.

Henry held my eyes expectantly.

"All right, *fine.*" I sighed. "I will give you *a date.*"

He raised an eyebrow. "A date?"

"Yes," I said. "A date—*one* date." I snorted. "If I'm going to pretend to go out with you, you need to pretend to *work* for it."

"Fair enough." Henry chuckled and presented me with my treat. "When can you pencil me in?"

"Next week," I told him, gently tearing open the Good & Plenty box before pouring some pink and white candies into my palm. "After my parents leave for France."

As a general rule, I didn't talk to my parents about my love life (not that there was much to broadcast), but I definitely didn't need my mom sniffing around this. She'd been enamored with Henry ever since meeting him last year; she even let him call her "Monica."

"It's a plan," Henry agreed. "Should we discuss terms and conditions?"

Terms and conditions.

My mind suddenly melted to mush. This conversation had eaten up the last of today's brain cells, and Henry didn't mess around when mulling over anything resembling a contract. Drafting Golightly Glass's return policy had taken an hour (and there was not a single loophole to be found). "Let's see how the date goes," I proposed, taste buds going wild as I unlatched the passenger door. "If it's promising, then we'll talk T&Cs."

"Okay . . ." Henry sounded amused. "Which train are we catching tomorrow morning?"

"The one that allows us to grab coffee beforehand," I said.

"So, early?"

"*So* early," I concurred, inelegantly sliding out of the car. My glassblowing class started at nine, and the train was a couple of hours, so I usually left Essex Harbor not long after the rooster crowed.

"I better get to bed, then," Henry joked before turning over his engine, ready to head home. "Good night, Natasha."

"Sleep tight, Tolstoy," I replied, for once in the know. We'd slogged through *War and Peace* in English this winter, and iconic Audrey had played the iconic Natasha in a 1950s adaptation. "Don't stay up too late musing . . ."

But Henry, a notorious night owl, predictably made no promises.

All he did was wink.

CHAPTER 3

A WEEK AFTER HAMBURGER HILL WITH HENRY and the other cater-waiters, we had Friday off school for a teacher in-service day. I slept until eight-thirty, then pulled a sweatshirt on over my pajamas and headed out to the hot shop to fire up the furnace. Things had grown nice and toasty a few hours later, and by noon, the glass was ready for me to work.

Some people might say glassblowing was a niche art form, and they weren't wrong . . . but if you *really* thought about it, glass was all around us. The glasses we drank out of, the vases my mother arranged flowers in, and even ornaments on a Christmas tree. It was everywhere.

My eyes had been opened three years ago, when my family had moved from Philadelphia to Vienna for my dad's job. After school one day, I'd been exploring, not ready to face my mom at home yet, and stumbled upon a glasswork gallery. And I just felt this *tug;* before I knew it, I'd seemingly teleported inside and was admiring a sculpture of a bird about to take flight from its nest. It was robin's-egg blue with silver-gold-tipped wings and shiny ebony eyes, both beautiful and whimsical, and I resisted the urge to touch the nest. How could the thin twigs and dried grass be *glass*? They were so lifelike.

"Kann ich Ihnen helfen?" someone said, and I turned to see a woman standing behind me. Streaks of silver shot through her curly brown hair and she had what looked like an oversized pair of tweezers tattooed on her arm.

"Es tut mir Leid." I winced at my pronunciation. I was getting better at reading German, but my conversational skills were terrible. "Ich spreche . . . kein Deutsch."

"Ah." She waved her hand in a no-worries manner. "May I help you with anything?" she asked again, this time in accented English.

"Oh, no, not really." I shook my head and smiled. "Just curious."

Bemused, she tilted her head. "About?"

I pointed at the bird. "It's incredible."

"Thank you," she said. "Although I disagree." She chuckled. "I worked very hard, but it's not my best."

"No way." I gawked. "How . . . ?"

The artist gestured to the far side of the gallery. "My hot shop is back there. Would you like to see?"

And there was that strong *pull* again. I found myself nodding and stepping forward before fully computing the question.

Emilia, glassblower extraordinaire, became my mentor for the next nine months. She taught me how to gather glass from the furnace with a long blowpipe by dipping it into the molten mixture and swirling until the tip was coated enough that it looked like a glowing honeycomb. She taught me how to blow into the hollow pipe, to create the bubble I'd sculpt with various tools. I quickly realized her forearm tattoo was a pair of jacks, steel tongs used to both warp and control the shape of the glass. "Play with it for a moment," Emilia said after I'd blown my first small bubble, and as I poked, prodded, twisted, and stretched the glass with the jacks, I couldn't believe how much it felt like taffy.

Emilia's sculptures were considered conceptual, but my education was strictly production glasswork. To strengthen my lungs, I blew bubble after bubble until I had a collection of marbles, and eventually, after blowing ornaments, Emilia promoted me to cups. "This will teach you how to use all the tools and perfect many techniques," she'd said after my shoulders slumped (at the time, all I wanted to do was sculpt pretty birds like hers).

Ironically, I fell in love with production glasswork. Emilia had been right: It involved both technique and repetition—or, more accurately, repetition that improved my technique. Cups fascinated me. No matter how simple they seemed or how many I made, each one presented a challenge. I felt like each and every one of my brain cells dialed in whenever I blew one, ready and eager to hone my skills.

Emilia and I shared photos of our work and kept in touch via WhatsApp, and I'd stopped by her hot shop when I visited

Vienna for Christmas. But I missed spending hours there after school. Saturdays with Nico in Brooklyn weren't the same.

I wanted to be in the thick of it again. It was the only way I was going to get where I wanted to go.

Today I felt scatterbrained, anxious about my parents jetting off for France, so I decided to center myself by blowing a cup. The tuition deadline for the Blue Ridge fellowship was looming (as in, the day after *tomorrow*), so I needed to talk to my parents about my Master Plan, and I couldn't be all over the place when I did. My dream for the future was too important to express through word vomit.

By now, the repetition of glassblowing almost felt like a form of meditation. First, I heated my blowpipe until its tip turned a dull cherry red, and then I quickly moved to quench it in a nearby bucket of water. The hissing steam was so satisfying. "What are you doing?" Ellie had sputtered the first time she saw me quench, and I'd explained that the water rid the pipe of any surface bubbles. Henry, naturally, had deduced that on his own. "I like to think of it as sanitizing a needle with alcohol," he'd said.

Next came the first gather, the first layer of glass. I rested my pipe on the yoke—the V-shaped apparatus in front of the furnace—and spun until I had enough liquid glass for a bubble. Right next to the furnace was the marver, which helped shape glass. Instead of a professional one, mine was totally DIY: an old restaurant cart that I'd salvaged by refurbishing the top with a flat slab of steel. I rolled the glowing honeycomb against the cool metal, rounding it out. The movement was mesmerizing—almost soothing.

But before I could grow too zen, I raised the pipe to my lips and blew.

"Not your best, not your worst," I murmured to myself as I covered the blowhole with my thumb after my first puff. Capping the pipe provided enough pressure for the air to shoot to the front. Once the bubble inflated, I removed my finger so it didn't get too big.

The next step was to move to what Henry referred to as the cockpit, but which was universally known in hot shops as the bench. My uncle had helped me build the workstation; we'd attached two metal rails to the front of an old vanity table stool for my pipes to ride on while I sat and worked. I used my jacks to carefully reshape the bubble's walls while rolling it on the bench's rails. Everything needed to be evened out before adding another coat of glass. My bubble was currently red orange, which meant I needed to let it cool a bit. If I gathered again now, the bubble would collapse. Emilia had let me learn that the hard way.

Glassblowing demands speed, she once said, *but it also requires patience.*

Waiting, I grabbed my phone to queue up Spotify. Griff had created a playlist for the hot shop while I worked on his grandmother's vase, and its astronomical energy level boosted my productivity. It was mostly Coachella bangers from the 2010s; by the time I dipped my pipe back into the furnace,

I was bopping along to Calvin Harris's "This Is What You Came For."

I harmonized with Rihanna while I let the pipe hang down to stretch the glass. Hot glass was spellbinding, and any intrusive thoughts that snuck into my head were quickly banished. For example, *why* hadn't I been able to muster the courage to bring up Blue Ridge with my parents earlier? Why had I saved it until the very last minute? I wanted to kick myself; maybe they would've warmed to the idea of me sidestepping college if I'd mentioned my fellowship acceptance more than once—if I truly acted like it was an *achievement*. I wasn't just doing this on a whim.

Not to mention, I was going on a *date* with *Henry* tonight. Everything had been normal between us this week, but my stomach stirred whenever I thought of him today.

Those were issues for Future Audrey. She could handle them.

Glassblowing was athletic, like a dance. I alternated between the bench and the furnace, using tools from my arsenal to continually shape my cup and flash it to keep the glass malleable. Otherwise it would cool and crack, and no one wanted that.

"You've got this, Audrey," I muttered, resting my blowpipe, with the tumbler still attached to one end, on the bench's rails so I could grab a long metal rod, called a punty, from my stash. Henry usually helped me with the punty, but alas, it was all up to me right now. After heating it for a few minutes, I gathered a little glass and quickly shaped it on the marver. All I wanted was enough for a point of contact. Using a pair of tweezers to guide the punty, I gently pressed it against the bottom of my tumbler. Was it a perfect bull's-eye? No, but it was still centered. With the cup now attached to the rod, I tapped the tweezers against my blowpipe.

The cup broke off cleanly.

From there, the dance resumed. Furnace, bench, furnace, bench, again and again. Sweat trickled down my back as I rolled my punty on the bench's rails, the cup rotating as my shears snipped away at the top. The glass cut like taffy and, punty still spinning, I alternated between my tweezers and jacks to form the mouth. The piece was really looking like a rocks glass.

I flashed it in the furnace again, and after a few more finishing touches, the final step was to transfer the cup to the annealer; the kiln would slowly cool the glass to prevent it from cracking. I pulled open the oven's lid before carefully knocking the glass off the punty rod and onto a flat paddle. It was still hot, but over the next sixteen hours, my tumbler would cool to room temperature.

When I closed the annealer, a wave of bliss rolled through me. Was my cup flawless? No, but I'd learned that sometimes the process itself was more beautiful than the finished product.

But unfortunately, when I left the hot shop, my stomach twisted.

My parents were leaving in several hours.

Which meant I was running out of time.

You can do this, I told Future Audrey.

NO ONE—AND I MEAN *NO ONE*—WAS MORE organized than Monica Barbour. My mother had hired a town car to drive my father and her to JFK, had their luggage standing at attention by the front door, and even drafted a *list* to go over with me. While I ate a roast beef sandwich at the spotless marble island, she paced the kitchen and read aloud from her trusty leather notebook. "Water the plants" fell somewhere between "pick up the dry cleaning" and "supervise the pool cleaners next Tuesday."

"We have a pool?" my dad joked, glancing out the kitchen's French doors at the tasteful rectangular pool in the backyard. It was saltwater and surrounded by a dark slate patio. Four wrought iron loungers sat poolside, with beige cushions and black-and-white-striped throw pillows. Summer had decided to arrive early.

My mom looked up from her list and smirked at him. In response, he flashed her an award-winning grin. I rolled my eyes, though I had to admit my parents fascinated me. I'd never seen them more in love, despite the fact that they lived on different continents.

Vienna hadn't agreed with my mom. She loved our life in Philadelphia and hadn't wanted to move to an unfamiliar city where she knew no one. A little over a year later, I realized she was barely leaving our apartment. She binged a lot of Netflix, read every cozy mystery series in existence, and became obsessed with the interior design corner of social media. She diagnosed herself with depression, and after seeing a therapist, she was *professionally* diagnosed with depression. "What will make things better, Mon?" my dad had asked at dinner one night, and I could tell it pained her to admit it, but she said, "Home."

It was quickly and neatly decided that my mom would move back to the States after Christmas, and I said I would join her, assuming we would return to Philly.

But in a plot twist, we ended up moving to Connecticut. My parents bought six acres on the Long Island Sound; the pièce de résistance was a gorgeous colonial mansion, stately white with black shutters. After moving, my mom spent the next six months renovating it into the Nancy Meyers house of her dreams.

Meanwhile, I started school.

And even though she and my dad were long-distance, they seemed really happy. They spoke on the phone every day, sometimes for hours. She wanted to know all about work and he asked all about the house and they talked about trips they wanted to take together. She actually *looked forward* to her occasional visits to Vienna. The only problem was that because my dad still hadn't moved to Connecticut, he seemed more like a visitor when he came home every few months.

At least, that's how it felt to me.

I took a deep breath, again cursing myself for choosing to procrastinate until the final moments before my parents departed for the airport. They wouldn't be back until the week of my graduation.

The tuition deadline would be long gone by then.

"Audrey," my dad said, "will you drive the Spider while we're away? It's been sitting in the garage for too long and should be driven."

Driving my parents' cool car—it was every kid's dream, wasn't it?

I swallowed the last of my sandwich. "I would, Dad, but I don't know how to drive it."

His brow furrowed. "What do you mean? You haven't learned to drive stick?"

I shook my head. He'd given me one or two lessons years ago, but they dropped off when he'd gotten too busy. "If you want, I can ask Griff to take it for a spin," I said. "He drives a Camaro."

"Griffin Keeler is a nice boy, Jeff," my mom filled in when my dad didn't respond. He had yet to meet Griff.

"What about Henry?" he asked.

I shook my head. Henry hated driving in general. It had apparently taken him three tries to get his license.

My mom shifted the subject by announcing I could use my American Express card for food and food alone; she also reminded me that I'd only be alone for three nights. My cousin James was coming to stay with me; he'd just finished his freshman year at Boston University. "But until then," she said, "use your best judgment. We trust you."

Then why did you recruit James? I wondered. James was the last person to use his best judgment about anything.

"Can we talk about something?" I blurted when my mom

ushered me and my dad into the foyer. "I know you guys have to leave, but it's important."

"Of course." My mom surreptitiously glanced at her watch. Their car was due to arrive any minute. "What is it?"

I took a deep breath. "So, okay, I know we've talked about this already, but I feel like it would be better in person rather than over FaceTime." I closed my eyes. "I know Wharton's a huge deal, but I still *really* want—"

"Audrey," my dad interrupted, "if you say 'take a different path' one more time . . ."

"Dad, why not?" I tried to keep my voice level. "I have a plan, I promise. It's not like I'm asking to go backpacking in Europe to *find myself*."

My mom pinched the bridge of her nose.

"Blue Ridge's fellowship is basically impossible to get into," I continued, echoing what I'd said when I announced my acceptance two months ago. "But I did, and it's too amazing of an opportunity to pass up! I'm going to become a better glassblower . . ." I swallowed; I needed to lay it on thicker. "And also learn new skills, like career resources for the future. Connections like that will really give me a leg up. My head isn't just going to be in the hot shop."

I remembered emailing my parents information on Blue Ridge Glass School's fellowship program as soon as I discovered it. **Business school for glassblowers!!!** I'd written in the subject line. The fellowship was both an educational and professional yearlong program designed to help young artists take the first big step in their careers. While I'd be strengthening my skills in the hot shop, I'd also tighten up my résumé, develop a website, learn about portfolio documentation, and get future glassblowing application tips. Going there would help me get into other prestigious courses and residencies around the country.

Only my mom had responded to the email: Thank you for sharing, sweetheart.

Now my parents exchanged a look.

I sighed. "Please don't say you're happy I found a hobby I'm so passionate about. Glassblowing is *more* than an after-school activity to me. You've seen my Etsy store."

"Yes." My dad nodded. "Golightly Glass is pithy."

"The program is for a full year?" my mom asked.

Ignoring the fact that she clearly hadn't read my email, I nodded, heart suddenly skipping. Were they finally getting it?

"Yeah, it starts in July," I said. "It could be a good stepping stone to future programs. It'll beef up my résumé."

My dad chuckled. "Sounds like we're applying to college all over again."

The back of my neck heated. "Dad, *I* applied to college."

"Oh, Audrey, come on," he said. "You know that's not what I meant." He smiled. "*You* applied, and we were there cheering you on."

A beat passed.

"What about Blue Ridge?" I asked quietly. "Can you cheer me on there?"

I didn't want to play the I-already-paid-the-deposit card unless I had to.

My dad stroked his beard thoughtfully, but I knew he was stalling, waiting on my mom. "Sweetheart," she said. "Getting into Wharton is such a remarkable accomplishment, and I worry . . ." She trailed off, then sighed. "I worry about you throwing away an incredible education."

"I wouldn't be throwing anything away," I countered, because if Blue Ridge and other glass schools were going to teach me the business ropes, did I really need to go to business school?

"How much is the fellowship?" my dad asked just as I heard a car pull into the driveway. "Are there scholarships?"

"Blue Ridge's scholarships and donors cover most of the tuition," I replied. The school had unbelievable funding. "But I have to cover the rest . . ." I bit the inside of my cheek, not yet able to utter *ten thousand dollars.*

My parents did support my glassblowing by paying the astronomical gas bill, but I bought my glassblowing materials and paid for my classes in Brooklyn.

Jeff and Monica weren't going to fund a glassblowing program, and I just couldn't afford it myself.

The three of us were silent until we heard my mom's phone ping with a text. "Our driver is here," she reported, then looked at me. "We love you, Audrey."

"The tuition is due tomorrow!" I blurted in a last-ditch Hail Mary. Their driver could wait a few minutes, right?

A lump formed in my throat and I felt tears in the corners of my eyes. "And Blue Ridge is holding my spot," I added. "I already paid the deposit, but I can't actually go unless I pay the last ten thousand—"

"Audrey!" my mom cut me off as my dad folded his arms over his chest.

"Can you get it back?" he asked.

My brows knitted together. "Get what back?"

"The deposit," he said. "You don't want to throw that money away, do you?"

Blood pounded in my ears. No. This was their way of saying *no*. They weren't going to pay my tuition, therefore rendering my deposit a complete and utter waste.

"We'll talk about this more later," my mom said after three beats of silence. "There's bound to be traffic . . ." She slung her travel tote over her shoulder and beckoned me over for a hug. "We love you, sweetheart."

"I love you, too," I whispered, because I didn't know what else to say. *Thank you for ripping away my dreams and stomping on them for good measure?*

My mom pulled back and smiled at me before touching the end of my ponytail. "Make an appointment at Blush," she said, tugging it lightly. "This is looking a little street-urchin scraggly."

I forced a laugh. "Really? Street-urchin scraggly?"

She was only suggesting a haircut, but I felt something in my chest start to churn.

"See you in three weeks, kiddo." My dad hugged me one last time, and I barely managed to say bon voyage before he let me go.

DO SOMETHING YOU'VE NEVER DONE BEFORE. Griff's words came to mind only minutes after my parents' chartered car disappeared down the driveway. *Say what the hell and shoot for the moon!*

Okay, it *was* cheesy, but Griff had a point. The closest I'd ever come to stepping out of line was applying to Blue Ridge. I'd never, for lack of a better word, *rebelled.*

Was it sad that the only thing I could think of was destroying my mom's perfect kitchen by making breakfast-for-dinner later? A mess of scrambled eggs, pancakes, and crispy bacon that would smell up the room for days?

Yes, Audrey, the little voice in my head said. *That's pretty pathetic.*

Especially because, like my mother, I preferred my life *neat.* The disaster zone would never last; I'd clean up the mess within a few hours of making it.

Hmm...

Before I knew what I was doing, I charged down to the basement and veered right, toward the wine cellar. It was a point of pride for my parents, bottles upon bottles arranged in mahogany built-ins behind a sleek glass wall. The humming wine fridge was stocked too. My mother always offered a glass of chilled sauvignon blanc to her friends.

I shifted from one foot to the other on the flagstone floor as I studied the shelves. The wine was organized by origin: Australia, France, Italy, North America, Spain . . .

My eyes backtracked to France and locked on the Loire Valley. How appropriate, since it was Jeff and Monica's destination. Smirking to myself, I selected a bottle nestled below my knees, one that wouldn't appear missing upon first glance. It was a 2021 Bourgueil Franc de Pied, whatever that was. All it looked like to me was a bottle of cabernet.

My parents would be upset, but not *too* upset—especially since I suspected they'd return home with plenty of souvenirs. They always did. I marched back upstairs feeling triumphant, and it was only when I'd pulled my dad's fancy electric bottle opener out of a cabinet that I asked myself what the hell I was doing. Drink an entire bottle of red wine? At three p.m.? By myself?

Heart rate hitching a little, I unlocked my phone and texted Henry. Busy?

Why? he responded a few minutes later. Are you lonely already, Gabrielle?

I rolled my eyes; another Audrey Hepburn reference. And as an only child, I didn't get lonely. I'd always been excellent at playing by myself as a little kid. The backstories I created for the family living in my dollhouse were masterful.

Gritting my teeth as I walk into the dentist, Henry added,

actually answering my question. See you at 7.

SHARP, I replied, then took a breath. Henry had offered to be the ultimate "book boyfriend" tonight, by taking me to the bookstore and watching me browse before dinner. "But you read more than me," I'd pointed out, to which he replied, "Who cares? Instagram will *love* it."

I wondered how many people would realize it was something resembling soft launch. Henry and I didn't post photos of each other often, and when we did, it was a goofy shot in the hot shop.

I locked my phone and went back to the wine, even though I had no intention of uncorking it. *What to do, what to do,* I thought, until I realized I was absentmindedly twirling my ponytail—or *scraggly* ponytail, per my mom.

And just like that, I found a way to fill the day until my "date."

My hair had its pros and cons. It was long and thick, and, thanks to Pantene's lavender volumizer shampoo and conditioner, had some bounce. But its natural color . . . on a good day, it could be described as *ashy blond;* on a bad day, *dishwater brown;* and on a regular day, *mousy.* I also wasn't really into styling it beyond a biannual trim. My mom always encouraged me to get some highlights and layers to spice things up a little. I didn't really see the point; I was a huge fan of ponytails, braids, and messy buns.

Instead of calling Blush, my mom's expensive salon, I reluctantly texted Ellie, who had connections elsewhere. But when she didn't respond right away, I grabbed Brigitta's keys off the mudroom hook and left without setting the alarm.

Ellie's house was an easy ten-minute drive, and Griff's just happened to be on the way there. My heart flipped when I saw him in his front yard, tossing the football around with his younger brothers. It was a gorgeous day, so he had gone full sun's out, guns out in a gray muscle tee and Oakley sunglasses. I thought about rolling down my window and calling his name, but my voice died in my throat when I noticed two girls on his front stoop. They were in bikini tops, sipping lemonade.

My cheeks warmed. *Keep driving.*

There were four cars in the Hoppers' driveway, including one with an unfamiliar Massachusetts license plate, and I spotted Ellie's Prius among them. I parked on the street, near the mailbox, and took a breath before unbuckling my seat belt. She still hadn't replied to my text.

Whatever, I told myself. Showing up out of nowhere would be fine. Maybe Ellie hadn't ever invited me to sleep over, but I knew the Hopper family from Constellation Catering and occasional cookouts at Henry's house and I could tell they liked me.

Their house was a historic saltbox, painted pale blue with big windows and a navy front door. I heard voices as I walked up the brick pathway and debated whether or not to wink at their Ring camera.

I went with *not,* since Caroline, my boss, also lived here.

Ding-dong went the doorbell.

"Nah, don't worry, I'll get it!" someone shouted from inside, and five seconds later, the door swung open and I was hit with a wave of what could only be called *devastating handsomeness.*

The guy standing before me looked like a Disney prince, tall with red-gold hair and twinkling blue eyes. His worn Sperrys and faded green shorts made him look no less royal, and even with his sleeves pushed up to the elbows, his white linen button-down looked familiar—I was pretty sure Henry owned the same one.

He aspired to own the silver Rolex on this guy's wrist.

Please, I prayed. *Please do not let this be Chase!*

"May I help you?" he asked when my brain couldn't formulate a hello.

"Are you Chase?" I squeaked.

"Dear god, no." He snorted just as I noticed his gold wedding band. "I'm Charlie, Ellie's second-favorite cousin."

I raised an eyebrow. "*Second*-favorite?"

"She prefers my twin," Charlie explained. He sighed. "But it's fine—I'm her sister's first favorite."

"Good for you," I joked.

Charlie chuckled and waved me into the house. "You just missed Ellie. Chase picked her up a half hour ago."

"Oh, okay," I said, even though it wasn't Ellie I needed to see (and *bleh,* she was on a date with Chase). All credit for her pink hair had gone to her sister, after all. "Is Tate around?"

"Tater Tot!" Charlie called. "You have a visitor!"

58

"Is it Tommy?" a little voice called back. "Because I have zero interest in talking to him!"

"Nope, not Tommy," her cousin confirmed, and soon Ellie's thirteen-year-old sister found us in the foyer. Her cinnamon-colored topknot bounced with each step, and I noticed her black and yellow FAIRFIELD MIDDLE SCHOOL T-shirt had been cut into a crop top.

My mom would be horrified if she knew I was about to ask a seventh grader to do my hair.

"Hi, Audrey," Tate said. "What's up?"

"Do you have any availability today?" I made a big show of tugging my hair free from my ponytail.

Tate's eyes widened, and soon we were studying her Pinterest together. It was an archive of actresses, singers, and influencers. A YouTuber named Steph was her current muse. "What are you looking for?" she asked. "Classic?" She clicked on a photo of Margot Robbie as Barbie, all cascading butter-blond waves. "Or drastic?" She switched to Billie Eilish circa neon green roots.

"Mmm," I considered. Drastic was tempting, but not dyeing-my-hair-two-colors tempting. "Keep scrolling..."

"Oh yes!" Tate squealed when I finally made my choice. "Audrey, this is gonna be *iconic*."

"Do you have all the stuff?" I glanced around her bedroom. Ellie had mentioned that Tate worked out of her en suite bathroom. Sure enough, there was a sign on the door that read THE HAIR DOCTOR & ASSOCIATES.

I both rolled my eyes and felt a pang in my chest. Henry, wannabe esquire, had definitely dreamed that up. He'd been close with Ellie's sister.

"Most of it." Tate nodded. "I can totally get the rest, though." She paused. "Would you mind driving me to CVS?"

CHAPTER 4

HENRY MIGHT'VE HATED DRIVING, BUT HE insisted on picking me up later. With Brigitta back from the shop, I assured him that I was cool grabbing him instead, but he shook his head and said, "Audrey, you are my *date*."

Oh, how I pretended to swoon.

At 6:58 p.m., his Toyota Highlander passed through my front gate and rolled up the driveway. I'm in the kitchen, I texted him, and two minutes later, he let himself in through the wide front door.

"Do you feel like sushi?" he called into the house, boots clomping on the hardwood floor. "Because I made a reservation—"

I tried not to giggle when he walked into the kitchen and stopped dead in his tracks. "You look really nice," I commented, as if nothing were amiss. He wore one of my favorite Henry Chen outfits: Chelsea boots with tapered blue pants—sorry, *trousers*—and a cream sweater. It might've felt like summer during the day, but the temperature slipped at night. His hair was, per usual, artfully disheveled.

"Doolittle," he finally said. "What am I looking at?"

"Oh, I don't know." I played dumb, glancing around the kitchen. "Marble countertops? Subzero fridge? Porcelain farmhouse sink?"

Henry blinked thrice. "No, I mean . . ." He trailed off to gesture at me.

I kept up my charade. "My outfit?"

Tonight, I'd chosen an all-black ensemble: a turtleneck tank and jeans with my favorite mules whose gold buckles matched my earrings. (I might not have much interest in my hair, but clothes were a different story.)

"Holly." Henry gave me a cut-the-bullshit look. "Your hair—what happened to your *hair*?"

"Cut it," I quoted in a British accent. "Do you like it?"

He rolled his eyes. "Hallie Parker masquerading as Annie James. *The Parent Trap*, 1998."

I smirked, then said: "I was a walk-in at the Hair Doctor & Associates this afternoon."

"Let me guess . . ." He assessed my newly short hair as I playfully tousled it. "There was a specific inspiration photo?"

"Taylor Swift at the 2016 Met Gala."

Not only had Ellie's sister chopped off my ponytail and expertly styled my hair into a layered bob with bangs, but she'd also bleached my hair blond.

Truth be told, I was horrified at first; terrified I'd made a serious mistake, my heart slid into my stomach. But after a couple of hours, the cut was growing on me. It felt cool and fresh—and my mother would absolutely *despise* it. While she loved the word *highlights,* she'd *never* said "dye."

"What's this?" Henry moved on to the other elephant in the room: the stolen bottle of wine sitting on the island.

"Oh, I took that from the cellar," I said. "My parents shot down Blue Ridge again before they left, and I was super pissed." I shrugged. "I guess I wanted to rebel."

"By drinking an entire bottle of red wine?"

"Hey, it's still corked, isn't it?" I said, then nodded toward the mudroom. "You want me to drive?"

"Nope." Henry gave me an almost painful smile. "I'm a gentleman."

"Yes, from head to toe," I agreed. "But not every gentleman can parallel park."

All the public lots in town filled up by dinnertime on Fridays.

His smile wavered. "I'll drive," he said somberly. "You park."

"Hey, look at us compromising!" I replied, laughing as I grabbed my jean jacket off the barstool. "Let's roll, Hank."

Grumbling, Henry followed me.

⁓

IT DIDN'T TAKE HENRY LONG TO ASK ABOUT
Ellie. Technically, he phrased it as *How are the Hoppers doing?*

but I knew what he meant as we drove toward town. What did I tell him? Did I paraphrase or directly quote Tate? "Ellie is happier than ever with Chase," she'd said during today's salon appointment. "But no one else in our family is . . ."

I played it cool. "Ellie wasn't there."

Henry snorted. "Nice to hear Chase hasn't changed," he said. "He never spent any time with Pinks's family. When she and I started dating, everyone was *shocked* that I accepted their invitation to stay for dinner and board games." His hands shifted on the steering wheel. "It's mind-boggling that someone who loves her family so much can be with someone who doesn't give a shit about getting to know them."

I didn't respond. Tate, with all her seventh-grade wisdom, had said something similar. "Chase is love-bombing Ellie," she'd told me while snipping my hair, seemingly at random, "but Henry *loves* Ellie. Chase just texts her that he's in the driveway." More hair fell to the floor. "And sometimes he's not even in the driveway yet. She waits on the front stoop."

"Chase is home from Davidson," I told Henry as he stopped at a yellow light he totally could've made, "but only for a couple of weeks. He's staying in an Airbnb in Boston before he starts his Bank of America internship. Apparently, Ellie and her parents are arguing over how often she'll visit him. She wants to skip her grandmother's ninetieth birthday bash."

"Okay, no way," Henry said. "She'd *never* miss Adelaide's party."

"Tate told me Chase invited her to Maine that weekend."

Henry wrinkled his nose. "That's just so . . . not Pinks."

"Well," I ventured gently, "it doesn't really sound like she's 'Pinks' anymore, Henry."

Henry thought for a beat, not noticing when the traffic light turned green. "No, it doesn't," he admitted after the car behind us honked. I fumbled for the safety handle when the Highlander lurched forward. "At least, not right now."

My heart twisted. He so wanted Ellie to be *his* again.

Something told me we really needed to commit to this fauxmance.

After circling all the public lots, we did indeed need to parallel park. "Unbelievable," Henry said when an opportunity opened up right outside the bookstore. It was if the parking gods were daring him to parallel park.

"Watch and learn," I joked once Henry flipped on the hazard lights and we deployed from the Highlander, quickly switching seats. I skillfully maneuvered the car between a Mercedes G-Wagon and what was undeniably Griff's hideous orange Camaro. It was Friday night. Was he grabbing pizza before heading to a party?

Maybe we'll see him, I couldn't stop myself from thinking.

Bedtime Stories was both our town's beloved indie bookstore and a New England icon. My mom worked there a few days a week, mostly coordinating author events and creating gorgeous window displays. I loved the store's midnight-blue facade and old-fashioned sign, hand-painted in gold block letters. Inside was a maze of mahogany shelves with various nooks and crannies, not to mention a hidden café. The bookshop was the perfect place to get lost on a rainy afternoon. I'd never call myself a reader, but the store was so cozy that I felt inspired to become one.

"Henry, hi!" Mia called when he and I pushed through the door. At the sound of the jingling bell, a cat appeared and weaved between my legs.

"Hello there," I cooed, and scooped up the gray and white Scottish fold to cuddle her close. Five cats freely wandered the store, but Poppet always rolled out the welcome wagon.

"Hey, Delphinus!" Henry called back, using Mia's Constellation Catering code name. "Still working two jobs?"

We walked over to the staff recommendations section, where Mia was updating her shelf. It appeared she was a huge fan of hockey romances.

No thanks, I thought as her eyes widened at my bleached hair. *Sports and spice aren't my thing.*

Mia told us about her plan to scale back her shifts at Bedtime Stories once Constellation Catering's schedule picked up next month. "I love the bookstore," she whispered, "but the caterwaiter money is way better. Like, the tip I got after Jack and Casey's welcome party—"

"Jake and Cassie," I corrected her in my best all-business Ellie Hopper voice.

"Oh, right." Mia nodded, while Henry looked bemused. He offered me his hand, and I hesitated before carefully depositing Poppet on the floor so I could take it.

His fingers were warm.

"We'll see you later, Mia," Henry said as the blood pumping in my ears became practically audible. "I promised to buy my love interest a latte and as many books as she wants tonight."

"With unlimited browsing time," I added.

"Wait, *love interest*?" Mia asked. "Are you—"

"He's a certified book boyfriend," I chirped, but regretted it almost immediately. Why had Henry called me his love interest, and why had I followed up with *boyfriend*? Tonight was only a trial run! I swallowed hard. "What's this week's specialty latte?"

Ten minutes later, Henry took an artsy photo of me sipping an orange blossom oat milk latte while I read the back of a mystery novel that sounded like *Downton Abbey* meets *Clue* meets *Groundhog Day*.

He posted the photo on his Instagram story.

I reposted it on mine and wrote: *Why're you so obsessed with me?*

Then I swore under my breath and quickly deleted it; there was no way I wanted my mom to see my new hairstyle yet. She would shriek all the way across the ocean.

"Okay, you're not giving me much content," Henry said after I'd gone from thoughtfully browsing to aimlessly browsing. I had one book; I was all good.

"No, you're just missing it," I shot back, because he put down his phone whenever a book caught his eye. Which was pretty much every five seconds.

"That's not . . ." Henry started, but got sidetracked by a flashy cover.

Henry bought the book for me, and we agreed to reverse roles. He browsed the store while I captured moments of him running a slow hand through his hair (if a book sounded good) or rolling his eyes (if a book came off as contrived) or wrinkling his nose (no, nope, no thanks). He picked out four books: a dark academia novel, an absolute brick of a bestselling history book, something with dragons, and a collection of essays by his favorite comedian.

"Thank you," he told me when Mia rang up his winners at the register. They were all hardcovers. "You're the best book girlfriend ever."

"I'm not sure that's a thing," I said, "but you're welcome."

Mia smiled at us. "Jared owes me a coffee," she said. "I told him there was something between you two, but he thinks you have a thing for Griff, Audrey."

Shit, I thought, willing myself not to flush. *It's that obvious?*

Henry knew, of course, and even though Ellie had never said anything, I suspected that *she* suspected, but—

"It's new, Delphinus," Henry said, lightly kissing my cheek after I tapped my debit card against the register's PIN pad. "We're just seeing where things go . . ."

Don't tell anyone! I almost added, even though the point was for Mia to tell *everyone.* We wanted her to stir up some gossip.

By the time we walked out the door, my phone had

pinged with a text from Venmo: *Henry Chen has paid you . . .*

I sighed. "I don't mind."

It was the truth . . . mostly. I'd ordered more glass supplies this week and those shipments were never cheap.

"Nope, don't even," Henry said. "That history book alone was forty dollars." He shook his head. "You can fund dinner."

"All right." I nodded, but regretted bumping our terms-and-conditions talk until later. Because this felt like we were *actually dating*. We could've googled *rules for fake dating* before leaving my house, or taken notes during *To All the Boys I've Loved Before* . . .

Henry unlocked the Highlander to stash his treasures; the Little Tuna was only a few blocks away, so we'd walk. I was fantasizing about a dragon roll when I heard voices.

Before I could turn and look, Henry closed the car door and leaned against it with a smirk curling the corners of his mouth. "What?" I asked.

He moved fast, reaching out to take my hand. I let him tug me toward him, now able to clearly hear Griff and his friends talking about their fantasy baseball league. A shiver rolled up my spine when Henry put a hand on my waist and shifted us so that I was now the one up against the car. I felt my spine straighten. "*Do not* kiss me," I whispered before he got any ideas. "I don't kiss on the first date."

"No?" Henry tilted his head. "Not even *halfway through the first date?*"

I rolled my eyes, all too aware that our hip bones were nearly touching. I regretted telling him about me and Brody Jones in the boys' locker room at JProm last year. Brody had been a senior, so nothing came of it, but it'd been a fun night.

I admittedly hadn't had many *fun nights* since then. Guys weren't exactly lining up to ask me out. "Audrey, it's because you're this badass glassblower," my cousin Grace told me when I'd confided in her over Thanksgiving. "You intimidate them." She comically brought her hands together in prayer. "May they someday be enlightened . . ."

What is wrong with you? I wondered now. Why was I resisting this? Why couldn't I *just kiss* Henry? It had been a long time since I'd kissed someone, and now the perfect opportunity was presenting itself. And it wasn't even a real kiss! It'd be a *stage* kiss, with zero emotion behind it.

Part of me wondered if that was the problem. I didn't want to find out what Henry was like when he went on autopilot, going through the motions with any of his feelings.

"Hey, Chen!" Griff shouted, making my heart lurch. "Is that you?"

My first inclination was to jump away from Henry, but he had one hand on the car window, half shielding me from the sidewalk. I couldn't move without it being incredibly awkward.

"Hey, Keeler," Henry said casually as Griff left his friends on the corner. "What's new?"

Griff sounded uncharacteristically and delightedly villainous. "Your friend," he quipped. "Are you gonna introduce us?"

Introduce us? I thought, confused. *Griff, you know me!*

Except he *didn't,* I realized. Because right now, all he was seeing was some bleached blonde whose face was obscured by Henry's arm. My guess was he hadn't yet seen Henry's Instagram story, where @audreyb had debuted her new look.

"Griff." I wriggled away from Henry. "Griff, hey."

Griffin Keeler's eyes widened and his jaw dropped, basically falling to the sidewalk. "Audrey?" he managed after a few beats.

I smiled. "Per my birth certificate."

"You . . ." He took a step backward and blinked, almost as if hallucinating.

"What's he doing?" I whispered to Henry.

"Having a moment," he whispered back.

"You changed your hair," Griff stated.

"This afternoon." I nodded, then attempted to bat my eyelashes. "What do you think?"

He shook his head, still in disbelief. "Thumbs—I mean, *double* thumbs-up."

"That makes two of us," I said, then nudged Henry. "This guy hasn't weighed in yet."

"I'm still composing my compliment," Henry deadpanned.

Griff chuckled. "No, seriously, you look incredible."

"Thanks." I tucked a lock of hair behind my ear, feeling myself blush. "We should probably go. Our reservation is in . . ."

"Five minutes," Henry supplied smoothly.

"Cool, cool, cool." Griff nodded, then furrowed his brow. "Are you two . . . ?"

"Yeah, we're grabbing dinner," I told him. "The Little Tuna."

"Right, okay . . ." he said slowly, as if trying to piece together tonight's context clues. His eyes snapped back to mine, deep blue even in the low lamplight. "Will I see you later? At Jason's?"

I glanced at Henry. Was Griff inviting me out?

"You should come," he added. "It'll be fun."

"Potentially." I tried to play things cool even though butterflies had swarmed in my stomach. "I'll definitely see you tomorrow, though."

Griff gave me a look. "I didn't think you were working the retirement brunch."

"I'm not." My heart rate heightened. Even though the idea had only popped into my head three seconds ago, I told myself to go for it. "But I am having some people over tomorrow night."

"You're having a party?" both Henry and Griff exclaimed, but in very different cadences. Griff was psyched; Henry sounded shocked.

"A small gathering," I corrected them, and took Henry's hand. I wondered if he could feel my pulse pumping in my palm. "I'll text you details later."

Griff grinned. "Embracing your freedom, huh?"

"Exactly." I grinned back as I noticed him clock Henry's and my hand-holding. "Embracing my freedom."

CHAPTER 5

HENRY AND I WALKED TO THE LITTLE TUNA mostly in silence. "So," he finally said when we were two storefronts away. "You're throwing a party."

"I guess." I shrugged. "Maybe."

"Maybe?" He shook his head and laughed. "You said the word *party*—"

"No!" My voice jumped an octave. "I said *gathering.*"

"Same difference," Henry said. "We're cater-waiters. *Gathering* is an automatic synonym for *party.*" He gave me a look. "Did your mom leave behind her Costco card?"

I groaned. He knew that, deep down, I was just like my hostess-with-the-mostest mother. If I was going to host a party, I was going to *commit* to hosting a party.

"Let's focus on the positives," Henry continued. "Griff had a total *She's All That* moment back there."

"A she's-all-*what*?"

"She's All That." Henry paused our promenade to give me a

look. "Romantic comedy from 1999 with Freddie Prinze Junior?"

"Doesn't ring a bell," I lied, knowing it would annoy him.

Sure enough, he let out a heavy sigh. "High school jock bets he can turn the nerdy girl into prom queen?"

"Let me guess," I said dryly. "She takes off her glasses and suddenly she's *gorgeous*."

"How'd you know?"

"Because Taylor Swift spoofs the scene in the 'You Belong with Me' music video," I said. "I've also seen the movie, Hank."

Henry flashed me the middle finger with one hand and used the other to zap my waist. "The equivalent of that happened earlier," he said after I tried to swallow my squeal. "Griff saw your new hair and now thinks you're a goddess."

"Sure he does."

"No, honestly," Henry said. "He could barely get any words out. For a second, I thought he was going to faint. He looked like he'd reached the peak of Mount Olympus."

"I think you're exaggerating," I told him, even though something had sparked in my chest at his words. Was Griff really seeing me in a new light?

"I think our plan is going to work," Henry countered, holding open the sushi restaurant's door for me. "We just need to give it some time."

You still haven't said you like my hair, I thought before stopping short by the hostess podium. The Little Tuna was all contemporary minimalism with moody lighting, but still, Ellie's pink-blond hair glowed in the dim light. She and Chase sat at a nearby table. I never would've thought it was possible to look lovestruck while eating edamame.

I could only see Chase's back. He had dark hair and broad shoulders.

"Henry," I hissed at the same time he said, "Chen, party of two."

The host scanned his list and nodded. "Yes, if you'll please follow me," he said, collecting a couple of menus.

"Henry." I grabbed his sleeve before he walked into the lion's den. "Ellie's here."

"What?"

"Ellie is here," I repeated. "With Chase."

His face paled, and I didn't blame him. It was one thing to see his ex-girlfriend solo, but seeing her so happy *with* Chase . . .

"What do you want to do?" I asked quietly. "Stay? Bail?"

"Does Hamburger Hill sound appetizing?"

I meant to nod, but then found myself shaking my head, lacing my fingers through his, and subtly tugging him toward our table. Henry and I had orchestrated this scheme to make Ellie jealous, so Ellie actually seeing us might be a strong start.

Our table was, as fate would have it, on the banquette wall. Two tables over from the lovebirds. There was no one dining between us.

Ellie noticed us as soon as we sat down, mid-sip of water. "Oh my god, Audrey!"

"Hey!" I plastered on a smile. "I didn't know you liked sushi."

"Neither did I," Henry mumbled.

If Ellie heard him, she didn't let on. "Your hair is really something else," she told me. "Tate sent me a photo earlier." Pause. "I think it's her best makeover to date."

Makeover? For some reason, the word stung. Yes, my haircut was making everyone's head spin, but I was still *me*.

"Thanks," I said brightly, then caught Ellie glance between Henry and me. I felt a pebble land in the pit of my stomach, hoping she didn't feel betrayed. Ellie Hopper and I only hung out due to proximity and/or convenience, so I didn't feel like I was breaking girl code by sitting here with Henry . . . At least, I didn't think so. "You must be the infamous Chase."

"Infamous?" His lips curled up in a cheeky smile. "What makes me *infamous*?"

Oh, I don't know, I thought. *Maybe the fact that you stole the love of my best friend's life?*

Henry cleared his throat. "Nice to see you, man," he said to Chase, always the bigger and better person. "How's Davidson?"

He nodded along as Chase talked about college, but I imagined the words were going in one ear and out the other.

"What about you, Chen?" Chase asked after Henry and I had ordered Thai iced teas. "You still doing improv?"

"Whatever gets me closer to Weekend Update on *SNL*," Henry said dryly.

Everyone laughed, but I noticed a slight hitch in Ellie's. I'd known Chase for all of five minutes, so I couldn't pen a

Google review on him yet, but I *did* know that he didn't have Henry's wit.

No one did.

"If you'll excuse me a moment . . ." I inched out of the banquette. "I'm going to run to the bathroom."

A high level of don't-leave-me-here alarm flashed across Henry's face, but he quickly recovered, pushing back his chair so he could stand up before I did.

His manners were also unrivaled. My mom said that men stood whenever a lady left or returned to the table.

My phone pinged three seconds after I locked the restroom door. You call HH and order takeout, **Henry had texted.** I'm brainstorming a way to get us out of here.

Really? **I replied.** Double dates aren't your thing?

He countered with a snarky *New Girl* GIF.

Fair, I thought. Ellie and Chase hadn't even gotten their sushi yet; they weren't on their way out anytime soon. Chase would probably chill out if we stayed, but I had a feeling Ellie and Henry—no matter how hard they tried not to—would eavesdrop on each other. Meanwhile, I'd feel like I was part of the world's most awkward performance piece.

A sighting of Henry and me together was enough for tonight, right?

"I'm sorry, but we need to go," I said anxiously when I got back to the table (Henry stood again). "I left the furnace on."

"Oh, crap." There was a glint in Henry's eye that I knew only I could see. It made me want to smile. "Yeah, we better—"

"Don't you leave the furnace on all the time?" Ellie asked. "It takes hours to heat up."

"Furnace?" Chase inquired.

"Audrey blows glass," Henry explained.

Chase snickered like a twelve-year-old boy.

I pointedly ignored him. It was always annoying how sexualized glassblowing was. My furnace's reheating chamber was commonly known as a "glory hole."

"Yes," I told Ellie, "but I'm pretty sure I left the hatch open, so the glass isn't totally contained." I forced a laugh. "My parents will murder me if I burn down the house!"

"Schumacher wallpaper *is* expensive," Ellie conceded.

Henry, the only person I knew who still carried cash, dropped a ten on the table to cover our drinks before putting his hand on my lower back to usher me outside. I stifled my surprised shiver, in case Ellie was watching. "Great to meet you, Chase!" I called over my shoulder.

"Very heartfelt," Henry noted as we raced each other to his car.

⁓

"WHAT DO YOU WANT TO WATCH?" I ASKED. The Highlander smelled like Hamburger Hill heaven. I was driving, and Henry had been obediently feeding me fries on the way home. Now we were finally at the front gate. *"Modern Family?"*

"Mmm," Henry mumbled.

"Early *Modern Family*?" I clarified, because out of the eleven seasons, the earlier episodes were best.

He was quiet while I rolled down the window and punched in the gate code. "I don't think I'm going to stay," he said. "Is that okay?"

"Oh," I said, sort of surprised.

"I'm sorry," he added. "It's not you . . ." He let out a long sigh. "Honestly, all I want to do is climb into bed with a good book."

"How fitting," I joked, and offhandedly gestured to his haul from Bedtime Stories in the back seat. "You have some strong contenders."

Henry chuckled. "I'll text you tomorrow," he said once I'd put his car in Park. "We can go to Costco when you're back from Brooklyn. I should be finished working the retirement brunch by then."

Right, we needed supplies for my *small gathering*.

"I'm going to text Ellie," I said, partly as a way to assuage my guilt about not giving her a heads-up about my date with Henry and partly to stall going inside. My house seemed spooky tonight, looming large in the darkness.

Not to mention, totally empty. I didn't even have a pet goldfish to keep me company.

You don't get lonely, I reminded myself.

"No need," Henry said. "I invited both her and Chase while you were in the bathroom."

"Seriously?" My eyebrows knitted together. "You couldn't even be in the same restaurant as him. How is my house going to be better?"

"I was being polite," Henry said. "There's no chance Chase Reynolds is going to a high school party." He shrugged. "He said he has 'business with the boys.'"

"As in the superheroes?"

"He wishes." Henry smirked. "No, just high school friends. Guys I *know* Ellie despises."

I laughed and finally unlatched the car door. Henry followed suit. "Start counting down the days," I told him. "Their relationship is doomed."

"She seemed pretty into him tonight." Henry sounded like he had a lump in his throat.

"Maybe," I said. "She wasn't *comfortable*, though."

"We certainly know how to kill the mood."

"That we do," I agreed. "But even before we sat down, I could tell she wasn't fully relaxed . . ." I rounded the hood of the Highlander to meet Henry at the front stoop. "At least, not the way she used to be with you."

Henry looked thoughtful but stayed quiet and offered me the brown bag of greasy takeout. My mouth watered at the thought of my burger.

"Thank you," I said. "Have fun snuggling up with your books."

"I fully intend to," he replied, but didn't get back in the car until I'd unlocked my front door. One foot in the foyer, I heard him start the engine before quickly killing it and rolling down his window.

"Is everything okay?" I called.

"I forgot to say good night! So . . . good night!"

"Good night," I said, giggling, then couldn't help but ask: "Do you like my hair?"

Henry was quiet for a moment. "You've definitely stepped up your reputation."

Then his window went back up, and he started the car and rounded the rotary-situation in the driveway.

I smiled as he honked twice in farewell and passed through the gate. He was a fan of the new look.

At least, I thought so.

CHAPTER 6

THE NEXT DAY, AFTER BLOWING GLASS IN Brooklyn, I tried to nod off on the train back to Connecticut. My class had been five hours; half of it was spent watching my instructor demonstrate blowing the foot of a goblet, and the latter half was dedicated to copying him. My usual partner had been sick, so I'd worked with our TA.

Goblet making was *not easy,* and our conversation only made things worse. "I believe congratulations are in order," Vin had said during a flash in the furnace. He was somehow managing glassblowing and a PhD program at Columbia, which sounded wild to me.

"For what?" I'd asked.

"Blue Ridge!" my TA answered. "What else?" He broke into a smile. "Nico told me, and it's really incredible, Audrey. I've applied to that fellowship *three* times . . ."

I managed to say thank you, but each one of his words felt like a cut. Even if my parents called me tomorrow with a change of heart, the Blue Ridge ship would've already set sail without me. Because at midnight tonight, tuition for the fellowship was due.

A lump formed in my throat seconds before I felt my iPhone buzz in my backpack. *Please leave your name and number,* I thought, but ended up fumbling for the phone in case it *was* my parents. They'd texted me after their plane had landed but we hadn't spoken yet.

Instead of my mom and dad, my cousin's name popped up on the screen.

What's he calling about? I wondered, since James was mostly a texter. Blinking to wake myself up, I tapped to answer. "Hi, James."

"Hey," he said, upbeat. "I'm just checking in. How are you?"

"How thoughtful," I said, because my cousin appreciated a healthy dose of sarcasm. "I'm good—I'm on the way home from Brooklyn."

"Right." I could almost see him nod. "You had class from nine to two."

"How do you know that?"

"It's on the schedule Aunt Monica emailed me last week."

"Of course." I sighed, because *of course.* It was so on-brand for my mom. "Tell me, what are my plans for this afternoon?"

"A few chores, but otherwise you're wide open . . ." James trailed off. "Have you driven the Spider yet?"

"No," I said.

"Why not?"

"I don't know how to drive stick."

My cousin was quiet, then said: "Do you think it might be worth learning? To pull off the 'old man's car' bit?"

The old man's car bit.

It was ironic that James was the cousin my parents had asked to come stay with me; he was polite, charming, and seemingly responsible but also never ran out of stories about his shenanigans. In high school, he'd pulled so many pranks and skipped class so many times that the principal encouraged him *not* to come back to visit after graduating last year.

Maybe my mom and dad thought college had changed him?

"Driving the Spider would be more of a chore than a joyride," I told him. "My dad did ask me to take it out for a spin. It's just been sitting in the garage."

"Mmm," James hummed. "Bummer."

"Are you on the train, too?" I asked when I overheard someone ask James if the seat next to him was taken.

"Yes, I'm staring wistfully out the window," he answered. "Isa still has finals, so I'm making a pit stop at Brown before heading to your place on Sunday."

Isa was James's girlfriend, and the most has-her-shit-together person on the planet. Opposites attract, I guess.

"Sounds good," I said, then closed my eyes, bit my lip, and asked if he had any advice for throwing a party.

"You're throwing a party?" James sounded both bemused and delighted.

"Well, actually, a small gathering," I corrected him, stomach swishing.

Was I about to make a huge mistake?

My cousin laughed. "Don't give anyone the gate code," he said. "Buzz them in yourself. Otherwise, attendance is going to multiply."

I nodded. Henry and Griff knew the gate code, but I could trust Henry to keep it a secret. Ellie too, if I told her. I'd probably need to talk to Griff. Per the mass Party at Jason's house @ 9 PM! texts I'd gotten in the past, he was definitely a "mi casa es su casa" guy.

Even if it wasn't his casa.

James offered some more pearls of party wisdom—always include "Mr. Brightside" on the playlist, dilute vodka with water, lock every door except the bathroom so people stay in common areas—and we signed off when my train pulled into the station. "Thanks for the tips," I said. "Say hi to Isa for me."

"Will do," he replied. "Text me if you need anything." Pause. "Or don't."

"Okay." I had no idea what that meant. "See you soon."

"But will you?" James asked coyly.

"Yes," I said. "It says so on my mom's agenda."

"That it does." A laugh. "Bye, Audrey."

"Bye, James."

I PULLED UP TO HENRY'S HOUSE BEFORE GOING home. His Highlander was diagonally parked in the center of the driveway, blocking in both his mom's and stepmother's cars. "Yikes," I muttered, and even though no one was around to hear me, I whistled for emphasis.

"Audrey, hello!" Charlotte, Henry's mom, greeted me when I slipped in through the kitchen door. There was flour, sugar, and brown-speckled banana peels on the counter, and she was pouring chocolate chips into her blue KitchenAid mixer. A sweet pang hit my stomach—Charlotte made the *best* chocolate chip banana bread.

"Hi, Charlotte." I smiled. "Did you see your son's parking violation?"

She sighed. "No . . ."

"But I did!" Tess said, waving a piece of paper around as she breezed out of her wife's office. She'd written *ESSEX HARBOR P.D.* over the letterhead, which actually read CARRIAGE WORKS. Tess Bauer specialized in restoring vintage Mercedes. People all over New England brought their cars to her garage.

"Brilliant." I giggled at the fake ticket, then pointed upstairs. "His room?"

Charlotte nodded. "Someone spilled a carafe of guava juice on him, so he's showering."

"Naturally," I said. A Constellation Catering brunch was never complete without our signature mimosa bar.

I wondered who was responsible for the party foul.

"Keep the door open!" Charlotte called once I was halfway up the stairs, and I stumbled even though she meant it all in good fun. Henry hadn't told his parents about our scheme yet, but if we grew more serious, I knew he would. He never kept things from them.

What are they going to think? I thought, a little anxiously. *That we're total idiots?*

I continued climbing the stairs.

Henry's room was painted navy blue, which somehow made the space feel cozy instead of dark, and he had long, low bookcases up against the walls. They were filled with books and topped with various mementos and pictures—everything from a cool weathered brass clock to his Marshall Bluetooth speaker to a framed photo of him and Ellie at JProm last year. She'd styled her pink hair in a classic chignon, and Henry was softly smiling as he twirled a tendril around his finger. I'd gag if I didn't know them.

For Henry's own good, I thought about putting the frame face down, but the picture was collecting dust. Perhaps it was a sign that Henry didn't pay it much attention.

The corners of my mouth turned up when I glanced at his desk; on it were both an LSAT prep book and a stack of *People* magazines. They suggested that Henry's internal battle between entertainment lawyer and hotshot Hollywood agent was still raging. "But you never know," I'd once overheard Ellie say to Henry, "you might get to college and realize you want to go to med school."

Does she not know about his delicate constitution? I'd wondered. *He vomited after helping me with a minor hot shop burn!*

The *People* issues were held in place by one of Golightly Glass's extremely limited-edition black diamond paperweights. I'd only blown one, an experiment gone horribly wrong. The paperweight was a glimmering ebony, but it didn't resemble a diamond at all. "It'll still do the job," Henry had said before pocketing it.

I was skimming the most recent magazine's "One Last Thing" interview with Selena Gomez when I heard a knock on the doorframe. My eyes snapped up to see Henry in the doorway in a striped bathrobe, wet hair standing on end. "How was work?" I asked, as if nothing about this were odd. "Fruity?"

Henry caught my drift and casually settled on the edge of his bed. "Jared has no spatial awareness," he responded, then added, "He also wants to come tonight." He took a breath. "Griff invited—"

I cut him off. "Please don't tell me he invited every constellation in the sky."

Henry shook his head. "Just the newbies. Kenzie, Mia, and Jared."

"Okay." I dug my phone out of my pocket after doing a mental tally of how many guests I'd be welcoming later. With the addition of cater-waiters, I'd hit my small-gathering max.

Hey, **I quickly texted Griff.** We've got a baker's dozen for tonight! All set.

Really? **he replied.** 12 people's nothing . . .

I stifled a grin, then typed: I really want the 13 of us to hang out. If I invite more, we might not even see each other!

Fair, **he said.** Especially in your mansion.

I haha'd his text. See you tonight, Griff.

He replied with some emojis: fire, a confetti canon, a salsa dancer, a volleyball, and a winky face.

This will be good, I told myself, despite feeling something in my chest clench. *You won't be alone when the clock strikes midnight and your dream slips through your fingers . . .*

I locked my phone and looked up to see Henry had shed his robe. He wore pajama bottoms, but his chest was bare. I spotted a scar on his collarbone, which I knew was from a childhood trampoline accident.

No matter how hard I tried, I could not picture Henry on a trampoline.

"Everything sorted?" he asked, making me blink. He started running a comb through his hair.

I nodded. "Are you ready?"

He put the comb down. "For what?"

I grinned. "Party prep."

MY MOM CALLED AT THE WORST POSSIBLE TIME

that night. "Bonsoir, sweetheart," she said when I was expecting the doorbell to ring. "How are you?"

Fine, I thought. *Can we talk about Blue Ridge again?*

"We'll talk about this more later," she'd said before taking off for the airport, but I could still hear her shutting me down the other day.

And I wasn't sure I could take that again. I already felt an ache.

"How am I?" I asked as I finished filling one of her big glass apothecary jars with gummy bears. Henry and I'd raided Costco's candy section, joking that tonight's spread should be so sweet that someone craved an actual salad after leaving (or feared multiple cavities). "Mom, how are *you*? Isn't it almost two a.m. over there?"

She laughed lightly. "We had a late dinner before meeting friends for drinks. Time slipped away from us."

I made a face, wondering if I'd missed something. "Friends?"

"Marc and Stacy Gallant. They're American, but his French relatives own one of our favorite vineyards here."

"Mmm," I said. Had she ever mentioned these people before?

"Audrey, your father and I went to their daughter's wedding last year. They're *very* good friends of ours."

"I believe you." I almost expected her to add that the Gallants would most definitely be invited to *my* wedding someday. "I'm sorry I forgot their last name."

My mom yawned.

I tried to capitalize on it.

"Well, I don't want to keep you up," I said as the doorbell rang. Dammit! Henry must've buzzed someone through the gate. "I'm glad you're—"

"Audrey Barbour!" Kenzie's voice echoed in the foyer. She sounded like she'd pregamed somewhere. "Why didn't you tell me you had a pool? I would've brought a suit!"

I closed my eyes and cursed Kenzie right before my mom said, without even a hint of exhaustion: "Who was that?"

My stomach twisted; there was no point in lying. "Kenzie Collins from work," I told her. "I'm having some people over tonight."

A pause, and then: "There's nothing wrong with having some friends over, honey. Thank you for telling me. Just use your best judgment, all right?"

"Of course," I told her, and managed to hang up before feeling guilty about the army of Jell-O shots ready and waiting in her beautifully organized fridge.

Maybe I knew a thing or two about rebellion after all.

Kenzie found me in the kitchen, Mia at her side. They both wore white tops with ripped jeans. "Griff didn't text you to bring a suit?" I asked, because he'd alerted me to have a swimsuit on hand . . . even though this was my house.

The girls shook their heads.

"Don't worry." I waved a hand, picturing my basket of bikinis upstairs. "I've got you covered."

"Unless skinny-dipping is more your style," Ellie joked, walking in from the front hall. I had given her the gate code earlier, and she must've let herself in. She and a couple of her theater friends joined us at the island, each person equipped with either a tote or backpack. I watched Ellie assess the candy-filled jars and glass cake stands showing off homemade Rice Krispies treats, cupcakes, and pretzel M&M bites. Plus, bowls of Doritos, potato chips, kettle corn, and they're-so-disgusting-they're-good cheese puffs. "You and Henry do love a theme," she said.

"Tonight's a classic house party," I supplied, and as if on cue, Zac Brown Band began to play over the speakers. The Bluetooth connection was malfunctioning earlier, but Henry and Jared, who was in the A/V club at school, had been determined to fix it. Thankfully, we hadn't needed to put much effort into tonight's music. Spotify boasted hundreds, if not thousands, of house party playlists. We'd decided to give listener_up_the_anthony's a shot.

Griff and the rest of the guys arrived a few minutes later, armed with six-packs of beer, spiked seltzer, hard cider, and more beer. Enough alcohol to force tonight's party into a sleepover. I'd put Griff on drink duty with a request for variety, but he'd taken liberties with quantity. Still, I couldn't help but laugh when he cheered. There were few things more infectious than Griffin Keeler's enthusiasm. "Are we up for a friendly match?" He raised a box over his head, and it was neither alcoholic nor a beverage.

It was an inflatable volleyball net.

That explains the emoji, I thought as one of his basketball-player friends spun the white volleyball on his index finger.

I wasn't even into sports, but when Kenzie and Mia asked for suits, I raced them up to my room so I could grab my favorite one for myself. Black with a ruffled top and cheeky bottoms . . . not super practical.

Henry, already in his trunks, handled compiling and placing a massive pizza order for later. "This party should be an intervention," he told me, a list of pizzas in hand, after I returned to the kitchen. "*Way* too many people like Hawaiian."

"Do you have a tire pump, Audrey?" Griff put a hand on my shoulder, and I felt my heart flip. "The one in the box is crap."

"In the garage," I heard myself say as I noticed him low-key scanning my body. More heart gymnastics. "Near the bikes."

Once the net had been inflated and Henry hung up with Ottimo, I led the way outside—the sun was sinking, but the sky hadn't lost its light. Our group crossed the pool deck but didn't stop there. Griff whistled when I unlatched the gate that led to the great beyond. "Hell, yeah!"

The Barbour family's pebbled stretch of the Long Island Sound might not have been sugary sand, but I loved the ocean. The waves were nearly nonexistent and its bottom didn't drop until you were yards and yards from shore. The sun-warmed water lapped up against my thighs as we waded out and chose teams. Griff and Bridget—one of Ellie's friends—had been nominated as captains, and with an uneven number of players,

Ellie had graciously volunteered to ref and DJ. Someone had brought out a waterproof speaker.

My pulse leaped when Griff chose me, and Henry took being last in stride. "Excellent," he said, pumping a sarcastic fist. "Because after much consideration, I had no dream team!" He lightly flicked my arm, and even though his touch felt like a feather, I rubbed goose bumps from my skin as he waded through the water toward Bridget. Maybe it was from the breeze.

Both teams took their positions, the floating net bobbing between us. With Henry directly across from me, I drew a slow but dramatic line across my neck. He responded by falling to his knees, water now skimming his upper chest, and pretending to choke on his own blood. "Where were you during *Sweeney Todd* auditions, Henry?" Bridget asked, at the same time Griff called: "Your serve, Bridget!"

Ellie's friend tossed the ball up in the air, and as soon as she sent it over the net, it became very clear who was playing for fun and who was playing to *win*. Griff passionately returned Bridget's ball, and Kenzie all but pushed Jared aside to hit it back. Most people, including me, would shout, *Got it!* but Griff and some others went, *Mine!*

Meanwhile, Henry: "Hey, ref, are you taking song requests?"

Ellie's lips twitched, as if to hide a smile.

"Get in the game, Perseus!" Kenzie shouted, using Constellation apron code.

"I'm literally *on* the court, Andromeda," Henry said simply, then leaped and executed a textbook spike.

"Shit!" Griff's friend shook his head.

Henry, unfazed, turned back to Ellie. "Hit it."

"I'm Just Ken" from the instant classic *Barbie* started playing.

Mia lobbed the ball over to me and bent to ready herself for a return. "Seriously? Aren't we over this song by now?"

"Never!" Ellie called, as I said, "It's Henry's anthem."

We both flushed.

"You're not even blond, Henry!" Bridget called.

"But I've got Kenergy," he countered, a smirk pulling at one corner of his mouth. One of his favorite pastimes was making people cringe. "Watch this!"

Another spike.

"Is being a main character really Kenergy?" I posed, but a stunned Griff spoke over me. "Dude, why aren't you like this in gym?"

No one on our team, not even Griff, had managed a spike yet, and now we were behind three points. "Pick it up, team!" Griff splashed the water for emphasis, then crouched low. We made eye contact, and he smiled and held my gaze before tapping his shoulders.

From many a pool party, I knew what that meant.

It took me two tries to climb up on his shoulders. The first was a failure, in part because we were both wet and slippery, but also because I was nervous. I'd never been so close to Griff before; we were talking skin to skin. My pulse pounded when he clamped his hands down on my knees, and I didn't dare look at Henry.

Griff had been especially touchy-feely tonight, a step above his typical casual coquetry. He had to know that something was sparking between Henry and me, right? He'd seen us together on Main Street last night, and Mia had most likely told Jared or Kenzie about our bookstore flirt fest, which meant someone had potentially told Griff. If so, he must've known it was nothing serious, because while Griff was *Griff*, he was also a good guy. He wouldn't cross any lines.

As Griff rose like King Triton out of the sea, I wondered how long things with Henry would go on, and how much they'd need to escalate. Until Griff developed feelings for me? Until Ellie realized what a mistake she'd made and broke up with Chase? Until we graduated?

We really needed to discuss our fauxmance's fine print.

I rolled my shoulders back, pushing away my thoughts. Griff and the rest of my team were counting on me. Henry and I could—and *would*—figure it out later.

Right now, I wanted to focus on the feel of Griff's flexed . . . everything.

And the game, of course. I wanted to make a comeback.

Once Bridget served the ball again, I watched it fly through the air. "Got it!" Mia shouted, which somehow signaled Griff to make a dash for it.

"All you, Audrey," he told me, squeezing my thighs in encouragement. Heart skipping and half clinging to him for dear life, I gritted my teeth and managed to hammer the ball back across the net . . .

Only to bonk Kenzie right on the head.

~

KENZIE TOOK THE HIT LIKE A CHAMP, BUT IT brought our game to a natural end. We were losing the sun, the blue-gold glow dimming on the horizon, and when Jared asked what time pizza was happening, a collective rumble rolled through everyone's stomachs. We splish-splashed to shore, and I waved people toward the pool house. It wasn't as spacious as Richard and Emily Gilmore's, but it was still big enough to store plenty of towels. Kenzie laughed when her teeth started uncontrollably chattering. "Whoops, sounds like someone's cold," Griff joked, and I felt something in me deflate when he wrapped his plush towel around her shoulders.

Dinner was delivered five minutes later, and I pretended nothing was weird about accepting the boxes with my hair twisted up in a towel. "Gather around, children!" I waved while Mia helped me arrange the boxes on the dining room table—the smell of melted mozzarella, garlic, and sausage was *heavenly.* I'd never understand the hype about pineapples on pizza, but I was so hungry that even the Hawaiian pies didn't smell half bad.

I welcomed that warm and fuzzy food coma feeling after three slices and a cold, crisp beer—which meant when Griff brought up moving the party down to the basement, I didn't blink. In fact, I wondered why I hadn't suggested it myself.

The basement, the most recently renovated space in the house, was my parents' favorite place to entertain. It saw way more ladies' nights than couples' evenings, but again, my dad didn't really live here. A set of spiral stairs snaked down to a sprawling moody room whose walls and wainscoting were painted an elegant hunter green. There were gold wall sconces and a trio of chandeliers. Cozy jewel-toned velvet couches and armchairs were artfully arranged, channeling classic cocktail lounge vibes, with a wet bar to match. Its marble bar top was a statement piece, the bright white slab the perfect contrast to the dark walls, and endless open shelving showed off the glassware my parents had collected over the years.

I could only dream of blowing my dad's Prohibition-era art deco coupe glasses, but it meant a lot that he'd saved all my wonky tumbler experiments for when he wanted a simple pour of scotch. "These are wonderful, Audrey," he'd said when I gave him a pair for his last birthday. I'd been playing with indentation; this particular glass had thick walls with a subtle depression that wrapped around the entire cup. "The curve feels like the natural place to hold the glass." He shook his head, impressed. "Very inventive."

I knew he was proud of me—I mean, he'd once spent an entire afternoon watching me work at Emilia's hot shop—but as a big-shot businessman, he didn't see anything artistic as a career path. Or a successful one, at least. Glassblowing was, like my mom said over and over, a hobby. It made my stomach twist. How could he be so proud of me yet not truly support me?

"Audrey." Ellie's voice made me blink. I turned to see her flop down on one of the couches with a black cherry seltzer. "This place is *amazing*."

"Thanks," I said. "I'll pass along the compliment."

For only picking up interior design a few years ago, my mom was extremely talented. "Mom, this could be your *job*," I'd said after the basement was finished, but she only smiled and shook her head. "I already have a job," she told me, referring to her coordinator position at the bookstore. "This is for fun."

"Okay, public service announcement!" I called when everyone had made it downstairs and finished oohing and aahing. Little did they know, there was also a bedroom, full bathroom, and a cute private patio with a Jacuzzi (and the wine cellar, of course). "The bar is totally off-limits, except for food." Henry and the other Constellation cater-waiters, ever the professionals, had brought down all the treats from the kitchen and arranged them on the bar top. "Any and all available beverages are the ones Griff brought."

"Keeler! Keeler! Keeler!" a few guys chanted, and Griff gunned for laughs by pumping his fist. Not knowing what else to say, I told everyone to have fun.

The night soon shifted into montage mode. I devoured half a chocolate cupcake before Griff offered me a fresh Budweiser and dragged me over to my dad's top-of-the-line golf simulator, where he and his friends had congregated. It was massive, the projection screen almost taking up the entire wall, and we stood on a sizable patch of Astroturf. A set of clubs and a basket of balls were all ready for tee time, and the screen and surrounding netting prevented any dents in the wall. "How do we turn this on?" Griff asked me. "It's different from the one Polasky has."

"Beats me." I shrugged, then deepened my voice as I quoted my dad. "If you don't learn to use it properly, then you can't use it at all." (He took everything about golf way too seriously.)

The guys gave me blank looks.

"I might've almost broken it the day my dad installed it," I explained, then jokingly elbowed Griff out of the way so I could work some magic to get the simulator up and running. The guys cheered when the menu popped up on-screen.

"Practice or play?" I asked.

"Play!"

Once I got them settled on the St. Andrews course in Scotland, I killed my beer and bowed out. "Not so fast, Audrey," Griff said with a teasing smile. "You don't know how to use it?"

"Didn't," I corrected him with a wink. "I eventually read the manual."

On rainy days, I occasionally practiced my drive.

"What a shame . . ." His eyes twinkled.

I was suddenly very aware of how fast my heart was beating.

"Dibs!" One of his friends grabbed my dad's driver before Griff could (hopefully) suggest getting up close and personal to better my swing.

"Just don't break any of Jeff Barbour's records!" I warned, then saluted the guys with my almost-empty beer bottle. "I'm getting another one."

"Out of Budweiser," Henry reported when I circled back to the drinks. He was leaning against the bar, calmly sipping a cider and taking in the chaos. "But there's *plenty* of Natty Ice."

I pretended to gag. Beer couldn't get much worse than Natty Ice.

"Forget that." I slipped behind the bar to steal a Stiegl from the hidden fridge. Henry gave me a bemused smirk. "My house, my rules," I justified, popping off the cap and taking a dramatic pull. "What have you been doing?"

"People-watching," he said as I sidled up next to him. I took a step back when our hips brushed. "I think Jared and Bridget are going to hook up," he said. "They were singing karaoke with a bunch of people"—he gestured to the karaoke corner, where someone was currently butchering a brokenhearted country ballad—"but left and have been cuddled up on the far couch ever since."

I looked and sure enough saw Jared and Ellie's best friend whispering to each other. Even in the dim light, Jared's eyes were bright, like he couldn't believe his luck. Bridget was a senior to his junior, and she'd stolen the show as Ophelia in our school's production of *Hamlet* last month. I whistled and took another sip of beer when she snuggled into Jared.

My pulse lurched when Henry's arm crooked around my waist.

"What are you doing?" I asked. "People will think *we're* going to hook up."

He clinked his cider can against my beer bottle. "As they should."

Because we're dating! I remembered, rolling my eyes at myself. The alcohol had made things a little hazy—dreamy, almost. It felt like we were in a snow globe. Our entire world was right here, right now—this party.

"Give me a Hollywood kiss," Henry murmured.

Give me a Hollywood kiss.

I could only assume that was Henry-speak for *give me the best fake kiss ever not filmed.*

It was a good line—dare I say, a *swoony* line—but I whispered, "Not yet."

"Why not?"

"There are people everywhere."

Henry gave me a funny look. "Isn't that the point?"

Yes—it was the point, the game, the set, and the match. After laying the groundwork last night, this party was the perfect place to hard launch our relationship. Neither of us needed to tell the other that.

"We haven't ironed out the details," I told him, my stomach somersaulting. "I'm not kissing you until we do."

Henry responded by moving closer to me. Again, his hip brushed mine, but I didn't step away this time. In fact, I may or may not have felt the hair on the back of my neck rise. "What are your terms?"

"Here?" I breathed. "You want to talk *here*?"

He gestured around the basement, as if to emphasize: *Tonight is too big of an opportunity to waste.*

"All right, fine," I agreed, knowing he was right. "We should put an approximate timeline on this. How long is our relationship's lifespan? When am I dumping you?"

"Excuse me, who says *you* get to dump *me*?" Henry whispered, incredulous. "I don't deserve to be dumped twice in less than six months!"

I giggled. "I'm kidding." I put a supportive hand on his arm. "It'll be amicable."

Not Ellie's fictitious *mutual*.

"How about graduation?" Henry suggested right as Jared got up the guts to kiss Bridget (I silently thanked James for advising me to lock the bedroom doors). "It's a natural, mostly drama-free parting."

"I like it," I said, glancing around to make sure no one was eavesdropping. "But if our plan works out before then? What if Ellie and Chase blow up and she wants to fall into your arms?"

"Mmm." Henry nodded. "Or if Griff finally sees how incredible you are . . ."

"How about," I said, "we end things if it's obviously clear Ellie or Griff is interested?" I paused. "I don't want it to seem like we're willing to cheat on each other."

"Never." His voice was solemn. This wasn't a joke. "I would never do that to you."

"And I would never do that to you," I echoed, then took a

breath. "Okay, timeline sorted. What's next?"

"Schedule?" Henry offered. "How many times a week do we go out, or post on social media that we're hanging out?"

"Three," I basically blurted. "Three times a week."

Henry raised an eyebrow. "That was fast."

I tried to dial back my enthusiasm with a shrug. Back when my parents were first dating, they had gone out three times a week . . . and I always thought that sounded so breathlessly romantic. "It was certainly a breakneck pace," my dad once said, my mom smiling as she added, "But we really just couldn't wait to see each other."

"Timeline, schedule . . ." Henry ticked them off on his fingers. "Anything else?"

It was a dumb question that made me blush. We both knew we had to establish some physical guidelines. "We can hold hands . . ."

Henry agreed by taking my hand.

I rolled my eyes but smiled and squeezed his fingers.

He was, I had to admit, adorable.

"We can touch each other." I winced as the words came out of my mouth, and awkwardly clarified, "You know, face, neck, arms, hips, lower back." I swallowed, finding myself nervous but also a little excited in a twisted way. This felt risky—fun. "You can run your hands through my hair."

One nod. "I appreciate your specificity."

I groaned. "We need to be convincing, don't we? Holding hands is only going to hit the point home so hard. People need to believe we're more than infatuated third graders."

"Yes, which means we should kiss at some point."

"You're just desperate to kiss me, aren't you?" I teased, and could almost feel the heat of Henry's blush. "We kiss when we need to," I continued. "How does that sound?"

"Up for interpretation," Henry said, but before we could narrow the PDA microscope lens, someone called our names.

"Henry! Audrey!" Mia shouted from across the room. "Either come sing some karaoke or get a room!"

Oh my god, I thought. Did we really look that cozy?

Henry gave me a look. "Just not a ridiculous eighties duet, all right?"

I hummed a familiar tune. *You were working as a waitress in a cocktail bar . . .*

"Fuck me," he mumbled.

"I plan to," I joked, and when Henry sighed, I tugged him toward my mom's idea of a piano bar. A very sweaty friend of Griff's had just finished "Old Time Rock and Roll" and Ellie had taken the mic when Henry and I joined the group. There wasn't much space, so my only seating option was Henry's lap (which I guess was allowed). People shouted song requests, and Ellie casually tossed her pink hair over one shoulder before sitting down at the baby grand piano on the stage. "Audrey, your parents should charge a cover fee for this place," Kenzie told me, and I didn't disagree. *Are you going to Monica's on Friday night?* was actually whispered in reverent tones by fortysomething women in town.

My favorite karaoke numbers were throwbacks, but with a karaoke machine that offered everything ever recorded, Ellie opted for something contemporary—*very* contemporary. I shifted on Henry's lap as the opening of "deja vu" began to play. Had I known she was an Olivia Rodrigo fan? "Henry..." I murmured when Ellie started singing.

Henry's only response was a grunt; I kept awkwardly shifting on his lap and had seemingly hit a sensitive spot. "Please sit still," he muttered.

I looped an arm around his neck, which may or may not have prompted Ellie's eyes to snap over to us. She seemed to know the lyrics by heart, and I had to remind myself that she was an actress; she was committing to tonight's performance. Heartbroken and haughty.

But when she hit the badass bridge, I felt absolutely eviscerated. She sounded *furious.* "Holy shit, Hank," I breathed. "Our stupid plan might work."

CHAPTER 7

"AUDREY, DID YOU THROW PARTIES IN VIENNA?" Griff asked. A few of us were clustered at the bar, all drinking fresh beers. I'd ditched the karaoke scene as soon as the applause for Ellie died down, not wanting to risk eye contact with her. The current knot in my chest told me I should've asked for her blessing to go out with, let alone flirt with, Henry.

Oops.

"It's like you have this down to a science," he added as I took an anxious sip of my fourth or fifth beer. The basement had grown very warm. "Jason had to throw, like, *ten* before they got good."

"Try *three*." Jason rolled his eyes, then looked at me. He was pretty smashed. "He's right, though. Parties are"—he made sloppy air quotes—"'a learning experience.'"

"Not for Audrey." Griff grinned, and I wondered if he noticed Henry's arm around me. "Tonight's been *electric*."

"Wow, thank you!" I heard myself gush, both blushing and brightening. "My cousin actually—"

"Hey, what's that?" Jason blurted, and we turned to see him pointing at a glass sculpture behind the bar. It was one of my few conceptual pieces; most people interpreted it as a wave. I'd blown it after a father-daughter trip to Hawaii last year, and given it to my dad as a birthday gift.

"That's Audrey's," Henry said proudly. "She blew that."

Jason snickered. "Blew?"

"Made," I simplified, to discourage middle school humor. "I *made* that."

Griff whistled. "You're ridiculously talented."

"She is," Ellie chimed in, popping the tab of a fresh LaCroix. No more hard seltzers for her. "It's too bad Blue Ridge isn't going to happen."

"Huh?" Griff said. I was also confused. I hadn't told many people about applying to Blue Ridge. Ellie had twisted it out of me a couple of months ago, after catching me smiling at my phone. I'd been rereading my acceptance email for the hundredth time.

But Henry must've let the part about my unsupportive parents slip . . .

I elbowed him in the ribs.

He took that as permission to enlighten everyone.

"Audrey got into this competitive blowing program for next year," he said. "It's at Blue Ridge Glass School in North Carolina. But her parents won't let her go."

"Holy shit." Griff looked impressed. "Why not? Haven't they seen you blow glass?"

"Not as often as you'd think," I said lightly, then shook my head. "It's complicated, but basically, they want me to go to college. Most of the program's tuition is already covered by scholarships and donor funding, but they refused to pay the rest."

"How much is left?" Mia asked.

"Ten thousand dollars."

A lot of eyes widened.

"You have to go, Audrey," Griff said, killing his beer. "This is a huge deal."

I know, I thought sadly. *It might be the hugest deal ever.*

"When does the program start?" Kenzie hiccupped. "You can spend this summer working your ass off, right?"

"The fellowship starts in July," I said, but the light died in Griff's and his friends' glazed-over eyes when I mentioned that the tuition was due tomorrow.

"Oh," Kenzie said weakly. "That's . . . well . . ." I actually saw her gulp. "Soon."

I nodded. "Yep."

"Are you sure you don't have the money, Audrey?" Mia asked. "Not even a little emergency fund? My mom makes me keep a thousand dollars set aside at all times. You know, just in case."

Emergency fund.

My mind started to wander, but then Henry caught my eye and imperceptibly shook his head.

Right, I thought. *Right, this is not an emergency.*

Or was it?

Blowing glass at Blue Ridge was my dream; I wanted it more than I'd ever wanted *anything*. And in a couple of hours, my chance would slip through my fingers.

The gnawing in the pit of my stomach told me I would never forgive myself if I let that happen. I tried to ignore the ache by shrugging Henry off so I could hop up from the couch and clap my hands before gesturing at the piano bar. "Who wants to harmonize with me?"

After all, I still hadn't sung a song.

~

BY MIDNIGHT, ONLY HENRY AND I WERE LEFT IN the house. Curfews existed and were apparently followed. Unbeknownst to me, several people had been sober monitors, so Griff, Kenzie, and anyone else unable to walk in a straight line had DDs. Ellie was one of them; I'd given her extra Rice Krispies treats to bring home, but I couldn't remember her thanking me. She'd just given me this anxious, wary look.

"What a wild night, right?" I asked Henry as he made us late-night grilled cheeses. "Didn't you have, like, the best time? My dad's going to be pissed Griff got a bogey on St. Andrews's tenth hole, but whatever." I smiled an award-winning grin. "We deserve a Grammy for our performance!"

"I'm glad you think so," Henry said wryly. "I, however, have to disagree . . ." He flipped our sandwiches onto two paper towels and handed me one. Who needed plates? "Considering there was no performance."

"What?" I said through a mouthful of melted cheddar and Gruyère. We Barbours were quite passionate about our cheeses. "We didn't duet?"

He smirked and shook his head. "You're so wasted, Hepburn."

I gave him the middle finger, even though I couldn't count the number of Griffin Keeler–sponsored drinks I'd had. "What did you think about Ellie's act?" I asked, because we hadn't talked about it yet.

Henry chewed with his mouth closed, like a civilized human. "Chase opted to hang out with the rest of the douche canoe club tonight, so it was probably less about us and more about her being pissed over that." He paused. "Things will be much more telling when he leaves for his internship."

"Oh my god," I groaned. "Again, you and long-distance romance . . ."

"It never works!" he countered.

"Yes, it does!" I disagreed. "It can!"

"Oh yeah? Give me an example."

"Taylor Swift and Travis Kelce, especially during the Eras Tour."

"Okay, but they're not *real* people," Henry said. "She's a billionaire with a private jet. Chase can't move the same mountains she does."

"He doesn't need to," I pointed out. "He's only going to be an Amtrak ride away, not entire continents."

Henry opened his mouth, then closed it.

Declaring myself victorious, I grinned and toasted him with my grilled cheese before shoving the last of it in my mouth. "I don't think their relationship is perfect," I clarified. "I just don't think it'll crumble because of the distance."

"Touché," he said begrudgingly, then gestured through the kitchen archway. "Do you want to watch something?"

After sprawling on the family room's expansive sunken couch, we ended up scrolling through the entirety of Netflix before settling on *Anyone but You*. I wanted to watch it for Glen Powell, and Henry acquiesced, tired of me unconvincingly musing "Maybe..." to his suggestions. "This is a terrible movie," he said after a while. "Truly."

"What? You don't like the plot?" I nodded at the flatscreen, currently seventy inches of Sydney Sweeney poolside.

"She's not my type," Henry said evenly, before turning to me. We made eye contact. "You feel comfortable with me, right?"

I laughed. "What kind of question is that?"

"A regular one."

"Random, though."

He sighed. "Okay, a random but regular question."

"You literally watched me gobble up a grilled cheese like a scraggly street urchin," I said. "*Of course* I'm comfortable with you. You're my best friend."

"Good." He smiled before his expression shifted to serious. "Then why," he said, "are you so jumpy when we try to act like something more?"

Mind somehow both spinning and slowing from tonight's festivities, I didn't fully comprehend his question at first.

Why are you so jumpy when we try to act like something more?

Oh, I realized at the same time I said aloud, "Oh."

Henry raised a brow and paused the movie, waiting for me to answer.

"I guess it's just a little strange," I admitted. "I know we need to do this, but we've been friends for so long . . . it's going to take some time to figure out how we fit together as an *us*." I shrugged. "I'm used to seeing you with your arm around Ellie, not feeling it around *me*."

He nodded, pensive. "It seems wrong somehow."

"Yes, but also no." I shook my head. "I don't know."

"Thank you for clarifying," he deadpanned.

"It doesn't feel very natural," I went on. "We've only touched in public. It's not like we're all close and cozy together when we hang out alone."

"I suppose that's fair," Henry said. "Sixty percent of the time we're alone, you're blowing glass and I'm managing Golightly Glass's affairs."

"Right," I agreed, pulse picking up.

Neither of us said anything for a few beats.

"Well . . ." Henry ventured. "We're not in the hot shop now."

He cleared his throat. "Maybe we should practice a little."

"Practice how?"

"Like this." He moved down the long couch, coming closer and closer until he was right next to me. There was barely an inch between us. "May I?" he asked, gently wrapping one arm around me once I nodded.

My body stiffened. This felt different from the play we put on at the party.

"Yep, you're doing it," Henry said. "Your vertebrae have straightened—"

"They have not."

"—*and* you're holding your breath."

I exhaled. "That's not fair," I told him. "You're pointy!"

"Pointy?" Henry looked at me, bemused. "What does *that* mean?"

"It means *pointy*," I said, residual alcohol preventing me from flipping through my mental thesaurus. "Your sharp bones keep poking me."

He responded by lightly poking my cheek with his index finger. "You mean like that?"

"Henry."

Another poke.

"Stop!" I started laughing. "I'm serious."

To combat the third poke, I launched a tickle attack on his ribs. His mom had once mentioned he'd been incredibly ticklish as a little boy. Was he still?

Affirmative, and I had to admit his squirming was

pretty cute—the way he squeezed his eyes shut, turtled his shoulders, and protectively wrapped his arms around himself. I felt his abs tighten under his T-shirt. His breathing grew short, but I only let up when he panted: "I'm—going—to—pass—out."

He took advantage of my mercy by throwing all his energy into tickling *me.*

"Go for it," I told him. "I'm not ticklish."

"Bullshit." His fingers danced across the inside of my elbow. Something swooped in my stomach, but it wasn't because I was ticklish.

We messed around until Henry faced the truth that he was not going to get any giggles or gasps out of me. I was leaning against his chest, able to feel his heartbeat, and he had an arm lazily draped across my collarbone. There was nothing pointy or sharp or edgy about it; in fact, it was quite cozy. "Should we go back to the movie?" I asked when my eyelids started fluttering.

What time was it?

When Henry didn't respond, I tilted my head back to look at him, wondering if he had fallen asleep. But no, his gaze was warm, wry, and trained on me.

Without thinking twice, I stretched up and pressed my lips to his. They tasted sweet like honey—the secret ingredient in his grilled cheese—and I sensed a strong wave of surprise ripple through his body, but he didn't pull back. In fact, he did the opposite, taking my face in his hands and deepening the kiss. My eyes fell shut.

I wanted to simultaneously melt into the couch and kiss Henry harder.

Audrey... The voice in the back of my head was distant, but still there. *What is happening?*

I don't know, I thought, because I didn't. What *was* happening? When I was excited or anxious about something—or *someone*—my mind tended to wander. Max, the guy I'd dated in Vienna for a hot second, could tell I paid more attention to my thoughts than to him. *Audrey, I don't know what we're doing,* he'd said. *Every time we're together, it feels like you want to escape to some other place...*

That wasn't exactly true, but I hadn't had the nerve to tell him; I was worried he'd think I was weird. Which I was! It made no sense that I wanted to check out from kissing someone I *wanted* to kiss. Or I *thought* I wanted to kiss.

And I sure as hell wanted to kiss *Griff.* Nothing had happened between us, but in all my daydreams of stolen moments in his car, kissing him was easy. There were no stakes. It was my fantasy, so everything was bound to be perfect. He wasn't going to reject me.

But here and now, I couldn't stop thinking about Henry. Henry's mouth on my neck, Henry's hand on my hip, Henry stoking the fire in my chest.

Henry, Henry, Henry.

It was simultaneously confusing and logical, as I was spectacularly drunk.

Several heartbeats later, Henry broke away to look at me.

A lock of dark hair fell across his forehead, somehow turning his intrigued but innocent gaze into something more suggestive.

The back of my neck burned white-hot. "Was it terrible?" I worried, because why else was he looking at me like that?

"Are you serious?" Henry said, and I sat up so we were looking each other in the eye. I saw a glint in his. Was there an iota of a chance that he felt the same way I did?

I groaned, not sure enough to find out. "Is this the part when you offer to give me kissing lessons?"

Henry laughed. "How do you know *I'm* not the one who needs kissing lessons?"

"I don't recall you snaking your tongue down my throat," I said dryly, then grumbled, "This is the inanest conversation."

"Oh, absolutely," Henry said. "But I think we've broken the ice, right?"

And with that, I rolled my eyes and got up. I retreated to the disastrous postparty kitchen, grabbed the bottle of wine I'd hidden in the cabinet under the sink, and uncorked it with plenty of chutzpah.

I returned to the den with two small jam jars. Henry accepted his and hit Play on the movie when I rejoined him on the couch. We sipped together, the wine turning things wonderfully sepia-colored and hazy again. The movie even seemed better—decent, actually. All was well until Glen's and Sydney's highly problematic characters spiced up the screen.

"Do you think I could try it again?" I quasi-squeaked. "You know, kissing you?"

If our kiss *had* been bad on his end, I wanted to wipe his memory of that.

"Sure..." Henry said slowly. He leaned forward and set his barely drunk wine on the coffee table. "Would you like me to kiss you back?"

Ignoring him, I closed my eyes and took a deep breath. Maybe it would be better if I pictured Griff instead. It would ease the strange swirl in my stomach. I imagined Griff during the volleyball game tonight, looking like the beach's hottest lifeguard in his red swim trunks. I thought of the way his hands had felt on my skin, when he'd helped me onto his shoulders.

Give me a Hollywood kiss, I thought.

Nothing happened.

"You asked if you could kiss me, Hepburn," Henry said after my brow furrowed.

Oh, I realized, the breakneck pace of my pulse slowing. *Right...*

"Would you like *me* to kiss *you*?" he asked when I didn't say anything.

"I kissed you last time," I answered, eyes still closed. "So..."

Visions of Griff vanished as soon as I felt Henry run a hand through my hair. My heart rate quickened—I could smell the wine, feel his breath. "So..." he picked up.

"So do it," I whispered. "Kiss me."

LATER, AT I DON'T KNOW WHAT TIME, I drunkenly navigated my way upstairs and down the dark hallway to my room. I mean, the lights technically *were* on, but someone had dimmed them, so the hall *felt* dark. *"Shit,"* I screeched when I stubbed my toe on my doorstop, an abstract hunk of blue and green glass. Pain swirled in my pinkie toe. "Call an ambulance!"

"What?" Henry slurred from down the hall. He was spending the night in one of our guest rooms. "Are you okay, El—Eliza?"

"Fine!" I called back as I thought, *Was he about to say Ellie?*

After using all my strength to move the doorstop, I stumbled into my room and slammed the door shut. *Pajamas*, I told myself, but was suddenly distracted by the bulletin board above my desk. It was covered with family photos, eclectic pins and bumper stickers, and postcards from my travels. There was also a Blue Ridge School of Glass brochure pinned front and center.

I blew it, I thought, a lump rising in my throat. *All my hard work, only to blow my shot.*

It was officially Sunday, deadline day.

As if on cue, a tear slipped down my cheek.

"What do I have to do?" I whispered to no one. "What do I have to *do* to go?"

I thought about my savings, as if doing so would multiply the amount, bibbidi-bobbidi-boo. *"Are you sure you don't have the money, Audrey?"* I vaguely remembered Mia asking earlier. *"Not even a little emergency fund—"*

Emergency fund.

Emergency fund!

My mind hooked on those two words, and then I practically launched myself toward my desk, determined to log in to my laptop.

By the time I finally fell into bed, I was grinning so hard my jaw hurt.

CHAPTER 8

IT FELT LIKE SOMEONE WAS BEATING MY HEAD like a drum when I woke up the next morning, my mouth hanging open and throat too dry to swallow. The light beaming through the half-closed blinds was bright, but thankfully a glass of water sat on my nightstand.

How thoughtful, Drunk Audrey.

After gulping down the water, I located my phone in my tangled sheets and saw that it was a little after ten. I vaguely remembered Henry and me enduring *Anyone but You* and calling it a night around three a.m. Where had he slept? His favorite guest room?

I swiped to open a text he'd sent around nine a.m. Heading out, it read. Thanks for an ELECTRIC night!

My cheeks warmed. What had I been so worried about? The party had been easy!

Anything for you, Keeler, I joked, then added some nonsensical emojis that would've made Griff proud. I wondered if I would hear from him today.

I forced myself to climb out of bed so I wouldn't stare at my screen and try to manifest his response. My bikini and dress from last night lay discarded on the floor. I tossed them into my hamper before experiencing a jump scare when I looked in the full-length mirror. My sleep-rumpled blond hair made me look like a Muppet. "You've looked better," I muttered. "*A lot* better."

Did I actually like this haircut?

I winced when I touched my mouth—it was tender, maybe even *sore*. Parts of last night might've been blurry, but Henry's and my after-party was crystal clear. *We made out*, I admitted... and I vividly remembered liking it. I'd *really* liked it. In fact, my swollen lips suggested it was the highlight of my night.

But did you like kissing Henry? I asked myself. *Or just kissing* someone?

I didn't let myself ponder that too long, instead chalking it up to my being drunk. Henry's next text also helped clear up any potential confusion.

Nothing can stop us now.

Right, I thought. I could really lean into my role now. Thanks to last night, whatever weird energy I'd had with Henry had been rechanneled into something that felt more like natural romance instead of an awkward sixth-grade play.

I emphasized his message with exclamation points, then took a step toward my door—only to step on something. Paper crumpled under my bare foot, and I glanced down to see the Blue Ridge brochure. Why was it on the floor? For the past year, it had been pinned prominently on my bulletin board. My chest tightened, wondering if it was some weird sign. The brochure symbolized my dreams, and my dreams were now worthless enough to be stepped on. I hadn't been able to pay the tuition—

Every bone in my body jolted, as if I'd been struck by a bolt of lightning. My eyes darted to my desk, where my MacBook sat half closed. *I didn't*, I thought. *I didn't, I didn't, I didn't . . .*

Did I?

I held my breath as I crept over to my desk and woke up my laptop to see the worst sight imaginable: an open Google Chrome window with Blue Ridge's logo in the top left corner and CONGRATULATIONS! stamped across the center of the screen.

Underneath it was a payment confirmation number. "Oh—my—god." I could barely breathe the words, every ounce of blood draining from my face. My fellowship tuition had been paid.

Oh my god.

Oh my god, I was going to Blue Ridge.

Oh my god, I owed my parents ten thousand dollars.

Because by paying my tuition, I had *stolen* ten thousand dollars from them.

⌒

MY FAMILY'S PRIMARY BANK WAS WELLS FARGO, but they also had an account at the Bank of Fairfield, a local bank. My parents had nicknamed the account "Expect the

Unexpected." It was an emergency fund of sorts: When our basement had flooded, my mom drew from the account to install French drains. When my aunt needed to borrow some money for reasons I wasn't supposed to know about, it came from the Bank of Fairfield.

I never kept tabs on how much money was stashed away—it wasn't my account—but I had a debit card and knew the login credentials. Because: "We trust you, Audrey."

Why? I wanted to wail. *Why did I do this? Why did I stoop so low?*

I was absolutely fucked, but before I attempted to take a metaphorical fire extinguisher to the dumpster fire that had become my life overnight, I wanted to run away from it. So I buckled my seat belt in Brigitta and sped into town for coffee.

Essex Harbor was idyllic, sitting right on the water with brick sidewalks, streetlights with hanging flower baskets, and not a single chain restaurant in sight. Starbucks? Sorry, Howard Schultz. Nothing beat Rise & Grind!

I'd recently reloaded my Valentine's Day gift card. My mom slipped one into the goofy card she gave me every year.

Taro latte, I chanted to myself as I pulled open the coffee shop's front door. I'd sobbed all the way there; now it was time for a temporary cheer-up. *Taro latte, taro latte, and oh! How about—*

I put a pin in debating which pastry I wanted when I spotted Ellie waiting in line. Her hair was wet; she'd probably come from the athletic club down the street. Henry once mentioned she liked to swim on weekends. My shoulders slumped.

There was no way I could avoid her unless I left.

And no one could possibly understand how much I *needed* this latte...

Plus, I literally had no reason to avoid her. She hadn't openly dedicated her karaoke performance to me.

"Hey!" I said upon joining her at the end of the line. "Tate text you her drink order?"

Everyone in town knew Tate Hopper and her fellow seventh graders were Rise & Grind regulars Monday through Friday afternoons.

"London fog with whipped cream," Ellie recited, but eyed me carefully. It was weird enough that I wondered if she *knew*. Did I drunkenly text people last night? To brag that I'd emptied my parents' emergency fund?

Ellie coughed. "Are you and Henry dating?"

Oh, okay.

She didn't sound particularly pissed. Just curious.

"Well, I don't know yet about *dating*." I tried to sound nonchalant, I tried to play it cool. *Anything* to avoid thinking about money for a few minutes. "But we've been hanging out more."

Ellie nodded, though she looked at the tile floor instead of at me. "Do you like him?"

"Yeah, I do." I played my part, laying things on thicker. "It kind of came out of nowhere, but I *really* like him." Something in my chest clenched, and while I knew I didn't need her blessing to date Henry, I wanted something close. "I mean, that's okay, right? I don't want to hurt you..."

"Why would it hurt me?" Ellie tucked a lock of pink-blond hair behind her ear. "I loved Henry, but I'm with Chase now." She smiled. "We're going to see *A Quiet Place* 6 later."

"That's great," I said. Ellie hated horror movies.

It went silent between us. We took a few steps forward in line, and I started studying the glass case of pastries. "I always thought you only had eyes for Griff," Ellie said as I zeroed in on the guava and cheese Danish.

My spine straightened. I'd been right: She *had* suspected.

"For a little while," I admitted, shrugging. "Though it's hard to hold out hope when he's holding out for someone else."

"Oh, he didn't tell you?" she said. "He and Libby officially called it quits. A couple of hours before your party yesterday."

My eyes stopped just short of widening. *Wait, what?*

"Anyway, it makes a lot of sense why you and Henry happened," she resumed. "You spend *so much* time together in the hot shop..." She smirked. "It's sexy, isn't it?"

Sexy? I thought about the hot shop and the last day Henry and I'd been there together: sweat dripping from my eyelashes and feeling so frustrated that I dropped a litany of swear words after I broke something, while, in the background, Henry proposed we slightly increase prices to combat the USPS's rising shipping costs.

"Mmm," I hummed. Sexy, sure—whatever Ellie wanted to

tell herself. Her upbeat cadence suggested she definitely wanted to tell herself *something*.

But had Griff let go of Libby? Or had Libby let go of Griff? My mind spun.

"Hi, Ellie!" one of Rise & Grind's baristas called before I could focus. "What's Tate in the mood for today?"

⁓

EVER THE BEST FRIEND, HENRY IMMEDIATELY responded to my 911 text—I DID SOMETHING REALLY BAD!!!—by calling to see if I was all right. "Yes," I told him. "But we need to talk." I swallowed. "In person."

Henry proposed grabbing lunch. His mom had taught him that most problems could be solved over good food. Telling him my colossal mistake in public didn't sound very appetizing, but lunch did. Even though I'd devoured a Danish earlier, my stomach was rumbling like distant thunder.

Sandwitch was the gourmet sandwich shop down the street from Bedtime Stories. Its sign appropriately featured a witch's hat, and inside it was spooky season all year long. "I'll pay," Henry told me after we met up and slipped through the side entrance. "Two more punches and I'm there."

"No way." I shook my head. Sandwitch's punch cards were no joke. Ten punches equaled a free lunch. "I only have three, so this would at least get me halfway—"

"Audrey!" I heard my name, the familiar voice sending a

shiver up my spine. The sandwich shop was packed, and my head swiveled until I found Griff near the plastic-spider-ridden drinks case. He held up an Arnold Palmer. "Want one?"

Okay, what is with the surprise cameos today? I wondered, at the same time Henry said, "Oh yeah, I invited Griff." He nudged me. "To give you guys some more face time."

I internally squirmed. "Hank, I told you I messed up," I whispered after giving Griff an enthusiastic thumbs-up. "Why would I want to see Griff right now? I need *help*."

Henry didn't respond as he scanned the blackboard menu. I didn't know why he wasted his time; he always got a number 14. Sliced chicken breast with melted Gouda, lettuce, tomato, avocado, cranberries, and honey mustard on sourdough.

His silence made me think of last night's party. Playing volleyball on Griff's shoulders in the Sound. Griff confiding that he abstained from candy because he'd had a Halloween choking incident as a little kid. And, okay—*wait*, did *we* do karaoke together? I vaguely recalled coercing him into a song. I also thought of Ellie's words earlier: *He and Libby officially called it quits.*

Something is going to shift, I told myself. *Something is going to shift between us.*

"Right," Henry finally said. "You need help." He gave me a look. "Griff might be flattered that you're asking for his."

I opened my mouth, but Griff's voice rang out before I could speak. "Strawberry lemonade for you, Chen?"

I laughed. Last year Griff had been the one who spilled Henry's undying love for fruity drinks. "The guy literally drank nothing but Capri-Sun in elementary school," he told me. "He once dropped his Mountain Cooler in the hallway, and I accidentally stepped on it—"

"Thanks, Keeler!" Henry said, and when we reached the front of the line, he whipped out his punch card first.

"Dammit," I muttered, but ordered my number 8: Cracked Pepper Mill turkey with Swiss cheese, coleslaw, and Russian dressing on toasted rye. Henry also ordered potato salad and chips for our respective sides. I liked some crunch with my sandwich.

"So, what is it?" Henry asked while we waited near the pickup window for our orders. "What'd you do? Was it before or after I left this morning?"

"Before . . ." I said slowly, then shook my head. "Let's talk about it after we eat, okay?"

Henry's brows furrowed in concern, but in tip-top procrastinator fashion, I ignored him. I needed to pretend everything was all right just a little longer.

Griff had somehow snagged a coveted high-top table, and I resisted the urge to smooth down his hair. "This is giving me *life*," he groaned after taking a massive bite of his sandwich. "Seriously the best hangover food."

"Oh, are you hungover?" I quipped.

Griff gave me a look. "I can hold my beer, but those Jell-O shots were *lethal*."

Henry nodded thoughtfully. "You didn't agree to karaoke until you'd done three."

The three of us laughed, then gave lunch our full and undivided attention. It wasn't until I'd finished the last of my potato chips that Griff said: "So what's next?"

I demurely licked salt and vinegar from my fingertips. "Excuse me?"

"What's next?" Griff emphasized with a gleam in his eye. "First you dyed your hair, then you threw last night's rager—"

"It was thirteen people," Henry cut in. "I was under the impression attendance had to be at least fifty for a rager, no?"

"Well, yeah, whatever." Griff waved a hand. "The point is"—he exhaled an exaggerated breath—"*what* is Audrey Elizabeth Barbour going to do next?"

"Elaine," Henry said as Griff smiled and wordlessly offered me a bite of his chocolate chip cookie. "It's Audrey Elaine."

I broke off a chunk of cookie, my pulse picking up. I didn't want to say *I don't know,* but I truly didn't know. I mean, I'd already thrown a party (if not a *rager*). What else was there to do when your parents were gone?

Plus, James was coming tomorrow. He was far from a chaperone, but still. I wouldn't be playing "home alone" anymore.

Not to mention, it was hard to see past my current problem.

"I'm not sure," I told Griff for fear of floundering. "I need to ruminate."

"Totally," he said. "Although I've got some ideas . . ."

"Ooh, I'm intrigued." I forced a smile, slipping off my stool and gesturing to the cobwebbed counter. "Who wants another cookie?"

Henry shot to his feet. "I'll get them!"

"Forget it," I told him. "Despite your motivation being less than altruistic, you paid for my sandwich."

I didn't give him a beat to argue.

"I'm sorry," Sandwitch's cashier said after I grabbed the cookies and absentmindedly inserted my debit card. Sandwitch still hadn't entered the age of the tap feature. "It's been declined."

"Can we try again?" I asked.

She nodded, but the second time I inserted my card, the PIN pad flashed DECLINED in my face.

No, I thought, heart hammering. *No, no, no—no!*

Had I also drained *my* bank account? In addition to Expect the Unexpected?

"Well, that's weird!" I chirped, trying to keep my composure. "Let me get my other card . . ."

My American Express passed with flying colors.

"Everything okay?" Henry asked when I returned to the table.

"Less so with each passing second," I mumbled, unlocking my phone and swiping to the Wells Fargo app. My heart hammered as I FaceIDed into my bank account, only to see . . .

The exact same balance as yesterday.

I let out a deep breath. *"Phew."*

"Phew what?" Griff asked amusedly.

"Nothing." I locked my phone. "My debit card was declined twice, but the chip must be dirty or something." I grimaced, knowing I couldn't stall any longer.

"It's okay," Henry said gently. "You can tell us."

"Tell us what?" Griff asked, glancing between Henry and me.

I gritted my teeth and explained. Blood pumped through my ears the entire time, and I was grateful when Henry took my hand and squeezed it.

I felt like I wasn't so alone.

"Whoa, Audrey," Griff said afterward, a mischievous grin pulling at the corners of his mouth. "I didn't know you had it in you!"

Henry was quiet. He didn't let go of my hand, but he was silent.

"I mean, good for you." Griff beamed. "This fellowship is a huge deal, and you desperately needed the money for it. That money was meant to be used—" He dropped off, the bell above Sandwitch's door chiming. "Hey, Cristina!" He raised an arm in a wave. "You feeling better?"

Throat thickening, I turned to Henry once Griff walked away. His eyes looked a little glassy. "I shouldn't have left you," he whispered, gripping my fingers tightly. "I was right behind you when we called it a night—I wanted to make sure you got to sleep okay—but then my stomach suddenly revolted and I took a detour to purge Jell-O and vodka from my system . . ." He winced. "God, I'm so sorry, Audrey."

It's not your fault, I wanted to say. *None of this is your fault.*
But it was hitting me now, *really* hitting me.

"How . . ." I began, fighting tears. "How am I going to . . ." I hunted for the right word. "Fix this?"

And how long until my parents checked the balance? I had no idea how often they monitored that account, but I couldn't have much time, right? What if something *unexpected* happened in France?

"We can figure this out," Henry said, staying calm. "Blue Ridge's deposit didn't clean you out. You still have some savings, and we can chip away bit by bit. There's about five hundred in Golightly Glass's PayPal and some money in Venmo."

I nodded quickly, trying to keep it together, but this was *ten thousand dollars.*

How had I not crumpled to the floor yet?

"Henry . . ." My voice wavered.

"What'd I miss?" Griff hopped back up on his stool and took a sip of soda. "Are you gonna get it all back or what?"

"Huh?" My eyebrows knitted. *Get it all back?*

He must've been talking about recouping the money. *Was* there a way to get it all back? There had to be, right? Something more dignified than calling Blue Ridge and begging for them to cancel the transaction. They didn't even need to return my deposit. Just the tuition.

Or *did* they? I shifted in my seat. Blue Ridge was paid for, paid for *entirely.* Besides my parents and a plane ticket, there was nothing stopping me now from achieving my dream.

Henry nodded, in actual agreement with Griff. "We should brainstorm a plan to reimburse your parents," he told me. "It's—"

"Totally doable," Griff said. "You've always been all about the hustle, Audrey."

The hustle.

Griff was right. If there was ever a time to hustle, it was now.

"By doing what?" I asked. "Even if Golightly Glass has a flash sale, it won't be enough, and it's not like I'll have a whole summer of Constellation paychecks."

After Blue Ridge accepted me, I'd prematurely told Ellie's mom that I wouldn't be around after June. The fellowship started in July, and I had been so confident that I'd somehow make it to North Carolina.

"Well," Henry said, "when your parents shook their heads at Blue Ridge on Friday, the first avenue you brainstormed was robbing the Gardner."

At that, I miraculously found it in myself to laugh. I remembered making that joke while we'd wandered Bedtime Stories on our date. Henry and I had watched Netflix's documentary about the 1990 Isabella Stewart Gardner Museum heist so many times, and with enough enthusiasm and hope that *we* might crack the case. "Okay, no," I said. "I'm *not* robbing the Gardner."

"You don't have to," he replied. "Blue Ridge doesn't cost Rembrandt money."

But Rembrandt money included ten thousand dollars!

"Well, what do you suggest?" I asked dryly. "A lemonade stand?"

"No, a yard sale," he parried, annoyed I wasn't taking reimbursement seriously.

"A car wash," I countered.

"Online poker."

"Momfluencer."

"You don't have any kids."

"*Yet.*"

"I've got it!" Griff exclaimed.

Henry looked doubtful. "Uber driver?"

"No." Griff shook his head. "But close."

"DoorDash?" I asked cautiously.

"Nope," he answered, then winked. "I know how you feel about food in your car."

It was true. Unless it was *my* food or Constellation leftovers, I wasn't a big fan of food in Brigitta. Ellie must've told him about the one time she spontaneously ordered Indian for a study session and asked me for a ride.

"Everyone does," Henry said, irritated. "Now cut to the chase."

I swallowed a dig about his use of the word *chase*.

Meanwhile, Griff could barely contain his excitement. "Airbnb!"

The suspense that I hadn't realized was building inside me suddenly deflated. "Oh, yeah," I said without much effort. "That'd be funny."

"Funny?" Griff gave me a look. "Audrey, come on! It's *genius*."

"Mmm, DoorDash sounds more promising," Henry said. "If you drive with your windows down, the smell won't—"

"All right," I cut him off, the bit now stale.

Griff reached across the table and rested his hand on mine. "Hear me out," he said as I almost choked on my own saliva. "Please?"

I must've nodded.

"Airbnb is the perfect plan," he said. "It will *rake in* money, trust me. My aunt owns a condo in Nashville and it gets booked like clockwork. Mostly for bachelorette weekends, but, you know, Nashville's a cool city. Plus, the condo's Taylor Swift–themed."

"What does that mean?" Henry asked.

Griff shrugged. "Each room is decorated as a different era, and I'm pretty sure there's a huge painting over the fireplace of her holding her cat."

"Oh man," I whispered. "That *is* genius."

"That's what I'm saying!" Griff grinned. "You can become an Airbnb host and rent out your house while your parents are gone. You'll make bank, Audrey."

Henry opened his mouth, but before he could explain that I'd specifically meant the Taylor Swift thing was genius, I pointed out that my parents were only away for three weeks. In the grand scheme of things, that wasn't very long.

"Right." Henry nodded. "How is that enough time for 'bank,' Keeler?"

If anyone even books it, I thought. *Doesn't it take time to build a reputation?*

"Audrey, come on!" Griff said. "Your house is a mansion on the Long Island Sound—we can charge whatever." He smiled, his slightly chipped tooth so charming. "I can help too. Seriously, anything you need. This is going to be electric."

Electric, I thought. It was such a Griffin Keeler word, but he didn't throw it around lightly. Did he really believe in this? Believe in *me*?

"It'd be legal, right?" I asked, my voice unintentionally breathy. "How old do you have to be to host?"

"Mmm..." Griff unlocked his phone, and after a couple of seconds of tapping, said, "Eighteen."

All right, I thought. I'd turned eighteen in February; I could use my actual driver's license instead of my fake ID.

If there was a way to keep this as clean as possible . . .

Other obstacles popped into my mind, but three words— *ten thousand dollars*—suddenly made them seem less important. Maybe James, who would be here in less than twenty-four hours, would find running an Airbnb fun.

"What do you think?" I asked Henry.

He glanced up from his phone, in the middle of texting someone—Ellie, once upon a time. *Audrey is about to go off the rails,* I imagined the message reading.

But I didn't care; that text didn't exist. He'd probably been messaging his mom or something.

"I think it could work," I prompted, and even though I knew

Henry liked to meditate on things for more than three minutes, there wasn't really time. I felt bolstered by Griff, and if I let that feeling shrink, I would change my mind.

"You really want to do this?" Henry asked me. "You *really* want to rent your home to strangers?"

"Chen, that's like Airbnb's entire philosophy," Griff said.

"Well, no," I answered. "Not my home—at least, not the *main* house." I shifted in my seat, flustered but forging onward. "We could do the carriage house."

The carriage house was a fancy way of saying *guesthouse,* which was a fancy way of saying *apartment above the garage.* Because above my hot shop was an adorable flat my mom had decorated to perfection.

Henry didn't respond.

Please, I thought after one beat, two beats, three beats had passed. *Please help me. I am organized, but so much more organized with you by my side.*

Whether friends or a fake couple, I was my best self with Henry.

"Okay," he finally relented. "The carriage house it is."

Griff whooped, and unable to express my gratitude, I grasped Henry's sleeve and shook his arm until he let out a laugh.

"What's step one?" he asked.

"Audrey registers as an Airbnb host," Griff responded. "I remember my aunt saying it's a piece of cake."

I nodded but bit the inside of my cheek. "We should move

this strategy session elsewhere," I said, glancing around us. Sandwitch was far from secluded. "I don't want anyone we know overhearing and snitching to my mom."

"To Casa Barbour we go!" Griff pushed back his chair. "Right after I hit the restroom . . ."

"Tell me right now," Henry whispered once Griff was gone. "Are you doing this for him?"

"What?" I gave him a look. "Henry, no."

He waited.

"It didn't even cross my mind," I told him. "This is all for"—I made air quotes—"the hustle." It was the truth, but now that he'd mentioned it, spending more time with Griff would be a nice bonus. "Whatever it takes, I need to make back everything I just drained from the Unexpected fund."

"You *will*," he told me, then sighed. "Because as risky as I think this is, we're going to pull it off."

PAINT A PICTURE OF YOUR PLACE.

That was the first phase in becoming a Here-to-Stay host. In the time it had taken to exit Sandwitch, cross the parking lot, and buckle our seat belts in Brigitta, Henry had discovered a snag in the plan. "Airbnb is outlawed in Essex Harbor," he informed me. "As of last year."

"No way," I said. "Really?"

Henry showed me his phone, which displayed the headline

ESSEX HARBOR FINALLY BANS AIRBNB. I skimmed the article enough to spot the phrases *little supervision* and *quality of life disrupted* and *newly drafted zoning codes*.

"Why didn't we know about this?" I asked.

Henry gave me a look that said, *Why* would *we*?

Everyone knew Essex Harbor's population swelled in the summer, and over the past several years, it had also apparently become the perfect place for a quiet, off-season retreat. Tourism boosted our economy!

But I'd never put much thought into where tourists stayed while here.

I scanned Henry's phone again. It turned out most people in town didn't like the short-term rental scene—Airbnb, Vrbo, Booking.com, etc.—but the only *problems* were specifically with Airbnb clientele. Other platforms were still fair game. "Fear not," I told Henry, smiling a little. "This says nothing about Here-to-Stay."

Here-to-Stay was one of my mom's recent obsessions. It was a short-term rental platform that specialized in curated, thoughtful getaways. You booked a weekend stay in Newport, Rhode Island, in order to experience *Newport, Rhode Island*. Here-to-Stay was about more than finding somewhere to crash after your fraternity brother's wedding. "It even offers you suggested trips!" I remembered my mom mentioning while we watched a montage of one lifestyle guru's weekend in Palm Beach (dinner at the Breakers, of course).

Henry's jaw tightened as he retrieved his phone, but he

immediately started typing something. "Hosts are twenty-five and older," he said after several beats.

My stomach sank. My fake ID said I was only twenty-two.

"Here-to-Stay needs to verify your identity and possession of the property," he continued, then looked at me. "You don't own your house."

"True," I agreed. "But we know the people who do."

Henry sighed. "Sabrina, don't tell me—"

"How do they verify it?" I asked, not ready to give up yet. "Because we can submit a copy of last month's electric bill as proof, and my mom's passport—"

"Is with her in France," Henry finished for me. "Along with her driver's license, right?"

"Shit," I mumbled, but then my pulse jumped. "Wait, I have a photo of her license! She forgot it at home one day, but needed it for an appointment so I texted it to her."

"Thank god you never delete your photos," Henry deadpanned. But he didn't say no. Instead, he offered to drive so I could download Here-to-Stay's app and take office as chief researcher.

"Share the finer details," I read aloud on the way home. "Where you live, how many guests can stay, et cetera."

Henry nodded. "After that?"

"Make it shine," I said. "Add photos, plus a title. Here-to-Stay will make some recommendations."

"How generous of them."

I cleared my throat. "Finish up and broadcast. Choose if

you'd like to start with a seasoned guest, set a nightly rate, and post your listing." I shifted in my seat. "Okay, that's a lot to consider."

"I'm sure they'll offer standard suggestions."

"Is it ironic that I wish my mom were here to help?"

Henry flipped Brigitta's blinker. "Very, but remember we've got Griff." Pause. "Who could be better?"

Griff and his Camaro had beaten us back to the house, but I couldn't pinpoint how I felt when I spotted Ellie's Prius also in the driveway. "Were you texting Ellie earlier?" I asked, voice sounding a little pitchy. "Did you invite her over?" I wanted to pinch Henry, totally mortified. "Did you *tell* her?"

"I did," Henry said, then dared to add, "She's good at this stuff, Holly."

He received the middle finger in response.

Ellie had changed since the morning and now looked put together in a cute dress with her no-longer-wet hair pulled back in what I called the "suburban mom bun." It implied she was going to get shit done.

Okay, I couldn't disagree with Henry on this one.

Her hair didn't look as pink as usual, though—it had been lightened back to its natural blond. I'd been too distracted lately to notice. Maybe Tate needed to restock supplies before she could touch it up?

"You know this is stupid," she greeted me, definitely judging. "Right?"

I nodded.

She plastered on a no-teeth smile. "What do you want me to do?"

"You really want to help?" I asked. If it were me, I wouldn't want to spend more time with my ex-boyfriend and his new girlfriend than absolutely necessary.

Unless . . .

Remember the goal, I reminded myself, thinking of Ellie's rendition of "deja vu" and our tense Rise & Grind talk this morning. *If Ellie has lingering feelings for Henry, we want her to reveal them.*

Ellie folded her arms over her chest. "It would be nice to make some extra money," she said. "I need to save my paychecks for college, but I know the Amtrak tickets to Boston this summer are going to add up."

I blinked. *Extra money?*

"Griff texted that you were going to give us each a cut," she clarified to my clearly clueless face. "For helping you?"

So not only had Henry called in the hospitality big guns, but Griff had too? I glanced over at him. He was leaning against his car, preoccupied with his phone. His Camaro was even more hideous in the sunlight. *I drained the coffers for this car,* he'd said after buying it a couple of months ago. *Bring on the cater-waiter tips this summer!*

Griff was also strapped for cash.

"I'll be right there, guys!" he called. "Just asking Aunt Lynn a question."

"We've aborted Airbnb, Keeler!" Henry called. "Here-to-Stay checks more boxes, and won't feature a visit from the police."

As long as "Monica Barbour" doesn't get caught, I thought.

"Of course I'm cutting you guys in," I told Ellie, squaring my shoulders. "I haven't done the math yet, but . . ."

Do you take Monopoly money? Because I need every nickel and dime!

"Thanks, Audrey." Ellie smiled as I held back an eye roll. "Just tell us what to do."

Even as eager as I was to snap photos of the carriage house and slap them online, I suggested we walk through the upstairs apartment to see what we were dealing with; my mom visited every now and again to run the water and flush the toilet, but it'd been a while for me. My reasons for visiting the carriage house started and ended with my hot shop.

The building's base was the original stonework, while the second floor was the same stately white with black shutters as the main house. Its brick chimney added some exterior charm, as did the small front and back balconies. Griff and I charged up the winding stairs to the apartment, Henry and Ellie on our heels. "You should hang up a wreath," Griff suggested once I unlocked the door. "The ones at your house are always really welcoming."

"Good idea," I said, bemused. Griff had noticed our seasonal wreaths? "I'll raid my mom's office later. She has a whole stash."

Ellie sighed when we stepped inside, and I totally

understood; the apartment was beautiful. All the walls were painted bright white, to "lighten up the space" and highlight various accents, like the wood beams running along the ceiling. The living room, while snug, felt airy, with a white couch, glass coffee table, and teak armchairs with pale-blue cushions with white scalloped edges. The brick fireplace had been whitewashed; two framed watercolors of ships casually rested on the mantel, along with a pair of antique candlesticks and a small cut-glass fishbowl filled with matchbooks from seaside restaurants. We stood on a rope area rug. *Tastefully nautical,* I remembered my mom calling the concept, to which I'd replied, *As opposed to what?* Gift shop *nautical?*

That had made her laugh.

"Well, this is awesome," Griff said after we'd toured the living room, bathroom, bedroom, and cozy kitchen. Everything was neat as a pin. "Looks like we have nothing to do!"

"Are you kidding?" I asked at the same time as Henry.

"Jinx!" I exclaimed, and when Henry opened his mouth, I snapped my fingers. "Not until someone says your name."

Griff chuckled and offered me a fist bump. "Nice."

I accepted, but after our knuckles knocked, I said, "The place might look neat, but it needs to be vacuumed, Swiffered, and dusted before we take photos."

Henry raised his hand.

"Yes, you can Swiffer," I told him.

He rolled his eyes but leaned over to kiss my cheek. One of his hands went to my waist—I felt its warmth through my shirt. Per our terms and conditions, this was all aboveboard. And after "practicing" last night, I had a hunch we were going to make a more convincing couple.

Griff pretended to gag, while Ellie aggressively unlocked her phone.

Mission accomplished.

The cleaning supplies were stored in the hall closet. Ellie volunteered Griff to vacuum, and while the Dyson—at the top of my mom's Christmas list last year!—was in the main house, the Dirt Devil did well enough. Henry grabbed the Swiffer wipes. Ellie was a meticulous duster and wiped down the kitchen countertops. "You assess the big picture," she suggested. "Make sure everything works and that everything is where you want it."

I tested the TV, lights, air conditioning, even the heat. Then I went through the kitchen cabinets to see how well stocked they were—someone might want to cook—and made a list of things to buy. Some basics in the fridge might be a nice touch.

It's almost like my mom designed this place as a getaway, I couldn't help but think. It was so cheerful, so damn coastal Connecticut. Perfect for Here-to-Stay. *Monica, this was lovely,* my aunt Kim had said the last time she and Uncle Scott visited. My mom had offered them the carriage house rather than a guest room. *It felt like we were on a little vacation.*

"Who has the latest iPhone?" I asked after cleaning had concluded, everything now sparkling as the sun streamed through the windows. "It's photo shoot time!"

Griff did, but Henry, after teaching himself to take professional photos for Golightly Glass, had the best eye. "Just don't look at my camera roll," Griff said before handing over his phone.

"TMI," I said, as Ellie wrinkled her nose.

"No, no, nothing like that!" He flushed and rubbed the back of his neck. "I have a lot of photos of Pheebs, that's all."

Phoebe was the Keelers' pug. She dutifully attended all Essex Harbor High football games and even made it into the team yearbook photo.

I smiled and shook my head, then looked at Henry. "Okay, Henry—"

His full name slipped out before I could stop myself; jinx broken, he raised his hands in the air and cheered. "Freedom!"

My spine almost straightened when Ellie giggled. "Movie, TV show, or late-night interview?" she asked.

What? I thought, before remembering it was a game. *Their* game. While Henry and I spoke in movie quotes, he and Ellie did trivia.

Henry winked at Ellie. "Movie."

"Hmm . . ." She put a finger to her lips, as if flirting with him.

Wait, *was* she flirting with him?

"Braveheart!" I blurted before we could really find out. "Mel Gibson's *Braveheart*." I smiled and gestured to the door. "Should we take exteriors first? Before we lose the light?"

Henry smiled. "Didn't we decide *I* was the professional photographer?"

I flashed him the middle finger, and he sweetly kissed my cheek before the four of us went outside. If Ellie had been purposefully flirting with Henry, she didn't try again.

Griff and Ellie stayed until we were unanimous on the final photos . . . and agreed on their percentage per night. Ellie happily fled to meet Chase, and Griff's mom called to ask him to pick up a chicken roaster and salad stuff for dinner. "You've got this, lovebirds!" Griff patted both me and Henry on the shoulders on his way out. He gave mine a subtle but undeniable squeeze. "Shoot me the link to the final product, all right?"

"Of course," I told him, unable to hide my smile.

Charlotte texted Henry that our dinner would be ready and waiting in the oven whenever we wanted to come over. "You don't have to host me," I said, but Henry shook his head.

"Hepburn, my mom knows you can't cook."

I acquiesced; a frozen pizza couldn't compete with whatever Charlotte had made.

On Here-to-Stay, Henry and I input *Essex Harbor, Connecticut* for our location, and noted our four-guest capacity. I thought of the narrow bunk room, the two tiny beds with their light-blue-and-white striped comforters with red piping. It was so adorable, but . . .

"Actually, make it two people," I told Henry. "Families need not apply." A family sounded like potential chaos, and I thought of Aunt Kim and Uncle Scott again. "A two-person stay suggests a dreamy getaway."

"It also suggests more sex," he commented.

"I will murder you if you put that in the description," I said, then gestured to the candles on the mantel. "In the living room, with the candlestick."

"Fine," he said. "If only because I'd prefer my death to be a little more original than Clue." He smirked at me. "Perhaps you should provide complimentary condoms?"

I groaned. "Henry!"

"Yeah, yeah." He nodded, refocusing on his laptop. "Back to work..."

No lie, my heart had sped up by the time we finished step two—the title, photos, and description. Rather than perusing Here-to-Stay for inspiration, I pulled up a YouTube clip from *The Holiday,* where Cameron Diaz reads about Kate Winslet's quaint and cozy and cute Rosehill Cottage. "We need to name the carriage house," I said. "It'll up the charm."

"Fair Winds . . . ?" Henry suggested after we spent a few minutes dreaming up some duds.

"Oh, I'm driving up to Fair Winds this weekend," I tried out, my heart flipping when Henry laughed. It *did* sound catchy. "Fair Winds" was a perfect shout-out to Fairfield County and the fresh, salty air that rolled off the Sound.

I was surprised how quickly I wrote a paragraph and change about Fair Winds and the town. Buzzwords like *dreamy* and *serene* for the carriage house, and *picturesque* and *lively* for Essex Harbor. I even threw in the phrase *coastal grandmother living.*

This place was a Nancy Meyers home meets Stars Hollow

meets romance novel community, and I was going to paint it as such!

"Mission accomplished," Henry said once he proofread the description. "Now . . ." He navigated to the next page. "Should anyone be able to book? Or do you want 'jet-setters' only? It looks like that's the Here-to-Stay equivalent of Airbnb's experienced guests."

"Jet-setters," I said without hesitation, and then, after a beat of hesitation, "I'd rather they be older, too."

Predictably, Henry made a crack about me being reverse ageist.

"No, you know what I mean," I said. "As a temporary landlord, I want to avoid any"—I searched for the right word—"*shenanigans.* This needs to stay low-key."

The town was already wary of short-term rentals.

He nodded. "You can't specify an age range," he said, "but potential renters need to write you a little message upon preliminary booking, so that should help you screen people."

"Excellent," I said, and then it was time to crunch the numbers. Here-to-Stay suggested $650 per night, but to quickly hook some guests, Henry and I both thought we needed to position Fair Winds as a *steal.* We agreed on $450 a night, at least to start. Right now, the math absolutely didn't math to ten thousand, but I'd decided earlier to contribute the vast majority of my own savings toward refilling Expect the Unexpected.

Part of me felt like an idiot for not telling my parents I'd contribute my own money toward Blue Ridge, but I knew it wouldn't have changed their minds. The financial implications had nothing to do with their decision.

Anyway, instead of ten thousand dollars, we now only needed seven.

And once Henry pledged a grand to the cause, seven became six. "Don't worry, it's not a donation," he told me as my eyes stung with tears. Could anyone be more wonderful than Henry Chen? "I'm going to calculate an appropriate interest rate . . ."

The only step left was to submit Fair Winds to be verified. I felt seasick even though the breakfast nook's wicker chairs weren't riding any waves. In one fell click, I would officially be trying to pass myself off as my mom. Although "Monica" had mentioned that her daughter Audrey would be handling all the scheduling.

And so I turned the laptop toward Henry. "You do it."

"Holly, this was your idea."

"No, it was *Griff's* idea."

"Well, he isn't here," Henry said. "He's getting a chicken roaster and salad stuff."

I groaned.

"Come on, submit it," he encouraged. On-screen, the cursor hovered above the magic button. "The vibes are immaculate." He sighed. "Not to mention, I'm getting hangry."

A hangry Henry was not a fun Henry.

"All right, all right . . ." I closed my eyes and took a deep breath.

Blue Ridge, I told myself. *You're doing this so you can inhale that mountain air and blow glass with the best of the best.*

And so my parents wouldn't kill me.

I counted to three.

Eins.

Zwei.

Drei.

Then I opened my eyes, bit my tongue, and double-clicked on the trackpad.

Fair Winds was officially live.

Well, it would be in twenty-four to forty-eight hours, after someone at Here-to-Stay stamped Monica Barbour as legitimate.

Henry whistled. "Congratulations."

"How long do you think until someone requests to stay?" I asked. "You know, after we're verified?"

"Time will tell." He rose from his chair. "Let's go eat."

After staring at the screen for five more seconds, I reluctantly agreed. We locked the newly christened Fair Winds behind us, but before we reached the stairs, Henry stopped in his tracks. "What's wrong?" I asked.

"Nothing," he said. "Well, nothing except a *tiny, insignificant* detail."

Love Actually, I recognized. *Liam Neeson and his stepson's storyline.*

I nodded. "Which is . . . ?"

"Truly pretty big, and extremely important."

I let out a melodramatic sigh.

"Audrey." Henry kept his voice controlled. "Did you cancel James?"

My pulse spiked. Per my mom's agenda, my cousin was due to arrive tomorrow. And per my phone call with James—which now felt like a *week* ago instead of yesterday—he was *still* scheduled to arrive tomorrow.

Shit.

CHAPTER 9

I CALLED JAMES ON THE DRIVE HOME FROM Henry's, after sweating off at least five pounds thanks to Charlotte's enchiladas. "They're spicier than usual," she'd warned. "I was on the phone with Tess's brother while cooking, so I forgot to deseed the peppers . . ."

"Milk!" Henry had gasped after his third bite. My mouth was also *ablaze*. "Get me a glass of milk—*please*!"

Phone in my cupholder and AirPods in my ears, I shifted my hands on the steering wheel, waiting for my cousin to answer.

"Hello, Audrey!" someone answered after the second ring.

But it wasn't James.

"Hey, Isa," I said, smiling. "What's up?"

"My Russian exam," she told me. "It's tomorrow morning, and I'm screwed."

"No way," I heard James say. "Tell the truth."

"I'm *screwed*," his girlfriend emphasized.

"Have you been studying?" I asked.

"All day," she replied. "We're getting ice cream now."

I affectionately rolled my eyes. According to James, ice cream was the answer to most of life's greatest conundrums. "You're going to totally crush your test," I told Isa. "I'm sending good vibes."

"Good vibes received and much appreciated," she said, then laughed before reading my mind. "Would you like to speak to J?"

I slowed to a stop at a red light. "Yes, please."

"Hey, what's happening?" James asked. "Everything okay?"

"Mm-hmm," I answered, blood pumping in my ears. "I was just wondering if, um, you'd bought your train ticket already?"

The line was silent.

"Not yet," James said carefully, as if trying to feel me out. "Why?"

"Because you don't need to come anymore!" I blurted, never one for subtlety. "I'll be fine on my own. You should stay at Brown with Isa."

"Huh," he said after I sucked in a deep breath. "Interesting."

"Hi!" Isa said brightly in the background. "May I sample the potato chip caramel crunch, please?"

"I'm not going to ask what you're planning," James said lightly. "But there *is* a plan, right? Preferably one that ensures your safety?"

"Affirmative," I told him, hoping that Here-to-Stay's

pool of "jet-setter" guests weren't axe murderers, human traffickers, or members of a drug cartel.

Too many movies, I told myself. *You and Henry watch too many movies!*

James paused to consider my one-word response (and to give Isa his ice cream order—two scoops of black raspberry chocolate chip in a waffle cone). "Fine," he said. "Here's the deal: I'll forgo my R&R in Essex Harbor on two conditions. First, you share your location with me."

With no intention of skipping school or town, I readily agreed.

"Second, you shoot me Henry's number."

My brows knitted together. "You want Henry's phone number?"

"Yeah," James said. "Emergency contacts are useful . . . especially in the case of an emergency."

I inwardly sighed. *James . . .*

"I have Hank's number memorized," I told him. "Do you have a pen?"

"No, I have an ice cream cone."

"You're exasperating," I said.

"Thanks for the compliment," he said back. "Just send me—"

"Two-oh-three," I recited, pulling into the driveway and speaking over him. "Five-nine-five, six-two-three-five."

A beat.

I fake coughed. "Did you get that?"

"Yes," he said as I rolled down my window and stretched to

punch in the gate code. "And it's incorrect." He mimicked my fake cough. "You said six-two-three-five for the last four digits. It's six-two-*five-three*."

Hold on, I thought, eyes narrowing. *He's right—how is he right?*

"James . . ." I said slowly. "Do you already *have* Henry's number?"

"Oh, Audrey"—I heard the smirk in his voice—"I already have *everyone's* number."

I groaned. My mother's list of instructions must've come with a whole roster of people to call in a crisis. I bet Ellie's mother—my Constellation boss—was even on there.

"Text me if you change your mind," James said, serious for the first time in the whole conversation.

"Thanks, James," I said. "Enjoy your ice cream and Isa's company."

"Always do!" he chirped, and then hung up. I parked Brigitta in her garage bay between my mom's Range Rover and the dormant Spider, then picked up my phone to share my location with James—only to see several notifications.

One was a text from Henry: Did you get home okay?

I felt my lips twitch up at the corners, bemused. It was endearing that Henry pretended he couldn't see me on Find My Friends. Yes, safe and sound, I texted.

Another text was a sequence of emojis from Griff: fire emoji, house emoji, first-place medal emoji, starry-eyed emoji, fire emoji again. I'd sent him my Here-to-Stay listing before dinner.

My fingers were crossed that it would be verified by the time I woke up tomorrow.

Thank you!!! **I dashed off.**

No joke, you did such a great job, **he wrote, then added a freaking** *pink heart.*

It gave me the confidence to type: Ellie told me about Libby. I'm really sorry.

That means a lot, **he replied.** I'll miss her, but it's time to find a new dance partner.

For prom? **I asked.** *Or the so-called dance that is life?*

His answer? A winky face.

I sighed. Could this guy get any flirtier?

My thumbs twitched over a response I hadn't figured out yet, but when a message popped up a minute later, it wasn't a text from Griff. My hammering heart slowed, then skipped some beats. Henry had texted again: Would you like to go out tomorrow after school?

We said goodbye less than an hour ago, **I quickly wrote back.** You aren't going to play it cool?

Not even a little bit.

Oh, my heart!

Keep it in your chest, Doolittle.

I grinned.

AFTER MY LAST CLASS ON MONDAY, HENRY MET me at my locker. "Where are we going?" I asked, excited. It had been difficult to stay focused in German; my mind kept spinning potential afternoon dates with Henry. He hadn't mentioned a plan, and I hadn't asked.

A little mystery never hurt, right?

We crossed the student lot toward Henry's car. It was very cute that he thought he had to drive us everywhere.

But before we could make a getaway, I heard the familiar *beep-beep* of Ellie's Prius . . . and glanced over my shoulder to see her approaching us. "Hey, Audrey," she said as I wondered how Henry had timed this so perfectly. Her eyes flicked to him. "What are you guys up to?"

"After-school activities," Henry said, which I suspected was code for *It's a secret.*

Ellie must've surmised the same. "How's Here-to-Stay going?" she asked me. "Any developments?"

I shook my head. "I'm still waiting to be verified," I told her. "But as soon as I am, Fair Winds is going to be featured in a *New Hot Spots* newsletter."

It was an amazing way to get the word out, and I had all my fingers and toes crossed that my mom didn't subscribe to Here-to-Stay emails.

"I know. I subscribed this morning." Ellie smiled a little. "I want to stay in the loop." She awkwardly gestured to her car. She looked like she both wanted and didn't want to leave.

Henry made the decision for her. "We'll see you later, Ellie," he said easily. "I'm taking Audrey Christmas shopping."

Ellie's brow furrowed, and I all but gasped. "Really?"

"Yep." Henry unlatched the passenger's side door for me. "Really."

I beamed as I climbed in his car, forgetting Ellie entirely. *Christmas shopping* referred to nearby Westbrook, specifically the Pink Sleigh. Housed in a historic brown barn right off the road, the Pink Sleigh was a tourist destination that exclusively sold Christmas ornaments and decorations—two entire floors' worth of inventory, everything from whimsical Old World glass ornaments to German nutcrackers to dazzling tree toppers to retro Technicolor lights to Nativity sets. It was all, in its own way, *art*.

"Oh, Hepburn . . ." Henry tried to keep a straight face when we walked inside, but his eyes shined and he laughed at my awestruck expression. He tilted his head. "You are so predictable."

My face warmed. "Christmas ornaments are an underappreciated art form!"

"Yes, and the Pink Sleigh has been fighting fearlessly since 1963 to change that."

I giggled. Did the owners have any idea what treasure was under their roof? Henry muttered that the place was one big fire hazard. "Bite your tongue," I said before snapping a photo of him assessing intricate white-lace snowflakes.

Then he took my hand and tried to twirl me around. My cheeks warmed as I narrowly dodged a tree covered in gold tinsel and fast-food ornaments. Griff would love the sausage, egg, and cheese breakfast sandwich.

The barn was so narrow that the first time my mom and I'd gone there, we joked that we couldn't turn around without making out with someone. It was beyond packed.

I remembered us snickering while surrounded by Byers' Choice Carolers—or, as Monica Barbour so inappropriately but also appropriately called them, "blow job dolls."

Now, I felt a tug in my chest. I suddenly missed her—and my dad, too. They sent a photo earlier, but we hadn't talked much since they left. *Maybe that's for the best,* I thought, as Henry and I climbed the rickety stairs to the second floor. *Even over the phone, they might be able to tell something is wrong...*

"I repeat," Henry said a few minutes later. I was admiring the old-fashioned Snow Village on display. It looked retro, circa the fifties. One of the villager figurines wore a red scarf and varsity letter sweater. "The fire marshal must be called."

"Oh, come on." I laughed. "Where is your Christmas cheer?" I turned to face Henry, my hip knocking his when I did. Only inches apart from each other, I could feel the heat radiating off his skin. His warmth tempted me to tip my head back to see if mistletoe hung above us.

I thought about kissing him.

I *really* thought about it, but before I could lean forward, Henry took one step sideways and snagged his arm in a web of twinkle lights.

"Graceful," I murmured, thankful for the sudden ping in

my pocket. I dug out my phone to see a new notification . . . then blinked to make sure I hadn't imagined it: a DM from the newly installed Here-to-Stay app.

It informed me that not only was Monica Barbour a verified host but also that her new listing had gone out in this afternoon's newsletter.

Fair Winds was officially live.

~

THE NEXT DAY, GRIFF WAS INCREDULOUS. "YOU said no to them?" he asked. "Audrey, *why* would you do that? Aunt Lynn would say that's an incredible first catch. I mean, think about the *exposure*."

I sighed. It was lunchtime, and so sunny out that Henry and I were eating at a picnic table in the quad. Equipped with cafeteria trays, his improv buddies were heading toward us. Ellie was nearby with Bridget and their fellow thespians, while Griff had made a pit stop at our table on his way to rendezvous with the football team.

That was a new development. If we made eye contact, I usually just got an enthusiastic wave.

"The exposure," Henry said lightly, "is exactly why she said no."

Griff cocked his head, as if to say, *I don't follow.*

"We want the word spread about Fair Winds," I tried to explain, "but it also needs to stay quiet. I don't want it buzzing all over social media; my parents might find out. I mean, my mom follows women like Erica."

Erica Lupo was a content creator on Instagram with over a hundred thousand followers (and counting). She touched on everything from her style to the books she read to her floral arrangements to her passion for New Jersey. And, naturally, her vacations.

Hi, Audrey, **she'd messaged me.** For the first time in a while, my husband and I have a wide-open weekend and are hoping to sneak away for a few days. I haven't been to Essex Harbor since college (I'm a Fairfield University alum!) and Fair Winds looks heavenly . . .

She seemed nice (and responsible), but I'd lied and said that someone had reached out about Fair Winds right before her, requesting the same dates. I had investigated her Instagram enough to know she'd probably vlog the entire time she was here. Which would one hundred percent put Fair Winds on the map . . .

One good thing, though, was that the Here-to-Stay newsletter was *clearly* effective. Erica had messaged me only hours after Fair Winds had gone on the market.

Griff nodded after I finished explaining. "I guess that makes sense. Bummer, but I get it." He stole one of my apple slices, and as embarrassing as it was, my heart fluttered—Griff had been stealing my food more and more lately. "Has anyone else reached out?"

"About what?" Rory, one of Henry's friends, asked as he

joined us at the table, swinging a leg over the bench. Alec and Cam, Henry's other improv buddies, followed suit.

"Nothing," I quickly said. "Just waiting for an update from my parents."

"Oh, yeah." Alec unwrapped a ham sandwich. "How's France treating them?"

I showed them a photo my dad had sent yesterday, a sweeping shot of whatever vineyard they were visiting. The leafy green grapevines were in neat rows, and the sky was nothing but blue. My mom was in the foreground in her black Celine sunglasses and a straw hat, toasting the camera with a glass of white.

We miss you! my dad had written.

Certainly looks like it! I'd texted back, feeling a little guilty about Here-to-Stay. But only a little bit, and not for very long. It was in their best interest.

"Living their best life," Griff declared, then nodded at Henry and the rest of the improv club's senior council. "See ya, guys." He smiled at me, chipped tooth and all. "We'll talk later, Audrey?"

"Definitely." I smiled back, but before it could grow into a grin, Henry accidentally knocked over his uncapped sweet tea.

It dripped through the slats in the picnic table and dribbled onto my jeans.

"Jeez, Chen." Griff whistled, then jogged back to the cafeteria for napkins.

"I'm sorry, Holly." Henry gave me puppy dog eyes. "Forgive me?"

I glanced over at Ellie's table to see Ellie not minding her own business. "Always," I told Henry, and planted a kiss on his shoulder as what could've been at the Pink Sleigh yesterday flashed in my mind. "You're a total klutz, but I'll always forgive you."

"Would someone mind walking me to the nurse's office?" Cam commented dryly. "You guys make me sick."

"We know," Henry and I said at the same time.

But under the table, I stomped on his foot.

IN TANDEM WITH THE STUDY HALL BELL, MY phone buzzed with a message. My stomach swirled when I saw it was a Here-to-Stay DM, from someone named Sandra Taylor. That couldn't be a momfluencer name, could it? I quickly unlocked my phone and scanned Sandra's note while navigating the science wing's mobbed hallway.

Hello, Audrey, Sandra had written. My name is Sandra—call me Sandy!—and I am inquiring about Fair Winds' availability. I'm a professor, and after a busy semester, my husband and I are looking to unwind and explore the charming seaside Connecticut towns I've heard so much about. We would love to stay Thursday through Sunday, if that works for you.

Warmly, Sandy

P.S. Are you named after Audrey Hepburn? Ron, my husband, loves Funny Face!

"Which one is *Funny Face* again?" I asked Henry when

I showed him the DM later. We stood in the doorway of an empty classroom; improv club was commencing shortly.

"Late-fifties musical rom-com with Fred Astaire," he said. "You play Jo, a shy shop assistant and amateur philosopher who thinks the fashion industry is ridiculous."

I sighed. "Do you just memorize IMDb pages?"

"Sometimes." Pause. "I also watch the movies." He laughed when I rolled my eyes. "I like these people. I think you should let them book you."

I hesitated. I'd talked a big game about renting out the carriage house, but now that I had an *actual* opportunity to . . .

"They're your target demographic," Henry pointed out. "They've seen *Funny Face*."

"So have you," I countered.

Henry shrugged. "Yeah, but I'm . . ."

"An original," I filled in the blank. "You're a true original."

"Thank you," he said. "Ellie preferred the term 'goofball,' and Chase Reynolds used to throw around 'gay.'"

My breath caught. "No way."

He shrugged. "It was sophomore year. Ellie and I were lab partners, and he knew I liked her. It was the only thing he could come up with."

"What a prick," I muttered.

"I have to go." Henry jerked his chin toward Bridget, who stood impatiently, her arms folded across her chest. Despite her theater commitments, she still managed to participate in improv. Today was their end-of-year party.

"You should write Sandy back and confirm their stay."

"Yeah, okay." I nodded, then felt some goose bumps when Henry looped an arm around my waist and whispered, "Give me a Hollywood kiss, Jo?"

Bridget will pass this on to Ellie, I thought, so I teasingly slung my arms around Henry's neck . . . but only kissed the corner of his mouth.

"Yikes," Cam joked, as Rory called, "*D*enied!"

"It's important to keep him striving," I said, then exited with a wink and a smile and excitement coursing through me.

CHAPTER 10

THERE WERE TWO WAYS I COULD PLAY Thursday's check-in. Griff suggested I leave a key in a lockbox on Fair Winds' front door. According to his aunt, it worked like a charm for the Swifties staying at her condo—and, unless disaster struck, it also ensured zero host-guest interaction. The idea was tempting, but I kind of wanted to meet Sandy and Ron; I wanted them to know that someone was *around*. "Audrey, relax," Griff said. "You sound paranoid. These people are pros, remember? Twenty vacations!"

We'd scoured their profiles for intel.

I admit I was on edge, but *of course* I was! Plus, as a new host, my payout could potentially be delayed a couple of weeks after my first reservation. I *had* to believe my parents were disconnected from real life in France, but when they returned home? I knew my dad would be touching base with our bank accounts.

I told Sandy check-in was at four p.m. and gave her the gate code as well as instructions to park in front of the carriage house garage. She and Ron were driving up from Washington, DC.

"I still can't believe I won't be blowing glass for three weeks," I lamented to Henry on Wednesday as we prepped for the Taylors' arrival. We'd gone to Whole Foods to buy some basics for the fridge—milk, eggs, butter, and ketchup—as well as a loaf of sourdough and local strawberry jam. Our coffee options included a basket of Nespresso pods, and there was also an array of herbal teas.

Moroccan Mint was my favorite.

"I know," Henry said, "but look at it this way: The gas bill won't be as outrageous this month."

"That's what I'm worried about," I mumbled. "Jeff and Monica will know something's up if they notice the lower bill. Why would I dial back blowing glass?"

"You don't have to," Henry pointed out. "The only person barring you from blowing glass is you."

I let out a sigh; it was a fair point, but it didn't change my mind. Once the Taylors were officially booked, I'd decided Golightly Glass was taking a hiatus. We hadn't exactly disclosed that Fair Winds was above a hot shop, and I wanted guests to feel like they were on vacation. If I was hard at work downstairs, I worried they would feel like they were living above a factory.

I couldn't let that color any reviews.

Plus, I didn't really want to talk or think about glassblowing for a while; I needed to devote all my energy and focus to Here-to-Stay.

I also thought it would be welcoming to put together a dossier of recommended restaurants and activities, so I stayed up late Wednesday night—or rather, into the wee hours of Thursday morning—dashing off a Google Doc for Henry to cosign. Thanks a lot, he texted me at 4:15 a.m. Now I'm craving Sister Act's lemon ricotta pancakes!

Rise & Grind was where you got your coffee and pastries and camped out with your laptop, but Sister Act Café was the holy grail of brunch spots.

On that note, I included a map for the local bird-watching beat, which I'd found on the Essex Harbor Chamber of Commerce website. "That is a nice touch," Henry commented while I printed out everything in our school's deserted computer lab. "Based on Sandy's profile pic, she looks like she could be into ornithology."

(The tiny snapshot showed Sandy with a pair of binoculars around her neck.)

There was going to be a caravan back to the Barbour house after school ended at two-thirty. Henry, obviously, and Griff also wanted to witness Sandy and Ron's arrival. "Only if you watch from the house with Henry," I said, because the last thing I wanted was an overeager teenage welcome wagon; my guests didn't need any weird vibes. This meet and greet had to be as professional as possible.

And, preferably, *short*.

"Do you need any help later?" Ellie found me at the tail end of lunch. Griff must've told her about the viewing party.

"Chase is picking me up, so if you want, we can—"

"No, thanks," I said tightly. "It's all covered."

Ellie nodded, but slowly—like she had something else to say.

You'll still get your seventy-five dollars, I almost said. *I just really don't want Chase at my house. I don't know him, and I don't ever plan on getting to know him.*

He sounded like a jerk.

I had to question whether I'd actually said that aloud when Ellie's brow furrowed. "Is this about Henry?" she asked, her voice going up an octave. "Has Henry said stuff about Chase?"

"When's your next appointment with the Hair Doctor?" I inelegantly changed the subject. Ellie's natural hair color was beautiful, but she didn't look like herself without her pink streaks.

"I haven't scheduled one." She half smiled, then shrugged. "It was time for a change."

∽

AT 4:23 P.M., I WANTED TO THROW UP.

Because at 4:23 p.m., a blue Volvo stopped at the gate, punched in our movie trivia question code, and then proceeded to drive down my driveway. "They're here!" Griff exclaimed before quite literally popping a piece of popcorn into his mouth. He'd helped himself to my mom's homemade kettle corn.

I felt Henry's hand on my back. "Are you sure you don't want me to go out there with you?"

I nodded. "I'm the host. It should just be me."

And with that, I marched out the mudroom door and into the sunshine.

Fair Winds was situated yards from the main house, close enough that Griff and Henry had a magnificent view from the living room window, but far enough that no one could mistake it for an ordinary detached garage. Our driveway splintered; continuing straight escorted you to the mansion's garage, while rounding the bend led to the carriage house. It was nestled among the flower beds my mom had tirelessly planted—the woman had a vision for everything—with a great view of the Sound.

By the time I walked over, heart thumping, Sandy and Ron had gotten out of their car and were assessing their accommodations. "Hello!" someone-who-did-not-sound-like-me-at-all called cheerfully as Sandy raised her phone for a photo. She and her husband both turned. "How was your drive?"

"Lovely!" Sandy said at the same time Ron said, "Arduous."

She shot him a look.

"What?" he asked sheepishly. "You managed to hit every single pothole."

I tried not to laugh. Was Ron a passenger princess like Henry?

"You must be Audrey." Sandy smiled after waving off her husband. She was maybe five ten with shoulder-length gray hair and glasses, and wearing a breezy white blouse with plaid capris and red Keds. Ron was a few inches shorter than her and stocky in a black quarter-zip and khaki shorts. I liked his Army green Crocs.

"Yes," I said, smiling back. "Welcome! I'm Audrey."

My stomach flipped. "Monica" had messaged Sandy earlier to remind her that *her daughter* would be meeting them today. It didn't say anywhere on Here-to-Stay that the host needed to be on the premises.

"This looks even more beautiful in person." Sandy shook her head in wonder. "We're so happy to be here."

"You seem rather young to own this place," Ron remarked after we shook hands. "How many grades did you skip in school?"

"Ron," his wife said. "Were you even listening in the car? When I told you about—"

"This is my parents' property." I kept my cool. "I'm managing it while they're temporarily away on business."

For some reason, *business* sounded better than *vacation*.

"Huh," Ron said but didn't question me further. I gestured toward Fair Winds, and Sandy eagerly followed me upstairs with her husband in tow.

"My mother decorated it herself," I found myself saying proudly as Sandy gushed over the apartment and Ron plopped down on the couch.

"Gorgeous," she said. "What's downstairs?"

"Storage," I lied, pulse quickening a bit. The last thing I wanted was for someone to discover and mess with my hot shop.

"Nobody's ever in there, so you won't be disturbed."

Then I swallowed, smiled, and handed Sandy the carriage house's key. I told her the kitchen was stocked with some basics, and that I'd left a *Things to Do in Essex Harbor* list on the coffee table. The Wi-Fi info was posted on the fridge.

"And if you need anything, feel free to text me," I said. "I'm around, and you might see"—I hesitated, but went with it—"my boyfriend."

The word *boyfriend* crackled; I felt a strange tingling sensation on my lips. It was the first time I'd ever called Henry that.

"Thank you for everything, Audrey," Sandy said, her face buried in my recommendation dossier. "I'm sure we're going to have a wonderful time."

"My pleasure," I said, and with that, left to let them get settled in.

~

"HOW WERE THEY?" HENRY ASKED WHEN I walked into the living room, but before I could answer, Griff clapped me on both shoulders.

"Audrey, it's real!" he said as my pulse jumped. "Shit just got so real—you have *guests*."

"That I do." I grinned nervously. "They seem nice."

"This is incredible," Griff said, still shaking me. "I *have* to text Kenzie."

My heart stopped. "Kenzie?"

"Yeah." He nodded. "She wanted—"

"Keeler," Henry groaned. "You *didn't*."

Griff gave him a funny look. "What?"

"You told Kenzie that Audrey's a Here-to-Stay host?"

Crickets.

"I might've," he allowed.

Oh, Griff . . . My stomach soured. "She knows not to say anything, right?"

"Totally," he said. "She knows it's chill."

Chill.

I *hated* that word. What did it even *mean*? Was it the same as *super casual* or *in-the-vault secret*?

Henry snagged the bad-cop role. "That's not a good enough answer," he said, unlocking his phone. "I'm starting a group chat. Audrey, you, me, Ellie, and Kenzie."

"Plus, Mia and Jared," Griff added.

"What!" Henry and I screeched.

"Whoa, don't blame me," he said. "Kenzie told them."

Blood thudded in my ears. "Forget the group chat," I told Henry. "Tell them to be at Hamburger Hill at six." I took a deep breath. "Now that people know, we need to outline expectations."

CHAPTER 11

ON FRIDAY MORNING, I WAS A LITTLE ANXIOUS about leaving Sandy and Ron alone on the property. I woke up earlier than usual, got dressed, and ate breakfast while glancing out the window every five seconds. Their car still sat in the driveway, and there was no sign of movement inside the carriage house (though, in all fairness, it wasn't even seven a.m. and they were on vacation—of course they were asleep).

It wasn't that I worried about them breaking into the house. The keypad locks my mom had recently installed on all the doors were more comforting than a guard dog, and I doubted the Taylors were the smash-and-grab type. Leaving them alone was just . . . well, *weird*.

Henry usually met me in the quad before homeroom, but surprisingly, today it was Griff. I waved, and saw he was holding a white bag with Rise & Grind's signature magenta stamp. My lips curved in a smile when he offered it to me; inside was a guava and cheese Danish, my new favorite pastry. How did he know?

"How was the first night?" he asked cautiously, as if he wasn't totally sure I'd forgiven him for spilling the beans yesterday.

Everything was good now—I mean, he'd meant well, and our Hamburger Hill Summit had been a success; in fact, I felt bolstered by it. We'd huddled together in the *Sgt. Pepper*–themed booth in the back, where I very quietly explained to Kenzie, Mia, and Jared the reason for Fair Winds, and that there was absolutely no world in which they could tell anyone. "But can we help?" Jared asked, to which I answered, "Yes, by taping your mouth shut."

All three cater-waiters nodded.

"Where is Henry?" Ellie ventured after everyone signed the NDA Henry had pulled off Google earlier. I swallowed a giggle at the crossed-out sections and highlighted paragraphs—seriously, it was so *Henry*. My heart sparked with excitement to get back home and fill him in on the meeting.

"He's back at my house," I said. Griff's leg accidentally brushed mine under the table. For the first time ever, we were sitting next to each other. "You know, in case the Taylors need anything."

Which was partly true. According to my mom, sometimes you had to jiggle the shower's faucet a little to get the hot water to work. Sandy and Ron didn't know that.

Remind me to draft a list of FW's quirks, I texted Henry.

He thumbs-upped my message, then wrote: Nothing to report here. Looks like they left to grab dinner somewhere.

It sounded like we were spying on them; we weren't, I

swear. But I'd only been a host for several hours. I needed more time to settle into the role.

Ellie nodded, then handed over her NDA. "Please tell him he's as clever as ever," she said before scooting out of the booth. "I can't stay for food; Chase is waiting for me outside. We're getting Italian."

"Are we ever going to meet Chase?" Kenzie asked.

"Trust me, Kenz, you don't want to," Griff joked, then muttered under his breath, "Dick."

Interesting, I thought. *Griff doesn't like Chase either?*

"Maybe." Ellie shrugged. "He leaves for Boston soon."

I couldn't help but notice she didn't seem very excited over Chase anymore. She waved before slinging her purse over her shoulder and heading toward the exit. Kenzie, Mia, and Jared started talking about the Constellation wedding next week, and as I sipped my mint chip milkshake, Griff leaned close—close enough that I could feel his warm breath against my ear. "That guy doesn't deserve her," he whispered. "Bad news all the way."

I squinted in Ellie's direction, but she'd already disappeared out the front door. "Yeah," I whispered back. "He sounds like it." I paused. "Do you think he has something to do with her ditching her pink hair?"

Griff sighed. "It wouldn't surprise me. She didn't have Tate dye it until after she and Chase first broke up."

"Huh," I said, intrigued. Maybe her pink hair signified her time with Henry? Had it really ended in her mind? I cleared my throat. "Did you ever hear—"

"Hey, Griff!" Kenzie said. "Can I try your shake?"

He grinned. "Of course."

I wanted to roll my eyes but resisted. Griff could flirt with whomever he wanted. Instead, I tapped my passcode into my phone and texted Henry:

Do you want pepper jack on your burger?

Cheddar, please, **he said.** Thanks to the Enchilada Incident, I'm now spice-free.

I smirked. Roger that.

How're things?

Good, **I wrote.** Circle of trust established.

I left out the part about Ellie being amused by his NDA.

It didn't seem that important.

~

GRIFF AND I TALKED ABOUT THIS YEAR'S

rumored prom theme—"When in Rome," whatever that meant—until the bell for homeroom rang. I hadn't responded to his cheeky prom text, even though Henry hadn't asked me yet. I couldn't crap out on our fake relationship so soon. We needed to hook Ellie.

Henry caught the last five minutes of homeroom, per usual. He spent most of it in the front office, broadcasting the morning announcements. Somehow, he managed to make something as mundane as cap and gown distribution sound like the biggest event of the semester. "I'm sorry I missed you earlier," he said before first period. "I had an eleventh-hour pop quiz."

In Henry-speak, a *pop quiz* was when he put on his peer-tutor hat and quickly grilled one of his many pupils before an imminent exam. Griff always scheduled his before Spanish presentations.

"It's cool," I told him, squeezing his fingers as he took my hand so we could brave the bustling hallway together. "Who was it?"

"Kenzie, actually," he said. "Medieval history debate."

"And she needs your help? She already likes to talk."

"Well, not about the Church of England." He chuckled and guided me toward the math hallway. We both had calculus, but with different teachers in different classrooms. "What was that eye roll? I like Kenzie."

"I do, too," I said, nodding for emphasis. Because I did. "She just . . ." *Greatly enjoys flirting with Griff!*

Henry let me trail off. "Did you get your Danish?" he asked. "Or did Griff eat it himself?"

"Oh no, he gave it to me." I sighed happily. "It was delicious."

"Good." Henry beamed. "It was their last one."

"Wait . . ." I blinked. "*You* bought it for me?"

"Yeah." He nodded. "Ellie and I stopped at Rise & Grind on the way to school."

I stopped short. "You drove Ellie to school?"

"Her dad needed to borrow the Prius," Henry explained. "And Chase is resting up for his internship, which translates to sleeping until noon." He shrugged. "She compensated me with an iced coffee."

It didn't strike me until we got to Mrs. Nystrom's classroom that Henry had probably loved chauffeuring Ellie to school. They hadn't been alone together since their breakup. If she'd called him, that was promising.

"Anyway," Henry said. "Hopefully the Taylors are out later, because Golightly Glass processed a few orders last night, and we should pack them up to ship." He gave me a look. "I know you've technically issued a moratorium, but . . ."

I couldn't help but grin. Even if I wasn't blowing it, *glass* was a magical word—and orders meant money. Henry's packaging was also amazing: Tiffany-blue Chinese take-out boxes sealed with our company sticker.

"Fingers crossed," I told Henry, and let him kiss my cheek in the busy hallway before I headed into class. His lips were as light as a feather. There one second and gone the next.

"Turn to page 324, please!" Mrs. Nystrom called a few minutes later, red lipstick smudged on her teeth. "We need to tackle antidifferentiation before the year ends."

I opened my textbook but was much more interested in learning about what Henry and Ellie had talked about on the way to school today.

It's all good, I told myself. *This is our plan. We're sticking to the plan.*

PER HERE-TO-STAY GUIDELINES, SANDY AND Ron loaded their weekenders and all Sandy's souvenirs into their car and were off by noon on Sunday morning. I could barely wait until the front gate closed behind them before making a beeline for the carriage house. Fair Winds needed to be cleaned in preparation for its next guests. I'd had a few inquiries, but no one who fit my requirements. Except for one couple who seemed so perfect I *knew* there had to be a catch. Jim and Janet Reynolds lived in Florida and wanted to have their "own space" while visiting their grandchildren for ten days. "Yep, it's just as we feared," Henry confirmed after some light internet sleuthing. "They're Chase's grandparents."

But the cleaning could wait; I *needed* to get into the hot shop. It was more than a week since I'd blown glass. "Hello!" I singsonged to the empty studio. Then someone cleared their throat and said, "I don't think you've ever sounded that happy to see me."

I spun around to see Griff in an old lifeguarding windbreaker and gray sweats, with a bemused look on his face.

"Griff, hi," I said, suddenly self-conscious. I'd haphazardly pulled my blond hair back in a clip and wore old, pilled leggings and an oversized green, black, and white Philadelphia Eagles T-shirt. "What are you doing here?"

"I knew Sandy and Ron were splitting this morning and figured you might want a head start with the cleaning." He paused. "What *is* Here-to-Stay's cleaning fee, anyway?"

"Thank you," I said, a little taken aback. Griff had come

over to *clean*? "Although I won't be playing Cinderella for a couple of hours..."

"That's okay." He smiled. "I'm good to just hang, if that's cool."

"Yeah." I nodded, still dazed. "That sounds—"

"I'm sorry I'm late." Henry appeared out of nowhere with a cardboard tray of iced coffees. "Ten a.m. mass ran over and Rise & Grind's line was out the door by the time I got there." He set our drinks down on his base of operations, then comically blinked upon noticing Griff. "Keeler, what brings you here?"

"He's going to hang out while we attend to business," I explained. "Then help us freshen up Fair Winds."

"You might regret it," Henry told Griff. "Ron must've cooked Sandy a romantic dinner, because all I smell is Old Bay."

Simultaneously, Griff and I channeled our inner bloodhounds, sniffing the air. "I'm not getting anything," he said, but I wrinkled my nose. Now that Henry had pointed it out, I couldn't *not* smell paprika.

Fantastic.

"Shall we?" Henry nodded at the worktable where we ritually packed all Golightly Glass's orders.

"We shall," I said, and Griff took that as a signal to wander over and flop down on the groupie area's couch. He connected his phone to the hot shop's Bluetooth speaker, and the opening beats of whatever EDM song he'd chosen pulsed as Henry pulled up Golightly Glass's order history.

For the next hour, we packed up cute red-and-white

toadstool ornaments, pineapple paperweights, rocks glasses, small strawberry sculptures, and my signature pendants. I called them mermaid teardrops because of their shape and shimmer.

It was amazing to see the shipping labels, to know that my artwork was traveling to places like Kansas City and Little Rock and San Francisco. There was even a necklace headed to Ireland!

But the adrenaline coursing through my veins wasn't only from pride. I desperately wanted to fire up the furnace and work. It was almost impossible to stand in the hot shop without a blowpipe in hand. "You're fidgeting," Henry noted after a while.

"No, I'm vibing with this," I joked, gesturing to the speaker. We were listening to Griff's master playlist, which blended every genre—*ever*.

"You really don't need to do this to yourself," he said. "But the lost time will be worth it, right?"

I shrugged. "Do you really believe that?" It was hard when I had a potentially messy apartment upstairs and no payout in my bank account yet. Why did the short-term rental gods have to withhold it?

"I've already told you we're going to pull this off," Henry said. "You'll reimburse your parents, and you'll have the chance to turn up your nose at Blue Ridge's cafeteria food, don't worry."

"I've actually heard it's really good—" I started, but a gasp across the hot shop cut me off. I glanced at the groupie couch, where Griff was grinning at something on his laptop.

"Audrey, c'mere," he said, frantically waving me over. "Someone left a review on Fair Winds' profile!"

My breath caught. "Sandy?"

It seemed impossible. There was no way the Taylors had made it home yet.

"Maybe Ron's driving," Henry mused. "Or, more likely, they're at a rest stop."

We joined Griff on the couch and leaned in to see:

Jet-setter Sandra
Washington, DC
★★★★★

"Look!" Griff exclaimed. "Five stars!"

Oh my god, I thought, my stomach dropping in shock before it roller-coastered back up. We had the most wonderful weekend stay at this serene (and very clean!) spot, Sandy had written. Fair Winds is a secluded and cozy guesthouse with a waterfront view, beautiful decor, and a kitchen that included all the essentials. Our hostess was SENSATIONAL! She made sure we had everything we needed, and even went above and beyond to provide a recommendation guide for charming Essex Harbor and its neighboring towns (order a #8 at Sandwitch—you'll thank me). We hope to come back in the autumn to see the leaves change!

Heart swelling, I beamed when Henry and I made eye contact. "Now do you believe me?" he asked, beaming back.

I nodded. Sandy's review was *glowing*.

"You're amazing, Audrey," Griff said. "That review's worth some *serious* legend points."

"It was a team effort." I blushed. "What are legend points?"

"They date back to seventh grade," Griff said as Henry sighed heavily. "Henry helped Jason and me devise a point system where—"

An unfamiliar ping came from my computer, idle on the worktable. I remembered I had a Google Chrome browser pulled up, with a Here-to-Stay tab open. Either it was a delayed announcement about Fair Winds' first review . . . or . . .

Might the *sensational* Audrey have another interested party?

CHAPTER 12

MY MOM CALLED AS I WAS WALKING OUT OF school on Monday afternoon, so I sat in Brigitta while we spoke. Spine rigid, I kept waiting for her to bring up the drained bank account, but she didn't. The student parking lot had almost emptied out by the time she finished recapping her and my dad's latest adventures. "I'm bringing back a case of this wonderful chardonnay," she told me. "Our wine ambassador called it her 'date night' wine. It has an attitude, if that makes sense—a bit spicy."

"Awesome," I said. My dad was the one who enjoyed wine's technical terms—body, legs, and "oak" levels—while my mom was more informal and creative with her descriptions. "A wine with gumption!"

She laughed. "I'm long overdue to rewatch that movie." She sighed, as if swooning over bespectacled Jude Law holding a cup of coffee in *The Holiday*. "How are you? How is James?"

"I'm good . . ." I said slowly. "James is good, too." My pulse picked up a little as I fumbled for something more concrete to say. "He's been playing me some recent In the Luxembourg Gardens songs."

In the Luxembourg Gardens was the name of my cousin and Isa's band, inspired by a famous painting. They weren't gunning for a record deal, but they did have a Spotify page and performed at various New England colleges. They could pretty much play anything, but their bread and butter were covers, transforming big-band songs from the fifties and sixties into dreamy contemporary duets. I knew their fans were hoping for original music soon. *Not yet*, James texted whenever anyone in the Barbour cousin group chat asked.

"And you?" my mom asked. "Have you made—*blown*—anything interesting recently?"

I closed my eyes. "No," I heard myself say, unable to lie to her. A lump rose in my throat. "Not really. Golightly Glass has gotten a rush of orders, so Henry and I've been shipping stuff out, but . . ."

"Your pendants are very pretty," she said when I trailed off. "Coincidentally, Stacy Gallant and I both wore ours to dinner the other night. Her daughter Katie gave one to her for Mother's Day last year."

I perked up a little. My mom had brought her mermaid teardrop with her? As far as I knew, she'd only worn it a few times.

"What about Henry?" she asked when I didn't respond. "You two been spending a lot of time together?"

For some reason, that ruffled my feathers. "Of course we have," I said. "He's my boyfriend."

Boyfriend, I mouthed again, just to feel the word on my lips.

I didn't realize my mistake until it was too late.

"Your boyfriend, huh?" my mom teased. "Well, isn't that an interesting development..."

Heat rushed to my cheeks. "Yeah," was all I said. Again, my mom and I didn't really talk about my love life. "I suppose."

She laughed. "Has he stood outside your window with a boom box and asked you to prom yet?"

"Actually, no," I said, hoping Henry would be a little more original than imitating Lloyd Dobler in *Say Anything*... "He's cutting it close."

Prom was ten days away. I hadn't forgotten about it per se, but becoming a Here-to-Stay host had shuffled my priorities. My guess was Henry hadn't promposed yet because he was holding out hope that he and Ellie might end up going together.

I thought of their junior prom photo, sitting framed on Henry's bookshelf. Collecting dust or not, it suddenly felt more significant than ever.

"Oh, sweetheart, I have to go," my mom said as I wondered what Griff's prom thoughts were. "Kim's calling."

"No problem," I said. "I love you, Mom. Say hi to Dad for me."

"I will. I love— Oh, shit!"

"What?" I asked, suddenly nervous. "What is it?"

"Dave Matthews's signing is tomorrow night," she said.

"And I collected all those concert posters for the collage but forgot to drop them off at the store before we left. Would you be able to swing by?"

"Oh, sure!" I prayed she didn't notice the squeak in my voice. Dave Matthews's memoir had been published last week, and my mom had successfully pitched Bedtime Stories as the Connecticut stop on his book tour. It was a ticketed event, and I knew for a fact some out-of-towners were driving in for it.

Fair Winds' next guests, for example.

"Thank you," she said. "I'll text Maureen to let her know you're coming."

"Perfect," I said, and then we hung up so she could catch Aunt Kim's call.

―

INSTEAD OF GOING STRAIGHT HOME, I DROVE to Trader Joe's to exercise my *food-only* American Express card. Their chicken fried rice sounded like the dinner of champions, but after I'd filled my basket with the rice and an assortment of other goodies—Everything but the Bagel mixed nuts, mac and cheese bites, chili and lime tortilla chips, and dark chocolate peanut butter cups—I overheard recognizable voices from the next aisle. "Are you serious?" Ellie was saying. "You brought me to *Trader Joe's* for an intervention?"

A shiver went up my spine. Please hide me, seltzer section...

"This isn't an intervention, Adelaide," Caroline Hopper

said to her daughter. "We're shopping. All I did was ask if you wanted the chocolate lava cakes."

"Even though you know I—"

"But yes," her mom interrupted, quietly but sharply, "if you want this to be an intervention, we can turn it into one." I knew they deserved privacy, but I found myself unable to move. "Is something bothering you, honey?" Caroline asked, her voice softer.

"No," Ellie said, and I pictured her folding her arms across her chest. "I'm fine. I've just given up dessert."

Had she? I could still see her devouring three slices of margherita pizza at my party, but had she eaten any dessert? She'd declined the Rice Krispies treat leftovers I offered, but I thought that was just because she was pissed about Henry and me.

And she didn't get a root beer float at the Here-to-Stay summit, I realized. Ellie always got an old-fashioned root beer float at Hamburger Hill. She'd left early to rendezvous with Chase, but the first thing we did at that meeting—before I even explained the precarious situation that was Fair Winds—was put in our milkshake order. They'd arrived minutes later.

I felt stupid for only noticing the disappearance of her pink hair.

"I know you've given up sweets," Caroline said. "What I'm wondering is *why*. I can't help but notice you've lost some weight. I know you're swimming more, but if it's not deliberate . . ."

Ellie was quiet, but after a couple of beats, she admitted she was stressed.

About what? I wondered. *Chase? Graduation? College?*

My heart twinged. We never talked enough for me to know.

Maybe that was my fault. I should've tried harder to be her friend.

"Have you tried talking to Henry?" her mom asked as I shifted my shopping basket to the other arm. "You two used to tell each other everything. What you found in each other is truly special, and I don't think you should let it go . . ."

"I hate to break it to you, Mom," Ellie said, a waver in her voice, "but what I had with Henry is gone, and whatever he had with me is *long* gone. He happily went and found something with Audrey."

Wow, I thought, a little sick to my stomach. *We must be putting on an incredible show.*

But at the same time, on Henry's behalf: *What did you expect? You dumped him for your asshole ex!*

"I know breakups are hard, El," Caroline said. "But they pass. It'll pass."

A lump formed in my throat. I stood still, guiltily listening to them push their cart farther down the aisle. The last thing I heard was Ellie saying, "Tate asked for vanilla meringues . . ."

What are Henry and I doing? I wondered. It sounded (and looked) like Ellie was really going through something—and here we were waving a fake relationship in her face.

"Excuse me, Miss Barbour." Someone coughed behind me. Stomach dropping, I turned and was relieved to see

Mrs. Nystrom, my math teacher. She pointed at the case of seltzer I was blocking. "Do you mind?"

⁓

BRIAN AND LESLIE FISHER WERE CHECKING IN today, but there was no rush to be home by four since they wouldn't arrive until ten. Even though chances were I'd still be awake, I had no intention of welcoming them in my pajamas. Instead, I went to the hardware store and bought a lockbox to hang on the door.

Fair Winds was back in *Architectural Digest* photo-shoot shape thanks to Henry's and my cleaning service. Griff cut out after two minutes of vacuuming, because he needed to drive his brother somewhere. "He can forget about a piece of this tip!" Henry had joked when we noticed an Andrew Jackson left on the coffee table. Sandy and Ron were so sweet—and *neat*. Besides an easy vacuum-Swiffer combo, taking out the trash, and washing the towels and sheets, the only challenge was fumigating the place of Old Bay.

Although in the process of opening all the windows, I did notice that a few things had been moved around. For example, my mom had inherited an antique silver tea service from her grandmother, and instead of displaying it as a set, she'd split it up. The small oval biscuit box with an intricate handle and working lock had sat next to the Nespresso machine. My mom used it to store tea bags. But now, it was gone.

Huh, I thought. It was probably on the back balcony—Sandy and Ron had had coffee there this morning—but I didn't stop working to check. There was no way I wanted the Fishers to wrinkle their noses upon arrival.

The reason for my second guests' visit was simple: Dave Matthews. Brian had emphasized what superfans they were—they followed his tour up and down the East Coast every summer, getting the same seats at each venue—and how excited they were for his memoir. Unfortunately, they lived in Rhode Island and Dave's publisher hadn't scheduled an event there.

So they'd decided to drive to Connecticut.

When I woke up Tuesday morning, I saw a Subaru parked by Fair Winds, and on my way out the door, I almost stepped on something wrapped in tinfoil. *That was close*, I thought, and picked up a glass pan that, upon further investigation, revealed itself to be brownies.

I opened the note perched on top of the foil and read:

Audrey, thank you so much for having us, especially on such short notice! These are Leslie's famous "mind-boggling" brownies—we hope you enjoy!
 Eat, drink, and be merry,
 B & L

My stomach, not quite full from breakfast, rumbled . . . but I got a grip and left the pan on the kitchen counter. *I'll be back later*, I told the baked goods.

It was a gorgeous day, so I rolled Brigitta's windows down before putting the VW in reverse and executing a perfect K-turn in the driveway. Spotify on shuffle, I shout-sang along to the 1975's "Chocolate."

And then, in a moment of perfect poetry, I caught a whiff of what smelled *a lot* like a Dave Matthews concert as I drove by Fair Winds. My pulse spiked.

No, I thought. *No, no, no!*

I sniffed the air again.

My guests had definitely indulged in some weed last night. *Don't forget to forbid smoking,* I remembered Henry saying as we wrote the Here-to-Stay copy. *Even if it's a strawberry vape pen, the smell might linger.*

Good call, I'd agreed. If there was one thing Monica Barbour despised, it was smoking. She'd asked my dad to give up his holiday cigars after my grandfather died of lung cancer.

Did I forget? I wondered, but upon checking Fair Winds' profile, my shoulders untensed in relief. I *had* specified that we were a nonsmoking property.

And even though I wanted to believe that the Fishers only wanted to unwind last night, I couldn't give them a total pass.

Good morning,
Thank you for the brownies! Who told you about my sweet tooth? I hope your drive went smoothly, and you slept well last night. I just wanted to remind you

that Fair Winds is a nonsmoking property. I hope this doesn't dampen your stay.

Best,
Audrey

I received a reply halfway through the school day.

Hi there,
How inconsiderate of us! I apologize—there was a lot of traffic on the drive down last night, and we needed to zen out before bed. It won't happen again. We brought some gummies and other treats, ha! Will we see you at Dave's signing tonight?
-L

"Why did you approve these people again?" Henry asked after scanning the message, but it took me a second to comprehend the question. He'd slipped a hand inside my jean jacket, and his fingertips were now dancing along my hip bone. My brain felt like it was blinking on and off like a neon sign.

I kept glancing around to see if Ellie or Griff was nearby, but if they were, I couldn't focus on them. I couldn't even return the enthusiastic wave Kenzie gave me as she passed by.

"They're retired with a yellow lab named Cheddar," I managed to say.

Henry stopped drumming his fingers to give me a look. *That's it?*

"And I thought it was strategic," I added, reaching out to smooth his already smooth hair. "Hosting someone during the week in addition to the weekend. More money."

"Didn't your mom leave you two tickets for the signing?" Henry asked. "We can always push back our dinner."

I nodded. "She did, but I gave them to Mrs. Nystrom as an early teacher appreciation gift. Tickets sold out before she and her son could get them."

Of course, it suddenly hit me that I should've sold them. Who knew how much some people would pay to breathe the same air as Dave Matthews?

Henry chuckled. "Okay, well, there goes your excuse to skip tonight's meal." He paused. "My mom has a late meeting, so Tess is at the helm tonight . . ."

I sucked in a dramatic breath, remembering the last time Henry's stepmother had cooked. Trying to cut my pork loin had been like trying to cut through a pack of index cards.

"So we're ordering sushi," Henry finished. He'd invited me over for dinner and homework. I had no doubt we'd open our books but end up watching a movie.

"Dragon roll, please," I told him, then thought of the hostess gift sitting on my kitchen counter. Leslie's "mind-boggling" brownies, whatever that meant. "I'll bring dessert."

"No complaints here." Henry smiled right as the warning bell rang for the last class of the day. "How does six sound?"

"Way too late." I fake yawned. He leaned in to kiss my cheek, but I impulsively turned so that we *actually* kissed. Henry straightened a little, surprised, but then I felt his arm crook around my waist. My palm prickled when my hand went to his warm cheek. *He tastes like a lemon-mint cough drop,* I noted as his tongue—

"Get a room!" someone shouted.

Oh, perfect! I thought, recognizing the voice of Griff's friend Jason. Griff had to be nearby, right?

Henry pulled back to respond. "The bell just rang!" he called with a smile in his voice. "We're about to be out of . . ."

He trailed off. Ellie stood in front of us, having appeared out of nowhere.

My stomach squirmed as I remembered how upset she'd been about Henry at Trader Joe's. Now, though, she didn't give anything away. "Do you have a second, Henry?" she asked.

"No, but I have a short commute to Italian," he answered. "You're welcome to join."

Ellie nodded. "I have a message from Tate."

If I didn't know how close Henry was to Ellie's sister (who I liked!), I would've rolled my eyes and thought, *Sure you do . . .*

Henry caught my eye. "I'll see you tonight?"

"In a sweatshirt and pajama bottoms," I confirmed, and forced myself not to watch them walk away.

CHAPTER 13

"THANK YOU SO MUCH FOR HAVING ME," I SAID as Henry poured glasses of water and Tess transferred our sushi and sashimi from their take-out boxes to two large platters. As it turned out, Henry's parents knew he and I weren't actually dating. "I want to avoid a *talk*," Henry had explained the other day, but after telling Charlotte and Tess about our scheme, he got one anyway. They thought fake dating was incredibly stupid and that Henry needed to respect Ellie's decision, but they weren't going to interfere.

Charlotte laughed. "Audrey, this is the fourth or fifth time you've had dinner with us since your parents' plane took off," she said. "Your gratitude is always appreciated, but not necessary."

"We love having you!" Tess echoed, and after serving herself some of the Little Tuna's Endless Summer roll, the topic of conversation switched to summer plans. She and Charlotte eyed Henry, who sighed.

"Relax," he said. "Dad and I spoke today. I'm moving into the Beach House a week after graduation."

"Good." Charlotte nodded. "I'm glad your departure date is settled."

I tried to swallow the giggle bubbling inside me. "The Beach House" was Henry's childhood nickname for his dad's house, which was literally in Essex Harbor. It was on the Sound like my house, only a ten-minute drive away—*tops.* Henry's parents had divorced when he was nine. His dad, a pretty well-known comedian, lived in Manhattan when he wasn't touring, but he spent June through September in Essex Harbor. He and Henry were close enough that Henry gave him feedback on his jokes, and his latest Netflix special was titled *Stuff My Son Says.*

"What about you, Audrey?" Charlotte asked. "Blue Ridge starts in July, right?"

"Yes," I said. "About a week after the Fourth of July." The fish in my stomach started to swim. Henry's parents had been so happy when I told them about my fellowship acceptance; they didn't know my parents were totally opposed to my dream.

Blue Ridge is *on the horizon,* the voice in my head encouraged. *It's paid for, and you're going to make sure it stays that way. Hosting a pair of wholesome potheads is going to pay off!*

Tess was looking at me thoughtfully. "What about after your fellowship?" she asked. "What's the next step?"

"I don't know yet," I admitted. "It depends on what happens at Blue Ridge." I shifted in my chair. "Ideally an instructor will invite me to take courses or work at another hot shop. My Brooklyn teacher says these programs involve a lot of informal networking." I glanced at Henry, but he didn't look like he was listening, instead too busy mulling over which piece of sashimi to eat next. "For example, Gemma Hollister will be teaching a class at Blue Ridge. If she likes me and if I'm good enough, maybe she'll invite me to assist her in her hot shop sometime. Antolini Glass is based in Philadelphia."

"It sounds like a lot of 'who you know,'" Tess noted. "With a dash of flying by the seat of your pants."

I nodded. "My plan is to work really hard and make as many connections as possible so I can pick and choose opportunities."

Charlotte swallowed a sip of water. "Have you officially deferred Wharton?"

"Not yet . . ." I snuck another peek at Henry, who still *would not* make eye contact. He was carefully mixing soy sauce and wasabi together, ensuring the proportions were on point.

"They're very proud of you," Henry's mom said. "I remember running into your mother at Bedtime Stories right after you got your acceptance letter." She smiled. "I'm sure they're just as proud about Blue Ridge."

"The mountains are amazing," Tess added. "My grandparents had a cabin up there when my brother Josh and I were kids. We spent *every* August with them."

We finished our meal, and then Henry and I washed and dried the dishes. "Does anyone want a brownie?" I asked.

"Leslie—" I cut myself off, but it was too late.

"Who's Leslie?" Charlotte asked.

Willing my face not to burst into flames, I fumbled for a lie. "A new neighbor," I said. "She and her husband just moved here from Rhode Island." I swallowed as I retrieved the pan from where it was sitting by the crisper. "She brought over brownies this morning."

"They look delicious!" Tess exclaimed, then sighed. "But it looks like they have walnuts."

"Shoot," I said. Tess was allergic to tree nuts. "Charlotte?"

"I'm also going to pass," she said. "If I have one, there won't be enough for you and Henry."

I giggled. Leslie's square pan easily held brownies for ten people.

Henry nodded upstairs, two forks and some napkins in hand. "Homework?"

"Homework," I confirmed.

"Enjoy the movie!" his parents chorused as we climbed the stairs.

HENRY'S HOUSE HAD A SMALL UPSTAIRS DEN,

but he and I shut ourselves in his room since his bed was way more comfortable than the couch. Tonight's feature film was *Ocean's Eleven,* which we'd both seen at least twelve times, but it never got old. "'I'm gonna get out of the car and I'm gonna drop you like third-period French,'" we simultaneously quoted as George Clooney and Brad Pitt recruited a crew for their heist, laughing like it was the first time we'd heard the line.

Henry paused his MacBook about forty-five minutes into the movie to go to the bathroom, and I unlocked my phone to check Instagram. *Holy crap,* I thought when I swiped through Bedtime Stories' newest post, a series of photos. *The Fishers' drive was worth it!*

Did someone say a sold-out show? the caption read. **We loved seeing Dave Matthews onstage tonight and chatting about his new memoir!**

The first picture was pretty iconic: Dave taking a selfie with the overwhelmingly enthusiastic audience, who all wore various DMB concert T-shirts. Bedtime Stories audiences ate up a group shot.

The final photo, to my delight, was of Dave and the Fishers. Brian and Leslie flanked the music icon as he signed their book, the identical expressions on their elated faces reading *Don't pinch me! I'm dreaming!*

"They're definitely going to need their gummies to calm down tonight," Henry commented when I showed him the post. He smiled and shook his head. "Good for them."

"Brownies?" I proposed before we resumed the movie. They'd somehow been forgotten in all the excitement over rewatching George, Brad, and friends knock over a triumvirate of Vegas casinos.

"Yes," Henry agreed. "Where did you put the forks?"

We ate the brownies straight from the pan. "Oh my god..." I said, eyelids fluttering shut in sugary-sweet ecstasy. "These are *so good*."

"*I know.*" Henry sighed. "It's almost *mind-boggling*."

I nodded. The brownies were somehow both fluffy and fudgy, and the walnuts added a satisfying crunch.

"Okay, I need to take a break," I said after a few minutes, embarrassingly breathless. Half the pan had disappeared. "I don't want my stomach to totally revolt."

"Good call." Henry put down his fork. "We'll circle back for seconds later."

I leaned forward and hit his laptop's space bar, resuming the movie. Henry settled back against the pillows, and I nestled into his side so I could relax too. My body buzzed, sugar spinning through my veins, and I sighed happily. "You of all people should know, *Terry*," Julia Roberts said toward the end of the movie, "in your hotel, there's *always* someone watching."

I giggled.

"What's so funny?" Henry asked.

"This." I pointed to the MacBook screen and giggled again. "It's hilarious."

Henry's brow furrowed. "No, it's not," he said. "You always say it's badass and empowering."

"Oh, and that I *love* her dress." Now outright laughing, I leaned forward—closer to Henry's laptop, which was resting on his thighs. "Look at it shimmer!"

Julia Roberts's sparkly halter dress almost looked 3D.

Henry abruptly sat up and glanced toward the closed bedroom door. "What's wrong?" I asked when he started rubbing the back of his neck.

"Nothing," he answered. "Just that my mom or Tess might come in."

"And see what?" I waggled my eyebrows at him. "We still have most of our clothes on."

I watched Henry's brown eyes scan me—no, I watched his eyes *take me in*. My heart started singing in my chest. "You only took off your sweater," he observed.

"I can take off more," I offered.

It seemed we had officially committed to this bit.

"My mom might come in," he repeated, this time in a stage whisper.

"She never comes in," I stage-whispered back.

Henry shook his head, somehow in slow motion. "No, that's *your* mom."

I laughed.

"Shh!" Henry clapped his hand over my mouth.

I licked his palm.

He gasped and grabbed his hand as if I'd bit him. "Holly!"

"I'm seeing *La La Land*," I said, looking around his room. "I mean, the room looks like *La La Land*—like, the end. The in-another-life epilogue. An old-fashioned camera. My vision is a"—I grappled for the technical term—"Super 8 lens." I grimaced. "Does that make sense?"

"Yeah, it does." Henry was wide-eyed and nodding. "I'm seeing you as *The Theory of Everything*."

"Oh, I love that movie," I breathed.

"Do you remember how they filmed it?" he asked. "It looked like there was an Instagram filter over every scene?"

I nodded, then put a hand on his chest. His racing heartbeat made mine quicken, too—as if it wanted to synchronize or harmonize with Henry's. "You would look so good in a tennis sweater." My voice was wistful. "And tails, too. You'd be *dashing* in a pair of tails."

"Should I get a pair? For prom?"

I gasped. "You want to go to prom together?"

"Of course." Henry frowned. "You're my girlfriend."

You're my girlfriend.

The three words danced around in my head, spinning and twirling and leaping. They sounded so true. I knew they weren't, but *could* they be?

"What about Ellie?" I asked. Because if Henry didn't see her that way anymore . . .

"You and I are a couple," he answered sagely, but goofily. "Not a throuple."

"No, for real!" I sighed. "You want Ellie to go to prom with Chase?" I remembered eavesdropping on Ellie and her mom at Trader Joe's. I opened my mouth and the story spilled out. Henry nodded along emphatically, seeming unsurprised.

"Of course she's stressed," Henry said after I finished telling him about their conversation. Deep down, I felt guilty for sharing, but I hadn't been able to stop myself from speaking. In fact, I could *feel* my lips flapping. "When she and Chase first dated..." Henry shook his head, a lock of dark hair falling across his forehead. I wanted to push it back, and take my time doing it. "He never pressured her or anything, but she felt like she needed to solely focus on him. There was no time for anything or anyone else. If he wanted to do something together, no matter how spontaneous, she always abandoned her plans."

I wrinkled my nose. "Why did she even go out with him?"

Henry shrugged. "He was popular; he was charming. He has an X factor."

"No, *you* have an X factor," I corrected him as I stretched to finally comb back his hair. It was thick, soft, and smelled like lemons. Maybe even Italian lemons, if that was possible. My mom had brought some back from Italy last year. "You're handsome, smart, witty, charismatic, and just..." My breath caught. "Technicolor. You're *Technicolor*, Henry."

A shy smile played at the corners of his mouth.

"I would never break up with you," I added.

"Really?" he asked after glancing at the door again. "Not even for a walking-red-flag ex?"

I vehemently shook my head. "Red's never been my favorite in the rainbow."

Henry grinned and fell back against the pillows. He was flickering and fuzzy at the edges, like Super 8 film, but perfectly framed in the center of my vision. It made me want to melt. "You're Technicolor too, Hepburn," he said. "You are strong, clever, genuine, funny, and talented and ambitious beyond belief." He blushed. "And even though I don't love your new hair, I think you are beau—"

"You don't like my hair?" I blurted.

You've definitely stepped up your reputation, he'd said. Why had I thought that meant he liked it?

Henry's cheeks went from pink to red. "Wait, that's not what I meant," he word-vomited. "Sorry—I mean, I don't *not* like it, but it's really different." He took a breath. "I knew you wanted me to compliment it that night, and I didn't want to hurt your feelings . . ."

"How else was I supposed to take it?" I was quiet for a moment, then said, "You *never* compliment me, Hank."

Why am I being so damn dramatic? I wondered.

Because I was actually tearing up.

"That's not true," Henry said. "Not true *at all.* I love your brain, and I bow down to your glassblowing." He tilted his head. "You are *amazing.*"

When he moved to pull me into his arms, I let him. There were definitely Italian lemons in his shampoo, straight from the Amalfi Coast. "Remember when I didn't like touching you?" I asked.

"Vividly," he said softly. "We were the most middle school couple ever."

"No, I know," I said dreamily. "Now we're an aspirational couple."

Henry laughed. "High praise."

I laughed too, and propped myself up on an elbow so that we made eye contact. Henry's brown irises swirled with liquid gold. "I like being together like this," I said softly—truthfully. "I wasn't sure at first, but—"

"Shit, what was that?" Henry bounced up on the mattress when we heard something in the hallway. "Mom . . . ?"

"Why are you paranoid?" I said when neither his mom nor Tess responded. "You're never this anxious."

Henry let out a deep sigh. "I don't know; I can't shake this jumping in my chest." He pressed his hand to his heart. "I'm sorry, I'll relax. I promise."

"Me too," I agreed, because my shoulders had now tensed. This whole night had been . . . an adventure. Besides my Super 8 vision, I almost felt like I was drunk. I mean, I'd just told Henry about feelings I hadn't yet told myself . . .

And why was he talking as if I were the bane of his existence and object of all his desires?

Without warning, my stomach grumbled. Henry and I searched for the forks so we could dig into our dessert again. The only thing that would make it better would be a glass of cold milk.

"God," he said a couple of minutes later. "*What* is in these brownies?"

At that, my blood went cold, a line from the Fishers' message racing through my mind:

We brought some gummies and other treats, ha!

Other treats.

OTHER TREATS.

"Henry, stop!" I whisper-screamed. "Stop eating!"

"What?" he asked mid-chew. "Why?"

Unable to speak, I shook my head and grabbed my silenced phone from the nightstand. Among other things, I had three missed calls and a string of texts from Leslie Fisher.

And the most recent one read DON'T EAT THE BROWNIES!

CHAPTER 14

SLIGHTLY DIZZY, I WOKE UP NOT KNOWING where I was at first. I didn't see my reflection in my mirror when I sat up in bed or the glass bird sculpture that Emilia had gifted me before I moved back to the States. My pulse leaped a little when I heard a knock at the door. "Audrey?" a familiar, warm voice came from the hallway. "Are you awake?"

It was Charlotte.

Which meant I was at Henry's house.

Why was I still here?

"Yes," I heard myself say, but my voice sounded far away. "Come in."

Henry's mom opened the door and slipped in with a mug of coffee and a slice of her mouthwatering banana bread. "I checked on you earlier," she said as I inelegantly gobbled it up, "but you were passed out. Henry, too. It's almost eleven."

Blood pumped through my ears. "Did Brigitta not start last night?" I asked. "She's been making this weird *clunk* sound..."

Charlotte gave me a look. "You don't remember?"

I bit the inside of my cheek, trying to rewind last night. We had sushi for dinner before going upstairs to watch *Ocean's Eleven*. But somehow *La La Land* and *The Theory of Everything* had come up? I also remembered talking about Ellie and Chase and smelling Henry's citrus shampoo and being so happy while snuggling with him—

My stomach dropped.

And eating the brownies.

Pot brownies.

"You and Henry came tearing down the stairs last night," Charlotte gently said. "Henry slipped and actually fell down the final few, and you were both shouting about getting high from your brownies. It sounded like gibberish at first, but eventually you synchronized and it made sense."

"Great." I sighed. "We couldn't even be cool about it."

"It was very dorky," she agreed. "Though I'm glad you told us. You were in no condition to drive home, Audrey. Tess sat with you until you fell asleep."

I groaned, suddenly remembering. "I had the chills . . ."

"Yes, and I've never seen you so off-kilter." She paused. "Did a neighbor really give you those brownies?"

I hesitated before nodding. Because it was true, in a sense. Leslie and Brian had lived next door, if only temporarily. "It was an accident," I said. "She texted me that she'd baked two batches of brownies—one laced, one not—and mixed them up. I didn't see the message until it was too late."

"Ah," Charlotte said, but I could tell she was more upset than she was letting on. "Well, I called school and told them you and Henry were sick today. Rest up, take a shower." She gestured to the bathroom. "Stay as long as you need." She smiled. "And if you would like to stay here for the rest of your parents' trip, you are more than welcome. Henry mentioned something important came up for your cousin, so you're alone."

"Yeah, James couldn't catch a break," I said, then shrugged. "But I'm okay."

Charlotte took my hand and squeezed it. "Just say the word if you change your mind."

Warmth bloomed in my chest. "I will."

⁓

HENRY WAS EITHER STILL ASLEEP OR recovering by the time I'd finished my coffee and showered. The hot water made me feel like a new person. Call me later, I texted him before tapping on James's parental/parole officer–sounding text from this morning: Where did you sleep last night? Why aren't you in school?

Really? I thought, surprised. James was seriously monitoring me?

Maybe he *was* the responsible person my parents believed him to be, after all.

Henry's, **I replied.** Went for dinner and a movie, and it got late. I wasn't feeling well this morning.

James didn't need to know about the brownies, did he?

Were Henry's parents home? **he asked.**

OMG, James. **I rolled my eyes.** You're supposed to be the cool cousin!

I AM the cool cousin, **he said.** Isa wants to know.

Ah, that made sense.

Once I sarcastically told him that he could call Charlotte for confirmation—because he *did* have her number—I started Brigitta and drove home. A lump rose in my throat when I turned in to my driveway, desperately hoping the Fishers were gone. Checkout was at noon, and it was now half past, but I worried that Leslie and Brian would stay until I got home to apologize in person.

Audrey, I am SO SORRY, she'd written in her follow-up message. **Brian mixed up the brownies. When ours didn't hit last night, I realized we were eating yours! We both feel terrible . . .**

It's fine, I wrote. The damage was done, and what was I going to do? Charge them more money? Report them? Try to have their jet-setter status revoked? I wasn't even supposed to be running a Here-to-Stay!

And at the end of the day, Henry and I were both okay.

I hope you had a wonderful stay! I'd added to end the conversation.

Thankfully, their Subaru was nowhere to be seen. I let out a deep breath, and even though I knew I had to clean the guesthouse for the coming weekend, I was so not doing that right now. I didn't want to think about being a host for a while.

Especially when I got a text from Griff. Hey, it said. Hope you're okay, haven't seen you in school. Just wanted to let you know that my dad went to the Dave signing last night and met this random couple from out of town. They mentioned they were staying at the nicest HTS called Fair Winds.

Yikes-face emoji.

My blood thickened. Instead of responding, I took a screenshot and sent it to Henry. He called me thirty seconds later. "We're screwed!" was my greeting.

"I'm feeling great, thank you for asking," Henry said dryly. "How about you?"

I grimaced. "I'm sorry. How are you feeling?"

"Better now," he told me. "I twisted my ankle falling down the stairs last night, but sleeping for thirteen hours works wonders. I'm sorry I wasn't awake when you left."

"It's okay," I said. "I would've stayed, but I was anxious to see if the Fishers were gone."

"Are they?"

"Yes." I sighed. "But Griff's text . . ."

"Don't worry about it," Henry said. "It's not like they gave Mr. Keeler your address, right?"

"But what if he looks up Fair Winds on Here-to-Stay?"

"Then he'll see photos of a guesthouse in Essex Harbor. When was the last time the Keelers were at your house, anyway?"

"Labor Day, maybe?" I answered. "I don't remember."

"Then I wouldn't worry about it," he said, and when I didn't respond, he tentatively added: "Why don't you blow something today?"

My stomach flipped.

"Unlock the hot shop," he continued. "Fire up the furnace."

"But I told you," I said, "Golightly Glass is currently on a production hiatus."

"I know, but it doesn't need to be." I could *hear* Henry's shrug. "No one's checked in right now; you're bumming yourself out for no reason."

I didn't respond. It was a little *more* than bumming me out, and Henry knew that. I'd never really been into sports, but right now I felt like an athlete who was sidelined for whatever reason, chomping at the bit to get back in the game. Without glassblowing, my life felt—to quote Charlotte Chen—"off-kilter."

"Fair Winds will be empty until Thursday night," he continued. "You can blow something cool this afternoon."

I smiled. "Thanks, Hank."

He chuckled. "You don't need my permission."

"I know," I said, "but I always want your support." I paused, suddenly missing him. "Do you want to come over?"

The line was quiet for a moment. "I can't," Henry said. "My mom has sort of grounded me."

"Oh."

"I mean, it's fine," he added. "Reading on the back porch isn't exactly the world's worst punishment . . ." He dropped his voice. "I'm not supposed to be on the phone, though."

I giggled. "I'll talk to you later, dearest one."

The words had slipped out so easily.

"Dearest one?" He sounded amused.

"Oh, you know what I mean!" Heat flared on the back of my neck. "I'm, you know, playing my part."

"As am I," Henry said dutifully.

"Yes," I whispered, though I could've pointed out that we didn't need to play our parts right now.

There was no one, not even a ghost, in my house who needed convincing we were a couple.

CHAPTER 15

THE FURNACE TOOK A COUPLE OF HOURS TO heat up, and I had to stop myself from dancing around the hot shop as I worked, almost able to hear the adrenaline humming inside me. I first tried to make a vase, and after blowing my first bubble, I rolled it in a bowl of blue-green frit—sugar-sized granules of glass—to change the color to a shade called seafoam.

In the end, I failed miserably. The vase soon grew too heavy for my blowpipe, and without an assistant to help me, it broke off and smashed on the concrete floor. I swore under my breath, then couldn't help but laugh.

It felt so damn *good* to be back.

After that, I switched to my mermaid teardrop pendants and moved quickly. I'd just placed my tenth in the annealer when I heard someone shout my name.

Trying not to visibly jump in surprise, I took out my AirPods and turned to see Ellie standing in the doorway. "Hey," I said. "What's up?"

"I was running an errand in town," she said. "You and Henry weren't in school today, so I wanted to make sure you were okay."

"Uh, yeah," I said, a little confused. A check-in text would've been easier. "I wasn't feeling well this morning, so . . ." I shrugged.

"All of your work is so incredible," Ellie said before things could become awkward. She pointed across the hot shop, at the inventory shelves.

"Thanks," I said. "Half of it is good, half of it was a learning experience."

Ellie laughed. "Henry always said you were humble."

Except I'm not, I thought. I knew I was a *good* glassblower, and with the right instructor, I could become a *great* glassblower. *I feel it in my bones,* I'd once said to Henry. *I can be amazing at this someday.*

"So . . ." Ellie took a deep breath. "I heard."

My stomach swished.

She'd *heard*? About the brownies? Had Henry told her?

"Griff found me at lunch," she continued. "His dad met the Fishers at Bedtime Stories?"

Oh, okay, I thought, relaxing a little. She gave me a wary look when I half lied that I wasn't too worried. "Griff's mom likes to talk," she said. "If his dad mentioned it to her . . ."

"I'm not worried," I repeated.

Ellie folded her arms over her chest. "I'm just trying to help."

"I know." I smiled gently. "And I really appreciate it."

"Has anyone booked for this weekend?" she asked.

"Yes," I said. "A woman from Brazil. She arrives tomorrow."

"Wow." Ellie looked impressed. "Where in Brazil?"

"Rio. She's originally from here, though." Valerie was in her forties, and had a third-round job interview in Manhattan on Friday.

"When should we clean the apartment?" Ellie offered, almost sounding hopeful.

"Oh, thank you." I felt caught a little off guard—a little *nervous*. Ellie and I hadn't hung out alone in . . . well, I was glad I could say, "Once Griff gets here."

He'd texted me while I was sweeping up my shattered vase.

"Fine with me." Ellie started browsing my shelves. "How did you get the flowers on this?" she asked, picking up a cup, and after I told her, she moved on to my pendants. "Is Golightly Glass going to have an 'everything must go' sale soon?"

"Uh, no." My brows knitted together. "What makes you think that?"

"No reason." She shrugged. "I've been thinking a lot about change lately. If you're blowing glass at Blue Ridge and Henry's busy at NYU . . . won't things be different? Hard?"

I shifted from one foot to the other; Henry and I hadn't talked about that yet. It wasn't like Golightly Glass was firmly rooted here—I could rent studio time to blow my pendants in any big city (and with better equipment!) and Henry could potentially work out of his dorm room—but was Ellie right? Would we both be too busy?

And even if I could blow pieces in my spare time, would

Golightly Glass still feel like Golightly Glass *without* Henry?

My heart quavered at the thought of not being able to look over at the worktable to see Henry sipping iced coffee while printing out USPS labels or packaging glassware and humming along to our new playlist. Golightly Glass was *more* than just tumblers and Christmas ornaments.

I tried to subtly clear my throat. "How's Chase been?"

"Fine." Ellie was nonchalant. "He left this morning for his internship."

"Really? I thought that started next week."

Did I remember Ellie mentioning the first week of June? Vaguely?

"It does, but he's at Lake George with friends right now," Ellie said. "My parents might let me go up this weekend."

I nodded, wondering if she really *wanted* to go to the Adirondacks. It sounded more like a chore than something she was excited about, and I found myself wanting to cheer her up. Ellie had come to clean, so we were going to clean. "You know what," I said. "Forget about Griff. Let's head upstairs and whip Fair Winds into shape!"

Ellie smiled and we climbed Fair Winds' steps together. I felt my phone buzz in my back pocket as I entered the four-digit code to the lockbox anchored on the door handle. Sure enough, the Fishers had left the gold key inside—along with a teensy-tiny folded piece of paper. It fell out and Ellie swept it up before I could.

"'Again, we're so sorry,'" she read aloud. "'We truly didn't know!'" She gave me a quizzical look. "What does that mean?"

"They smoked some pot the other night," I said casually. I was so not going to tell her the whole truth. "I listed Fair Winds as a nonsmoking property, but they missed that part."

"Gross." Ellie wrinkled her nose. "Gummies would've been much more considerate."

I laughed a little, tapping my phone to see a text from Griff.

He was going to be late.

My heart dipped a little, but at least he'd offered to bring milkshakes.

"Looks like it's just you and me," I said, showing Ellie the text.

"Mmm," was all she said.

The Fishers hadn't been as neat as Sandy and Ron, but the aroma of their chai tea was less pungent than Ron's Old Bay. They did use more towels than I'd known were even in the linen closet, and there were some stains I preferred not to identify on the bedsheets, but all in all, nothing to vomit over. "No need to brag that you have a stronger stomach than me!" Ellie exclaimed after I teased her for gagging, to which I replied, "Tampons in the trash would've been a different story . . ."

Ellie wiped down the kitchen while I vacuumed and straightened up the bedroom. There were a couple of books on the nightstand, one of them an old copy of Joanne Fluke's *Cherry Cheesecake Murder* and the other a guide to mushrooms.

Okay, then, I thought, but decided to add them to the

eclectic assortment on the bookshelf.

The only other weird thing was the dresser. Despite the decorative silver tray that sat on top, it looked a little bare. It took me a moment to realize that the ship's bell clock was missing. My mom had found it in London, and it was gorgeous and timeless with its shiny hardwood base and brass case. Perfect for "tastefully nautical."

My guess was Leslie or Brian had tucked it away somewhere to muffle the noise. Per tradition, the clock chimed eight times—at four, eight, and twelve—to mark the end of a mariner's four-hour watch. The setting was easy enough to disable, but my mom didn't want to compromise the clock's authenticity.

Maybe in the bunk room? I guessed, but on my way to check, Ellie called my name and I made a detour to the kitchen. She held up one of Rise & Grind's signature bakery boxes.

For Audrey & Boyfriend, I read the accompanying note as Ellie said, "This is addressed to you."

"What's inside?" I asked, even though I had an inkling.

"Brownies."

My stomach swished with revulsion. I never wanted to eat brownies again.

"Have as many as you want," I told her. "I know you've given up desserts, but . . ."

She cocked her head. "I told you I'm off sweets?"

Shit, I thought, pulse pounding. *You aren't supposed to know that! She told her mom in confidence at TJ's!*

I had to play this cool, so I shrugged. "You might've? I think?"

"Oh, maybe," she replied. "But Rise & Grind's brownies have always been my weakness..."

I waved my hand. *Go for it!*

"Henry has met guests?" Ellie asked three brownies later.

"Nope," I said. "I've just mentioned him a couple of times."

As your "boyfriend," the voice in my head whispered. *And it makes you feel taller, it makes you smile more...*

My heart twisted. I know I didn't need a boyfriend to be happy, but...

Having one, even a fake one, made me feel more like a glass-half-full person.

Ellie nodded. "How're things with him?"

"Good," I answered.

"That's it? Good?"

What does she want me to say? I wondered. *Am I supposed to gush about how much I love her ex-boyfriend?*

I mean, of course I was supposed to—this was a golden opportunity in our evil plan to make Ellie jealous, to make her realize what she had given up and then see the light and run back into Henry's arms. Henry this, Henry that, let's talk everything Henry and only Henry!

But I found that I didn't want to talk about Henry. Ellie hadn't sounded like she was totally over their breakup, and I didn't want to rub it in even more. Guilt felt like slime coating my skin.

I also wanted to keep Henry to myself. I didn't want to share what we talked about together or our inside jokes or how determined he was to find my nonexistent ticklish spot. That stuff was all ours.

Henry, in a way, now felt like mine.

Would he still feel that way when we went back to being just best friends?

"He asked me to prom last night" was the one tidbit I finally gave Ellie.

"Oh, really?" She blinked. "How?"

Fortunately, I'd remembered more from last night, despite having been high as a kite. "We were talking about *The Theory of Everything*—you know, the Stephen Hawking movie—and he asked me if he should wear tails to prom. Go really old-school." I rolled my eyes affectionately.

Ellie smiled weakly. "If anyone can pull off tails, it's Henry Chen."

"No way," I said. "I love him, but he's not tall enough."

"Did you tell him that?" she asked, a little coolly.

"Deep down, he *knows* that." I started to laugh, but my stomach somersaulted when I realized what I'd just said.

I love him.

Three seconds ago, I told Ellie I *loved* Henry.

How did she interpret that? I wondered. *Like I loved Henry casually? Or not so casually?*

Wait... My heart suddenly skipped. Was *it casual? Or not so casual?*

"It's funny," Ellie said as I tried to decipher it. "I *really* always pictured you with Griff."

I gave her a look. "You did?"

"Yeah, you guys look like you have so much fun when you hang out." She reached for another brownie. "I know you said your crush kind of stalled, but I was surprised it fizzled . . . *especially* after that water volleyball game. You were all over each other!"

I don't not *have a crush on Griff,* I thought, pulse quickening. *Right?*

I mean, lately I'd felt like my mind was happily occupied with Henry, but I still had a thing for Griff. I still imagined him picking me up and spinning me around, the two of us laughing until our ribs hurt. He still hadn't stopped by with our promised milkshakes, though, which bummed me out.

"He asked Kenzie to prom after school today," Ellie added. "You saw it on his Instagram story, right?"

My stomach dropped. "Oh, yeah," I lied. I hadn't been on social media much today; everything faded away when I blew glass.

Ellie laughed. "I hope he asked her parents if it was okay to shoot an arrow at their front door."

I didn't need to check out Instagram to see the footage; I could just picture it. Griff, square-shouldered and chestnut hair shining in the sunlight, walking down Kenzie's front path with a bow and a PROM? note dangling from Cupid's arrow.

"What about Chase?" I asked, half to change the subject and half because I wanted to know. "Is he coming back for prom?"

Ellie nodded. "He says he wouldn't miss it." She glanced away before looking back at me and smiling, her eyes strained.

"You know he doesn't deserve you, right?" I asked, because what was the harm? "You're too good for him."

Ellie blushed. "Maybe," she said quietly.

I gave her a smile, waiting and wishing for her to add something about breaking up with Chase. Hopefully this was a start.

⁓

IT WAS MY IDEA TO PUT ON MUSIC WHILE WE finished up cleaning Fair Winds, and I laughed when Ellie put down the Swiffer to show me a few of today's popular middle school dance moves. "Don't tell her I told you, but Tate is almost as tragic a dancer as our dad!"

"Her talents lie elsewhere," I rephrased, pointing to my hair.

"Indeed!"

I felt a twinge. Henry and I'd talked about being only children—neither of us had ever particularly wished for siblings, but there were fleeting moments when we did. Usually when Ellie spoke about her brother and sister. *No one loves their siblings more than Pinks,* Henry long ago remarked. *She sometimes wants to kill them, but mostly wants to kill for them...*

There were more than enough brownies left for Ellie's family, so I sent her home with the bakery box once the guesthouse looked straight out of a Serena & Lily catalog. It was pristine. "I hope I can pay you soon," I said by way of goodbye. "Here-to-Stay is still holding my money hostage."

"Don't worry." Ellie smiled. "There's no rush."

No rush.

She really must be rethinking things with Chase, I thought. If there was no rush for her cut, then there must not be a rush for a train ticket to visit him.

Meanwhile, Griff had texted me this morning: Funds hit account yet?

Later, I ordered a margherita pizza from Ottimo and zipped into town to get it (I was lazy, but not lazy enough for DoorDash). The restaurant was packed every night of the week; I could barely hear my thoughts over diners' conversations. My pizza waited expectantly behind the bar, near the brick oven with its blue, green, and white tile mosaic. "This one's on me!" I swear I heard someone shout just as I was about to hand over my credit card.

I flinched when I felt a hand on my shoulder, and turned to see a chipped-tooth smile. "Griff, hey," I said, but the words came out like I'd swallowed a bug. A sort of cough. "What's up?"

"Let me treat you to dinner," he said. "I'm sorry I never showed up to help you clean. I told you I'd be there, and I wasn't."

Yeah, I thought. *Why?*

"You owe me a milkshake," I quipped when he didn't explain. "Not a pizza."

Griff shrugged, and I didn't protest when he handed over his debit card.

"Thanks, Keeler," I said. "I'll think of you while I'm devouring this in twenty minutes."

"I'm flattered," Griff chuckled, then nodded outside. "I'll walk you to Brigitta."

"What about your family?" I asked.

"Oh, I'm not with my family," he said. "Just Jason." He winked as he held open the door for me. "We're talking strategy about his promposal to Cristina."

"Got it," I said, then mustered up some enthusiasm. "Congratulations on asking Kenzie!"

"You don't sound thrilled." For once, Griff was quick on the uptake, noticing my lack of cheer. "Are you good?"

Who cares if I'm not thrilled? I thought. *I don't need to be thrilled. It's not my promposal.*

"You're going with Chen, right?" Griff asked when I stayed silent. "I mean, since you're together?"

"Yeah, of course." I shrugged and then, embarrassingly, started laughing. "I'm sorry, Griff," I said. "I'm so tired today. Running a short-term rental is *not* for the faint of heart."

"No worries, Audrey." Griff gave me a lopsided smile and clapped my shoulder, almost knocking the pizza box from my arms. "You're doing awesome."

"Tell that to my bank account," I muttered as my phone chimed in my sweatshirt pocket.

"No, no, come on." Griff shook his head. "That *review*?"

I rolled my eyes. "It was *one* review, Griff."

He smirked. "Oh, so you haven't seen it."

"Seen what?"

"The *second* review."

There was a second review? My pulse jumped, but before I could shove my dinner at him and check Here-to-Stay myself, Griff pulled it up on his phone.

No way. I blinked upon seeing the screen. *Five stars from Brian and Leslie?*

You deserve it, I could hear Henry say. *Plus, it's an olive branch to avoid a lawsuit...*

I skimmed. They called Fair Winds cute, clean, and cozy, and the highlight of their trip was their sunrise and sunset walks on the Sound. It made Leslie's blood pressure drop "in the best way." They would've stayed longer if they could, calling me the consummate professional: extremely organized, considerate, and discreet.

And to sweeten the pot even more, *Sandy* had added an additional review: If you love Beach Cottage Chronicles, Fair Winds is perfect for you!

"I *told* you," Griff said when I finished reading. "You're killing it." He grinned. "You've got someone lined up for this weekend, don't you?"

"Of course," I said, straightening my shoulders. Because he was right! Look at me! In my entrepreneur era! "She's arriving tomorrow..." I balanced the pizza box in one hand so I could unlock my phone, but once I tapped on the Here-to-Stay app,

I trailed off . . .

They'd unfrozen my money.

My new-host delay had been lifted.

I could officially pay out and transfer five nights' worth of rent to my bank account.

"Fuck yeah!" Griff cheered when I showed him. "Let's pay the hell out!"

And then, without any warning, he picked me up and spun me around twice. A small zing went up my spine, but I just smiled and held on to my pizza for dear life.

CHAPTER 16

WE HAD WAY LESS MONEY THAN I'D THOUGHT we would. Four-fifty a night for five nights had sounded promising, but after all of Here-to-Stay's fees, it turned out we were only netting three hundred a night. And I also had to pay Ellie and Griff their twenty-five-dollar-per-night pie slices.

In short: I had made less than two thousand dollars.

How was I going to make up the rest? I had spoken to my parents a few more times, and they hadn't mentioned anything even vaguely related to money, but I could hear the clock ticking in time with my heart.

"We can raise the rate a little," Henry suggested when I'd called him with the news. "Increase it to five hundred?"

I groaned. "That's only a fifty-dollar difference."

On the other end of the line, he was quiet. "You know," he eventually ventured. "I really don't mind—"

"I'm not accepting any more money from you." I cut him off, pulse leaping. Why was he like this? The absolute best?

"In case you forgot, you already gave me a *grand*."

More silence. "I just feel like it's partly my fault," he murmured. "We were so drunk, and I left you alone . . ."

"Henry, stop." My eyes started to prickle. "This is entirely on me. I'm the idiot here." I swallowed hard, wishing I could fall into his arms for a hug. "Maybe we can raise it to five-fifty?"

"Okay, five-fifty," he agreed, releasing a deep breath. "It's a plan."

"AUDREY, WHY IS THERE SOME KID watching us?"

"What?" I was sitting on the diving board, focused on snapping a photo of Henry, who had fallen asleep floating in a classic red-and-white striped inner tube. A heat wave had hit Essex Harbor, so he and his improv friends had cornered me after class and asked if they could come swim. Henry's head lolled to the left, his wet hair shining in the sunlight, but he still looked too cool for school in his Ray-Bans.

Lifeguard off duty, I typed before posting the picture on my Instagram story.

"Over there." Rory nodded toward the pool gate. "There's a kid watching us."

I turned and saw, to my horror, a little boy leaning against the fence. He was maybe five or six, dressed in yellow shorts and a T-shirt with the Brazilian flag on it. *Oh my god*, I thought, heart rate escalating, as Cam called out, "Hey, bud!"

Henry jolted awake, nearly splashing me. "I'm not asleep, I never fell asleep!"

"Oh, dude . . ." Alec shook his head from the shallow end. "The footage we have tells another story."

"Hi!" the boy called back. "I'm Junior!"

"Hi, Junior," I said, a catch in my voice. Was he who I thought he was? "I'm Audrey. Where's your—"

"Junior!" someone shouted, and a beat later, a woman with curly brown hair appeared. "I'm so sorry." She waved to me. "He's adventurous like his father and has a tendency to wander off . . ."

"Okay, who is that?" Rory asked. "A neighbor?"

"Define 'neighbor,'" I mumbled, rising from the diving board. Did I want to meet my new guest in a bikini? Definitely not, but it was happening anyway. My stomach squirmed. "Henry . . ."

"Go, go," he said quickly. "I'll handle the guys."

"Hi, Valerie," I said, summoning a smile when I reached the pool gate. "I hope your flight was smooth?"

She laughed. "Traveling with a child always brings some turbulence." She ran a hand through her son's hair. "But we made it! Didn't we, Junior?"

"She yelled at me during our layover in Miami," Junior told me, but I barely heard him. Instead, I was opening up a new tab in my head, mentally scrolling through Fair Winds' Here-to-Stay description. *No children, please,* I remembered typing.

Valerie had also specified that she was coming alone. A party of one.

"Is there a problem with the lockbox?" I asked lightly.

"Oh, no." She dug the guesthouse key out of her pocket. "Worked like a charm."

"Great." I didn't know what else to say. I couldn't believe she'd brought her kid!

Valerie handed Junior the key. "Honey, why don't you go back to the little house and explore? We're going to be living here for the next few days!"

Junior looked at me.

"Have fun!" I told him in a high-pitched voice, hoping it disguised how pissed I was. All I could see were Magic Markers all over the furniture.

They were washable, right?

"I'm sorry," Valerie said as Junior raced off and we trailed behind him. "I know you don't normally allow kids, but my husband is an archaeologist and was invited on a last-minute dig, and Junior rarely sees his grandparents . . ."

Okay, then why isn't he staying with them? I wondered.

"Their senior living community is strict about overnight guests," she added. "That's why we aren't staying with them." She sighed a stressed-out-mom sigh. "You're doing us a huge favor. This location is perfect, and I knew we had to stay here when I read the reviews. It sounds like I might even get to relax!"

We reached the bottom of the guesthouse staircase, and

Junior had left the screen door wide open. "Junior has probably already discovered it," I said, "but Fair Winds has a small second bedroom with bunk beds."

Valerie lit up. "He will *love* that." She smiled. "I promise he will be well-behaved. We've brought plenty of games and books, and his grandparents will take care of him tomorrow while I'm in the city."

I nodded, telling myself I believed her. "You said your husband's an archaeologist?" I couldn't help but ask. The cinephile in me wanted to know. It was too funny a coincidence. "Is Junior . . . ?"

"An Indiana Jones reference, yes." She rolled her eyes and smiled. "My husband is Gregory Daniels Senior, so we couldn't resist when we had Junior."

I laughed. Indiana Jones's real name was Henry Jones Jr., and it always got on his nerves when his dad called him Junior.

Valerie raised an eyebrow, impressed. "You have excellent taste in movies."

"Thank you." I gestured to the pool. "My boyfriend's is better."

Why, I wondered after wishing Valerie a nice stay, *are you suddenly so obsessed with calling Henry your boyfriend?*

When we'd first started "dating," I'd had to force the word out of my mouth.

Now it rolled off my tongue like the most natural thing in the world.

IN THE TIME I'D SPENT WELCOMING VALERIE (and Junior), Henry not only told his friends about my Here-to-Stay scheme but also managed to grab his laptop and print three copies of the NDA from the printer in my mom's office. "Who knew you were so badass, Audrey?" Rory said.

"Says the least badass person on the planet," commented Alec as Henry shot Rory a look and said, "I did."

I blushed so fiercely that I was tempted to swan dive into the pool.

"You don't have to worry about us," Cam told me. "Our lips are sealed."

"Hopefully with Gorilla Glue," I said.

Alec winked. "We signed your boyfriend's NDA, didn't we?"

There it was again.

Boyfriend.

This time, I leaped into the pool and could have sworn that I felt the cool water turn to steam against my hot skin. I couldn't deny it was from more than today's relentless sunshine.

When I came up for air, Henry was an airborne cannonball and splashed me upon detonation. "You got me in the eye!" I whined once he broke the surface. The corners of my eyes stung from the chlorine.

He smiled and whipped back his wet hair before paddling over and wrapping his arms around me. "Wait . . ." he said when I squealed. "Did I finally find your ticklish spot?" He zapped my waist; my heart sprang. "I swear I've tickled you there before!"

Yes, I thought. *But, the thing is, we both had more clothes on...*

I was very aware of the rise and fall of Henry's chest against mine. Very aware of his teasing smile and also very aware of the goose bumps that had just bloomed up and down his arms. I was starting to wonder, truthfully maybe even *hope*, that—

"Audrey, your phone is ringing!" Cam called from the pool deck.

"And not to snoop," Alec added, "but it's your dad!"

"Perfect timing," I muttered before ducking underwater and swimming over to the pool steps. The slate patio was so hot that I walked to my lounge chair on my heels. "Shit, shit, *shit.*"

Sure enough, my phone screen read **Dein Vater**. *Your father.*

I tapped to answer. "Hello!"

"Audrey, this is your father," my dad said. It was how he greeted me every time he called, one of our favorite inside jokes.

But he sounded so serious that I worried it wasn't a joke this time. Was this it? Had he received an email about the money I'd recently deposited in our Bank of Fairfield account?

"Hi, Dad." I tried to stay cool. "What time is it there?"

"A little past eleven. Your mother is asleep, but I'm out on the balcony having a nightcap."

My stomach dropped like a roller coaster. A nightcap—my

dad was having *a nightcap*? I closed my eyes. "What poison did you pick?" I managed to ask.

If his drink was a scotch and soda, he was unwinding at the end of a long but good day.

But if it was a vodka martini...

Well, my dad sipped those when he was crunching the Barbour family numbers and wanted to take the edge off.

This is it, I thought as I moved away from the guys for a little privacy. My legs wobbled. *He checked the account.*

I was about to find myself in some deep shit.

"Scotch and soda," he said. "We had a fantastic day, but it was a long one."

I let out a very deep, very internal sigh.

Bless the Lord.

"Nice," I said. "What did you guys do?"

"We went on a hike with some people from our hotel, and afterward I read while your mom enjoyed the spa. We ventured into town for dinner and discovered this tiny restaurant..."

"Delicious!" I said after he'd described their eight-course meal (and wine pairings). "That sounds like a really great day."

"It was," he said, and I could hear the smile in his voice. "We'd love to bring you here sometime, kiddo."

"My passport is begging to be stamped," I quipped, making him chuckle. My dad and I were good at bantering, but sometimes I worried we never talked about anything real.

"What're you up to?" he asked. "It's fiveish there?"

"Mm-hmm," I said. "It's really hot today, so Henry—"

"Oh yes," my dad cut in. "Henry, my daughter's *boyfriend*."

I rolled my eyes. My mom must've told him. "That's him," I said before he could give me any sort of talk. "He and some friends are here swimming."

"In the Sound?"

"Pool."

A dramatic gasp. "We have a pool?"

I let a giggle slip.

"Oh." I heard my dad snap his fingers. "I'm supposed to ask if you could stop by the carriage house apartment to flush the toilet and run the water for a bit. Your mom says it's been a while."

I literally felt my blood thicken. "Already done," I managed to say. "Mom mentioned it before you guys left, so I assessed the situation yesterday." I swallowed. "Everything's fine."

"Wonderful, I'll let—"

"It's really pretty," I added. "Mom is so talented, Dad."

"Yes, I agree." He sounded like he was nodding. "What she's done with the whole property is incredible."

"Has she heard of *Beach Cottage Chronicles*?" I asked. "It's this miniseries that showcases unique waterfront cottages and, like, the stories behind them. I think Fair—I mean, the carriage house—would be perfect for it. She should apply."

After Sandy's comment, I'd watched the first episode of *Beach Cottage Chronicles* and was officially hooked.

"I'll ask," my dad said. "Don't let your expectations get too high, though. You know she only does this because it brings her joy."

"Okay, Marie Kondo," I deadpanned.

"Ouch," he said. "Too dated a reference?"

"We still lived in Philly during that phenomenon," I replied. "So, yes."

He chuckled. "You humble me, Audrey."

I smiled. "I love you, Dad."

"I love you, too," he said, then yawned. "I should get to bed. It sounds like you're doing a great job holding down the fort."

"Oh yeah," I told him, unable to suppress a smirk. "I have this place running like a well-oiled machine..."

CHAPTER 17

ON FRIDAY MORNING, I WAS TEMPTED TO CHECK on Fair Winds after Valerie and Junior left for the day. It felt strange having a little kid there, especially with all my parents' trinkets and treasures from their travels. *Relax,* I told myself as I buckled my seat belt and turned over Brigitta's ignition. *You're being overprotective. Valerie promised Junior would be on his best behavior.*

But you saw him bring in a bag of cheese puffs! another part of my brain fired back. *He's going to get them on the furniture, and they're going to stain—*

I slammed on my brakes at the end of the driveway. I'd almost driven straight into the front gate. *Get it together, Audrey.*

Get it together.

Get it together!

Henry was already in the quad, iced coffees in hand, when I got to school. "This doesn't look like Rise & Grind," I commented after accepting the cup, misty with condensation. Instead of the coffee shop's signature plastic magenta straw, this was a bamboo one.

"Excellent detective work," he said. "It's an iced orange blossom latte from—"

"Bedtime Stories!" I broke into a grin, remembering our "first date" there. *Do not kiss me*, I'd said. *I don't kiss on the first date.*

Now my knees went numb at the thought of Henry's fingertips on my waist. The moment, in hindsight, seemed so romantic. I'd really resisted kissing him?

It felt so natural now.

"Yeah, Ellie wanted to change it up," Henry said.

The first sip of my latte made my stomach curdle. "You drove Ellie to school again?"

Henry shook his head. "No, she drove me. My starter crapped out this morning."

"Tess couldn't do anything?" As a mechanic, she knew *everything* about cars.

"She'd already left for work," he replied. "Full slate today."

"Oh." I took another sip of my drink, but it didn't help cool off my flaming face.

Henry tilted his head. "Is everything okay?"

No, I thought. *Not really.*

"Holly—"

"Don't call me that," I cut him off. "I'm named after Audrey Hepburn, not any of her characters." I sucked in a breath. "And

I can't believe you asked *Ellie* for a ride to school."

"Why not?" Henry asked. "She's a friend who lives only five to eight minutes away."

I opened my mouth, then closed it. Henry had never referred to Ellie as his friend before; he'd probably go back to calling her "Pinks" by lunch.

"Okay, so you're back to being friends," I heard myself say, inexplicably pissed. "But I'm your girlfriend, Hank. I might be more like eight to ten minutes away, but still, I'm your *girlfriend*." My heart thudded in my chest. "You could've called me."

Then I shoved my iced coffee at him and walked away.

∽

I AVOIDED HENRY FOR THE REST OF THE DAY, mostly because I was embarrassed. I might've been his girlfriend, but I was not his *girlfriend*. Who cared if Ellie drove him to school? I definitely shouldn't.

And wasn't that what our whole ruse was about anyway? Maybe it missed the mark for Griff and me, now that he'd asked Kenzie to prom, but for Henry . . .

If anything, I owed him a congratulatory iced coffee.

Speaking of . . .

Griff found me after gym as we were walking back to the locker rooms. Our last unit of the year was pickleball. Everyone found it funny how seriously Griff took it, even our teacher.

I mean, it was *pickleball*.

"Hey, Audrey." He flashed me a smile. "How's the bank account?"

"Growing," I quipped, though my chest tightened. No one had booked Fair Winds after I raised its nightly rate.

He held out a fist for me to bump. I hesitated before knocking my knuckles against his. Was I irrationally annoyed with Henry? Yes, but I also couldn't stop thinking about running into Griff at Ottimo . . . and talking about prom. He'd seemed a little *off* after finding out that Henry hadn't promposed to me yet. Was he second-guessing asking Kenzie? Or at least kicking himself for not waiting until Henry had asked me?

It kind of felt that way.

"My parents get home in nine days," I added, not wanting to dwell too long. "I just need to squeeze in a few more guests, and then I'll be all set."

I sounded more confident than I felt.

But my heart sang with determination. I was closer to attending the Blue Ridge School of Glass than I'd ever been; all my hard work—glassblowing, catering, and Here-to-Stay hosting—was going to pay off. I'd make sure it did.

"Thank you, Griff." I smiled and reached out to give his arm a squeeze. "Without your help, this wouldn't be happening."

Really? I could hear Henry, and picture him with a skeptically raised brow. *Has he really been indispensable?*

"You're welcome!" Griff said. "And hey, I have another idea . . ."

"Are you going to make me guess?" I laughed when he didn't say more.

He shook his head. "But I can't tell you here." He gestured around. "It has to do with your current venture."

"Ah." I nodded, appreciative that he knew not to mention Here-to-Stay at school.

"We can talk later," he said. "Are you going to homecoming tonight?"

"Of course," I told him. "Homecoming" was the Constellation catering crew's affectionate nickname for the season-opener party Caroline Hopper threw at the beginning of every summer. It was always a ton of fun. This year's venue was an upscale restaurant called Swan, right on the water. Attire was semi-formal.

"Cool," Griff said, then rocked back on his heels. "Henry driving you?"

Yep! I thought, but swallowed the word.

"Actually, no," I said lightly. "I don't think so. His car didn't start this morning, and he's not sure when it'll be fixed, so it looks like I'm driving."

"No, you're not." Griff grinned. "I'll drive you."

My heart leaped. "Really?"

"Absolutely. I'll grab you, then Chen."

"That's not necessary," I said coolly, tucking a sweaty lock of hair behind my ear. It had fallen out of its tiny ponytail. "He lives closer to Ellie than he does to me. I'm sure she'd be happy to drive him."

"Perfect!" Griff winked. "I'll see you at six-thirty."

Then he pushed through the boys' locker room door,

heading for the shower.

"Are you shampoo-then-body-wash?" I blurted before he disappeared, remembering my dream/nightmare featuring Griff upstairs in the shower. "Or body-wash-then-shampoo?"

"Body-wash-then-shampoo!" he called back.

Huh, I thought as the door swung shut.

THERE WAS AN UNFAMILIAR CADILLAC PARKED outside Fair Winds when I got home from school and walked over to casually check on things. "You must be the hostess with the mostest!" someone called as I squinted through the Caddy's windows and saw a booster seat in the back.

My eyes snapped up to the balcony, where an elderly woman stood. She had short white hair and wore a green-and-white geometric-print tunic.

Junior's grandmother, I surmised.

"Yes, that's me," I replied. "I'm Audrey, and..." I searched for a reason to be here. "I was wondering if Valerie needed anything?"

"Val's not due back until late," her mother said, slowly starting down the stairs. I suddenly felt bad that Fair Winds didn't have an elevator. "I'm Susan, her mother, and my husband, Rich, is upstairs with Gregory."

I offered her a smile. "It's nice to meet you."

Susan continued her descent. "I hope you don't mind that Valerie gave us your gate code, but things were getting a bit loud at home and I didn't want to disturb our neighbors." She laughed and shook her head. "Our grandson has quite the imagination."

I tried not to wince at the thought of the breakables upstairs. Like the gorgeous white pitcher from my parents' trip to Tuscany when I was in middle school. Right now, it sat on the credenza, just begging to be accidentally knocked over.

"No problem," I told Susan, then gestured to the house. "I have a few things to do before going out later, but please text me if you need anything."

Susan smiled. "You're Monica Barbour's daughter, aren't you?"

My heart stopped. Wait, Susan *knew* my mom?

"I used to manage Bedtime Stories once upon a time," she explained when I didn't answer. "And I still stop in every now and again. It's become an even more wonderful store. Julie, my successor, was so excited when she hired your mom, and I can see why. She's such a gem—so personable, helpful, and capable. It sounds like every publicist in publishing has her email for tour stops, and my oh my, those window displays . . ." She trailed off as if she didn't have the words.

Gorgeous, whimsical, and captivating, I thought.

"My mom is the most talented person I know," I said, realizing it was true. She got shit done while also making her corner of the world beautiful.

Susan smiled. "Fair Winds is such a lovely place."

Please don't ask if my mom knows about Here-to-Stay,

I prayed. *Please don't ask, please don't ask, please don't ask!*

And, more importantly, please don't *tell*.

"Grandma!" Junior appeared on the balcony. "The timer's going off, but Grandpa's in the bathroom."

"I'll be right there, sweetie!" Susan called up, then said to me, "We made peanut butter cookies. I was going to leave some on your doorstep later, as a thank-you."

A shiver went up my spine as I flashed back to the Fishers' brownies waiting for me on the welcome mat. "That's really nice of you," I said, "but I'm allergic to peanuts."

I was also a big fat liar, but after that wild night at Henry's, I didn't think I could accept any more gifts from guests.

"Oh, that's a shame," Susan said at the same time Junior impatiently stamped his foot and whined, *"Grandma . . ."*

"Gregory, that's not polite," his grandmother said with a sigh. "Thank you again for your hospitality, Audrey. Your mother would be proud of you."

My ears perked up at her words.

Would, not *will*.

"Thank you." I smiled at her. "I hope the cookies are delicious!"

⁓

HENRY TEXTED ME BEFORE I STEPPED IN THE shower, but I didn't respond until after my bathroom had clouded up with steam and I smelled like lavender. Tess brought my car back to life, **the message read.** See you at 6:15?

Thanks, but don't worry about it, **I wrote back.** Something came up so I'll drive myself.

He hadn't mentioned Ellie driving him to school, so I didn't need to mention Griff, right? He'd find out later. Right before hitting Send, I added:

I might be a little late.

Because Griff was almost always late. He'd said six-thirty, but I didn't expect him to show up until 6:45 at the earliest.

Henry didn't respond for five minutes. Is everything okay?

Fire alarm went off in Fair Winds after baking cookies, I wrote, hoping I wasn't jinxing things. See you there!

Then I stared at our chat for several seconds, half waiting for Henry to reply and half wondering what the hell I was doing.

Like clockwork, six-thirty p.m. came and went, but I was pleasantly surprised when my doorbell rang at approximately 6:39. "Wow . . ." Griff said when I opened the door, his eyes widening a little. "Audrey, you look *incredible*."

"Don't I?" I winked. I was wearing a cocktail dress my mom and I'd found on a rare shopping spree together. The dress illustrated the night sky: black sequins with a silver-beaded crescent moon, stars, and clouds. I shined in the lamplight. "You look great, too," I told Griff, who was dapper in a navy suit. Vineyard Vines ties weren't my thing, but I couldn't help but laugh when I saw his was covered in pickleball paddles. Really?

Griff offered me his arm, ready to escort me to his car,

but my smile slipped off my face when the passenger window rolled down. "Audrey, *where* did you get your earrings?" Kenzie called out, because *Kenzie* was in the front seat. "I love them!"

"Oh, they're my mom's," I said, touching one of the firecracker-shaped silver and gold earrings. They were Swarovski, and no, I had not asked to borrow them.

She smiled. "They look really pretty on you!"

"Totally!" someone else agreed, and I discovered Mia in the back seat. She'd wrangled her curly hair into a slicked-back bun for tonight. "You're so on-theme," she told me, pointing to my outfit.

It took me a second, and then I pretended to groan. Constellation catering and my nightscape dress went hand in hand. "Oh my god, it was a complete accident."

"Buckle up, ladies!" Griff said once he was behind the steering wheel. "You three are precious cargo . . ."

Kenzie and Mia giggled, but I couldn't stop a chord from striking in my chest as I clicked my seat belt. When Griff had offered to drive me tonight, I thought that meant he'd be driving me and only me. This felt like a group date on *The Bachelor*.

I tried to shrug it off by asking to DJ.

"I know it's been two years!" Mia shouted during the chorus. "But I *still* can't believe this song is about Matty!"

"This one even *sounds* like a 1975 song," Kenzie said. "You like them, don't you, Audrey?"

I was only half listening.

Idiot, idiot, I thought, Henry running through my mind. *We're two idiots.*

Weren't we?

CHAPTER 18

ACROSS THE HARBOR FROM THE SAILING CLUB sat Swan, a long white clapboard building with the smallest parking lot in all of Essex Harbor. Griff circled for almost ten minutes before admitting defeat. "You're gonna get dizzy, Keeler!" one of the college-age cater-waiters called on his way inside, which Griff took as his cue to park up the street. My feet ached a little by the time we made it back to the restaurant, but I still smiled at the gold placard above the door: an etching of two swans kissing. Their necks formed a heart.

"We're here for the Constellation Catering party!" Kenzie told Swan's hostess after she greeted us. A curved staircase led upstairs to the main bar and restaurant, but the hostess directed us to the private room on the first floor.

Voices and music drifted toward us, and Griff whistled when we pushed through the doors. The room was timeless with its gleaming wood floor, lantern wall sconces, and white-marble-topped bar. Instead of round tables seating eight to ten, long oak farm tables ran parallel to one another. Each one was decorated with a navy-blue table runner, tea candles, and small, flower-filled vases. *This might be prettier than prom next week*, I thought.

"The bud vases were my idea," someone said, and I turned to see Tate in a cute violet jumpsuit. She sipped a soda. "We didn't need to break the bank on flowers."

I laughed. When your mother owned an event planning firm, I guess you learned all the tricks early. "When are you double-knotting your Constellation apron?" I joked, but whatever Tate quipped back turned to white noise when I felt a light hand on my lower back.

"Hey, Hepburn," Henry said when I turned. My heart quickened; he looked so handsome in a gray suit with the top two buttons of his white dress shirt undone. I noticed his black belt was the one I'd gotten him for his birthday. Henry surprisingly didn't love monograms, which I'd found out *after* I'd had his initials embossed on its silver buckle. HFC, for Henry Francis Chen.

And his hair—it was *Henry* hair, dark and thick and artfully unkempt. Hair I realized I desperately wanted to run my hands through. I'd had a hundred opportunities and hadn't taken nearly enough of them.

Oh my god, I thought, head spinning at Henry's mere existence. *How were we ever only friends? How did I ever put out that spark I first felt?*

"Tate, would you excuse us for a minute?" Henry asked as

I surreptitiously glanced around for Ellie. She was nowhere to be seen among Constellation's mingling staff. "I need to talk to Audrey."

"Of course." Tate nodded. "I'll get drinks."

"I'm sorry I'm late," I said once Tate was out of earshot, off on a mission to get two of Swan's signature mocktails. Henry already held one. "Parking was—"

Henry cut me off. "Did something happen to Brigitta?"

"No."

"Okay." He nodded. "Then why did Griff drive you here?"

I kept quiet, my pulse beginning to pound.

"You walked in with him," Henry said, as if I needed a refresher. "After blowing me off earlier, you showed up with him tonight." A pause. "Why?"

"Because he offered," I said, keeping my voice low. "And it was more like he just gave me a ride, because he chauffeured Kenzie and Mia too, so . . ." I shrugged.

Henry looked at me, his eyes heavy with something. Judgment? Disappointment? Maybe even *hurt*?

A lump formed in my throat. The last thing I wanted to do was hurt Henry; I'd never forget him showing up at the hot shop postbreakup with Ellie, tears streaming down his face and carrying his shattered heart.

Unsure what to say, I shifted from one high heel to the other.

Where was Tate with our drinks?

"We should talk," Henry said. "Let's go out outside." He

gestured to the far wall, with its floor-to-ceiling glass sliding doors that led to the back deck.

Hesitant, I said, "Caroline's probably going to make her welcome remarks soon."

"I don't think she'll mind." Henry offered me his hand. "The rest of the room will be rapt."

I let him lace his fingers through mine and lead me through the party. Hi's and hello's and oh-my-god-you-look-amazing's were dropped, but we didn't stop to talk to anyone.

Tonight's sunset was breathtaking, a warm golden glow on the blue horizon. I'd miss the summertime sunsets when I was at Blue Ridge—*if* I was at Blue Ridge. I loved watching them from our beach, bright pink bleeding into an endless orange. What would North Carolina's sunsets look like?

Henry and I walked down the deck and around the corner so the party wouldn't see us. I took a deep breath when he leaned against the wrought iron railing. The harbor breeze swept through his hair, tempting me to reach out and smooth it back into place. "All right," he said, our eyes locking. His brown irises shined in the market lights strung above us. "Tell me, really—why are you accepting rides from Griff?"

Because I have a crush on him should've been my answer.

But it wasn't the truth, at least not anymore.

I knew that now.

"Because I was mad at you," I said, chest clenching. "It was payback for asking Ellie to drive you to school this morning instead of me."

Henry quizzically tilted his head.

I felt myself flush. "Yes, I might as well be Tate's age. It was immature and stupid and petty, and I'm sorry." My heart hammered. "But at the same time, I'm also *not* sorry, because what *we're* doing is immature and stupid and petty, and I can't play along anymore."

Suddenly wide-eyed, Henry opened his mouth, but I didn't give him even a beat to speak.

"I don't regret agreeing to our deal," I said. "You were *crushed* after Ellie ended things. I wanted to do whatever I could to make things better, even if it meant pretending to date you to make her see her monumental mistake. It was never really about Griff. He's *Griff,* but it's always been more about *you.*" I blinked, coming to terms with the truth. First, I'd wanted to protect Henry, help him, and now . . . "This thing needs to end." I gestured between us. "I can't be your girlfriend anymore, because I've recently realized that I *want* to be your girlfriend. Maybe you're the love of Ellie's life, but I selfishly also want you to be the loss of her life." I paused. "You know, that sounded way less dramatic and horrible in my head, and I think I'm semiquoting a song. I just meant . . ."

"I know what you meant," Henry whispered once I trailed off. His left hand landed lightly on my waist and I felt his thumb brush across my hip bone as he gave me a long look. "Are you drunk?"

My pulse spiked. *Was I* what?

"Or high?" he asked.

"Are *you*?" I whispered, feeling sparks on my skin. "I tell you I'm in love with you, and your immediate response—"

"You didn't," he interrupted. "You basically said you didn't want me to be with Ellie, but you didn't tell me you loved me." He paused. "And we only ever talk like this when we're drunk." He grimaced. "Or unknowingly high."

I winced, because he was right. "I'm *me*," I emphasized, but my voice wavered, and for some inexplicable reason, I suddenly was fighting tears. "I'm your best friend, Hank."

"I hate it when you call me that," he replied, and a heartbeat after, his lips quirked into a cheeky smile, I took his face in my hands, and I crushed my mouth against his. Henry's lips were warm and soft, with a hint of spicy sweetness that might've been Swan's famous cherry-ginger mocktail—or it might've just been *Henry*. My heart ached before melting into molten glass.

We broke apart to breathe, then laughed before kissing again. My insides swooped and soared when he pressed me up against the deck's railing and kissed me like we had to prove something to everyone watching . . . except we didn't. There was no one here, only us. *Henry, Henry, Henry* was all I could think. The temperature had dipped and the breeze had picked up, but he felt like a furnace. I curled my fingers around the collar of his jacket and pulled him closer until his hips dug into mine. His hands were trembling but warm as his fingers came up to cradle the sides of my face, and I wished I didn't need to break the moment to breathe.

"*That* was a Hollywood kiss," I whispered once my lungs were full of sea air. "Wasn't it?"

"Yes," Henry whispered back. "It was Technicolor."

I wrinkled my nose. "Not your best line."

"Agreed." His brown eyes were mesmerizing. "It sounded more romantic when we were high."

HOMECOMING WRAPPED UP AROUND TEN,

and by 10:15, we high schoolers were in the Union Jack booth at Hamburger Hill. Tate, bless her, had tried to talk her way into tagging along, but her mom had nipped that in the bud. "Would you let me go if Ellie were here?" Tate asked, and I'd had to swallow a giggle when her mom said, "Since she's not, I couldn't tell you."

Ellie had said she was sick tonight.

I hope you feel better soon, I'd texted, but hadn't gotten a response. I suspected something else was up.

"Oh man, Audrey!" Griff said after we ordered milkshakes and fries. He was sitting across from me, pickleball tie loosened and holding court with Mia on his left and Kenzie on his right. "We never touched base tonight."

"Touched base?" I blinked. Under the table, Henry was idly drumming his fingertips against my thigh. It made things a little difficult to focus. Every single one of my brain cells was dialed in to his touch.

"My idea," he reminded me. "My idea for Fair Winds' expansion."

Henry's fingers stopped, and on my other side, Jared said, "Uh, *what* expansion?"

I couldn't think of a better question myself.

"Okay, so, Audrey and I were shooting the shit after gym today," Griff said. "You know, talking about Here-to-Stay rent and how much she still needs to pay back her parents."

"Uh-oh." Mia looked at me. "You don't have enough money yet?"

Not even close, I thought.

"I'm working on it," I said, pulse picking up. I *was* working on it, but could I do it?

"Well, I still think it's so cool, Audrey," Kenzie said. "Taking a gap year to do what you really love?"

Out of the corner of my eye, I saw Henry sit up straighter.

"Something like that," I lied, suddenly shy about admitting that I was choosing glassblowing over college. "If my year at Blue Ridge goes well, doors might open for me. Ideally, I'd travel for other courses or residencies."

"What about Penn?" Jared asked. "Wharton?"

I shrugged before explaining how important improving my craft was. "Henry and I want to build Golightly Glass into a real business someday."

Kenzie gave Henry a look. "I thought you wanted to be a Hollywood agent."

"Entertainment lawyer, actually," he said. "I've been

following some lawsuits recently . . ."

He is such a nerd, I thought, unable to hold back a smile.

"So how are you going to work for Golightly Glass?" Mia asked. "My older sister is in law school now, and she barely has time to eat lunch."

My unrivaled time management skills! I expected Henry to say, but when his mouth clamped shut, I felt my pulse falter.

"Milkshakes!" Hamburger Hill's owner announced, interrupting my train of thought. I unsuccessfully tried to track it down as she handed out our shakes—coconut for Mia, strawberry for Kenzie, banana chocolate chip for Jared, and chocolate peanut butter for Griff. As always, Henry got his black-and-white and I'd ordered mint chip. "Fries will be up in a few minutes," Heather told Griff before he could inquire.

"Okay, so what's your plan for Audrey?" Kenzie asked Griff, in a sweet effort to distract him until his chili fries arrived. "Expansion?"

Griff brightened. "Yes, *major* expansion . . ."

"We're already on the hook, Keeler," Henry said when Griff teasingly trailed off. "Time to reel us in."

"Chen, I'm trying to build the suspense."

"It's been built," I assured him, then took a sip of my milkshake. "Talk."

"Okay, so hear me out—"

"*Keeler.*"

"You should rent out your *actual* house," he said. "Before your parents get home. Fair Winds has been fun and all, but to get real money—*enough* money—you need to think bigger and better by posting the mansion on Here-to-Stay. It's gigantic, private, and has all the bells and whistles for a good time."

Rent... out... my... house...? White noise buzzed in my ears. Was he serious?

"Fries!" Heather was the one to cheerfully break the ice. Griff (and Kenzie) immediately dug into the chili fries, but I didn't acknowledge my sweet potato waffle fries until Mia asked if she could try one.

"That," Henry finally commented, "sounds terrifying."

"Oh, come on," Griff said. "*Think* about it, Chen."

Henry shot him a look that suggested he was most definitely *not* going to think about it, but I at least mentally ran through why the idea was so implausible. Starting with the fact that my parents would be back on American soil in only nine days! Nine days wasn't enough time to ready the house, market it, *and* host. A cozy guesthouse was one thing, but I had a feeling it would take *a lot* of bait to hook a reservation for a mansion. The booking wouldn't be instantaneous; someone special had to come along. Who knew how long that would take?

And this was all assuming I was totally cool with someone sleeping in my bed!

"Griff, I can't let people stay in my house," I said. "No way."

He raised an eyebrow. "Isn't Fair Winds your house?" He

shrugged. "If it weren't, you wouldn't be worrying about that kid breaking something."

I didn't know what to say. Okay, he wasn't wrong; I was extremely protective of Fair Winds. But my house was different. It was *my house*.

"You need to make more money," Griff continued, eyes locking with mine. His were as blue as the Sound on a sunny day, but no zing zipped through me this time. "This is the ultimate opportunity to be a little enterpriser."

"Entrepreneur," Kenzie whispered to him.

"They're interchangeable," Henry whispered to her.

I shifted in my seat as the whole table sipped their shakes in anticipation. "I'll think about it," I told Griff in an effort to answer without answering. "I have two booking requests for Fair Winds next week. Let me assess those to see where they'll get me."

That, thankfully, was true. Two people had reached out during the Constellation party.

But they still wouldn't boost me to six thousand dollars.

Griff grinned. "Hey, you could even rent *both* out."

Kenzie gave him an incredulous look. "Where would she sleep?"

"A tent in the backyard," Jared proposed.

"An air mattress in the pool house," Mia joked.

"I appreciate the suggestions," I said dryly. "But, if anything, I'd take the Chens up on the open invitation to their guest room."

"She brought us brownies during her last stay," Henry said as I popped a sweet potato fry into my mouth. "How thoughtful was that?"

I laughed so hard I almost choked on my food.

~

GRIFF DIDN'T OFFER TO DRIVE ME HOME, AND once he walked off with his arms around both Kenzie and Mia, neither did Henry. I tapped him on the shoulder while he chatted with Jared, who was waiting for his dad to pick him up. "Hey, I have a question."

He raised an expectant eyebrow. "A question?"

I internally rolled my eyes; he was going to make me work for it. "A *favor*," I amended after Jared rode off in his dad's Honda. "I need a ride home."

"Hmm . . ." Henry hummed, contemplative. "A ride home."

"Well, not *just* a ride," I said, smiling and reaching for his hand. "It would make my night if you could drive me home and see me inside safely."

"*Now* you're speaking my language." Henry smiled back and squeezed my fingers. "I'm nothing if not a gentleman!"

"The swooniest one in town," I quipped. I'd always known it, deep down, but I guess I never thought he was the swooniest one for *me*.

Several minutes later, we made it to his Highlander—which was horrifically parallel parked in front of Sandwitch—and

Henry opened the passenger door. "Don't look at me!" I told him as I tried to get into the front seat without my minidress riding up. "This is a *standing* dress, not a sitting dress."

He averted his eyes. "Okay, Midge."

I smirked. With a professional comedian for a father and an affinity for high-budget productions, Henry never stood a chance against *The Marvelous Mrs. Maisel*. It was his comfort show. He also couldn't get through an episode without saying how gorgeous Midge was.

"Thank you!" I chirped once I'd buckled my seat belt, and Henry leaned in for a brushstroke of a kiss before closing my door and walking around to the driver's side. Goose bumps bloomed on the back of my neck, and if Henry weren't a strict two-hands-on-the-wheel driver, I would've threaded my fingers through his while he drove. "So that's some strategy Griff came up with," I said once we were cruising on Main Street.

"Uh-huh." Henry nodded. "It's definitely a vision."

I bit the inside of my cheek. "Do you really think it'd be a shitshow?"

"Wait." Henry abruptly hit the brakes at a red light, hard enough that I pitched forward in my seat. "Are you *actually* considering it?"

"No!" I blurted, before I realized that maybe I kind of was—or was at least wondering if someone would pay for a couple of nights in the house. Rent would be at least a thousand per night, minimum. Right?

Here-to-Stay would suggest a range, I thought before kicking myself for thinking that.

"You're *going* to have enough money for Blue Ridge," Henry said.

"But what about enough for my parents' bank account?"

Henry was quiet, well aware we were four thousand short.

God, what was going to happen when they realized most of their money was missing? How was I going to explain? Here-to-Stay profits, plus my savings and a generous donation from Henry, put me in the six thousand and change ballpark.

It wasn't the full ten thousand, but it also wasn't *terrible*, was it?

Henry cleared his throat. "We should probably hide some of Golightly Glass's inventory at my house so it looks like you sold most of it while they were away. You'll need to be able to explain how you can suddenly afford the fellowship."

I shifted in my seat to look at him.

"What?" he asked.

"Nothing," I said, but smiled after he reached across the center console for my hand. My heart twisted and twirled in my chest when he kissed my knuckles. "Pay attention to the road," I joked.

"You pay attention to the road," he joked back, and it was only then that I realized Henry wasn't driving me home. Instead, he flipped his blinker to turn onto his street.

My open invitation to the Chens' guest room.

"But I didn't bring any brownies," I whispered over the sudden lump in my throat.

Henry chuckled. "Hepburn, no one wants your brownies."

⁓

EVEN THOUGH THE CARS IN THE DRIVEWAY said otherwise, it turned out Charlotte and Tess weren't home; they'd taken the train into the city for a concert. The thought sent a thrill up my spine, and I grinned in the darkness as Henry and I walked up his front path.

I decided to let him take the lead.

"Do you want something to eat?" he asked after switching on the kitchen lights. I watched him casually slide off his suit jacket and drape it across the back of a chair.

My heart swelled.

"We just finished our second dinner," I pointed out.

He flushed a little. "Oh, right."

We stood in silence for a few beats, until I gathered up the courage to ask when his parents were going to be back. Hopefully the question would plant the seed of an idea, if it wasn't already on his mind.

"I gave them a midnight curfew," he said, then consulted the invisible watch on his wrist. "Although it looks like they're going to break it . . ."

He looked at me, deep-brown gaze unwavering.

"Maybe we'd be moving too fast," I heard myself whisper,

"but—"

His phone pinging cut me off. Its chime was usually pleasant, but couldn't be more obnoxious right now. "Jeez," Henry chuckled. "At this time of night?"

"Your mom?" I asked when he pulled the glowing iPhone out of his pocket.

"No." He shook his head, brow furrowing a little. "It's Ellie."

I raised an eyebrow. "Ellie?"

Why was Ellie texting Henry?

"She's asking if we can talk," he said. "She wants my advice."

On what? I thought, which came out as, "How mysterious."

Henry shrugged while his thumbs flew over the screen.

A lump formed in my throat. "I'm going to head to bed, then."

"You sure?" He glanced up from his phone.

"Yeah." I nodded. "Can I borrow something to sleep in?"

"Of course." He moved in to give me a hug. His warm embrace, despite his arms' pointiness, had become one of my favorite places. "My sweats are in my bottom drawer." One more squeeze. "I'll see you in the morning."

"See you in the morning," I echoed, then climbed the stairs with heavy feet. My ears strained to eavesdrop on him speaking to Ellie, but his voice was too low to hear.

They're just friends, I reminded myself once I'd crawled under the covers of the guest room bed. *You and Henry are more than friends.*

Although he hadn't exactly said he loved me back when I professed my feelings, had he?

Just friends, I repeated to myself like a mantra. *He loves you, even if he didn't say it out loud.*

Just friends.

CHAPTER 19

ON SATURDAY MORNING, CHARLOTTE MADE breakfast for everyone. I'd stayed over, still stewing in the guest room when Henry's mom and Tess had gotten home a little after two a.m. What had Henry and Ellie talked about? What advice did she want? Was it something to do with Chase?

Pancakes had just been flopped onto my plate when a text from my mom popped up on my phone. CALL ME, it read.

My heart jolted. *Relax,* I tried to tell myself. Maybe this wasn't about the Bank of Fairfield account. Maybe my aunt Kim had figured out James was in Rhode Island with Isa instead of here with me and told my mom about it. To his credit, my cousin checked in at the end of each day. Last night he'd buzzed in around midnight: Staying at Henry's again, are we?

I swallowed hard, knowing I needed to face the music. "I'll be right back," I told Henry and Charlotte, sliding off my barstool. "My mom wants me to call her."

Fear flashed in Henry's eyes. "Everything okay?"

I shrugged, needing to keep my cool in front of his mother. "She's not the queen of context."

"She might just miss you!" Charlotte chimed in.

"It was an all-capitals *call me*," I told her.

She sucked in a melodramatic breath, then smiled and sipped her coffee. I slipped out the patio sliding doors into the foggy morning. My stomach clenched as I pressed my phone to my ear, listening to the ringtone.

One.

Two.

Thr—

"Audrey!" my mom exclaimed.

"Hi, Mom," I said, ready to take the hit. "Please let me explain—"

"Your hair," she cut me off. "*What* did you do to your hair?"

My shoulders sagged in relief.

"Your tagged photos on Instagram," she continued before I could fall to the flagstones and happily weep. "I knew the Constellation party was last night, and I wanted to see if anyone had posted photos."

Rookie mistake, I thought. I could police my own social media, but not everyone else's. After Caroline's welcome speech and dinner, the cater-waiters had migrated out to the deck to take pictures together. Kenzie, Mia, and I hadn't been able to stop laughing when Griff coerced Henry into reenacting the *Titanic* pose.

"You look stunning in that dress, honey," my mom said. "And I would've let you borrow those earrings if you'd asked, but..." She sighed. "Audrey, your hair."

I found my voice. "Mom, you're always telling me to spice things up. You even said I looked like a scraggly street urchin before you left. What was I supposed to do?"

"Not enter your *Reputation* era," she said. "You look like you're about to hit the dance floor with Tom Hiddleston!"

Well, at least the inspiration for my new look had come through loud and clear.

"Jealous much?" I lightly quipped, because my mom had a major crush on him. Most of her suggested YouTube videos were Tom Hiddleston interviews, and one of her ongoing beefs with my father was who deserved to be the next James Bond.

"This is not a joke, Audrey. Did Laurie at Blush do it?"

I ignored her; I wouldn't snitch on Tate. "I'm sorry you don't like it, Mom."

"No, I don't," she said. "But the real question is, do *you* like it?"

Not really, I thought, if I was being honest. It had been fun to turn things upside down for a while, but the haircut didn't feel like me. It felt like I was playing a part.

And every time I glanced in the mirror, I almost scared myself out of my skin, not recognizing my reflection.

"It's too short to pull back in a ponytail," I mumbled.

"Mmm," my mom hummed. "And it's hard to blow glass without a ponytail, isn't it?"

"Yeah," I agreed, my heart warming. She'd gotten it right.

Blow glass, not *make* glass. "I need to buy a clip or something."

"I have some in my bathroom," she said at the same time I asked, "What does Dad think?"

"Believe it or not, he didn't notice," she said. "He couldn't get past how short your dress was."

"Did you tell him *you* picked it out?"

My mom laughed, and I couldn't help but smirk when she didn't answer the question.

~

THERE WAS NO WAY I WANTED TO DANCE

back into my dress before heading home, so Henry let me keep the NYU sweats I'd slept in and offered me his favorite navy and orange anorak. It had started drizzling outside. He got a little worked up when I refused to swear that I'd return it.

I winked. "You know where I live."

Charlotte and Tess stopped us before we left. "One quick question," Tess said, gesturing between Henry and me. "Are we still doing the ridiculous fake-dating thing?"

I glanced at Henry and he glanced at me.

You take the lead on this one, I tried to communicate. *They're your* parents.

And it was your *idea!*

"Let us rephrase," Charlotte said after a few awkward beats. "Was this mistakenly dumped in the trash?"

And lo and behold, she held up Henry's framed junior prom photo of him and Ellie. My heart twisted.

"We should keep the frame," Henry said. "It's really nice." He rubbed the back of his neck. "But I think I'll soon have a much better photo for it." He took my hand and turned to me. "Audrey Barbour, will you go to prom with me?"

"You already asked me," I said.

"No." He tilted his head in his flirtatious Henry way. "I asked you if I should wear tails."

My heart did a pirouette.

"Absolutely not," Charlotte said. "You're not tall enough."

Henry flushed but didn't look away from me as he muttered, "Mom, I *know*."

"It would be my pleasure," I told him, then put a hand to my heart and pretended to swoon. "There's nothing better than a man in a tuxedo."

"What about a white dinner jacket?"

Charlotte, Tess, and I groaned. "Go, go!" Charlotte waved us away. "Take your date home, Humphrey Bogart."

"Really?" Tess said to her wife as I tugged Henry toward the garage. "*Casablanca*? I like James Bond best in that jacket."

TWO HOURS AFTER HENRY DROPPED ME AT home (I was thrilled when he escorted me inside for an extended goodbye), I grabbed Brigitta's keys and drove over to the Hair Doctor & Associates. "But I don't understand," Tate, still in her pajamas, said as I followed her upstairs to her room. "It looks so good!"

"You did an *amazing* job," I told her. "I just don't really feel like me."

Tate whipped around, an eyebrow arched. "Your mom hates it, doesn't she?"

"Oh, she despises it," I said. "But that's Laurie-from-Blush's fault, not yours."

"Oops." Tate giggled, and asked what I was thinking now. Alas, we couldn't do anything about the length. She hadn't mastered hair extensions yet.

Not to mention, high-quality ones were expensive.

"Could we consult . . ." I started to ask, but my eyes wandered down the hall to Ellie's room. Her door was closed, and I still didn't know what she'd wanted to bend Henry's ear about. He hadn't mentioned anything at breakfast. "Hey, how's Ellie feeling?"

"Fine, I think." Tate shrugged. "Our dad dropped her at the train station this morning."

"Wait, what?"

"The train station," she repeated. "She took an Amtrak to Boston to see . . ." She pretended to gag.

"Oh," I said, a bit surprised. Last night *must've* been about Chase, but now she was going to visit him? When Ellie had helped me turn over Fair Winds, it seemed like she was realizing they weren't the best fit.

"I don't know why," Tate added. "I went in her room the other day and found her looking through her Henry scrapbooks."

Something twisted in my stomach. *Henry scrapbooks?*

"She's realized what a mistake she made," Tate said airily, then smiled at me. "Don't worry, I've fully accepted that you and Henry are a couple."

"Thank you." I tried to genuinely smile back, but I didn't like the visual of Ellie revisiting her relationship with Henry. It made me nervous.

Henry might've called her, but he threw out their photo, the voice in my head said. *He only thinks of her as a friend.*

"It's also supercute that you thought no one would see you guys sneak off together last night . . ."

I felt myself go red. "Tate!"

She laughed and opened her Chromebook. Luckily, it only took a couple of minutes to settle on today's inspiration. Gracie Abrams's hair was short, with side bangs, so all we had to do was dye my hair deep brown. Tate hit Play on Gracie's Spotify (so we could really feel the vibes) before she got to work.

I sent my mom a photo of my new look, and she hearted the photo and texted back, MUCH BETTER! XO

That was it. There was no mention of anything else.

"In my professional opinion, you look more natural as a brunette," Tate noted, and I hugged her. My Venmo payment also included a well-deserved tip.

"Who was the inspiration?" Henry asked over FaceTime later.

"Tate's favorite singer," I said.

"Okay, well, I think you look like Audrey."

I raised an exaggerated eyebrow. "Hepburn?"

A blush crept up his neck, and his lips spread in a sly smile. "Who's that?" he asked.

My heart spun like a top.

VALERIE AND JUNIOR CHECKED OUT OF FAIR Winds at the crack of dawn on Sunday morning; they must've had an early flight back to Brazil. A plate of cookies *was* left as a goodbye gift, but they were chocolate chip. I heard you were allergic to peanut butter! the accompanying note read. I hope you enjoy these, just like Junior and I enjoyed the last several days here. Fingers crossed you'll see us around town soon! Val

I took it her marathon of interviews went well, and the note was so sweet that I couldn't resist biting into a cookie . . .

Before spitting it into our front stoop's planter. *God, that's terrible,* I thought, wiping my lips after expelling some extra saliva. *Did they accidentally use salt instead of sugar?*

It was the thought that counted!

Fair Winds' next guests—two septuagenarian BFFs from New Jersey—weren't arriving until Tuesday, so before I went upstairs to survey the damage, I unlocked the hot shop to turn on the furnace. Now equipped with a big clip to hold my hair back, I was excited to blow something. "Let's get this party started," I whispered as I loaded glass cullet into the furnace. Hopefully it would melt by the time I finished cleaning Fair Winds.

I felt my phone buzz in my jumpsuit pocket and, assuming it was Henry, fished it out and accepted the call without looking. "I have a great idea for a new Christmas ornament," I said without greeting. "Acorns, but we torch the lids to have this cool metallic sheen."

"You can definitely put me down for one," Not-Henry said. "Although that's not why I called . . ."

I smiled and rolled my eyes. "What's up, James?"

"Two things," he said, sounding weirdly serious. "Number one, Isa loves your hair."

"It's *so* Gracie!" I heard her shout.

"That was what my stylist was going for!" I shouted back.

"Yes!" James also shouted. "Break my eardrum, why don't you?" He sighed overdramatically. "In the Luxembourg Gardens just turned one of her songs into a duet. Isa wrote a verse from the ex-lover's perspective."

"Ooh, I love that," I said, and when James didn't reply, I asked what the second conversation topic was.

"Well, there's neither an elegant nor a subtle way to say this . . ." James began, then let a second of suspense build before he said, "Audrey, why is your carriage house on Here-to-Stay?"

No, I thought. *No, no, no!*

"I mean, I'm looking at it right now," he said. "Isa was searching for a Here-to-Stay for a weekend getaway with her mom next month, and *Fair Winds* came up as a Connecticut suggestion." Pause. "Last I heard, my mom still hadn't successfully convinced yours to rent it."

I opened my mouth. No words spilled out.

"This is why you told me to stay at Brown," he guessed. "To ensure I didn't get in the way, right?"

I somehow squeaked out a yes.

The line was silent for a few moments before James chuckled. "Oh, dear cousin, how little you know me," he said. "Just because your mom briefed me like a CIA handler doesn't mean I wouldn't go rogue with you."

Relief washed over me. "I didn't want you involved," I explained. "If I get in trouble, I don't want you dragged into it."

"Audrey, I agreed to leave you unsupervised," he said. "No matter what, it's a pretty safe bet that I'd be just as screwed as you." He paused, and I was able to picture his smirk. "What sounds good for dinner? Isa and I can pick it up on our way."

"What?" My eyes widened. "James, *no*. You guys can't come!"

"Relax—"

"I've got this," I interrupted. I was on a roll; I couldn't have James and Isa try to shut me down or get in my way. "I'm *good* at this. Have you read my reviews?"

"We have," Isa said. "They're *very* impressive. I had planned to reach out to you with some questions before James recognized Fair Winds. We just want to make sure you're being safe."

"Like you guys were that time Grace lied about being sick

so you could totally blow off school and spend the day in Philly? Without telling anyone?"

The line was dead silent.

"Your sister is super chatty when she's drunk on eggnog," I told James. Grace had called me on Christmas to say she missed me, then ended up confessing her deepest secrets for an hour. 'Twas the highlight of my holiday season.

He cleared his throat. "Well, for the record, I *ditched* school. I didn't skip."

Isa giggled.

"Audrey, these stakes are higher than Grace's day off, or any of my bullshit," James said. "If you don't want us to show up with pizza and ice cream later, you need to tell us why you're doing it."

I told them about needing money for Blue Ridge, but not the part about pretty much stealing from my parents.

"Call us," James said. "If anything gets sketchy or shit hits the fan or the house goes up in flames, call—"

"Nine-one-one," Isa cut in. "Call nine-one-one, and *then* call us."

"You guys are terrible babysitters!" I said lovingly, and after making a few more promises, I hung up, with a sigh of relief.

~

FAIR WINDS, SHOCKINGLY, WAS EVEN NEATER than before Valerie and Junior's arrival. "Huh," I said to myself, thinking for sure there'd be some dried cookie batter spattered on the kitchen counter. Nope, nothing. The kitchen was spotless.

And so was the rest of the apartment.

But after taking my initial lap around the apartment, I took a second—and a third. Something felt off.

The hot shop would have to wait until I figured out what that was.

CHAPTER 20

HENRY ARRIVED LESS THAN FIVE MINUTES AFTER I texted him, so he must've already been on his way over. "Okay, is it just me . . ." I said, recognizing his footsteps as he opened Fair Winds' screen door. I was busy staring at the kitchen. "Or is something weird?"

My heart leaped a little when I felt his hands on my shoulders, and my breath caught as he spun me around to face him. Our eyes locked. "What?" he asked, a smile playing on his lips. "No hello?"

I felt myself melt into a grin. "Hello."

He grinned too. "Hi."

"Kiss me?"

"As you wish."

"The Princess Bride," I whispered before his lips could touch mine. "1985."

"1987," he whispered back. "But close enough."

I gasped. "You really do memorize IMDb pages!"

He sheepishly rubbed the back of his neck.

In response, I grabbed his shirt and pulled him in for a kiss.

"What's wrong with you?" I asked afterward.

"Why do you assume something's wrong?"

I shrugged. "You marched up the stairs like you were on a mission."

"Well, I really want my anorak back."

"Henry, I've had it less than twelve hours."

He chuckled, then dug his phone out of his pocket. "I also wanted you to see this . . ." he said, trailing off as he showed me a text from an unknown number.

If Audrey needs help, it read, you help her, no matter what. Copy?

"Should I call this person?" Henry asked. "It's concerning that they know your name."

"No need," I told him, stealing his phone to message back: Copy.

Henry looked horrified.

"It's James," I said. "My cousin James."

"Okay . . ." He nodded slowly. "How does he have my number?"

I rolled my eyes. "Take a wild guess."

It took him five seconds. "Never change, Monica!"

"Exactly," I said, then took a deep breath. "James knows, Henry. He knows about Fair Winds."

Henry's face paled.

"He doesn't know about the drained account," I said quickly. "I said I was hustling to make enough for my tuition . . . which is *basically* true."

He let out a breath. "Basically."

"I also made him promise not to tell anyone. He wanted to come down, but I convinced him not to. He's just guaranteeing my safety and securing backup for any shitstorms."

"We have yet to experience a shitstorm," Henry said, taking my hand. "And if we do, we'll navigate it together."

I gave him a bemused smile. "You have a way with words, you know that?"

"Well, I suspected." He smirked. "Considering I have a Netflix special named after me."

"Henry Chen, everyone!" I proclaimed to the empty apartment. "Master of the humblebrag!"

Henry rolled his eyes, then gestured around. "The place looks great, but why did you clean it all alone?"

My eyebrows knitted together. "You didn't get my text?"

"No . . ."

"Hey, sorry I'm late," someone said, and Henry and I both turned to see Griff bang through the screen door. His eyes were on his phone as he texted. "My brother and I were throwing the football down by the harbor."

Oh jeez, I thought. *Did I accidentally text Griff?*

According to my phone, I had.

How embarrassing.

Though technically, I paid him to help me clean. He was

supposed to be here.

"Audrey, what do you need me for?" Griff exclaimed, one eye still on his phone. "I've never seen this place so spotless!"

"I haven't cleaned it yet," I said through gritted teeth. "My Spidey-senses are just tingling."

"Tobey Maguire, Andrew Garfield, or Tom Holland?" Henry asked at the same time that Griff finally looked at me. His eyes widened.

"Tate kindly redid my hair earlier today," I explained. "Based on the polls, I'm best as a brunette."

"Aw, why?" Griff chuckled. "Are you not fun enough to be a blond?"

Henry clapped his hands. "Keeler, you strip the bed and I'll grab the towels from the bathroom." He nodded at me. "You follow your Andrew Garfield Spidey-senses."

"Tom Holland," I clarified, and thanked him and Griff before scanning the living room again. The mantel above the fireplace was good; the ship paintings and fishbowl full of matchbooks were still there. The driftwood lamp on an end table had a crooked shade, but I straightened it. Someone had probably just knocked it.

What's your deal? I asked myself, my heart racing. *Why—*

Something across the room caught my eye—a glazed terra-cotta pitcher that sat on one of the kitchen's open glass shelves. It was yet another souvenir from my parents' travels; my mom had found it in Tuscany. It was white with yellow lemons and light-green leaves painted on top of blue stripes and swirls.

Was it "tastefully nautical"? Not in the slightest, but it was pretty and somehow still worked with the vibe.

It also belonged on the living room credenza. Why had it moved to the kitchen?

I crossed the room for an inspection. The pitcher's lemons were plumper than I remembered, and the leaves a brighter shade of green, but my blood didn't thicken until I turned the pitcher to discover a new detail. A painted banner across the front that read ACQUA in Papyrus-looking font.

I must've made a noise, because Henry came rushing into the room. "What?" he said. "What is it?"

"This." I held up the pitcher. "This isn't . . . My mom will see . . ."

"She'll see what?" he asked, but instead of answering, I turned the pitcher upside down.

Only to see a fucking Pottery Barn sticker on the bottom.

"Oh, shit," Henry said. "You're right."

Sweat beading on my back, I handed him the fraudulent pitcher so I could open a lower cabinet, the one that hid the trash can. Fair Winds' policy for guests was to double-knot their garbage bag, but then leave it to me. The carriage house's garbage cans were right under the hot shop's window. I didn't want guests to peek into the garage.

Sure enough, Valerie had tied the trash bag, and I took a deep breath before ripping it open and going through the contents. "You are one intrepid explorer," Henry murmured as he watched me sort through used tissues, eggshells, cheese stick wrappers, wet paper towels, an apple core, broken crayons, a torn-open Ghirardelli bag, and an empty iced-coffee cup from Rise & Grind—*Come on*, I thought. *Recycle!*—until, at the very bottom, I discovered the shards of my mom's pitcher.

"Should we try to glue it back together?" Henry suggested.

"Very funny," I mumbled, even though the exact same thought had crossed my mind. But no, as I examined the pieces, it was clear that the pitcher looked like it best belonged at an archaeological dig. *"Fuck."* My heart hammered. "I made an exception for a cute little kid and now I'm paying for it."

"You don't know Junior broke it," Henry said.

I shot him a glare.

He responded with a gentle smile. "It's one thing," he said. "Out of six people—including two who were definitely high most of the time—only one thing has been broken."

"But other stuff has gone missing!" I exclaimed, suddenly remembering and doing the math. The silver tea set's biscuit tin, the ship's bell clock—I thought they'd turn up, but here I was, in an exceedingly neat apartment, and those antiques were nowhere to be seen.

"Get Griff," I told Henry. "We need to check this place top to bottom."

The three of us spent an hour searching and scouring Fair Winds, but to no avail. In fact, after consulting the photos posted on Here-to-Stay, I noticed more MIA treasures. The purple, green, and gold Hermès Le Sirenuse ashtray? Gone. A rare leather-bound edition of *Moby-Dick*? Gone. Champagne bucket from Paris? Gone. The candlesticks above the fireplace had also disappeared . . . How had I not picked up on that? Even my grandparents' wedding china had been taken from the steamer trunk at the foot of the bed.

"I don't know what to do," I said, nearly catatonic on the couch. "I literally don't know what to do."

Griff sighed. "It's tough."

"Has your aunt ever had anything stolen from her condo?" Henry asked him.

Griff shrugged. "If she has, I don't think she cares. It's all Taylor Swift stuff from Etsy. Not her personal belongings."

I took a breath. "I should report this, right?"

Henry handed me my phone. "I think you should message everyone first," he said. "Tell them how happy you are that they had wonderful stays before bringing up the missing stuff. Don't accuse them of taking anything, but ask them to let you know if they saw certain items. It might be helpful when we report the theft."

I nodded. It definitely couldn't hurt. "Could you and Griff get some inventory from the hot shop?" I asked. "I'm not saying the place looks empty, but now that we know stuff's missing . . ." I bit my lip, not able to unsee it. "Just not anything *too* good."

"Not your best candlesticks," Henry agreed. "Only your wonkiest."

Tears pricked the corners of my eyes. "Thanks."

"Always," he said, and after he and Griff went downstairs, I groaned before unlocking my phone and composing a message.

~

BY THE TIME HENRY, GRIFF, AND I FINISHED staging the apartment, approximately no one had responded to my messages. Not Sandy and Ron, not Brian and Leslie, and definitely not Valerie. I mean, it'd only been twenty minutes, but still. I had written everyone a version of exactly what Henry suggested: I am so thrilled you had a wonderful stay at Fair Winds, and your kind review means so much to me. I'm reaching out to touch base on some beloved family belongings that I've discovered to be missing . . .

It had been painful to type out the list.

"Let's give them twenty-four hours?" Henry proposed on his way out. Charlotte had called to remind him about dinner with his grandparents. "Then we'll report it."

A lump formed in my throat when he kissed me goodbye. I'd never felt so unglued; I didn't want him to leave.

Griff didn't move from the couch, as if he had no one to see and nowhere to be for once. He didn't protest when I turned on Apple TV, needing some stupid, mindless noise. "You know what," he said while I considered Netflix options. "You're *really* talented."

I gave him a look. "Huh?"

"You're really talented," he repeated. "I know I said that after you blew the vase for Gram, but . . ." He motioned around the room, to my not-quite-identical blue candlesticks on the mantel to my rippled vase on the table to some small seashell sculptures. "Your stuff really is *incredible,* Audrey. I've seen you in the hot shop before, but seeing all of these different things here, I can tell how hard you bust your ass."

"Thanks, Griff," I said, smiling a little before telling him the truth. "I work so hard because I want to become the best."

He nodded. "That's why you want to skip college."

My eyebrows knitted together. "Skip college" seemed a little unfair. I'd always liked school. I was good at it, and I wasn't against the idea of college. But Blue Ridge and whatever opportunities lay beyond would help me achieve my dream faster.

"Golightly Glass won't be a successful business if I don't have the skills." I sighed. "And I don't think blowing glass on weekends in college will give me enough experience. I *really* want to commit to getting better."

Instead of saying anything, Griff looked at me and I looked at him. There was nothing romantic about it—instead, there was *realization.* "You should rent out your house," Griff said, then blushed. "Trust me, I know how nuts it sounds, especially now with this stolen stuff, but I believe in you, Audrey. You need to go for it to make that money back."

"You're right," I heard myself say softly. I didn't have much faith that someone would rent the house in time, but I could at least try. There was no harm in *trying.*

The mansion—*my house*—was my last shot.

Griff grinned. "What the hell, right?"

"Yeah," I agreed, hope flaming in my heart. "What the hell?"

"YOU'RE KIDDING," HENRY SAID AT SCHOOL the next day. We were under the quad's centuries-old maple tree, sitting on one of the benches. I'd told Henry I had something to tell him, and that it was probably safest if he heard the news while seated. "Are you *seriously* telling me you're listening to Griff? You're going to rent out your house?" His expression was incredulous. "Especially after stuff was stolen from the apartment?"

I glanced away for a moment, unable to deny that Griff's scheme sounded absurd. He'd even said it himself! "I need the money," I said. "We both know I'm not going to hit six thousand, even with the next guests." I shrugged. "My parents get home only a few days after their stay. It's not going to happen."

Henry opened his mouth.

"And this is *my* mistake," I added before he could speak. "I'm not taking out another loan from you. This is *my* hole to dig myself out of."

Five seconds of silence passed.

Henry shook his head. "It's a bad idea, Audrey."

"Well, Fair Winds wasn't a great one," I pointed out, "but we're pulling it off."

I thought of my most recent review. Valerie hadn't responded to my stolen-stuff query, but she'd rated me five stars and called me professional, attentive, and compassionate.

It was hard not to be flattered, but I couldn't believe she was ignoring me. Did she think a good review was an apology for breaking the pitcher?

"Yes, we are," Henry said. "If you turn a blind eye to your parents' missing antiques, we are pulling it off just fine."

"Then what's the problem?" Something deep in my stomach started to squirm. I knew convincing Henry wouldn't be easy, but why couldn't he help me accomplish this on my terms?

The warning bell rang. I hadn't taken a sip of my iced coffee yet. "I'll see you this afternoon," Henry said, rising from the bench. "I have a few pop quizzes with people at lunch."

Before he could walk away, I took his hand and squeezed it.

He squeezed back, but didn't say anything.

I WASN'T SURPRISED TO SEE ELLIE IN ENGLISH, but I *was* surprised to see the return of her signature pink-blond hair. "Tate did it last night," she said as I did a double take. "Right after I got home from Boston."

Right after I got home from Boston.

Was she giving me an opening? To ask about Chase?

"Pink is your color" was what I settled on saying.

Ellie rolled her eyes, but all in good fun. "Way to quote my mom."

I shrugged. "It's true."

"I know." She smiled softly, then pointed at me with her

pencil. "The bleach blond was cool, but this is much better."

"Way to quote *my* mom," I laughed, then told her about the CALL ME text.

Ellie laughed, too. "She and your dad will be home soon, right?"

"This Sunday."

She nodded. "Do you have people booked this week?"

"Ruth and Eileen arrive tomorrow," I said. "They're seventy-five and have been best friends since first grade. Ruth said that they desperately need a break from their retirement community." I shrugged. "Apparently there's been some senior citizen drama."

"Well, they sound interesting," Ellie said. "Did you ask if they can handle the carriage house stairs?"

"Yes, I sent them a video. Eileen has had her hip done and Ruth's recovered from a knee replacement, so they aren't worried."

Ellie shook her head, impressed. "You think of everything, Audrey."

Not wanting to talk about my hosting gig anymore, I tried to change the subject to our homework, but after admitting she'd only had time to skim the SparkNotes, Ellie circled back. "I ran into Kenzie in the bathroom this morning," she whispered, "and she told me the most ridiculous thing."

No, I thought, feeling my blood thud, thud, thud in my veins. *No, Griff, please tell me—*

"She said Griff texted her that you plan to post your house on Here-to-Stay."

The back of my neck flamed. I never thought I'd say it, but

I wanted to *punch* Griffin Keeler.

Ellie gasped at my silence. "Audrey!"

"Shh!" I anxiously glanced around the classroom.

"It's insane," she whispered.

"It's hypothetical," I whispered back.

"For now," she said. "I can tell you're going to go for it." Her eyes widened with shock all over again. "What does Henry think?"

"He's ruminating," I said, because I had all my fingers and toes crossed that it was the truth. I knew I didn't need Henry to make my final decision, but making my final decision would be easier if I knew I had his help. So I was going to let him think, weigh every pro and con, and run through various scenarios.

But again, it was my house.

My house, my rules.

And I was going to do what I had to do.

I NEITHER SAW NOR HEARD FROM HENRY FOR the rest of the day. He didn't stop by my locker between classes, send me any funny memes, or reply to any of my texts. *Come on,* I thought, annoyed. *Even if you don't like this plan, you're still my boyfriend!*

He was, wasn't he? I mean, I'd told him I wanted to be his girlfriend and he'd asked me to prom, so we were actually dating, right?

Yes, I tried to reassure myself. *Dating was implied!*

It wasn't until I got home that I realized none of my texts had even been read (Henry was a staunch supporter of read receipts). "Okay, this is ridiculous," I muttered to myself, then aggressively tapped my screen to call him.

"Hello?" someone who didn't sound remotely like Henry answered after four rings.

"Hello?" My eyebrows knitted together. "Who's this?"

"Nadine from Sandwitch," the girl said. "Is this your phone? It was found under a table after our lunch rush."

Ah, I thought. Whoever Henry had tutored today must've treated him to lunch.

"No, it's not mine," I said. "But I know—" I stopped, hearing the front door open and familiar footsteps in the foyer.

"Hepburn!"

I smiled to myself. "Hepburn" was special. *I* was special. To him.

"Who are you talking to?" Henry asked when he entered the kitchen. His hair was a little wild, like he'd run his hand through it a hundred times today.

"You," I answered, and showed him my screen.

Hank, it read. His contact photo was the snap of him asleep in the striped inner tube.

He sighed and took the phone from me. "Hi," he said. "Please tell me I don't have to pay a king's ransom . . ."

I'd only eaten an apple and peanut butter for lunch, so I offered to drive Henry into town so he could retrieve his phone and I could get a sandwich. Nadine was more than happy to take my order before we hung up, and fifteen minutes later, Henry insisted on paying for it—or not paying for it, because he'd finally filled up his punch card. "You're giving me your free sandwich?" I said, stomach growling with gratitude.

Henry crooked an arm around my neck. "I'm sorry for ignoring you all day."

"That's okay." I kissed his cheek. "I like to think it's because you lost your phone."

He grinned so wryly that my knees went numb. "Is there any way I can make it up to you?"

"Hmm." I pretended to ponder. "How about"—I tossed my wrapped sandwich in the air, then caught it with one hand—"you drive home so I can immediately devour this?"

Henry's eyes twinkled. "Deal."

WHEN WE GOT BACK TO MY HOUSE, I ASKED

Henry if he wanted to come in and hang out for a while. "Is that a trick question?" he asked, but instead of us making out in my room (my after-school activity of choice), Henry brought his backpack in and set up camp at the kitchen table.

Bleh, I thought. *Homework?*

Midnight was when I thrived academically.

"First things first," he said. "You need to cancel Friday night's Fair Winds booking."

Something in me tightened. "What?"

"Fair Winds," Henry repeated. "The septuagenarian *Thelma & Louise* trip tomorrow is fine, but I refuse to let you rent out both the carriage house and this house."

My heart warmed, relieved. "What made you change your mind?"

Henry opened his laptop, body language all business. "I didn't change my mind."

"Excuse me, but you told me it was a *bad idea*!"

"Yes, that's my *opinion*," he said. "After thinking about it more, my *decision* is to help." He gave me a look. "James texted me to help you no matter what, and I don't want to let him down."

Tears threatened to spill. "Henry Chen, have I mentioned I love you?"

"Yes, but the exact number of times depends on the context."

Grinning, I went over to the table and wrapped my arms around him from behind, hugging him close. "Thank you," I whispered in his ear. "Thank you, thank you, thank you."

"You're welcome," he whispered back, then focused on his laptop. He already had a Here-to-Stay tab on-screen. "Now let's pitch this house."

CHAPTER 21

WE ONLY HIT ONE SNAG WHILE POSTING MY house. Writing the copy was easy, especially after Fair Winds. I used a lot of the same key words—*dreamy, idyllic,* and how could we forget *coastal grandmother living*? We added *spacious* with *scenic views* and *private*. Henry also encouraged me to include *only fifteen minutes from picturesque Fairfield University.*

"That's strangely specific," I told him with some side-eye.

"Au contraire," he replied. "It's *strategic.* Trust me."

"I do," I said, but sighed when visual aids came into play. I had plenty of pictures of my house, but my house wasn't the *subject* of those shots. We needed to snap some photos ourselves. "I guess we should start on the first floor?"

Henry chewed on his lip. "The natural lighting isn't great."

Unfortunately, he was right. It had been overcast all afternoon. "Well, I don't know, then," I said. "There might be professional photos on Realtor.com, from when the house was for sale a few years ago, but my mom has since worked wonders on the place."

We sat in contemplative silence for a beat, before Henry snapped his fingers. "Wait, that's it!" he exclaimed. "I bet you anything she has photos on her computer."

My brows knitted together as he pushed back his chair, ready to charge upstairs. "Why would she have taken pictures? It's not like she wants to sell the house."

"No," Henry said, "but it was a substantial renovation, and I'm sure she's proud of it." He paused. "Plus, your dad wasn't really here to see it."

"Oh my god, you're totally right!" I nodded and pushed back my chair too. "She would've sent him everything."

We took the stairs two at a time, up to my mom's office on the third floor. It was small but still a showpiece room, not unlike Diane Keaton's writing nook in *Something's Gotta Give*. Everything was light and bright, whites and creams, with her cherrywood desk facing three big windows that overlooked the vast Sound. I slid into her swivel chair and opened her left-behind MacBook. She only traveled with her iPad.

Password? the laptop asked, and even though I knew the answer, my heart rate sped up.

Had I felt that way when I helped myself to my parents' emergency fund?

Probably not.

Stellablue1!, I typed. Stella was my mom's childhood dog, blue was her favorite color, and my dad always reminded us that special characters made passwords harder to guess. It was also our Amazon Prime password.

"Okay . . ." Henry said when access was approved. "Are you sure this is your mom's computer?"

"I know, I know," I told him. "She's a contradiction."

Because while my mom was organized in almost every area of her life, her laptop was not one of them. Her desktop was a mess of miscellaneous folders, documents, and screenshots. She even had some funny GIFs saved. I had to squint to sort through them and double-clicked on a promising folder labeled *inspiration*.

Henry and I scanned its subfolders. Each had a different vibe, from preppy to bohemian to mid-century to contemporary casual. None of them was what we were looking for, but I was impressed—my mom appeared to be a student of all styles.

"Try that one," Henry suggested once I'd navigated back to the chaotic screen. He pointed at the upper right-hand corner, at a folder between a PDF flyer for Dave Matthews's book signing and an old photo of me in a blue cap and gown at my middle school graduation. The folder read *house & home by monica*.

I double-clicked.

"Jackpot," Henry whispered, because the folder was filled with high-resolution shots of our house postrenovation. Our kitchen with its marble island and eight-burner stove, the cocktail lounge basement, and even the primary bathroom with a wet room. The photos were all stunning.

But there were also pictures of the Keelers' California cool–inspired den, and the Bedtime Stories owner's farmhouse-style mudroom. *I'm offering advice,* my mom had merely said when mentioning those projects, almost shrugging them off.

Was it more than that? I couldn't help but wonder. Had she done *more* than consult? Had she *designed* those spaces?

Because this folder didn't look like just an online scrapbook; it looked like the beginning of a portfolio. *house & home by monica* sounded like the name of an interior design firm.

My heart warmed. Could my mom be thinking of turning her hobby into a business?

I emailed several photos to Henry, and then we retreated to our base of operations to continue working. "I like that we named the carriage house," I said. "Let's name this place, too."

Holiday House, Henry typed.

I rolled my eyes. "How original." There was no way I was ripping off the name of Taylor Swift's iconic Rhode Island abode.

Five minutes passed.

"Okay, just call it 'Fair Winds,'" I said when no other ideas came to mind. "We can change Fair Winds to Fair Winds II or something."

"Works for me," Henry said. "I'm snoozing its availability, though. We can't have anyone requesting to stay there."

"Just delete it," I said. My parents would be home on Sunday. This was our last hurrah.

"No, I think it's important for potential guests to see your glowing reviews," he replied. "It'll help us hook them for the house."

I grinned. "Okay, *this* is why you're my business partner."

Henry hummed. "Mm-hmm."

We both held our breath as the cursor hovered over the List button. There was no going back after this. Here-to-Stay would include it in a newsletter email blast within the hour.

"You're sure?" Henry asked me.

"Yes." I nodded, then added a cool shrug. "And who knows? It might not even rent."

My house was beyond gorgeous, but it was expensive—we'd listed it for a steep two thousand a night. The chances of someone booking it were low, and if someone *did* want to rent it, now was not the time for us to accept a lowball offer.

What are the odds a bachelorette party without a budget needs a last-minute place to stay this weekend? I wondered.

Fingers laced together, Henry and I stared at his computer screen for a few minutes, waiting for a request to appear. Because "Monica" was already a verified host, there was no wait time for a new listing. Henry hit Refresh once, and after nothing new popped up, he squeezed my hand. "I have to go," he told me. "You'll let me know if anything happens?"

"Oh, sure." I nodded, a little dazed. Henry was leaving? I was going to offer to order dinner later. "Are you headed home?"

He shook his head. "I'm . . ." He paused, then said, "I'm actually going to the Hoppers' house. Tate invited me over for dinner and board games."

"Huh?" I blurted before even trying to understand.

Henry was going to Ellie's house?

They're friends, the rational side of my brain told me for the hundredth time. *Just because they dated doesn't mean they can't be friends.*

"Tate twisted my arm," Henry said. "Ellie's in rough shape, and Tate thinks this will help her feel better."

I groaned. "I will *pay* her to break up with Chase."

He gave me a look. "Hepburn, she *did*. Where have you been?"

A small wave of hurt hit me. "Planet Earth," I said. "When did she end things? We had class together today, and she didn't say anything."

Why didn't she tell me?

"This weekend while she was in Boston." He shrugged. "Maybe she's not ready to tell everyone yet."

She told you, I thought, the pieces finally fitting together. Ellie had called Henry last week to ask his advice on breaking up with Chase.

But why did she need his input? She was a natural at breaking up with people.

Henry smiled and gently tucked a lock of my hair behind my ear. "It's just pizza and board games."

Can I come? I wanted to ask, because Monopoly or Scrabble or Clue sounded a lot more fun than hanging out solo tonight. Maybe I shouldn't have fought so hard for James and Isa to stay at Brown. Things would be less lonely with them here.

I walked Henry to the door, and he spun me goofily before pulling me close for a kiss on the cheek. "I'll call you later," he whispered. "Okay?"

"Okay," I echoed, then messed up his hair. "Kick ass and take names during games."

"I usually do," he said, smiling and smoothing his hair back down. "But Tate's made everyone swear to let Ellie win."

I felt a pang in my chest. Why did Henry spending the evening with the Hoppers bother me? Especially when it was *Tate* who had invited him?

Ellie hadn't had anything to do with it.

At least, that was what I told myself.

~

AFTER PAD THAI FOR ONE, I PROCRASTINATED doing my homework even more by showering, changing into sweats, and collapsing on the couch. I'd been working my way through *Blown Away*, Netflix's glassblowing show. Had I seen every episode already? Yes, but it was fun to rewatch. "How do you not get it?" I shouted at the TV as they discussed one of the pieces. "The hamster tubes are a metaphor for the hardships of mental health—"

My phone chimed.

Finally, I thought. It was almost ten and I hadn't heard from Henry since he texted that Ellie's dad had broken out Catan. Henry had all the respect in the world for role-playing games, but they weren't his thing. He once said he'd rather play football with Griff than join Alec, Rory, and Cam's Dungeons & Dragons group. "I possess neither the creativity nor the passion," were his words.

But when I grabbed my phone from the coffee table, fumbling my bowl of M&M's in the process, I saw a Here-to-Stay DM instead of a text.

I quickly FaceIDed into my phone.

Hey there, Monica! the message read. My name is Joel, and your amazing house just caught my eye. I'm a class secretary for Fairfield University—we're celebrating our fifth reunion this weekend, but unfortunately our HTS fell through this morning. My co-secretary and I are VERY interested in Fair Winds (love the name!). Do you mind if I ask a few questions?

Looking forward to hearing from you,

Joel

My stomach stirred. *That son of a bitch*, I thought, and immediately tapped out of chat to shoot Henry a text: Did you know that Fairfield's alumni weekend is THIS weekend?

Because why else would we have included that detail about my house being only fifteen minutes from the college?

When he didn't respond, I checked his location and saw that he was still parked at Ellie's house. Why? Was he having a midnight snack? I took a deep breath and went back to my Here-to-Stay chats.

Hi Joel, I wrote while biting the inside of my cheek. Was this actually happening? This is Audrey, Monica's daughter. My parents are away on business, so I have taken over hosting duties. Congratulations on 5 years! Hit me with your questions . . .

He replied less than five minutes later. Hi, Audrey. This is Lana, Joel's co-secretary (and fiancée). I want to be totally transparent. Joel, me, and four friends will be the primary guests for Friday and Saturday, but we volunteered to host the after-party on Saturday night. Is that okay?

I bit the inside of my cheek. *No way, Lana Del Rey*, I considered typing. *That is* not *happening!*

Although, I'd mentally prepared for a bachelorette party to rage on my pool deck, so how different could this be, really?

Plus . . . money. I knew, deep in my bones, that this was an opportunity I couldn't pass up.

So I closed my eyes, and with the home keys memorized, I blindly typed: Yes.

And then, to make sure I sounded enthusiastic enough, I opened my eyes and way overcompensated by adding: The pool and outdoor entertainment area promote parties!

I thought so too! Lana replied before rattling off questions.

No, the house could not be seen from the street.

But yes, Uber and Lyft could easily find it.

Yes, there was beach access.

Yes, I would be staying on the property, in the guesthouse.

No, there was absolutely no smoking allowed.

I could tell she wasn't thrilled by that answer since she didn't reply right away, but she eventually said, Got it!

My heart hammered—I was so close to locking down the reservation. *What else?* I thought about typing to keep the conversation going, but I didn't want to push Lana too hard. Audrey Barbour was a cool, calm, and collected host!

I threw my arms in the air in victory when Lana finally confirmed they'd book my house. But even after the two-night reservation went through (my eyes turned into four-thousand-dollar signs), she wasn't finished with her questions. In fact, she turned things back over to Joel. Lana and I are flying in from Chicago, he wrote. Our flight isn't arriving until late Friday afternoon, so we'll need to book it to the opening cocktail party . . .

Best of luck, I thought, with zero idea where he was going.

We wondered if you would be willing to run some errands and oversee some party deliveries for us, he said. If you're able, we will make it worth your while. Price is no object; most of our classmates have offered to contribute for an epic night!

My heart thudded hard in my chest. *Holy shit.*

Price was no object? For accepting Amazon packages of fun decorations and games and going to Trader Joe's or picking up a catered order in town? Price was no object?

You could do it, I told myself. *You could fully refill the bank account.* Four thousand *plus* errand-running money would get me across the finish line, even with the cuts I owed Griff and Ellie.

My email is golightlyglass@gmail.com, I wrote after Joel agreed upon a price. Let me know what you need me to do!

Fantastic! Joel said. I'll have Lana send a list. The theme is old-fashioned kegger.

CHAPTER 22

AFTER SCHOOL ON TUESDAY, THE SEVEN OF US rendezvoused at Hamburger Hill. Henry, Griff, Ellie, Kenzie, Mia, Jared, and I slid into our favorite booth. "Okay, I called you all here..." I said, our usual order already placed. Everyone except Henry leaned forward when I took a deep breath. "Because I need your help."

"With tonight's guests?" Ellie guessed, and I felt something in me twist. I'd asked her in English why she hadn't mentioned dumping Chase, and she curtly said, "You didn't ask."

I can't read your mind! I'd almost said, but a sudden sneeze had saved me.

"No," I said now, shaking my head. "Ruth and Eileen aren't due to arrive until five. I left Fair Winds'—I mean, Fair Winds II's—key in the lockbox for them."

"Hold up," Jared said. "What's Fair Winds *II*?"

Blood started pumping in my ears, and before I could break the news, Griff grinned. "Fair Winds II is the original

Fair Winds," he enlightened the table. "Audrey and Chen renamed it."

Mia raised an eyebrow. "Why?"

"Because," Griff began excitedly, "Audrey is renting out her house. And since it's bigger and better, it should be the first Fair Winds."

No one said anything, but everyone looked at me.

I nervously sucked down some milkshake.

"Are you serious?" Kenzie asked. "You really want to rent out your *house*?"

"She doesn't *want* to," Henry said, shooting me some side-eye. "She *did*."

Ellie covered her face with her hands. *"Audrey..."*

I winced. What the hell had I been thinking last night? A college reunion after-party? I might as well light my house on fire myself! And offering to all but plan it? Yes, it had sounded fun, but when Joel emailed me the to-do list...

Henry had been pretty pissed when I forwarded him the email, which he made clear over the phone later. "Why didn't you call me?" was how he greeted me.

My voice jumped an octave. "You were busy!"

At Ellie's house.

"But it's *you*, Audrey," he said, dead set and determined. "I would've answered, because I will *always* pick up the phone when it's you."

Those words had hit me hard but soft in the chest. *It's* you, *Audrey.*

Henry hadn't told me he loved me yet, but wasn't this basically the same thing?

God, I felt terrible. Mint chip ice cream and milk now started to sour in my stomach.

"How much are they paying you?" Mia asked cautiously. "A lot?"

The juniors' eyes bulged when I named the price. Even Ellie remarked it was incredible. "You're actually going to be able to do it," she said. "Your parents are *never* going to know."

And they might even be proud of me, I hoped. *When I tell them I can pay for Blue Ridge myself . . .*

They had to let me go then . . . right?

Griff popped three fries in his mouth. "Are we allowed to attend the party?"

"Jesus, Keeler." Henry shook his head. "You never cease to amaze."

"Not only do we want you to *attend* the party," I added as I pinched Henry's arm, "but we also want you to *work* it."

Cue the collective: "Huh?"

"Audrey has been asked to coordinate the party," Henry explained. "But it's a much bigger deal than pitched, so it's all hands on deck for this one."

Jared cleared his throat. "Why us?"

"Because you're trained cater-waiters," I said with a smile. "Service industry professionals!"

"You're also members of the Circle of Trust," Henry said, a flattering reminder that they'd offered to help with anything and everything when they signed our NDA. "Avengers assemble!"

"And I'm going to pay everyone," I told them.

It was an empowering enough pitch that Mia, Kenzie, and Jared echoed Griff when he nodded and declared that he was in. Ellie hesitated.

"Ellie?" Henry prompted.

I need you, I tried to telepath to her. *I know you might be mad at me, or not even like me very much, but Henry and I need your help. You're the only other person with true leadership skills at this table.*

Griff could hype up a football team, but Ellie was captain of the Constellation cater-waiters. And, no offense to Griff, but whenever Ellie helped prep Fair Winds for its next guests, she was far more effective.

Finally, she looked at me. "Tell us what to do."

I grinned, my heart flooded with relief. "Okay, let me pull up the email."

Mia unlocked her phone and volunteered to take notes.

Henry snapped his fingers. "I like the way you think, Mia."

She blushed, and an hour and a second round of chili fries (Griff) later, we had a plan of attack.

Invitations: Lana was going to send them herself, via Paperless Post.

Decorations: Kenzie called dibs. The "Old-Fashioned Kegger" theme had apparently generated a million ideas.

Food: Ironically, Lana had placed a huge order with

Constellation Catering, but thankfully Ellie's mom didn't oversee that side of the business. "How are we going to get it, though?" Mia had asked. "Employees will recognize us if we pick it up, and wouldn't it be suspicious if it's delivered to Audrey's house?"

Henry volunteered his improv friends, also NDA-signing Circle of Trust members, to handle pickup duties. Alec agreed via text.

Alcohol: Joel had ordered kegs to be delivered. "Won't they card you?" Kenzie worried, and I tried to pull off a confident shrug. "I have a fake ID," I said.

"Another drink could be fun too," Ellie said. "Especially since some people don't like beer." She made a *yuck* face, and I noticed Henry's laugh above everyone else's. "Wine doesn't work with the theme, but—"

"Jungle juice!" I blurted. "Jungle juice, or some type of punch"—I thought of all the college movies Henry and I'd seen—"in a trash can."

Griff clapped. "Hell yes!"

I said I'd get those ingredients.

Music: Lana and Joel couldn't decide between a band or a DJ (good luck with wedding planning). The only thing they were set on was they didn't want an aux cord or Bluetooth speaker. "Isn't Cam teaching himself to DJ?" Ellie asked Henry, who nodded but said, "He isn't even passable yet."

We were stumped until Griff remembered that his cousin was in a cover band. He lived a couple of towns over and played some local open mic nights and parties. Griff insisted he would handle it. "I've got it, Audrey," he reassured me when I looked worried. "I'll even get him to sign one of Chen's little NDAs."

That was the end of the co-secretaries' list, but Henry had some amendments to discuss. "They'll most likely be using the pool," he said, "so we need a lifeguard for multiple reasons." He looked pointedly at Griff, who lifeguarded at Essex Harbor's country club when he wasn't cater-waitering in the summer. "Preferably *two* lifeguards."

Griff nodded. "I'll ask Kaitlyn and Mateo. They're chill."

Great, I thought, smiling nervously. *I hope they're* super *chill.*

I wasn't thrilled about telling *more* people about Here-to-Stay.

"Thanks, Keeler," Henry said. "I think we should also have a valet stand. I'm sure there will be a steady stream of Ubers and Lyfts, but we still want there to be traffic supervision."

When no one offered, he assigned the job to his improv buddies.

"We also need a security detail!" I announced, since the need for a valet signaled *a lot* of guests. It meant telling more people about my top-secret operation, but I knew my gut was right when Henry enthusiastically squeezed my knee under the table.

"Would Jason be interested?" I asked Griff, then glanced at Henry. "Maybe some of the other football players you tutor?"

"Oh yeah." Griff nodded, with Henry echoing him. "Maybe not for free, but—"

"Don't worry, they'll be paid, like you," I interrupted. "You guys are the Command strips that are going to hold this house together."

"What a thoughtful analogy," Henry said, smirking as the table laughed.

"Do you think it's going to work?" I asked Henry when the rest of the crew finally took off, leaving just me and him with our cheeseburgers.

He chewed, swallowed, and took a sip of Coke. "It's a lot of moving parts," he said, "but I think we've covered all the bases." He paused. "Personally, I think the party is the simple part."

My brows furrowed. "What do you mean?"

"Well, the next day is going to be rough. You're going to need to get all these hungover people out of your house and then clean it before your parents get back in the afternoon."

I groaned. The thought had crossed my mind, but after these past few weeks, we had deep-cleaning down to a well-choreographed dance. It was the hungover partygoers who were unpredictable. I had told myself that checkout was at noon, so one way or another, they would be gone by then, while my parents' plane would still be in the air.

Maybe I should've thought that through.

"Cheer up," Henry said with a faux smile. "Enjoy your burger!"

I pushed my plate away, no longer in the mood for it.

∽

WHEN I PULLED INTO THE DRIVEWAY AROUND six-thirty, Ruth and Eileen were sitting on the front balcony, enjoying a bottle of wine and a cheese plate. I knew they had dinner reservations in town later. "We love this place!" they called, while I smiled and waved. Normally I would've gone over to say hello, but I didn't have time for chitchat.

I had to call my mom.

"Audrey, hello," she said upon answering the phone. "This is a surprise!"

"That I called?" I wondered if she was tipsy.

She laughed and dodged the question.

"What are you sipping?" I asked.

"The hotel's signature cocktail," she said. "It's called Walk the Plank."

I gulped. She and my dad were spending the final days of their vacation in Paris. *If I don't pull this off,* I thought, *she's going to make* me *walk the plank.*

Or, more likely, *push* me off.

". . . sweet vermouth and tonic," she finished.

"Oh, that sounds nice," I said, fiddling with my seat belt. I was still sitting in Brigitta and hadn't even unbuckled it. "May I talk to you for a minute?"

"We're talking right now," she pointed out.

That made me giggle and lightened the mood a little. "I meant that I need to tell you something." I shifted in my seat, nervous but knowing I needed to test the waters. "I'm fine," I prefaced. "Nothing is wrong, but I was upstairs in the carriage house the other day—to flush the toilet and stuff—and I"—my eyes squeezed shut—"accidentally knocked over the biscuit tin."

My mom was quiet for a moment, then, "Why did you touch the biscuit tin?"

"Because we're out of Moroccan Mint tea," I said. It wasn't actually a lie; we *had* run out of my favorite tea. "I was hoping there were a couple of bags in the tin."

"How bad is the dent?"

I mumbled something about a corner, that the tin was now off balance. What I wanted to gauge was how upset she'd be—a mild preview of what to expect when she came home and inevitably noticed the stolen belongings. Because the only reply I'd received was from Brian, who said: **That's too bad, Audrey. We admittedly took a few matchbooks from the fishbowl (we'd been to the restaurants), but wouldn't touch personal items. Let us know if we can help. We still feel terrible about the brownies!**

I'd rolled my eyes; the fishbowl *was* a personal item! My mom had collected most of those matchbooks with my grandfather when she was a teenager.

Mark my words: I was going to hide every single valuable before the Fairfield alumni after-party on Saturday.

"How could you let that happen?" my mother said. Her voice was level, but she was undeniably upset. "You know that tin was part of my grandmother's tea set."

"I know," I whispered. "I'm really sorry."

She was going to go ballistic once she realized her Italian pitcher was a Pottery Barn imposter. I needed to get some nail polish remover to remove the sticker residue on the bottom.

After a heavy sigh, she handed the phone to my dad. "The tin?" he said. "Really? Kiddo, you're not usually such a klutz..." His voice drifted out, then returned as a murmur. My guess was he'd walked away from the hotel bar so my mom didn't overhear. "Why did you tell her now? Why not wait until we're home?"

My face warmed. "I didn't want her to think I was hiding it." This was going to be such a *mess*. Why hadn't I just hidden all the valuables before Sandy and Ron's inaugural stay?

"I'll talk to you later, Dad," I said. "I have a lot of homework—wait, one more thing."

At the thought of them coming home, an idea had sparked.

"Yes?"

"The house is looking pretty dusty," I told him, thinking about the potential damage from the Fairfield party. "Can I call Merry Maids? Surprise Mom with a nice clean house?"

The line was silent as my dad considered. He knew there were few things that relaxed Monica Barbour more than a spotless, shiny house. "Ah, what the heck?" he said. "Go for it. Put it on your credit card."

Yes! I grinned. *Victory!*

Five minutes later, the cleaning service was booked for Sunday morning.

Postparty.

CHAPTER 23

EVEN THOUGH I NEVER FORMALLY INTRODUCED myself to them, Ruth and Eileen rated me five stars. Notable quotes included She gave us the best restaurant recommendations, and Watch out Here-to-Stay, Audrey is a Platinum Host in the making!

The compliment bolstered me, because I admit, I was getting increasingly nervous about Saturday night. There had been no issues with preparation so far. Griff's lifeguarding friends had signed on and so had the football players, and everyone had signed NDAs. "This is so wild, Audrey," Griff's friend Jason told me. "How did I not know this was happening?"

I couldn't help but smile. For once, Griffin Keeler had kept his mouth shut.

Thursday night would be a good distraction: It was prom. Tate texted and offered to do my hair and makeup. *Is Ellie going to be there?* I almost typed back, but felt my cheeks warm in embarrassment. What was I? Ten? Of course Ellie was going to be at her house, and, okay, there wasn't technically anything wrong between us. Everything was just awkward, and would probably turn more awkward when Henry picked me up. Now that Ellie and Chase were over, I didn't know if she had a date.

I was really tempted to tell Tate I had hair and makeup appointments in town, but being pampered sounded nice. And I really wasn't sure how to style my short hair.

What time? I texted back.

The Hoppers' garage door was open, but instead of slipping in that way, I walked up the front pathway with my garment bag and backpack and rang their Ring camera's doorbell. "Don't worry, I've got it," I heard an unfamiliar voice call, then jokingly add, "Wouldn't want you to trouble yourselves!"

Three seconds later, a twentysomething guy opened the door. He was thin with tortoiseshell glasses, and his floppy black hair reminded me of Henry's. Would Henry ever wear a cable-knit sweater with Adidas track pants? In no dimension, but the outfit undeniably *worked* on this guy. He was really cute.

"Your name?" he asked dryly.

I blinked. "Huh?"

"Your name," he repeated. "So I can announce your arrival."

"Oh, Audrey," I said. "I'm Audrey Barbour, like the jacket but no relation."

"Pity," he replied. "My family is embarrassingly huge fans of the jacket."

I laughed. "Who are you?"

"Luke, Tate's favorite cousin."

"Actually, I think Tate's favorite cousin opened the door the last time I knocked. Red hair? Rolex?"

Luke rolled his eyes, but I saw a smile at the corners of his mouth. "Yeah, sounds vaguely familiar." He held up his hand, a wedding band on his finger. Cousin by marriage, maybe?

"Is Charlie here?" I asked after he welcomed me inside.

"Of course," Luke deadpanned. "It's *prom*."

His sarcasm deserved applause.

He looked like he was about to say more, but a *ping* sound stopped him. He dug around in his pocket for his phone. "Shoot, I have to handle this," he said, skimming a text before firing off a reply. "This case suddenly blew up . . ." He pointed upstairs.

Everyone's up there, I surmised.

Unsurprisingly, Tate was hosting a full-on pre-prom glam session in her room. "Awesome, you already took a shower!" she greeted me as I speechlessly took in the scene: the snacks, the freestanding rack of gowns, the treasure chest of nail polish and makeup, the full-length mirror outlined in fairy lights, and Olivia Rodrigo's latest concert movie playing on the TV. I could also smell a sandalwood-scented candle.

"Yeah . . ." I blinked a couple of times. "I thought you'd want wet hair to work with."

She grinned. "I've taught you well!"

Ellie appeared in the doorway wearing a cute pink robe covered in poodles. Tate promptly confiscated the bottle of sparkling cider her sister held. "Hey, Audrey," Ellie said.

"Thanks for coming." She shifted from one slipper-clad foot to the other, as if a little nervous. "It wasn't supposed to be this big of a production, but when Tate has a vision . . ."

I gave her a smile. "I'm happy she invited me."

Ellie smiled back, and after a few beats of noticeable silence, she suggested we start with mani-pedis. Her friend Bridget was already getting her hair done in the bathroom, and apparently her hairstyle involved so many braids that it was going to take a while. Tate had hired a couple of her friends as manicurists. "Hope and Deepa, this is Audrey," Ellie introduced me.

The seventh graders exchanged a look. "Tate bleached your hair, right?" Hope asked. "That was you?"

"Yes." I smiled fondly. "There's no one I trust with my hair more."

"And you're dating Henry now," Deepa said.

"But Tate said he was over here playing games the other night," Hope whispered to her.

I caught something flicker on Ellie's face, but she simply laughed and gave the girls our color choices. Essie's pale-pink Ballet Slippers for her and silver Cosmic Chrome for me.

Ellie and I sat on Tate's fluffy white futon and dipped our feet in tubs of soapy warm water. Tate's friends put in AirPods and went to work. I couldn't help but wonder if Tate's invitation was really a ruse to get her sister and me to talk. Because suddenly, now that we were sitting together, that seemed like the natural next step. "I'm sorry I didn't ask about Chase," I said once Deepa appeared to be engrossed in listening to

"Midnight Rain" and Hope some audiobook that sounded a little too spicy for her. Despite their opening questions, they weren't eavesdroppers. "I know you hinted in English on Monday, but I didn't totally know if you wanted me to ask..."

"It's all right," Ellie said. "I *did* want to tell you, but I guess I wanted to know if you really cared or not first."

My eyebrows knitted together. "Why would I not care?"

"I don't know." She shrugged. "You didn't really care about my breakup with Henry."

"That's not true," I said before I realized it definitely was. I cared so much about their breakup . . . but from *Henry*'s perspective.

"I mean, I get it," Ellie continued. "We've never really been *friends*-friends." She sighed. "You and Henry are best friends who ended up becoming something more—*of course* you were going to take his side." She paused. "I can't imagine how awful he made me sound, because I was awful. I told him I was *emotionally cheating* on him. What was I thinking?"

Unsure what to say without sounding harsh, I kept my mouth shut.

Ellie grimaced. "Honestly, I doubt I *was* thinking," she admitted. "Whenever Chase is involved, I never do much thinking. He has this way of sweeping you up, and suddenly the only thing you care about is how and when the two of you can be together. I didn't even second-guess breaking Henry's heart." She dropped her voice to a murmur. "At first."

I felt a twinge in my ribs.

At first. She hadn't meant to crush Henry *at first.*

Did she regret it now?

"It killed me to see him that hurt," I said slowly, knowing I had to say something. Ellie was being honest with me, so I owed her some honesty, too. "And I was also pretty bummed. I kind of loved you two together."

Ellie raised an eyebrow. "Really?"

Yes, I thought. *Bummed enough to fake date him so he could get you back!*

But I couldn't tell her that, right? It would just make everything exponentially more complicated, especially because I had no intention of dropping Henry's hand. I didn't want anything to come between us. But if something already had, right from the start . . .

Was a part of Henry still holding out for Ellie? After all, he'd never said, *Forget about our scheme, forget about Ellie.*

"That means a lot, Audrey," Ellie whispered when I didn't answer. "I think the two of you are cute together, too. Henry really loves you." She laughed. "'If I loved her less, I might be able to talk about her more.'"

"That's a nice line," I said, feeling my pulse speed up. Had Henry said that about me? Maybe this was all in my head. "Is it a quote? Or a Henry Chen original?"

"A Henry Chen–tweaked quote," she said. "Jane Austen's genius. You didn't read *Emma* last year?"

"No, I did." I sighed. "But I found Emma extremely annoying, so I can't say the book really *moved* me."

Henry quoting it did, though.

Heart swelling, I hoped he would quote it to me sometime. Even if he didn't love me yet, it would be nice to know exactly how he was feeling. I mean, I knew he liked me from the way he smiled, laughed, and kissed me. Affection, whether in public or private, was his specialty. Not to mention, absolutely no one supported me like he did. But it had recently hit me that I wanted to *hear* it. I hadn't expected Henry to be so stoic. He hadn't been this way with Ellie.

"It's been nice talking to him again," Ellie confessed. "I can't describe how much I missed him. How much I *still* miss him." She blinked and gave me a warm smile. "Not in a romantic way, anymore . . . but as a true *friend.* Henry really understood me, and I knew I could tell him anything and lean on him for support. Chase . . ." She trailed off. "Well, I didn't realize how much Henry's friendship meant to me until I got back together with Chase." She shook her head, disappointed in herself. "Never take Henry for granted, Audrey."

I slowly nodded, my stomach churning. I couldn't keep Henry's and my origin story a secret from Ellie. No way. She deserved to know how much she'd meant to Henry, and how far he was willing to go to get her back. Maybe our stunt didn't make her jealous, but the effort behind it might make all the difference. I didn't want Ellie to come between Henry and me, but if they were both holding out even a shred of hope for each other, chances were he and I weren't meant to be together.

"Listen, Ellie," I heard myself say. "Henry and I might be

together now, but he was all-in with *you* long after you ended things." I took a deep breath. "He was so determined to get you back that we pretended to date each other, hoping it would make you jealous." I swallowed hard. "And I know how incredibly *stupid* that sounds, but I agreed because it was killing me to see him so sad, and because a part of me also believed it might work." I winced. "I really didn't consider the possible side effects."

Ellie was silent. She wouldn't even look at me. Blood thumped in my ears as her gaze shifted to toes, now painted pale pink.

Mistake, I thought. *You've made a big mistake—a* huge *mistake!*

"One side effect being you falling for him?" she asked right as I was considering getting up and showing myself out. "Or realizing you'd *already* fallen for him?"

"I'm the worst," I squeaked. "Tell me I'm the worst."

"Try *overdramatic*," she snapped, but not unkindly. "It takes two to tango, Audrey. Henry's just as much of an idiot as you—and as *me*, for that matter."

What is she talking about? I wondered.

"I tried," she explained. "I tried so hard to steer you away from Henry by helping you with Griff. But you just seemed *so into* Henry."

"I guess I'm a better actress than I thought," I whispered, remembering Ellie's and my Rise & Grind run-in and then our cleaning the carriage house together. Both times Ellie had brought up Griff, but I hadn't taken the bait.

"Audrey, come on." Ellie shook her head. "That wasn't acting."

I couldn't disagree.

"And it was obvious to everyone how great you are together," she added, which made my stomach somersault. "I wasn't *happy* for you guys. Seeing you together sucked sometimes, especially when Chase was being such a dick."

"I'm glad you ended it with him," I whispered. "You deserve someone wonderful."

Someone wonderful didn't mean Henry, but still, I wanted Ellie to be happy.

"Thank you," Ellie whispered back. "I'm also going to *buy* myself something wonderful, with my Here-to-Stay money." She smiled and rolled her eyes. "Now that I don't need to spend it on train tickets to Boston."

"What do you have in mind?" I asked, and after joking around a moment longer, we fell into a comfortable silence. We sat quietly until Deepa took an earbud out and asked if we wanted coconut or lavender lotion for our foot massages.

"You seem tense," Ellie commented as Deepa worked on the balls of my feet. "Is something wrong?"

"I don't love foot massages," I admitted, then rubbed my temples. "And I'm stressed."

"About Saturday?"

"Yeah, but also . . ." I reached up to wipe away the tears pooling in my eyes. "Even if we get away with everything, I'm still going to be in huge trouble."

"Why?" she asked.

I let the entire saga of the missing-presumably-stolen-items spill out, and by the end, Ellie's face had gone white.

"Exactly," I said.

"Audrey, I feel sick—" she started.

"I haven't reported it yet," I spoke over her. "I guess I've been hoping that someone would eventually come forward."

"Audrey, *stop*." Ellie took my hand. "You don't need to report it. In fact, please *don't* report it."

I frowned. "Why not?"

She shook her head. "It was mean," she said, guilt swimming in her eyes. "But I wanted to get back at you because I was upset about you and Henry. I was jealous of how happy you were, because I wasn't happy and worried I'd made a mistake. I was going to come clean as soon as you brought it up, but you never did."

"What?" My breath caught. "When?"

"Right after we took the photos for Here-to-Stay," she said. "I know how thoughtfully your mom curated that apartment and what that stuff means to her . . . and I thought it was ridiculous that you were just going to leave everything there for strangers to touch." She sighed. "While you and Henry were obsessing over the photos—I think Griff was busy Snapping—I collected a bunch of stuff and brought it down to your hot shop."

I gaped. "How did I not notice that?"

She shrugged. "When you and Henry focus on something together, you are *focused*."

"Everything's in the hot shop?" I asked, flushed.

"Yes," she assured me. "Once I figured out how to disable that clock, I boxed it all up and stored it on one of your inventory shelves. I guess you haven't been blowing much glass?" She bit her lip. "Please don't be mad at me."

I was furious. The back of my neck flamed, but then I felt a few tears slide down my cheeks. "Oh, thank you," I said. "Thank you, I'm so relieved. My mom isn't going to murder me."

"Provided we survive Saturday night," Ellie pointed out, holding up two crossed fingers. I wiped my eyes, then did the same.

Thanks for inviting me, Tate, I thought. More than one problem had been solved.

―

BRIDGET—WHOSE HAIR ENDED UP LOOKING amazing—had been hooking up with Jared ever since my party, so he came with Henry to Ellie's house. "Oh, have Henry come here instead!" Ellie had said after I mentioned that he and I had made plans to meet at my house before prom. "It won't be awkward." She gave me a bright smile. "I promise."

I nodded, but was secretly relieved when Henry's friend Cam showed up too. Notoriously awkward with girls, he'd apparently leapt at the chance when Ellie casually promposed to him a couple of days ago.

Charlotte, our appointed photographer, arrived in a second car.

Henry wore neither tails nor a white dinner jacket; instead, he wore a sharply tailored navy tux with a black bow tie and lapels. Ellie's mom playfully catcalled him, and I laughed when he raised his Ray-Bans and said, "Excuse me, Caroline, but you're my *boss*!"

We took pictures in front of the Hoppers' peonies. Ellie looked beautiful in a strapless champagne-colored gown, and Bridget popped in pink. "You look incredible," Henry whispered as Mr. Hopper and his mom snapped pictures. *"Holly."*

"Shut up," I said through my smile. I hadn't purposely chosen a gown that looked like Audrey Hepburn's iconic *Breakfast at Tiffany's* black dress, but I leaned into her look a little. My hair was too short for an updo, so Tate had used Etsy-acquired jeweled barrettes to pull it back, and my mom had let me wear her sparkly wreath-shaped statement necklace (I'd asked!). Tate had done a light smoky palette for my eye makeup. I drew the line at the opera gloves—there was a line between an homage and a costume.

But I still felt like Audrey, with an edge.

Essex Harbor High's senior prom was held at the sailing club, but because Constellation Catering had done so many weddings there, the whole thing was a little underwhelming. "Are those the same Chinese lanterns from the Newfield wedding last summer?" I asked Henry while we waited in line for sparkling lemonade.

"They might be," he said, looking up. "I do remember one being punctured during tear-down."

"The decorations are amazing, aren't they?" someone squealed, and Henry and I turned to see Kenzie on Griff's arm. Underclassmen dates weren't allowed to wear gowns, so she had donned an embellished mint-green cocktail dress. She looked thrilled to be here, and I loved that for her.

Griff was dashing in a classic tuxedo. I couldn't help but swoon a little. In response, Henry snorted and zapped my waist, setting off a swirl of heat on my skin. *Griff and I would've had fun together,* I thought as he fist-bumped Henry. *But being here with the right person is better.*

We weren't eating dinner at the same table, so Griff double-checked that we were coming to the after-party. Since my parents weren't back yet, there had been an eleventh-hour campaign for me to host it, but I reminded everyone that Griff's friend Jason had volunteered last semester: *I don't want to take that from him, do you?*

There was no way I could handle two house parties in one week.

"Did Griff actually secure the band for Saturday?" I asked later, on the dance floor. After a series of fist-pumping songs, Henry and I were swaying to Billie Eilish. The lyrics weren't romantic whatsoever, but the melody and the feel of Henry's hands on me lulled me into a dreamlike trance.

"Believe it or not, he did," Henry said. "His cousin emailed me scans of the band's signed NDA. Illegible handwriting, but I guess that's rock and roll."

I giggled. "They're guys. Of course their handwriting sucks."

Henry squared his shoulders. "My handwriting doesn't suck."

"Yeah, but you're Henry."

"What does that mean?"

"It means you're special—an *original*."

He smirked. "That's the best compliment you've ever paid me."

"Really?" I gave him a look. "'I love you' isn't number one?"

We were still dancing, but I felt him bristle. My heart dipped. Why? What was wrong?

"I'm going to miss you," I murmured when he didn't say anything. "You know, while I'm at Blue Ridge. I'm *really* going to miss you, Hank."

"Me too," he whispered, not quite looking at me.

"And thank you," I added, squeezing his shoulder. "Thank you for helping me these past few weeks." I took a deep breath. "*Really*, Henry. Maybe it was Griff's bonkers idea, but I'd never be able to repay my parents and *actually* go to Blue Ridge without you."

Stone-faced, Henry nodded once.

"What?" My eyebrows knitted together when he reached up to rub his eyes. "What's up?"

I felt my heart start to hammer, and then I swear all of space and time stopped when Henry sighed and said: "Audrey, I don't think this is going to work."

I TRIED TO MAKE A CASUAL EXIT FROM THE dance floor, and Henry followed suit. My pulse had surged again and again by the time we made it to the perfect place for a private conversation: the sailing club's hall of prehistoric phone booths. "What do you mean you don't think this is going to work?" I asked after we'd shut ourselves into a space so small that it would make my claustrophobic mother sweat. "What's *this*?"

Was he talking about this weekend? My final Here-to-Stay hosting gig? Successfully keeping the truth from my parents? Something else?

"Skipping college," Henry told me, color rushing to his cheeks. "I don't think turning down Wharton is a smart idea."

Betrayal stung my cheeks. "But . . ."

"I'm so proud of you," Henry said. "The Blue Ridge fellowship is an incredible opportunity, and you absolutely need to do it. You're *meant* to go." He took my hands and squeezed them. "But, Hepburn, *why* are you writing off college entirely?"

"Oh my god," I said, my voice pitchy. "You agree with my parents."

"No." Henry shook his head. "I don't agree with them." He grimaced. "But honestly, I can't say I disagree with them either. I always stop myself from bringing this up with you, because I already know the answer, but . . ." He ran a hand through his hair. "Have you ever considered going to Penn *after* Blue Ridge? Taking a gap year?"

Blood pulsed in my ears. "I mean, not really," I said. The thought had crossed my mind, but only briefly. "Nothing can compete with Blue Ridge's level of exposure. If everything goes well, I'll have a shot at other fellowships or residencies all over the country. It's not like I can defer those until after I graduate college." I folded my arms across my chest. "If I just focus on glass, I'll be good enough to launch Golightly Glass *for real.*"

"You're amazing, Audrey," Henry said. "And you'll be in an entirely different *stratosphere* after intensive professional instruction." Pause. "You *also* got into one of the country's top undergraduate business programs."

"And I'm proud of myself!" I exclaimed. "But that doesn't mean—"

"It might," he cut me off. "Golightly Glass won't grow if the only thing you're capable of is blowing glass. It's a business, so you also need to have a head for business. Otherwise, it's not going to survive." He gave me a bittersweet smile. "I know you dream of something bigger than Etsy. You want a state-of-the-art hot shop right behind a gallery, like Emilia's. You want a booth at Philadelphia's Christmas Village, and for people to buy your vases and candlesticks as wedding gifts. You want an empire that rivals Simon fucking Pearce's."

The corners of my eyes started to prickle. I couldn't have said it better myself.

"Audrey, I love you, but I don't think the business end is going to be as easy as it is on Etsy. You'll need to know the ropes backward and forward. Golightly Glass is going to be about more than just glassblowing."

I opened my mouth, but nothing came out; instead, this weird moment of déjà vu came over me. *Okay, no.* I remembered Henry shaking his head. We were in my hot shop. *You're going to college. You* need *to go to college.*

Or what? I'd countered.

Or all this—he gestured around the garage—*disappears.*

Fuck. It hit me. My dream—my repetitive nightmare-dream! I'd always shrugged off the part about Henry saying he could end the party, but was he *right*?

Blue Ridge isn't your only big break, a voice in the back of my head said, sounding a little like my dad. *Not everyone gets into the Wharton School of Business . . .*

I didn't want to think about that now, so I latched on to something else Henry had said.

"You love me?" I breathed.

He looked stunned. "Yes, I love you," he said. "*Of course* I love you!"

My stomach stirred. "As your business partner? Best friend? Girl of your dreams?"

Because I wanted to hear it from *him*.

"Audrey," he said. "You are going to Blue Ridge next month, for the whole year, and after that, wherever glassblowing takes you." His voice cracked. "You need to be free to do that."

"I *am* free to do that," I responded. "I can walk out the door right now."

He shook his head. "I meant I don't want you to feel tethered anywhere. I'll be in New York for the next four years; I don't want you to feel tugged there if it's not the best opportunity for you. I don't want you to miss out on anything."

I couldn't help it; I rolled my eyes. "You don't think we'd last, do you?" I surmised, pulse pounding. "What was it you said about Ellie and Chase? They wouldn't last because long-distance relationships are doomed, even with the 'best intentions and purest hearts.'" I shook my head. "God, what movie is that line from?"

"It's not from a movie," he replied. "I made it up."

My heart twisted. "Well, for the record," I said, tears threatening to spill, "I would've at least liked to give it a shot." I started gathering up my dress and accidentally elbowed Henry in the stomach. *Oof.* "You would've been a touchstone, Hank. Not a tether."

I waited for him to say something.

He didn't.

CHAPTER 24

I SKIPPED THE PROM AFTER-PARTY, TAKING AN Uber home instead to pathetically fall asleep in Henry's sweats. *I can't believe he doesn't even want to try,* I kept thinking, and in between those thoughts: *Does he have a point about Wharton?*

The next day was Friday, but because of prom, seniors had the day off. Based on her social media, it looked like Kenzie had had the best night (Jared's Snapchat story caught her and Griff making out), but as a junior, she had to get up and drag herself to school. I ate breakfast in complete and utter silence, eyes red-rimmed from crying, then marched out to fire up my furnace. My mind *needed* to go elsewhere.

I felt my phone buzz in my pocket as I unlocked the hot shop door, and for a moment I hoped it was Henry. My heart sank when I saw it was only a text from James.

Morning! **he'd written.** Per my dossier, last night was prom.

Not in the mood, I wrote back: And?

He took a beat.

AND I noticed you were home pretty early, before midnight.

I rolled my eyes. He'd monitored my location.

I need to keep tabs on you, cuz, **he added.** Especially now with your enterprise.

Henry and I broke up, **I told him.**

Typing dots.

Wait, you and Henry were dating? That wasn't in my notes!

More typing dots.

Who broke up with who?

(Sorry, WHOM per Isa)

Great, I thought. Isa was reading my texts.

Does it matter? **I asked.** I'm looking for a little compassion.

James sent a hug emoji. I'm sorry, Audrey, **he said.** But if he can't keep up with you, he doesn't deserve you.

That's the thing, though, I thought. If anyone could keep up with me, it was Henry. If anyone could *challenge* me, it was Henry.

Thanks, **I texted.**

If it helps even a fraction, **James said,** Isa and I loved Ruth's review. You are a superstar.

I smiled a bit, and when he and Isa asked why I'd paused the listing—of course they'd noticed!—I lied and said it was because I'd made enough money for Blue Ridge's tuition. The carriage house was one thing, but I crossed my fingers and toes that Isa wasn't browsing bigger Here-to-Stay properties. After Joel and Lana had booked my house, I'd suspended that listing, too. I planned to deactivate my properties as soon as the party was over.

James not only texted me congratulations but also sent a goofy video of him actually bowing down to me. I could hear Isa giggling as she filmed. My cousin looked really happy.

It was a good look on him.

Ellie scared the shit out of me later as I was singing along to one of Griff's hype playlists and spinning my bubble in red frit. The color was called vermilion, but I'd discovered the shade never turned out quite as expected. "Holy crap!" I quaked when she snuck up on me. "What are you doing here?"

She looked tired. Not in a bad way, but in an I-had-a-lot-of-fun-last-night way. I hoped that was true. "I wanted to check on you," she said. "Did you and Henry skip the after-party?"

Ah, so Henry had ditched it too.

I nodded. "We skipped separately."

Ellie's brows knitted.

"We're done," I said, shrugging when she gasped. "We're putting our fifty-million-dollar mansion on the market, but I'm keeping the Hamptons house and Henry's going to rent in Brentwood for a while—"

"Audrey!"

I told her what happened. Henry supporting my

glassblowing dream, but not the path I wanted to take to make it come true.

"Let me guess..." I said when she didn't say anything. "You agree with him?"

Ellie somehow both nodded and shook her head. "I want you to be able to do what you want to do," she said. "I don't want you to choose college because you can't afford your dream. I think you deserve a true choice. That's why I'm helping with this absurd party." She smiled sheepishly. "And because I still feel guilty about hiding your mom's stuff."

I laughed. I'd put everything back in place while waiting for the furnace to hit two thousand degrees, which included intentionally denting the biscuit tin. Not as badly as I'd made it sound on the phone, but... I'd felt obligated to fully commit to my story.

The only loose end was the Tuscan pitcher. Hopefully Pottery Barn would buy me some time.

"Henry will come around," Ellie added. "To him, you are the greatest person to walk planet Earth. He will do *anything* for you."

Something twinged in my chest. I thought of Henry—my fellow foodie, cinephile, and, for a moment there, my heart. "You think?" I asked Ellie.

"Audrey, I've spent a fair amount of time with Henry." She gave me a long look. "I *know*."

FIRST CAME THE KEGS. I BUZZED THE TRUCK through the front gate that afternoon, ready to flash my fake ID, but all the delivery guy asked was where I wanted them.

There were a shit ton.

I texted Griff. Glassblowing required heavy lifting and constant movement, so my muscles were toned, but I needed backup here. Griff responded with an affirmative emoji sequence and brought Jason, and the three of us hefted the kegs down into the wine cellar. I'd read that storing kegs at room temperature wasn't ideal, and while the wine cellar wasn't *cold*, I hoped it would be cool enough. "This is awesome!" Jason said, looking like a kid on Christmas morning.

I had to remind him that Santa Claus wasn't coming to town.

I also had to figure out how to keep the guests from getting into the wine. Maybe we'd move the kegs right before the party or store them elsewhere?

The cups arrived next. Lana and Joel had ordered custom plastic pint glasses. They were red with the college crest stamped in the center. FAIRFEILD UNIVERSITY, it said in black. CHEERS TO FIVE YEARS!

Yikes, I thought when I noticed the typo.

Nevertheless, the cups were cute.

I wanted to send Henry a photo, knowing he would get a kick out of the typo. *"I" before "E" except after "C"!* I imagined him responding, but the thought didn't make me laugh.

Instead, all I texted him was: Will you be here tomorrow?

Because I needed to know . . . for planning purposes.

And as if reading my mind, Henry replied: Yes, I'll get ice.

A lump rose in my throat. Together or apart, he was going to help me.

No matter what.

⁓

THE FIRST THING I DID ON SATURDAY WAS

throw up. It was a bright, sunny day, but I was so fucking nervous. Lana, Joel, and their four classmates had checked in last night, so I slept in the carriage house. Ellie had helped me dust and straighten up as much as possible before we filled my parents' safe with valuables and hustled the rest over to Fair Winds II.

The co-secretaries seemed nice. Preppy Joel had brown hair and a toothy smile, while blond Lana was tall and willowy. They'd rented a Porsche for the weekend. "Incredible wine cellar!" Joel commented when I showed them the kegs, and I explained that I'd be moving the kegs to the pool house for the party. I also made a mental note to hang a bedsheet or tarp up to hide the cellar's glass wall. If people went in there . . .

My friends and I were allowed back into the house to prep for the party. Ellie, Kenzie, and Mia came over after breakfast, and once they dispersed to start decorating, I had to play it cool when Henry showed up with several bags of ice. I felt like a jerk for not offering to help him transport the ice into the garage freezer, but I was busy prepping Jell-O shots. Lana and

Joel hadn't asked for them, but I thought they'd be a fun touch.

"Do you need any help?" Henry asked when he was back in the kitchen, and while I nodded, I didn't say anything the entire time. My lungs had contracted so tightly that I could barely breathe, and no matter how much I willed Henry to talk—to say *something*, ideally along the lines of an apology—he kept his mouth shut too.

Our work was quick and methodical.

Trouble struck around noon, when Henry's friend Rory called; he and Cam were supposed to be picking up the food from Constellation Catering. "I had them check *three* times," he said as I felt the blood drain from my face. "There's not even a *record* of the order."

Oh my god, I thought, pulse pumping. *There is no food. We have no food. Who wants to go to a party without food?*

"I mean, we can go to Trader Joe's and get a ton of stuff," Rory continued. "No one hates those dark chocolate peanut butter cups."

"Unless they have a peanut allergy," Henry pointed out, which made me want to slap him in the chest. Not helping!

"Rory, go to Costco," I said. Lana had reassured me that I would be reimbursed for anything not already paid for. "I know it's farther out of town than Trader Joe's, but it'll have the stuff we need. I'll text you a list."

Then I ended the call and steeled myself to look at Henry. His brown eyes were alarmingly steady, while I felt mine could well up at any moment.

I let out a breath. "I have an idea."

"Never would've guessed," he deadpanned. "What is it?"

I gestured to the fridge, where the Jell-O shots sat on cookie sheets. "Let's fully commit to this theme."

He blinked, but before he said anything, I raced upstairs to my mom's office to grab her laptop. I needed to peek at her Google Drive, specifically a document titled something to the effect of *Jeff's 40th Birthday*. It had been years ago—more years than my dad would care to admit—and my mom had thrown him a huge party.

The theme had been "Toga Night at Sigma Chi"—my dad's college fraternity.

Ten minutes later, an on-board Henry texted Rory a list of ingredients. Twinkies? he responded. Seriously?

I stole Henry's phone and wrote: JUST TRUST ME!!!

Audrey, breathe, Rory wrote, then sent a salute emoji.

Henry nodded toward the French doors once I'd composed myself, and we stepped into the sun to check on the decoration committee's progress. I could feel Henry next to me just like I could feel the sun on my skin. "Kenzie, those are amazing!" I called when I saw Kenzie and Mia finish hanging strings of red Solo cups off the pool house's pergola. "How long did it take you to make them?"

"Not long." She smiled. "Mia and I watched *Animal House* while we did it."

Henry raised his hands in silent applause while I mimed a chef's kiss.

My heart twinged. *Animal House* was one of the first movies we'd watched together.

"We have fairy lights, too," Mia said. "It should look really cool once it gets dark."

Meanwhile, Ellie and Jared had arranged the tables we rented in a long line, ready and waiting for food. The table under the pergola was covered with the custom Fairfeild cups, with plastic tubs nearby. We'd fill them with ice later, before popping the kegs in. I hoped I would be fortunate enough to miss the inevitable keg stands.

Two cheesy lawn chairs sat on either side of the pool, for Kaitlyn and Mateo, our lifeguards.

"What time is the band getting here?" Ellie asked.

"Late this afternoon," I said. "I have no idea where they should be"—I gestured around the yard—"so I want them to have plenty of time to figure that out and do a sound check and stuff. Lana thought their class dinner would be over around eight."

"That seems weirdly early," Kenzie said.

I shrugged. "I figure we'd order pizzas for dinner?"

Ellie volunteered to pick them up; I told her I was eternally grateful.

Griff, Jason, and the rest of our security detail came over around two. "You need any help?" Griff asked, but ten minutes later, they were whooping and whistling and cannonballing into the pool.

Griffin Keeler is going to be the death of me, I thought,

but perked up when Henry's improv trio arrived with our Costco haul.

"Okay, *what* are you making?" Cam asked, setting everything on the island. A white box with Hostess's red, white, and blue logo peeked out of a reusable bag.

"Slutty brownies and a white trash wedding cake," Henry answered.

"Huh?"

"Don't worry about it," I said. "Not your monkeys, not your circus."

Because it was, unfortunately, my monkeys and my circus.

I suggested that Rory, Cam, and Alec head outside and scout the driveway and yard, to figure out how they wanted to run the valet line tonight.

"Don't need to tell us twice," Alec said. "We bought high-vis construction vests so no one runs us over."

I snapped my fingers. "That's the level of effort I'm looking for!"

After they smirked and sauntered out of the kitchen, Henry and I were alone again. I racked my brain for something else he could do, or for someone who could act as a buffer, but my concentration broke when he spoke. "Audrey..."

My heart jumped into my throat as Henry took a deep breath. *Yes?*

"Are you sure about keeping the kegs in the wine cellar? Because..."

"I'm relocating them later," I said in a little voice, and

swallowed so my heart would sink back down into my chest. Henry had always been a master at keeping things professional, so I had to do the same. I gestured to all the ingredients on the island. "Right now there are more pressing matters at hand."

We started on the slutty brownies, which were basically four-layer brownies. Layer one was Toll House cookie dough, the second layer was half a bowl of brownie mix, followed by Oreos arranged in the center, and topped off with the rest of the brownie batter. The smell brought me back to our kitchen in Philadelphia; I'd helped my mom make them for my dad's party. *Why are they called slutty brownies?* I'd asked. *Because,* she eventually said, *they're brownies that don't know they're loved, so they share themselves with everyone.*

(It turned out she'd been quoting Urban Dictionary.)

"Can we *please* eat a couple?" Henry asked after our third batch. We hadn't spoken since cracking a trio of eggs for batch one.

"Are you seriously suggesting that?" I eyed him, but my rumbling stomach gave me away and Henry sliced us a couple. My hand prickled where it brushed his as he handed me a square.

The white trash wedding cake was the pièce de résistance. With the kitchen oven occupied by the brownies, we baked three cakes in the outdoor kitchen's oven, and once they'd cooled, I recruited Jared to help unwrap the treasure trove of Twinkies, Hostess Cupcakes, Snoballs, and Donettes. Henry got the message to find himself a new task.

It killed me how relieved I was.

In between each layer of vanilla cake were the chocolate cupcakes, and after slathering the wonky wedding cake–like creation with Pillsbury's Funfetti icing, we decorated it with the other snacks. A ring of Snoballs at the base, Twinkies pressed against the sides, a small ring of Donettes, more Twinkies, and a cupcake as the angel at the top of the tree! "I pinkie promise I will not post this anywhere," Jared breathed once we finished. "But I *need* photo evidence."

"Same," I said, beaming. "Send it to me?"

I quickly reorganized the garage fridge so we could store the cake in it. The rest of the food was simple: potato chips, Doritos, Cheetos, pretzels, plus some seven-layer dip that Jared had volunteered to make from the contents of the fridge. "Kitchen sink dip," he called it.

Was it delicious? Was it disgusting?

I'd let the party decide.

The paper plates were red and white gingham, like a picnic blanket, the napkins black, and the plastic flatware white. Fairfield—oops, Fairfeild—colors.

I was texting updates to Lana, who'd checked in multiple times, and Joel, who hadn't checked in once, when the doorbell rang. "I've got it!" I heard Ellie call from somewhere as I thought, *Cue the band . . .*

I love everything about this! **Lana texted me back.** I only wish Joel had gotten everyone to dress up (he's the sales guy). Eighties costumes would've been so—

Someone tapped my shoulder.

"Yeah?" I asked, glancing up to see Ellie. "Was that the band? At the door?"

Strangely pale-faced, she nodded.

"Perfect! Can you find Jared? He's the A/V expert, so he can help with whatever."

Ellie didn't move.

I gave her a funny look. "What's up?"

Her lips were in a straight line. "I think you should meet the band."

"I will," I said. "But I have some stuff—"

"*Audrey!*"

"Okay, okay," I agreed, nodding quickly. I'd never heard her voice so sharp. "Take me to the band."

I entered the pool's splash zone approximately two minutes later. "Why the hell didn't you tell me?" I called to Griff.

About to launch himself off the diving board, he glanced around, as if to say, *You talking to me?*

"Yes, Keeler!" I said, my voice cracking as he hit the water.

"Why didn't I tell you what?" he asked once he surfaced.

"That your cousin's band"—I had to will myself not to detonate—"are all *freshmen*!"

High school freshmen.

Fifteen. Years. Old.

"Well, technically, they're *almost* sophomores," Griff said. "But yeah, sorry, I thought I mentioned that." He chuckled. "Also, Conrad is a sophomore, so he's basically a junior." He hoisted himself out of the water and slicked back his wet hair. If Kenzie and Mia weren't killing it as worker bees, I'm sure they would've gone weak at the knees. "Are they here?"

"They *were*." I folded my arms over my chest. "I sent them home."

(The mom who drove them had rolled down her SUV window and called out, "Wrong address?")

Griff grabbed a towel. "Aw, man, why?"

"Because they're *freshmen*!"

What was so hard for him to get? Having his cousin's band play was like hiring Tate to run a temporary tattoo table tonight. We weren't allowed-to-drink adults, but everyone here was eighteen—*legal* adults. And Kenzie, Mia, and Jared were mature for their age.

I hoped.

Griff sighed. "Well, we lost our music for tonight. Do you want me to make a playlist?"

"That would be *wonderful*," I said, even though I had no intention of utilizing it. Griff's playlists *were* electric, but Lana and Joel weren't paying us to plug in an aux cord.

I just wanted him to *do something* while I found a band.

Fortunately, I knew of one.

∽

IF YOU NEED ANYTHING OR HAVE QUESTIONS WITHIN the next twenty minutes, **I texted the growing Circle of Trust** group chat, Henry and Ellie are your point people.

Then I sank down on Fair Winds II's couch and sighed.

I really didn't want to make this call.

But I had no other choice. Henry had quit cello after three weeks, and while Ellie could sing, I knew her non–show tunes repertoire wasn't strong enough.

"Hello," James said after 1.5 rings. "What can I help you with?"

My pulse wavered. "How do you know I need help?"

"Because up until now, I've always been the one to call you," he said. "You never call me." A pause. "It hurts."

"James, can you be a real person for five seconds?"

"I'll try my best."

"Thank you." I swallowed hard. "Okay, I *do* need your help."

"Call 911."

"J!" (Isa, in the background.)

He laughed, then cleared his throat. "Audrey, are you physically all right?"

I nodded. "Yes."

"Situationally all right?"

"Mmm . . ." I hesitated. "Are you guys still in Providence?"

"No, actually," he said, "we're not."

Shit.

"Funnily enough, we're an hour from Essex Harbor," he continued, making my stomach drop. "Our entire family—Grammy and Poppy included—has been under the impression that we've been eating at least two meals a day together these past few weeks, so I thought it might be nice for your parents to see me when they get back tomorrow. You know, in the flesh."

Heart hammering, I gripped my phone tighter. I hadn't even thought of that. *Where's James?* I could imagine my mom asking, and I would've had to pull something out of my ass.

"But enough about my travel schedule," James said. "You said you needed help with something?"

My voice was small. "Did you happen to bring your keyboard? Or your guitar?"

"Of course," he said. "Isa and I are driving home to Pennsylvania after this, so we brought everything. Why?"

I bit the inside of my cheek.

"Oh, shit, Audrey. Did you volunteer In the Luxembourg Gardens to perform somewhere? Like a high school party? Are *you* throwing *another* party?"

"Uh-huh." I tried to control my voice. "Something like that."

He let out a deep groan, then took a deep breath. It was how he summoned his second wind. "Okay, okay," he said, reenergized. "I'm going to put you on speaker so you can give us three songs to set a vibe. Isa will put a set list together based on that."

"Cool," I said, feeling bolstered. "My best guess—"

"But first," he cut me off, "you're going to tell me *exactly* what this party's like."

CHAPTER 25

THE CIRCLE OF TRUST HAD DEMOLISHED TWELVE pizzas by six-thirty, and by seven-thirty, Lana had texted that she and Joel and their classmates were getting ready to head over. That gave us fifteen, maybe twenty minutes. "Sounds like Fairfield throws a pretty sad class dinner," Griff said as he pulled on a black Dri-Fit quarter zip. I'd told everyone to wear black tonight. Just like at Constellation Catering events, we were staff, *not* guests. We needed to be as invisible as possible.

But in hindsight, it would've been fun to wear togas to fully embrace the night's theme.

"Or they're sick of *behaving* at their class dinner," Jason suggested.

That was *not* what I wanted to hear.

"It's been over three hours," I said. "Their dinner started at four, right after their campus-wide parade." I nodded to the left. "Go talk to Henry in the hot shop. He has a chart for the security detail."

Jason snorted. "He *would*."

"And air horns, if things get out of control."

Griff's and Jason's eyes lit up. "Awesome!"

Once Griff and Jason walked off toward Henry's headquarters, I went over to the pool. Kaitlyn and Mateo—Griff's lifeguarding friends—were chilling in their chairs, whistles around their necks and wearing fluorescent suits. "Ready?" I asked, and after they nodded, I crossed the patio. Kenzie and Mia had been right about the pool house; the pergola did look amazing with the red Solo cups and string lights. Ellie was doing one last check on the food, holding one contemplative finger to her lips. The first couple of kegs sat nearby in plastic tubs of ice. "You can tap them," I told James, since it turned out he was the only one who knew how. We stuck to six-packs around here.

Isa was dumping a bowl of cubed fruit into the trash can punch Ellie and I'd mixed earlier. It had everything from lemonade and vodka to fruit punch and orange juice to Sprite and rainbow sherbet. "The fruit just gives it a bit more class," Isa told me. She'd borrowed my sequined nightscape dress and paired it with strappy sandals. Her glossy brown hair fell in an elegant sheet down her back.

James gave me a look. "I'm truly in awe of you, Audrey," he said. "But have you *ever* considered the existence of the police department?"

"No one is going to hear us," I replied. My house was set back on the water, and our nearest neighbors were away for their son's college graduation. Plus, I'd told Lana to spread the word that all rideshares needed to drop passengers at the end of the driveway.

James held up crossed fingers, then stretched out his hand to Isa. Their "stage" was the satellite patio in the rose garden. Of course, they'd sounded absolutely amazing during their sound check earlier.

Lana and Joel's silver Porsche rental rolled in minutes later. They looked bright-eyed from dinner but showed no signs of being buzzed. For seemingly no reason at all, Joel handed me a fifty-dollar bill after I told them to have fun.

I watched the trail of alumni, more or less dressed in Fairfield red and white, walk up the driveway, evidence of the Uber and Lyft drop-offs. But there were more designated drivers than I had expected. Dressed in black and their high-vis construction vests, the three improvisers had made a last-minute valet sign and were navigating the line easily. I giggled when Rory and Alec quickly played rock-paper-scissors to see who had to park an intimidating Yukon XL, but I left before one of them got behind the wheel.

If there was a problem, they'd text me. Henry might be tonight's troubleshooter, and Ellie our natural manager, but I was captaining this ship.

At first, the party seemed like a success. Everyone was smiling in our beautiful backyard, with the football security team on the periphery. Griff was all charm while dissuading a loved-up couple from disappearing into the pool house. People were having animated conversations near the kegs, Fairfeild cups in one hand and a hefty plate of food in the other. The co-secretaries must've sent out a text about the pool, because some guests were swimming. Joel and Lana were acting like the king and queen of the land, sipping their drinks and accepting compliments.

In the Luxembourg Gardens were professionals. James and Isa were mostly doing covers from the late 2010s and early 2020s, from the guests' college days, with a throwback song every now and again. Currently, they were crushing Harry Styles's "Adore You."

I hoped someone in the party noticed that James had written an original verse for Isa, to shift the song into a duet. *Does anyone here work in the music industry?* I wondered.

Give those two a record deal!

"Hey," someone said, and I turned to see Henry dressed in all black: T-shirt, trousers, and his beloved Thursday Boots. He *never* wore baseball caps, but tonight he sported one that said SCRATCH PAPER. Merch from his dad's latest comedy tour.

"Hi." I tried to ignore the ache in my chest. Dressed up or dressed down, Henry was devastating. "What's up?"

"Just wanted to touch base," he said, then gave me a look. I could tell he was treading lightly, trying to be nice. "Is it just me, or does this feel manageable so far?"

"Nope, definitely not just you." I unlocked my phone and tapped on the camera; I wanted to take a video to make sure I'd remember this. "I think everyone did a really great job."

Henry was silent for a moment. "*You* did a great job," he eventually said—slowly and softly enough to send shivers up my spine. "This is pure insanity, but it's *incredible*."

A lump rose in my throat. "I never could've done it without you," I said, even though I was so upset—so *frustrated* with him. Why was long distance so daunting? Why did he think he would drag me down or hold me back? I resisted the urge to knock off his hat and kiss some sense into him, reassure him that we would figure it out.

We're a team, I thought. *The* best *team, if you haven't noticed.*

But I swallowed the words and forced a small smile. "If anyone could pull this off, it's us."

"I agree." Henry shifted from one foot to the other. "Griff might be the idea guy, but execution isn't his strong suit."

"He sticks with his strengths," I said. If Griff Keeler could stop sloshed alumni from hooking up in my pool house, awesome.

Henry laughed, the sound so mesmerizing that I realized I couldn't let him go so easily. "Can we talk?" I asked, taking a deep breath. "Later tonight?"

Something flashed in his eyes, something that made him nod. "Later tonight," he agreed, then pointed toward the pergola, where Jason was approaching the food. "Jason's strayed from his sector to steal some cake."

I rolled my eyes. "If that's our biggest problem tonight . . ."

"I'll take it," Henry finished for me, but as he walked away,

I felt my stomach twist into knots. Had we jinxed ourselves?

I slipped into the house to find some salt to toss over my shoulder.

⁓

WHEN THE WHEELS CAME OFF THE BUS, IT FELT like a movie montage. It was a gorgeous night, starry and warm, and not many alumni were hanging out in the house. So when I spotted Lana and a friend sipping glasses of red wine on the living room couch, I did a double take. *Did she bring that wine?* I wondered.

My pulse skyrocketed when I noticed the bottle on the coffee table. It was a barbera my dad had brought back from Italy, the same trip where my mom bought the pitcher (RIP). And if that was my dad's wine, that meant . . .

Someone had been in the wine cellar.

"Oh my god, I hope it's okay!" Lana said when I asked. "Greer"—she gestured to the woman next to her—"doesn't like beer, and the punch is too sweet for her, so her husband grabbed us this bottle."

Dammit, I thought. Lana or Joel or another guest must've spilled the beans about the wine cellar. Even though I'd told them it was off-limits!

But really, they'd disregarded the tarp Griff and Jason hung?

Unless they never hung it, I worried. I'd had a hundred other things to do and decided to trust them instead of checking.

"I understand," I said as I internally winced. It was too late to confiscate the bottle. "If you would just please be careful, this couch is new—"

"Holy shit! *Lana?*" someone exclaimed. *"Greer?"*

And then, faster than the speed of light, a woman rushed over to the couch to reunite with her long-lost Intro to Psych classmates.

But she was clearly drunk, so instead of slowing to a stop, she banged into the couch and bumped Greer's shoulder.

Greer spilled her red wine all over the white—*pristinely* white—couch cushion. "Oh no!" she gasped. "It's all over me!"

My face flamed. Lana looked at me, but before I could blow a gasket—*How are your jeans more important than my couch?*—Ellie swept onto the scene. "Let me show you to the powder room, ladies," she said calmly, trying to usher them away. "I have towels, seltzer, and plenty of Tide to Go sticks . . ."

Of course you do, I thought, relieved. Ellie always had everything on hand.

"Carly, come with us!" Lana called to her plastered friend, probably to save her from my wrath. "I heard you have a toddler now?"

I flashed their backs double middle fingers before they disappeared into the front hall, then sprang into action, grabbing the half-full wine bottle and hiding it under the sink so I could retrieve the Shout stain remover and spray the defiled cushion. "Mia!" I waved her over when she passed through the room, a garbage bag over her shoulder. Our goal was as little cleanup as possible later.

We traded, and I took the trash while she brought the cushion to the laundry room, which had a huge porcelain sink. "Wait ten minutes and then blot the stain," I instructed her, reassuring myself that if the stain didn't come out, I could flip the cushion and deal with the drama another time. Maybe next week, when my mom inevitably discovered it.

"We have a problem," Jared said after I dumped the garbage into the garage's huge can.

"What is it?" I asked. Henry and I had made him a spy, since he shared the best wedding guest sound bites after service. Tonight, he was supposed to circulate and eavesdrop on guests to make sure they didn't do anything too out of line.

"Pool heater's busted."

I shut my eyes.

"I caught some guys messing with it . . ."

I held up a hand. "Is anything spraying anywhere? Or did something blow up?"

(That's how much I knew about pools.)

Jared shook his head. "Nope."

"Okay, tomorrow I'll call—"

I stopped, feeling my phone insistently vibrate in my pocket. I dug it out to see three texts from the improv comedians/valet crew. The first was from Rory: red siren emoji.

Then, Alec: Porsche is gone.

And Cam: Joe and friend took it for a drive.

Another text, this one from Henry: *Joel

WHERE? I fired off, heart revving.

I didn't need to wait for a response. "Audrey, there you are!" Kenzie appeared in the kitchen, breathless. "A car is doing doughnuts out past the fence, near the beach."

Give me something else, I thought, queasy bordering on carsick. *Give me something else to handle so I don't have to think about my entire backyard being torn up.*

The fates listened.

"Hello, everyone!" someone said, using the microphone. "Great night for a party, am I right?"

Kenzie, Jared, and I all looked at each other, as if to say, *Who the hell is that?*

We went to investigate.

"Oh my god," I groaned.

Chase Reynolds had taken the stage. He looked a little sloppy in faded jeans, but his T-shirt showed off his broad shoulders and his brown hair fell effortlessly across his forehead.

Objectively, I could see the appeal.

Ellie stood only a few yards away, near our peach-colored roses. Her face was ashen.

"I drove all the way down from Boston tonight," he continued. "Because I just *had* to see this girl—"

"Bro, she dumped your ass!" a fellow dude-bro shouted.

I felt my mouth twitch up. Henry. It was Henry. He called that his "douche canoe" impression.

A text came in seconds later: I'm giving him two minutes

to embarrass himself, then getting Griff to boot him from your property.

I replied with a thumbs-up.

"Excuse me," I told Kenzie and Jared. "Ellie probably needs a drink."

They nodded, and I weaved my way across the pool deck to the pergola. I grabbed a plastic cup and served myself some punch from the gleaming trash can. It was more than halfway empty, but Isa was right: The floating fruit did give it a special touch. "Hello," someone behind me said, and I turned to see a petite woman with a cute pixie cut. "By any chance, are you Audrey?"

I plastered on a smile. "Yes, hi."

She smiled back, and I noticed she was drinking water. "I'm Trina, one of Lana's sorority sisters. She said this party is all your doing."

"That's very kind of her." I paused, both pleasantly surprised and unsure where this small talk was going. I glanced at one of Griff's football teammates stationed a few yards away, but he shook his head. He didn't know either. "May I help you with anything?" I asked.

"No, no." She shook her head. "I'm just extremely impressed."

This is a trap, I almost heard Henry whispering in my ear.

I straightened my shoulders to ward off anxiety. But blood pulsed so hard in my veins it was almost audible as we continued to speak, and it sped up when she asked where I went to school.

"I'll be at Penn next year," I lied, not wanting to get into all the specifics of my future plans. Hopefully Penn made me sound like the most professional and mature teenager ever. "The Wharton School of Business."

Interest sparked in Trina's eyes.

Uh-oh, I thought.

"How funny!" she said. "I'm an admissions officer there." She took a sip of her water. "What made you choose Penn?"

⁓

AFTER AN INITIAL FROZEN MOMENT OF PANIC—

of *course* I'd stumbled upon the one person who represented the very future I was about to blow up—I talked about Philadelphia. How I'd grown up there, and how much I missed it.

I talked about Penn's campus. How it was in a city yet felt secluded.

I talked about the school spirit and diversity. I'd lived abroad, and loved learning about different cultures.

I talked about Wharton. The endless courses and renowned professors who were going to sharpen my mind for the business I hoped to start and grow someday.

I told Trina everything I'd told the admissions officer during my *actual* interview, back in the fall. Except this time, sweat was sliding down my back. I felt like she was going to call the cops on me any minute.

And then somehow have my acceptance letter rescinded by Monday morning.

My parents would be beyond pissed, and I was surprised how much my heart rate hitched at the thought of my letter being figuratively shredded. I'd worked so hard to get in; I deserved to go. *But wait, do you* want *to go?* my conscience asked, because suddenly I sounded like I *did*.

Trina asked more about my business dreams. "Some sort of start-up, I'm guessing?"

"No." I shook my head. "I'm actually a glassblower, so I want to pursue that. I already have an Etsy shop."

Trina raised an eyebrow. "Really?"

"Yes," I said, and because my heart was trying to hammer its way out of my chest, I offered to show her my hot shop. I knew I would calm down once I saw my blowpipes, and I wanted her to see that I was serious. This was far bigger than a hobby.

James, back from his break with Isa, caught my eye from onstage as Trina and I passed the rosebushes. I gave him a subtle thumbs-up.

"How did you get into glassblowing?" Trina asked after I gave her a quick tour. She was now admiring my teardrop pendants. "It's not as"—she searched for a word—"*mainstream* as painting or ceramics."

"Vienna," I answered. "When I lived there, I discovered a gallery . . ." I couldn't share my story fast enough, suddenly eager to tell her everything. Learning to blow glass, building my hot shop, launching Golightly Glass with Henry, Blue Ridge . . . and even my potential detour.

Shockingly, Trina took it all in stride. "Well, first off," she said, once I'd run out of breath, "where is this Henry going to college?"

I blushed a little. "NYU. He wants to be a lawyer—or a Hollywood agent."

"Hmm." She nodded. "Does he have an ego?"

"He's an original," was all I said.

Trina chuckled. "Now, about your detour . . ."

"Is it a stupid plan?" I asked. "From a college admissions standpoint?"

"Wharton has already accepted you," she reminded me.

My cheeks warmed.

"Have you ever thought about a gap year?" she asked. "They can be very beneficial. Depending on how they're spent, they can truly broaden horizons and enrich lives." She gave me a look. "You seem quite torn."

I bit the inside of my cheek, remembering Henry's suggestion. A gap year still didn't sound like much time to me, but maybe it could be enough? To at least get a taste of professional glassblowing? To find out if it was truly what I wanted?

"For the last nine months, all I've hoped to do is travel from hot shop to hot shop," I said. "But now I don't know if improving my craft will be enough for expanding Golightly Glass. I know it will *help*, but will it be enough to *succeed*?"

I sighed. "Wharton will teach me so much more than I can ever teach myself, and I feel like my classes will also give me a million things to think about and focus on. They'll help me decide what I want Golightly Glass to ultimately become. Right?"

Trina took that as a rhetorical question, selecting a pendant and a pair of rocks glasses instead of answering. "This is stunning." She held up the necklace, then the tumblers. "And my husband and I love to end the day with a nightcap. How do I pay?"

My heart sparked, and I smiled. "PayPal or Venmo."

"And you know," she said as I packaged her purchase in Golightly Glass's signature Tiffany-blue take-out box, "you wouldn't need to press pause on glassblowing should you come to Wharton this fall." She smiled. "If you give me your email, I would love to connect you with my sister. She is head of the Tyler School of Art and Architecture at Temple University, which, as you probably know, is in—"

"Philadelphia!" I blurted.

Trina laughed. "I'm confident that you would be able to take classes there while at Penn."

I blinked a few times. This sounded too good to be true. I had to tell—

There was a knock on the door. Polite but insistent.

"Come in!" I called, and when Henry pushed open the door, I sighed. Nothing between us was okay, but I was so happy to see him. "So, how're we doing out there?" I asked.

In response, he smiled wide, waved his arms, and said: "Sounds like the ten-year alums are headed over!"

Fuck, I thought. *Fuck, fuck, fuck!*

Someone invited another entire class?

"Shut it down," I said through gritted teeth. "We're *done*."

Henry saluted me, as if nothing were wrong between us.

"Was that Henry?" Trina asked after he left.

I nodded. "The one and only."

"You're right, he is an *original*," she said. "I can tell."

And I absolutely adore him, I thought, unable to stop myself from smiling. There was no one like Henry Chen. *We're going to figure this out.*

CHAPTER 26

THERE WAS NO SWEETER SOUND THAN AN AIR horn—except for the sound of *five* air horns. Henry gave his security team a signal (a text reading MAKE NOISE), and several beats later, the party vibes vanished. James caught the drift immediately. "Thank you so much for letting us celebrate with you tonight," he told the crowd. "I'm James, and this is the extraordinary Isa"—he smiled and took her hand—"and we're In the Luxembourg Gardens!"

They received impressive applause when they bowed, and then Ellie stepped onstage and quickly became the cruise director.

"If you drove here tonight, please form an orderly line at the valet stand," she said, sounding like her mom. "Jared will be leading a group down the driveway to our rideshare pickup area." She took a breath. "And if you did drive here, but are no longer in a condition to drive, please speak to Lana about spending the night." She plastered on her service-with-a-smile grin. "Congratulations on five years!"

"What happened to Chase?" I asked Kenzie once the chaos of everyone-trying-to-get-their-shit-together commenced.

"Oh, Griff pulled him off the stage after he said he owed Ellie a dance," she said excitedly. "Then Ellie shoved him in the pool! It was amazing!"

"She did?" I was thrilled, but there wasn't time to talk to Ellie right now. We had to focus on getting everyone off the property.

And since they were adults, it wasn't impossible. It took maybe an hour, and only about fifteen people needed to crash. "We're going to start cleaning up," I told Joel when he sought me out.

Thank god the Merry Maids were coming right after checkout!

"Sounds great," he said soberly. "I was, uh, wondering if you knew a good tow truck company?" He scratched the back of his head. "My car . . ."

My eyes narrowed. "Your car *what*?"

"It ended up in the Sound."

"Oh, Joel . . ." I said, probably sounding like his mother.

"Not deep enough for it to be washed out to sea," he quickly said. "But I can't drive it out."

Well, isn't this the cherry on top, I thought dryly. *And payback for probably tearing up my lawn!*

"I do know a tow truck company," I told him. "My friend Mia's brother is a mechanic . . ."

Because there was no way Tess could know about this.

"Phew." Joel sighed in relief. "You're a lifesaver, Audrey."

I smiled tightly. "Go to bed, Joel."

IT FELT LIKE THREE A.M. WHEN ALL WAS SAID and done, but in reality, it was only midnight ("Some afterparty!" Jason called). I was relieved most of my staff had another hour before their curfews. "Golightly Glass will Venmo you all by the end of the day tomorrow," I told them by way of goodbye. Joel and Lana still needed to reimburse me for the party. "Thank you, thank you—thank you a thousand times over!"

Not to mention, Alec had set up a tip jar for the valets. They were going home with a pretty sweet deal.

"I am giving Kenzie my keys!" Ellie declared before sucking down a cup of trash can punch. Not everyone had taken their Fairfeild cup as a souvenir. "She's driving home."

"You're incredible," I told Ellie. "I'm sorry I missed you push Chase into the pool."

"It's okay." She hiccuped. "I'm pretty sure Griff took a video."

"Sounds about right." I nodded, then looked around. "Where is Griff, anyway?"

"Oh, in the pool house," Kenzie said nonchalantly. "Hooking up with Kaitlyn."

Who's Kaitlyn? I wondered, before remembering that she was one of the lifeguards.

It had been a big night.

"Are you okay?" Ellie and I both asked.

"Yeah." Kenzie shrugged. "Why wouldn't I be?"

"Uh, maybe the nonstop flirting?" Ellie said before I could. "Or prom?"

"Guys, come on." Kenzie laughed. "It was fun while it lasted, but it's Griff Keeler." She rolled her eyes. "It's never serious for him." She turned toward the pool house and cupped her hands around her mouth. "Wrap it up in there! Audrey wants to go to sleep!"

Then she plucked Ellie's keys up and strolled off toward the Prius.

"Kenzie is an icon," I said.

"Yes," Ellie agreed. "Not nearly as iconic as Tate, though."

I shrugged. "Who is?"

"You are," Ellie said, and when I looked at her, she smiled. "I've always thought so, Audrey." Her voice softened. "I would also love to be better friends."

My heart warmed. "You took the words right out of my mouth," I said, and gave her a hug. "Thank you for your help these past few weeks."

"Yes," Henry agreed, popping out of the darkness, back from checking out Joel's waterlogged Porsche. "Especially for stealing all that stuff. That was *greatly* appreciated."

"You're just jealous you didn't think of it first," Ellie said lightly, clapping him on the shoulder before whispering something in his ear.

I looked away just in time to see Griff and Kaitlyn sheepishly emerge from the pool house. "Audrey!" he had the guts to shout. "Do you have our money?"

Oh, Griff, I thought. *Griff freaking Keeler.*

CHAPTER 27

NOT WANTING JAMES OR ISA TO HELP whatsoever with cleanup (they'd played our party last minute and pro bono!), I sent them up to Fair Winds II, our accommodations for the night. "I'll put on some water for tea!" Isa called down from the balcony, but Henry and I weren't climbing the carriage house's steps to join them anytime soon. We still had business to attend to; specifically, numbers to run and paychecks to organize. I wanted to cut all ties from this night as soon as possible. "Well," Henry said once we were settled at the hot shop's worktable. "At least we didn't have to call the police."

I groaned. *"Mood."*

He laughed, and the sound made my bones ache. They were still weary later, when Henry and I stared at my laptop screen . . . at my parents' account balance on the Bank of Fairfield's website: $10,019.88. "Isn't it a pretty sight?" Henry murmured.

All I could do was nod. Ten thousand dollars and change. Even after deducting everyone's wages for tonight. *Ten thousand dollars and change!* The total was technically pending, but still. Three thousand from me, a grand from Henry, almost six thousand from five Here-to-Stay check-ins and checkouts (well, as of tomorrow), and prompt compensation for all Joel and Lana's party needs. It was all *there.*

And a special shout-out to Venmo's instant transfer feature! I thought. The fee was worth it, because the Barbour family's Expect the Unexpected account was once again liquid.

My parents were not going to sink their teeth into me.

Not for this, anyway.

"Hey, what's wrong?" Henry asked. "Why aren't you dancing on top of the table right now? You recovered *ten grand* in less than a month!"

"I know." I released a deep breath, then echoed what I'd told him at the party. "Nothing would have been possible without you, Henry."

With a smirk, he nudged me. "You happy, Hepburn?"

Hepburn, a hit to the heart.

The corners of my eyes started to sting. "Can we talk?" I asked Henry, at the same time he sighed and said, "We should talk."

I gave him a look. "About what? We've compiled quite the list of viable topics."

"I know." He rubbed the back of his neck. "Let's start with Golightly Glass."

Golightly Glass? I thought. *Really? Business?*

Although maybe it *was* the easiest starting point.

"Okay..." I shifted in my seat. Henry's s brown eyes looked hesitant, but warm. My pulse picked up. "What about it?"

Henry cleared his throat. "I feel like I've been giving you the impression that I want to quit soon," he said. "That I plan to leave it behind when I go to NYU."

"I mean, I understand if you do," I told him, thinking of our uncertain plan for Golightly Glass after graduation. I swallowed the lump rising in my throat. It was going to be harder to say goodbye to high school than I thought. "It might be tough to find time, with your classes and stuff."

"Maybe," Henry allowed, "but I *want* to find the time. Maybe I won't be able to pack and ship out inventory, but I'll be all over our Instagram and I have an idea for a T-shirt design." He paused. "I love Golightly Glass, and even if we aren't side by side anymore, we'll figure out how to stay in sync..."

A sharp pang struck me in the chest. If Henry was so dedicated to our Etsy shop, why couldn't he show the same dedication to our relationship?

"Audrey," he whispered when I didn't say anything.

"Why are you so against long-distance relationships?" I blurted. "Why are you so determined to call them *doomed*?"

Next to me, Henry froze like I'd hit his most serious nerve. "Because..." he slowly said. "I have yet to see one with a happy ending."

"Henry, come on," I said. "You can't give up hope just

because Griff and Libby fell apart!" I laughed a little. "Don't tell me you thought they were going to be the paragon of a long-distance couple . . ."

"No," Henry said tightly. "But I hoped my parents might be."

My heart slipped into my stomach. *Oh.*

It was a sudden and swift reminder that Henry and I'd known each other less than two years. I didn't know much about his parents' divorce beyond it happening when he was nine and the whole thing being relatively drama-free. His mom and dad were pretty good friends now.

Henry slipped off his stool and paced the shop. "They were never in the same place at the same time," he explained. "My dad was working all the time. He was writing for *SNL*, doing comedy festivals, writing for awards shows, traveling for his tour, and then he started booking sets on the late-show circuit, and just like that, he had to be *everywhere* . . . while Mom was home with me." He paused. "*No one* supported him more than her—I remember her shrieking when he got his first Netflix special—but they *never* saw each other, Audrey. At some point, I think my dad's longest stretch home was a week." He rubbed his eyes. "And as easy as it is to say that sitting on the couch together isn't the height of luxury, it does *matter*. It matters *so much*."

The lump lodged in my throat was too large for me to speak, so I quickly nodded in understanding as I rose from my stool. I knew my parents missed drinking wine while playing Scrabble together.

Henry and his plight against long distance . . .

It made sense.

"I'm scared," he admitted once I joined him where he stood near the furnace. I took his hand and squeezed it. "I was confident in what Ellie and I had—Barnard and NYU are in the same city, how hard would that be?—but then she broke up with me so suddenly. No one in this town saw it coming, let alone me. And it really hurt, even though she was only one part of my life. A big part, but not the only part. While you . . ." His throat bobbed. "I've learned these past couple of months that if Ellie was a quarter of my heart, you are my *entire* heart. You're the fourth person at my family's dinner table even when you aren't actually there. It's been that way for a long time." He inhaled. "Yes, my mom and Tess thought we were idiots for fake dating, but they also thought we were smart—we unknowingly figured out the way to fall for each other." He threaded his fingers through mine. "You're the most important person in my life, Audrey."

"And you're the most important person in mine," I whispered, my pulse racing. "You know that."

"You've alluded to it once or twice," he quipped, then rocked back on his heels. "I want to make sure it stays that way. We need to stay best friends. I worry that if we tried and failed as something more, we'll lose that."

"You don't think we could go back to being friends?" I asked softly. "If we dated and it didn't work out . . . friendship wouldn't be possible?"

"No." Henry blushed. "For so many reasons."

I blushed back, using my imagination.

"I love you, Audrey," Henry whispered. "More than I can express."

My heart swelled, then exploded.

"I love you, too," I told him. "I love you so much, Henry."

He smiled and wriggled out of my grip so he could take my face in his hands and kiss me. I tasted the faintest but sweetest hint of rainbow sherbet.

"You helped yourself to the trash can punch," I breathed.

"And you didn't?" he breathed back.

I laughed and looped my arms around his neck to kiss him again, longer this time.

What does this mean? a corner of my mind wondered as Henry's lips on my neck sent zing after zing up my spine. *Are we—*

We're together now, I told myself. *Right now, in this moment, Henry and I are together.*

When we broke apart for air, my eyes darted around the hot shop until they landed on the far corner. Heart hammering, I caught Henry following my gaze before looking at me.

His deep-brown gaze didn't waver.

"Maybe we shouldn't," I heard myself murmur, "but—"

Henry took my hand and swiftly tugged me across the room, toward the groupie area (as cliché as it was). I laughed and let him lead me to the couch, where he turned and gave me a look, confirming it was okay.

I quickly nodded, and we collapsed onto the couch.

"Are you nervous too?" he asked a while later, when it became clear making out was going to lead to more. I lay on top of him, and I could feel his heart thumping hard in his chest. I'd pulled off his black T-shirt and he'd unbuttoned my jeans. He grabbed a foil square from his wallet.

The question both confused and charmed me. "You're nervous? What about Ellie?"

"Ellie isn't you," he murmured, pressing a kiss to my forehead.

"Yes, I'm nervous," I answered, heart rate at full throttle. Tonight would be my first time, but I wasn't going to overthink it. Henry made me feel confident and unstoppable—when I'd said I loved him, I *meant* it. "But I want this."

"Me too." He grinned, and I giggled when his fingers fumbled on my bra clasp. Soon our clothes had been kicked off the couch. "You're beautiful, Audrey," he said, tracing a fingertip along my collarbone. I shivered, but I had never felt so much heat swirling in my body.

I kissed Henry with everything I had once he was on top of me, hip bone to hip bone. Standing side by side or tangled together on an ancient couch, we were always the exact same height. He slowed the kiss down, then pulled away to say something.

I covered his mouth before he could.

"No Oscar-winning lines," I whispered. "Let's just be us."

Henry kissed my palm in agreement before he stretched to turn off the lamp on the side table. Pearlescent moonlight spilled through the hot shop window.

I grimaced when we started to move together, then winced. "Say the word and I'll stop," he told me, but I shook my head and focused on his heart beating against mine. Quick, light, loving. *Henry-and-Audrey,* it whispered. *Henry-and-Audrey.*

CHAPTER 28

I DON'T REMEMBER WHAT TIME HENRY AND I crept up to the apartment and ended up falling asleep in the bunk beds, but I bumped my head on the ceiling when I jolted awake at eight. "Ouch," Henry mumbled in my ear. We were like two sardines in the top bunk, but neither of us cared. "That didn't sound fun."

Ignoring him, I checked my phone to see that my dad had sent me a text a few hours ago: Activating airplane mode in 3, 2, 1 . . .

"We have to get moving," I said after quickly checking Jeff and Monica's flight status. "My parents' flight lands at 12:20. They'll probably be home around 2:45."

Henry threw back the covers with determination, but before we could burst out of the narrow bunk room, he pulled me in for a kiss that made me forget the world for a heartbeat.

"Okay, what's first?" Isa asked a minute later. She was dressed and sitting at the kitchen table with a mug of coffee.

She shot us a look. "James and I *are* helping bring this home."

"The Merry Maids are coming at noon, but we need to get rid of all the garbage," I said, willing myself not to blush. Hopefully she and James hadn't heard anything downstairs last night. "Every can is overflowing, and we have all the used kegs . . ." A solution sparked. "Our neighbors are away, but every May they rent a dumpster for spring-cleaning."

"Oh, I love a good dumpster," James said, emerging from the bedroom. "The only problem is that it's June."

I bit the inside of my cheek.

"We'll try anyway," Isa said with an encouraging smile. "And if it's gone, I bet your school has a dumpster?"

"Behind the cafeteria," Henry said, and five minutes later, we were stuffing as much garbage as possible into Isa's Mini Cooper. The black plastic bags were heavy, and I cringed at the liquid swishing around in them.

If one breaks, I thought, *I will pay to have her car detailed.*

No one had emerged from my house yet—I hated that they didn't need to check out until noon—but Henry and I didn't hesitate scouring the yard for leftover party detritus. We collected cups, bent paper plates, Twinkie halves, and even a bra and a used condom. It made me gag. Henry used an oven mitt from Fair Winds II to pick the condom up.

James and Isa returned from their trash run earlier than expected; they confirmed that a dumpster was still sitting in my neighbors' driveway, and I helped load up the car again. Who knew how many trips they would need to make?

Around nine-thirty, I got a text from Lana: Is the kitchen stocked for breakfast?

No, I said. I hadn't gone grocery shopping on purpose, not wanting them to feel too at home. But Rise & Grind has the best coffee and pastries in town, and Sister Act Café has a wonderful brunch!

She didn't respond.

Slowly but surely, hungover alumni began to emerge from the house. Before taking off for the night, Rory had given us the drunk guests' keys—all neatly labeled—and now Henry dutifully distributed them. My way of bidding them farewell was by buzzing open the gate.

But Joel and Lana were stranded for the time being. The nose of their rented Porsche had spent the night in the Sound, and we were waiting for Mia and her brother to arrive with his tow truck. I almost cheered when it pulled up.

"I'm so sorry, Audrey," Joel said as Elijah and a fellow mechanic got to work. "I don't know what I was thinking"—he gestured to the chewed-up yard—"I'm honestly embarrassed."

"You can write me a check for the lawn care company," I said.

Joel snorted. "Who has a checkbook these days?"

My mom! I thought, suddenly *supremely* annoyed. *Don't make fun of her!*

"How does Venmo sound?" he asked.

"Fine," I answered curtly. "Please make it a private transaction."

He sent me money right then and there.

"How *are* you going to explain the damage to your parents?" Mia whispered. The lawn didn't look as bad as the phrase *car doing doughnuts* had made it sound, but . . . it wasn't great.

"My dad has one of those supercharged golf carts," I said. "I'll just have to say that Henry and I were messing around one day."

Mia was quiet a moment. "Tell him Griff and Jason were messing around during the party you threw. It's something they would do."

I laughed a little. "Definitely, but I'll still get in trouble."

"I know." She shrugged. "But at least they won't think you and Henry *actually* did it."

Then the two of us had to cover our mouths so we didn't laugh as her brother pulled Joel's Porsche out of the Sound. Water came gushing out of it.

Joel was going to ride with them to the auto shop, Lana and their suitcases would follow in an Uber. I had an inkling that returning the rental car was going to be a headache.

And that they weren't going to make their flight back to Chicago later.

"Good riddance!" I called after the last guest was gone at 11:58 a.m.

The Merry Maids were prompt, arriving three minutes later. Even though my dad knew I was having the house cleaned, nervous adrenaline raced through my veins.

Landed! my mom texted at 12:08.

Their flight had gotten in early.

Can't wait to see you! I wrote back, hoping there was at least *a little* traffic on the way home from JFK.

I wasn't ready when Henry announced he had to leave, having lost track of time. Charlotte had been fine with him sleeping over—Henry's parents trusted him implicitly—but she was strict about Sunday mass attendance. "I missed ten a.m.," Henry said. "I need to sneak into the noon mass or else I'm screwed."

"Have I said thank you yet?" I asked as I hugged him, my eyelids fluttering shut. Only hours ago I'd fallen asleep in Henry's arms, feeling like I was wrapped up in a dream.

"Once or twice." He hugged me back. "Good luck with your parents." He pulled away to look at me, eyes alight but also unreadable. "May the odds be ever in your favor!"

"Really?" I wrinkled my nose. *"The Hunger Games?"*

"Oh, give me a break," he groaned. "I'm running on very little sleep."

He quickly kissed my cheek before taking off for his car. "I'll be back later!"

I put the back of my hand to my burning face as I watched him execute the most inelegant K-turn and zip up the driveway.

Last night happened, I told myself. *What happens next?*

The twinge in my heart told me it couldn't be friendship.

FOR THE MOST PART, I LET THE CLEANERS DO their thing, but I also needed to feel like I was doing something. Isa was currently emptying the safe of the breakables and valuables Ellie and I'd locked up for safekeeping, while James was out back inspecting the "busted" pool heater. Not broken, he'd texted me a few minutes ago. You just have a really dirty filter. I can change it, NBD.

I suddenly felt guilty for canceling the pool guy's visit last month. I hadn't wanted him to catch a whiff of my Here-to-Stay host gig.

BEST COUSIN EVER, I texted James back.

"Miss Barbour?" I blinked and looked up to see a cleaner by the kitchen sink. Lo and behold, she was holding an open bottle of wine. The barbera that Lana's friend had spilled on the living room couch and I'd stashed under the sink. "Would you like me to get rid of this?" she asked. "Or—"

"No, that's all right," I said quickly. "I'll take it!"

I wasn't especially proud of what I did next. The bottle was only half full, so I grabbed cranberry cocktail from the fridge and carefully poured what was left into the bottle. When that didn't quite do the trick, I added water. Last night I noticed that Lana had left the cork and seal on the island, so I'd hidden them in the utensil drawer. I retrieved them and pretty much hammered the cork into place before doing my best to glue the seal back on the bottle.

Nice save, Audrey, I thought after returning the bottle to the cellar, which had never been concealed behind a tarp (of course). I took stock of the basement bar and was unsurprised to notice a few liquor bottles missing. I'd known it was inevitable, and the only solution was to adjust the spacing between handles so it didn't look like anything had been swiped. My parents weren't as eagle-eyed about hard liquor as they were about wine.

Isa and I had just finished rearranging my mom's favorite crystal clock on the living room mantel when I squeaked, remembering the couch cushion. It was two-thirty and the Merry Maids were on their way out the door; I raced to the laundry room to find that the stain had not surrendered to the Shout. It was now a faint pink, but still there.

Close enough!

I flipped the cushion and fit it back into place on the couch. "It looks totally normal," Isa assured me, at the same time James shouted, "Audrey, their royal majesties have arrived!"

"Shit, okay." I made eye contact with Isa. My pulse was pounding. "Do I look anxious?" I swallowed. "Or guilty?"

"No," she lied, which somehow calmed me down.

I took a deep breath when the front door opened. "Hey there!" I heard James call. "You guys still drunk?"

Classic James Barbour.

Isa sighed and shook her head. "He's such a clown."

Together we headed into the foyer, and when I saw my parents—looking fresh-faced despite their eight-hour flight—my heart swelled. I didn't think I'd ever been so happy to see them. "Mom!" I shouted, and basically threw myself into her arms.

She smelled like her favorite Burberry perfume and her go-to hand sanitizer. "Audrey!" She laughed and hugged me. "Missed us, did you?"

"Oh, desperately," I said dryly, even though nothing had ever been truer. It felt like a serious weight had been lifted from my shoulders. Managing a huge house took a lot of work.

"James and Isa weren't good company?" my dad joked.

"We don't have the same taste in TV shows," James said smoothly, then offered to go to Rise & Grind to get coffee for everyone. Aunt Monica and Uncle Jeff had to be exhausted, right?

"Tell me about your trip," I said once we got the luggage inside and James and Isa left on their caffeine run. "How was the weather? What was your favorite vineyard? How are Marc and Stacy Gallant?"

(I remembered their names this time.)

"There were a few rainy days, but otherwise the weather was picture-perfect," my dad said, then launched into the thrilling tale of discovering the most idyllic vineyard in all the valley. I tried to listen, but I only caught the words *vine* and *barrels* and *delectable cheese plate*. We were walking through the house and I was distracted watching their faces, trying to read if they could tell something was off—if they could see that something had *happened* here last night. My spine straightened when my mom sighed.

"Audrey, sweetie, thank you," she said. "It was so thoughtful of you to have the house cleaned for us."

Oh my god, how does she know? I wondered. *I didn't—*

"It was me." My dad smiled sheepishly. "I let it slip."

Okay, phew.

Now I had to stop them from looking out the French doors. I didn't want them to see the tire tracks yet; I needed to buy a little more time.

"Did you bring back any wine, Dad?" I asked. "I can help you put it in the cellar."

His face lit up. "I did bring back a couple of bottles. The cases I ordered should arrive this week."

My mom followed us down to the wine cellar. She updated me on the Gallants, and I nodded along as my dad stopped in front of the cellar's French sector. "Audrey," he interrupted news of Marc and Stacy's elder daughter's recent engagement, "what happened here?"

Huh? I thought. Something had happened in *Italy*, not France.

He pivoted and gestured to an empty cubby. "Where is the Bourgueil Franc de Pied?"

Oh. The back of my neck heated. *Oh, shit.*

That was the cabernet Henry and I had drunk after my party. When we'd finally kissed. The cellar went fuzzy at the thought.

"I drank it," I heard myself admit. "I was bored after you left, and got curious, so . . ."

Yeah. So, yeah.

My parents exchanged a look.

"Did you drink it yourself?" my mom asked.

"Mmm." I kept my lips zipped, not wanting to narc on Henry.

But she nodded once, like she knew.

"Well, in any case," my dad said somberly, "it's gone." He raised an eyebrow, then started to smile. "What did you think?"

I wanted to use some of his wine terms, but for the life of me, I couldn't remember what the bottle's label had said or what the wine had tasted like. Were there some fruity notes in it?

In the end, my review sounded like how my mom described wine. "It was the perfect choice for a night in with friends," I said. "Cozy and comfortable, but still full of life and laughter."

He nodded thoughtfully. "Probably due to the cherry notes," he said, then snapped his fingers. "I think you'll like this cab I ordered."

"I sat next to a nice woman on the plane," my mom said once my dad had put away his new acquisitions. The three of us settled on the velvet couch near the golf simulator. Hopefully my dad wasn't keen to play St. Andrews anytime soon; Griff had beaten his record.

"Oh, yeah?" I asked cautiously.

"Mm-hmm." She touched her necklace, which I realized was the mermaid teardrop pendant. "She complimented my necklace." She smiled, almost proudly. "I told her my daughter made it and showed her Golightly Glass's Instagram. She thinks you're incredibly talented for blowing less than two years."

"That's really cool," I said as every fiber in me screamed, *This is the moment! Tell them you're going to Blue Ridge! Tell them you're actually doing it! Tell them you paid for it!*

But instead, I asked: "Mom, why don't you want to be an interior designer?"

She cocked her head at the seemingly out-of-left-field subject.

"I mean, you *are* an interior designer," I clarified. "You renovated our entire house, and I know you've helped friends with theirs, but why don't you make a website? People would hire you left and right. You're so talented!" I swallowed. "And I saw the *house & home by monica* folder on your laptop. It looks a lot like a portfolio."

My mom didn't respond, but I felt some tension swirling in the air. "Honey, why were you on my computer?" she asked.

"Just . . ." I couldn't tell her the truth. Empty bank account! Here-to-Stay! Kegger! "Looking for some old photos." I shrugged.

"Ah." She didn't push it; instead, she answered my question. "You're right," she said, "that folder is my first attempt at a portfolio. I *have* thought about launching a firm, but . . ." She pivoted a little. "I work at Bedtime Stories because I love to read, and I love helping others discover their love for reading. I feel professionally fulfilled." She took a breath. "Interior design and decorating are my *passion*, Audrey. Excluding you and your dad, nothing makes me happier than seeing a space live up to its full potential. I *love* it." She hesitated. "But I worry that if I do it professionally, I won't love it that way anymore. That it will become work and someday I will never want to look at fabrics or wallpaper samples again. It's a real fear of mine, as silly as it may sound."

"Oh," I said, puzzle pieces unscrambling themselves in my head. Could that have something to do with—

"And that is why I am hesitant about your glassblowing," she admitted. "Your father and I support you so much . . ."

I glanced over to see him give me a thumbs-up.

". . . but the last thing we want is for you to fall out of love when you professionally pursue it." She smiled wistfully. "You are so gifted, Audrey, and you have one of the greatest work ethics I've ever seen. Friends have marveled to us about how talented you are, and it takes a lot not to outright brag about you. What high schooler builds a hot shop? Has a successful Etsy store? We are so *proud*." She paused. "I'm just nervous. There's no pressure with hobbies."

I was speechless. Really? All this time? I knew on some level my parents were proud, but they were truly *that* impressed? They wanted to *brag* about me?

A lump rose in my throat. "I never thought about it that way," I said quietly. "I think that's a rational fear. But I'm never going to know if I don't try, right?" I gave my mom a look. "And neither will you."

"Touché," she acknowledged.

"I really want to go to North Carolina next month," I said, seizing my moment. "Golightly Glass had a flash sale recently, and combined with my Constellation money and savings, I can afford Blue Ridge's tuition. After that, I have some thinking to do." I paused, then took a breath. "Maybe I could at least do a gap year?"

I'd been turning it over in my head ever since my fight with Henry, and the idea had taken root after talking with Trina. Would going to Wharton and blowing glass at Temple be right for me? The best balance? The perfect match?

Teary-eyed, my mom nodded. "We were actually going to bring that up with you," she said. "We spoke with the Gallants, and it turned out Marc took a gap year once upon a time to live in France and work on his grandparents' vineyard. He swears it helped shape him into the person he is today."

"And it was *only* for twelve months," my dad added teasingly. "He *did* go to Michigan after that."

"So it's a yes?" I asked, hope flaring in my chest. "You'll let me go to Blue Ridge?" I held my breath as my parents held each other's gazes for a beat, then turned back to me in unison . . .

And nodded.

"Yes," my mom said, smiling. "It's a yes."

"Thank you!" I grinned. "I love you so much."

"We love you, too, Audrey." My mom laughed. "You might be our only child, but you are also our *favorite*."

"I've visited every continent," my dad mused, "but I've yet to see the Blue Ridge Mountains." He chuckled. "This should be an adventure!"

I GOT IN TROUBLE FOR THE TIRE TRACKS IN THE backyard right after James and Isa returned with coffee and muffins. I couldn't in good conscience throw Griff under the bus, but before I could cop to it solo, James stepped in: "I egged her on, Aunt Monica. She took me on a ride in the golf cart one night, and I dared her to do doughnuts."

My mom rubbed her eyes, exasperated. "James . . ."

You owe me, he mouthed at me. *Big-time.*

My cousin might've let my mom down, but the guilty party was funding the lawn repair.

Thanks for the Venmo, Joel!

What I didn't expect was my dad calling me into his office later, while my mom was cozy on the couch and exploring the many wonders of Squarespace on her laptop. We were trying out different templates for house & home by monica. "What's up?" I asked.

"I wanted to reiterate how proud of you I am," he said, holding a Golightly Glass tumbler of scotch and leaning against his desk. "I've been reading up on Blue Ridge and these other glass schools, and then fell down the Corning Museum's YouTube rabbit hole . . ." He shook his head. "*Congratulations* on your fellowship acceptance, Audrey. I'm sorry it took me so long to really tell you that."

"Thank you," I said. "That means a lot, Dad. I mean, better late than never!"

He laughed. "I do want to add that I still think Wharton is too good an opportunity to pass up. A business degree opens all kinds of doors."

I nodded. I'd emailed Trina's sister earlier to inquire about Temple's art school. After a year of exploration, could I really combine Penn and glassblowing?

"For example, if glassblowing doesn't work out," he continued, "I believe you have a promising future in luxury property management."

Luxury property management? I thought, before my blood pressure skyrocketed into space. *LUXURY PROPERTY MANAGEMENT!!!*

My dad took a casual sip of scotch, but there was a twinkle in his eye. "Wouldn't you agree?"

CHAPTER 29

"OKAY, OKAY, BUT *HOW* DID HE FIND OUT?" Henry asked. It was almost eight, and we were alone in the hot shop. He was perched on his stool while I focused on the furnace and twirled my blowpipe, gathering glass. James and Isa had left late in the afternoon, and my parents had gone to bed an hour ago, still operating on Paris time. Henry had raced over after I'd texted: My dad thinks "Fair Winds" has a nice ring to it . . .

"Do you remember Sandy and Ron?" I said. "Our first guests?"

"Of course. Sandy wanted to explore every corner of Connecticut while Ron wanted to binge every corner of Netflix"—he wrinkled his nose—"and season every meal with Old Bay."

I rolled my eyes. "Henry, I suspect it was only *one* meal."

"It certainly didn't smell like it!"

"*Well*," I said, "it turns out Ron and my dad used to work together."

His eyes widened. "What?"

"Yes." I nodded. "Before we moved to Vienna, my dad and Ron were colleagues. They weren't that close, but they're still *Facebook friends.* Sandy posted some photos from their trip and tagged Ron."

"Which means it showed up on your dad's feed," Henry concluded. His brow furrowed. "He didn't show your mom?"

Henry waited as I blew a bubble and then capped the pipe with my thumb so it would inflate.

"Nope," I said. Luckily, my mom found Facebook insufferable; she'd deleted her account ages ago. "It turns out he's always thought the carriage house would make a great Here-to-Stay, and he thought this looked like a promising trial run."

When I'd asked him why he didn't immediately call me about it, he reiterated my mom's mantra: *We trust you, Audrey.*

I was still shaking my head in disbelief.

Henry whistled. "Are you going to tell your mom? Now that it's over?"

"We agreed I should, but not until I'm like thirty-five . . . when it doesn't matter anymore." I giggled as I flashed the bubble. "She might even find it funny."

He looked at me wryly. "Here's hoping!"

We shared a smile, and as I worked on a vase, I told him about my conversation with my parents. About us finally being on the same page, or at least in the same chapter. "My dad said he'd help me plan a gap year, but I'm really excited to hear back from Temple, and to talk to Trina again. It could *work,* you know?" I sighed. "I mean, *of course* you know. It was basically your idea."

"Not really." Henry shook his head. "The gap year suggestion, sure, but the details are all you." He smiled. "Who knew that you would find something close to clarity by throwing a kegger?"

Laughing, I turned to flash the vase, but took a clumsy step and accidentally knocked it on the edge of the furnace.

It promptly broke off my pipe and shattered on the concrete floor.

"Shit, I'm sorry," Henry said. "I'm distracting you."

"No, it's okay," I replied. "I'm just messing around." I quenched my blazing pipe to cool it off, then started cleaning up the shards. Henry moved to help, but I waved him away. Even if my work broke, it felt like such a luxury to be able to blow regularly again.

But I found I had neither the patience nor focus to start over, not when I felt endless threads of energy coursing through the room, from Henry to me and from me to Henry. I had no idea how to bottle them, yet I wanted to—desperately.

"Henry Chen," I said, putting down my blowpipe. "I think we should be together."

Something flashed in Henry's eyes.

I held up my hand so he wouldn't speak. "I know part of why you don't want to be is because you want to protect our friendship, but I'm afraid I have some disappointing news." I took a breath. "It's too late to play it safe. After last night, I cannot be solely best friends with you. I can *try*, but it's not going to make me happy." My voice wavered a bit. "And I don't think it's going to make you happy either."

"Audrey, I meant what I said at prom," Henry said as I closed the distance between us. "I want you to be free to do anything and go anywhere you want. I never want you to pass up an opportunity because of me."

My cheeks warmed. "God, what is it about that line? Everyone's been using it lately." I snorted. "What if what I want is *you*? Why can't I have both? Why can't I work at becoming a great glassblower and also have you?" I reached to run a hand through Henry's hair, hoping it wasn't for the last time. "Whether I'm in North Carolina or Philadelphia..." Tears pooled in the corners of my eyes at the realization that I had a real plan in the works. One I was truly excited about, confident in, and that my parents would support. If glassblowing at Temple was possible, I knew my path involved Wharton after my Blue Ridge fellowship. My gut told me it *was* possible, and the perfect match for me. "I want other things, too," I resumed, "but I especially want *you*, Hank." I squeezed his hand. "Long-distance relationships are intimidating, but they don't always end. My parents are mostly long distance, and they *thrive* off it." I tried to smile. "And I know we're not like my parents, but we're also not like *your* parents. We're Audrey and Henry, and we can figure it out. Especially with the help of a calendar and an Amtrak schedule—not to mention the fact that I am obsessed with you." I took a deep breath. "And I know you feel the same."

Henry blinked before nodding slightly, and then we stood there in silence. The longer I waited, the more my heart throbbed.

Is this what heartbreak feels like? I wondered. I was teetering on the edge of it. He had to feel the same way, right?

"I had a dream last night," Henry finally said.

Before I could stop myself, I rolled my eyes.

A dream? Really?

"I have a point," he added quietly. "I promise."

I swallowed the lump in my throat and indulged him. "You *never* remember your dreams."

He shook his head. "Untrue. I remember one where—"

"You solved New York City's rat problem," I finished for him. "Fine, who could ever forget that . . ."

"I still think releasing all those cats could work."

I snorted. "What was this dream about?"

He smirked. "It's a real roller coaster."

I mimed buckling a seat belt.

"It all started at Sandwitch," he said. "You and I were getting lunch, but then Griff Keeler appeared out of nowhere and had this absolutely deranged plan to . . ."

As advertised, his dream went all over the place.

And it sounded like something I'd heard before . . .

Or, more accurately, something I'd *lived* already.

It involved renting my carriage house as a Here-to-Stay, an entire tin of Old Bay, getting high off pot brownies, falling asleep in my pool, wondering if I'd save Henry if he started to drown, a broken pitcher and stolen family heirlooms, Ellie in tears over him instead of Chase, Griff letting everyone down in little ways that never seemed to add up, Henry fighting with me in a phone booth, his Uber refusing to take him to my house after prom, my letting absolute strangers inhabit Fair Winds, and throwing a party that was not only unhinged but also highly illegal. It ended with Henry needing to navigate roadwork on the way to see me.

(Henry hated construction.)

"How is that a dream?" I asked once he finished, trying to keep a straight face. "It sounds like a *nightmare*."

"No way." He shook his head. "It wasn't a nightmare; it was *definitely* a dream." He tilted his head, smiled a little. "Because you were in it."

My stomach stirred. "Henry . . ."

Henry stood there looking at me, his deep-brown eyes numbing the backs of my knees. His voice was low. "I'm a little *more* than obsessed with you."

I sheepishly smiled, feeling heat swirl in my chest. "I know."

"If we can survive the craziness of the last few weeks, Hepburn, I know we can do anything together." His free hand went to my waist and my breath caught, my heart going molten when he leaned close. "I love you, Audrey. So much more than I can ever express."

"Try," I murmured before his lips brushed mine. "Give me a Hollywood kiss."

He grinned and did.

ACKNOWLEDGMENTS

Every time I read this book, I laugh.

Not because it's funny (it is), but because it's *fun*.

These characters and their shenanigans are *so much fun*!

Which is hilarious, because drafting this book was *not* so much fun. I found myself battling a terrible case of tendinitis for my first few months of work, and I also needed to pack my entire life into a U-Haul for a cross-country move.

It was an extremely emotional time.

There is no other way to start these acknowledgments than by thanking all the people who listened to me complain about my tendinitis pain and comforted me whenever it brought me to tears. I never, ever would've finished this book without your unconditional love, support, and hand massages.

Endless gratitude to Eva Scalzo, who remains the best teammate in the game! Six books together, and so many more on the horizon. I would not be where I am without you. And a special shout-out to Tom Scalzo for his help brainstorming both book titles and fake business names. "Here-to-Stay" is too perfect for words.

Thank you to Hannah Hill, editor extraordinaire. I knew Audrey's story needed a lot of work when I turned it in, and felt very validated when I received your notes! You truly push me to be the best writer I can be, and every moment is absolutely delightful. I am so happy with this book, and beyond excited for our next collaboration. Hopefully it doesn't involve any math.

Delacorte Romance, I've said it before and I will say it again: You are the *dream team*! Wendy Loggia, Makena Cioni, Noreen Herits, Joey Ho, Andrea Baird, Kristin Guy, Michelle Campbell, Casey Moses, Tamar Schwartz, Colleen Fellingham, Megan Shortt, and Tracy Heydweiller—my books are so lucky to have all of you as fairy godparents. Thank you to Heather Lockwood Hughes, my fantastic copyeditor, and to Monique Aimee. How is it that every cover you create instantly becomes my new favorite?!

I am also so grateful to Electric Monkey, whose enthusiasm knows no bounds. Lindsey Heaven, thank you for believing in this retelling, and, Liz Sellen-Bankes, thank you for helping polish this manuscript until it shone. Griff Keeler has no idea how lucky he is to be loved by you! And a huge applause to everyone in marketing for fiercely spreading the word about my books. I can't express how wonderful it feels to be part of the Farshore family.

Thank you, thank you, thank you a thousand times over

to Gemma Hollister and Tate Newfield of Antolini Glass! You are two of the coolest, kindest, and most talented people I know. While the hours I spent in your hot shop did not all directly translate to the page, Golightly Glass would cease to exist without your thoughtful tutelage and passion for your work. Any errors I may have made in depicting the fine art of glassblowing are mine and mine alone.

Readers, please check out @antoliniglassco on Instagram!

John and Erin Bautz, thank you for throwing the original old-fashioned kegger. You are the dearest of friends.

Mary and Peter Bransfield, thank you for hosting such dreamy weekends on the Connecticut coast. I cherish every visit to your gem on the Sound. Ashley's Ice Cream will forever be spoken about in a reverent tone.

My friends! Madison, Michael, and Anthony: I'm so fortunate to have you three in my life. Thank you for building me up, making me laugh, and inspiring me with your brilliance.

Kismet, thank you for your guidance in writing That Scene. I have no doubt it'll be a fan favorite moment, as it is one of mine! Mimi Matthews, thank you for rolling out the welcome wagon on the West Coast. I really can't believe we only played together one season, because reconnecting with you didn't feel like reconnecting at all. You are pure sunshine.

And Jessica L. Cozzi, author of *We've Hit Turbulence*! We text at lightning speed, and it doesn't matter if we're talking books, writing, movies, dogs, or weddings—I love it all. You are a true friend and destined for YA romance greatness.

Much love to the Costantini family. Thank you for welcoming me with open arms and supporting me every step of the way. Hopefully the Monza bookstore will stock my books someday!

Team W, Webbers and Walthers: I love you all so very much. Sarah Webber DePietro, thank you for letting me crash your and your sister's fall trip to the Farm in 2023! It might've rained and I might've spent most of it writing, but it was still idyllic, wasn't it? You are the most wonderful godmother, and it is an honor to be your goddaughter.

Tibbles, you know how awesome you are, right? You both inspire me to no end.

Christopher, husband of mine: I am eternally grateful for your love and support, especially during my "trying time of tendinitis." You hugged me during a meltdown on a street in Key West, you took my hand and squeezed it hard while driving a twenty-foot U-Haul somewhere in Kansas, and you coached me to the end of the manuscript during the dog days of summer. I love you to pieces, and those pieces will always find their way into my books.

Thank you, Mom, for being one of the most important players not just in my life but also in my writing process. "This can work!" I remember you insisting (red wine in hand) after we watched *Risky Business* on my laptop. We were building the plot aloud, stream-of-consciousness style. "This can totally work..."

As always, you were right, and I love you so much.

ABOUT THE AUTHOR

K. L. WALTHER is the #1 *New York Times* and *USA Today* bestselling author of *The Summer of Broken Rules, What Happens After Midnight, Maybe Meant to Be,* and *While We're Young.* She was born and raised in the rolling hills of Bucks County, Pennsylvania, surrounded by family, dogs, and books. Her childhood was spent traveling the Northeastern Seaboard to play ice hockey. She attended a boarding school in New Jersey and went on to earn a BA in English from the University of Virginia. She is happiest on the beach with a book, cheering for the New York Rangers, or enjoying a rom-com while digging into a big bowl of popcorn and M&M's.

KLWALTHER.COM
@klwalther9